12-25-2019

1967
a coming of age story

Richard W. Doornink

This book reflects the author's present recollections of experiences over time. Some names and characteristics have been changed, some events have been compressed, and some dialogue has been recreated.

ISBN 978-1-9995660-0-5 (Paperback Edition)
Coming of age / Memoir / Young Adult / Yorkton, Saskatchewan

Editor: Jennifer Dinsmore jdinsmore@rogers.com
Typesetting, Layout and Cover Design: Monique Taylor monique@ccdesign.ca
Front Cover Image: Used under license from Alamy Limited
Line Drawing: Mary Lynn Jones prettybirdportfolio@yahoo.com
Printed and Bound in Canada by: Island Blue Book Print Co. Ltd.
Distribution: IngramSpark
First published in Canada 2019 by: Richard W. Doornink

An imprint of vigomultimedia.com
40 Chetwynd Lane
Lion's Head Ontario
N0H 1W0
www.richardwdoornink.com

BIOGRAPHY

Richard William Doornink was born in Winnipeg, Manitoba in 1958, moved to Yorkton, Saskatchewan with his family in 1966, and lived there until 1969 when they moved to Toronto, Ontario.

Richard received his Bachelor of Arts from York University (Atkinson College), with a major in their film and video program (with a heavy dose of French and Italian cinema) and a minor in Political Science. He has also completed the Humber School for Writers post-graduate creative writing program, as well as screenplay and script-writing workshops.

He has been a book editor and book angel investor, has worked in film and video (S-VHS, 16 mm, and 35 mm formats) as credited production manager and post production coordinator, and has also studied painting and photography.

Richard has started up and run several successful businesses in both Canada and the US; launching his first start up at 23. He has been active in political campaigns since he was 16, and is now a full time writer.

Currently splitting his time between Buffalo, New York; Venice, Florida; and Lion's Head, Ontario, Canada, Richard is finishing his second and third books.

ACKNOWLEDGEMENTS

To Kathy Courteau, without whom this book would never have been completed. Your support made it possible for me to see this through to the end, and I will always be grateful.

To Red; once a little sister I took care of and protected, now a big sister to me. I love you.

Isabel Huggan; for teaching me to know my characters' shoe size. I could go on and on, but compression is key.

SPECIAL THANKS

My first readers, Carolyn Sherar, Sandra Scott, Cher Barry, Steve Crone, Andreas Schumacher, Marg Allen and my mom, thank you for the comments and support.

Rick Evans; for over thirty years a rock, a supporter, a sounding board, a friend.

Travis Wallace; for the support and encouragement to get started on getting finished.

Rosa Sivsco; for your edits, comments, and suggestions. Big Boy lives!

Peter Dobbie, a kindred soul and quiet wit.
Thank you for your patience, advice, and countless corrections.

Humber School for Writers program, including Kim Moritsugu, Antanas Sileika, and Hilary Higgins.

Humber Publishing Services (HPS), School of Creative and Performing Arts, Humber College, and Irene Merritt.

Jennifer Dinsmore; for your thoughtful copy edits, suggestions, and patience.

Monique Taylor; for your first read, vision, design, creative content, support, and hours and hours of talk time.

And lastly, a special thanks to Stephen King, for giving me permission to write.

www.richardwdoornink.com

CHAPTER ONE

September, 1966

His black, Brylcreemed pompadour gleamed under the dining-room light, a front wave rolled into place by a careful flick of his comb. That wave was the last thing he used to do as I sat on the edge of the bathtub and watched him get ready for work.

He would wash first, then whip up some shaving cream from the kit he had brought from Holland. After carefully examining the blade to make sure it was still sharp, he'd start by running fresh lines up his neck, head tilted back, little rows plowed as the blade pulled and tugged the hairs.

By the time he was done his face would be covered with torn bits of wetted toilet paper, stuck here and there to stop the flow of blood from the nicks and scrapes the razor had just scratched out.

Back then he did a lot of his selling at night, which meant many dinners at other people's tables while we ate without him. When he did join us, if there was any conversation at all, it was about *his* day.

"Everyone needs life insurance," he said, his moustache bristling as he spoke. "They just don't know it. A careless driver, a wet road, something you just don't expect. Your number can be called. Just like that!"

He spoke slow and clear, then snapped his fingers on the word "that" like a hypnotist waking a subject, his hand within inches of my nose. Work was always on his mind. He even brought a suit on our camping vacations saying, "You never know when your next client might pop up!"

He was trying to teach me a lesson, but, afraid he'd get angry over something plain as day to him, I didn't dare ask what that lesson was. I just kept quiet like we'd been taught; we were to be seen but not heard.

"A man's responsible for his family even when he isn't around anymore," he continued. "Once I was on my third dinner with this guy and his family, and he still couldn't make up his mind. Well, he up and died before he could bring himself to sign. The family, of course, was left in financial ruin."

▸▸▸◂◂◂

He had delivered bread door-to-door, sold magazines and insurance, and now, just before we left for vacation at Clear Lake, Dad had applied for a new job with the Rexall Drug Company. Every few days we'd leave our campsite and drive into town so he could use a pay phone to see if he got the job. Every time he hung up I hoped he'd heard a "yes," just so he'd stop talking about it while we tried to enjoy our vacation. Getting the job meant we'd be moving, but that, I thought, would be better than living with him while he got over *not* getting the job.

When he finally did receive word he had the job, Mom and him decided it'd be a good idea for us to drive to Yorkton—a straight line west of Clear Lake—to see the town before we moved. Even with the windows down it was a hot and dusty drive, and soon enough we were all wind-blown and sticky. Mom had forgotten to bring the Gravol and it was all Red, her red hair now damp with sweat, and I could do to keep from getting car sick. We did stop once so Little Sister could throw up at the side of the road, after which Dad made it clear to Mom to never forget the Gravol again.

We finally pulled into town just past noon, Sam Cooke's "Chain Gang" on the radio, Dad drumming his rings against the steering wheel, clicking time to the song. I could tell by the way his hands flew about he was in a good mood. I heard it in his voice too when he said, “You know, they sure are great dressers.”

Mom turned and asked, “Who are great dressers?”

“The Negroes,” he replied. “The Negroes really know how to dress.”

She managed an “oh” before returning to stare out her side window. The town appeared deserted, no one out and about. Like a *Twilight Zone* episode, something felt different, very different. Dad drove on until we spotted an old man in green overalls, plaid shirt, baseball cap, and tall, black rubber boots walking along the sidewalk. I looked up at the sky: a bright and sunny day, not a cloud in sight.

Did he think it was going to rain?

Mom told Dad to pull up alongside so she could talk to him.

As the car slowed and Mom leaned out her window the scarf tied around her hair fell forward. Pulling it back up she asked, “Could you please tell us where everyone is?”

The old man stopped and stared. Red sat perfectly still and started to crank up her window, at least until it got stuck. Very slowly she rolled the handle back down ’til it caught, then carried on until the window was closed. I stared at him, not caring whether he caught me looking at him or not.

He started toward the car. The butt end of an already smoked cigarette stuck in the corner of his mouth, the letters M and F and the words Massey Ferguson printed on his baseball cap.

Must be the name of his baseball team.

He placed one hand on the top of the car, the other on the door frame, and leaned into Mom’s window; she quickly pulled back in. I looked at the black, grey, and red whiskers that covered his face and then at the dark, wet line that ran along his collar where sweat had settled in.

I rubbed my own neck as little drops of water started to roll down my back, the breeze through the window now replaced by the heat rising from the pavement. I wiped my hand on my cut-offs, the material soon a darker shade of blue.

Mom spoke again. “Can you tell us why everything is closed? Where is everyone?”

The man pulled a red kerchief from his back pocket, dragged it along his neck, and then let out a long stream of words I'd never heard before. The girls shrieked as Mom and Dad turned to each other. Neither spoke, but from the look on their faces I could tell both knew what the other was thinking, then they burst out laughing.

"Welcome to Yorkton," Dad said, as he turned to face us. "See kids, we're so far from home they speak a different language!" I hadn't expected this, and from the look on the girls' faces they hadn't either.

The man stepped back from the car, turned, and started off while Mom called out "Thanks" while Dad put the car in gear and stepped on the gas.

"Come on kids," Mom laughed. "It's okay. You just met your first Ukrainian."

What the heck was a Ukrainian? Did kids here speak that way? Was I going to have to learn to speak like the man who cheers for Massey Ferguson*?*

I turned back to watch the distance between the man and us widen. Unlike Winnipeg, the streets in Yorkton were wide enough to drive down without worrying about hitting anything. The stubby trees were few and far between, as if deciding whether it was worth the effort to grow.

Mom spoke first. "The gas station up ahead looks open. Let's see what's going on."

The *ding ding* of the rubber hose brought out a man wearing a mechanics' uniform. Dad leaned out his window but before he could say anything the man asked, "Fill it up?" I breathed a sigh of relief.

"No thanks," Dad replied, "gas is good. Just wanted to ask you a few questions. We came to have a look around and find a place to live, but everything seems closed."

The man stood and chuckled while wiping his hands off on an oil rag. "Any other day there'd be lots of people out and about, 'cept Sunday of course. On Wednesdays, though, almost everything closes at noon for the day, the stores for sure. Gives us a break during the week."

Dad glanced at Mom, then back at the man. "Well, that explains things!"

"I could tell you weren't from around here," the mechanic continued before tucking the oil rag into his back pocket. I started to wonder how he knew, but before I could finish my thought he said, "Saw your plate as I walked over. Figured you to be from Winnipeg?"

"Yes sir." Dad chuckled. "Winnipeg it is. Can you tell us if there might be a restaurant open?"

"Yup, there's a couple of places you can try. If you want something for the kids there's a Dog n' Suds—country fried chicken, burgers, fries, stuff like that. Claim to fame is the world's creamiest root beer. Don't even have to get out of the car to eat if you don't want to."

Dad wasn't one to let us eat in the car. As if reading my mind the mechanic said if we wanted something a little fancier we could try the restaurant in the Corona Motor Hotel.

"Both places are straight down Broadway, in that direction" he said, now pointing his finger in "that direction."

"We'll also need a place to rent," Dad added. "Any suggestions?"

"Well, you can try the municipal office. Someone oughtta still be working. I'd stop in there and see what they have to say."

Dad thanked the man, and after a quick oil check and windshield cleaning, we were off. After a few turns Dad found the municipal office. Telling us not to move, the two of them went inside. The heat shimmered off the front hood as a welcome breeze passed through the open windows. Little Sister, hair matted against the side of her face, had fallen asleep up against Red. Red and I, too hot to poke at each other, stared out of our windows and waited.

I hadn't dozed off for more than a minute or two before Mom and Dad returned.

"Good news," Mom said. "According to the woman inside, the best place to rent is on the west side of town. The new part."

As we drove off "Soul Man" started to play and the DJ cheerfully announced we were listening to "Yorkton's one and only radio station." Dad's head moved back and forth like Ray Charles, but this time there wasn't any drumming against the wheel. I figured he didn't want to wake Little Sister.

All the streets were empty. Once in a while we'd see a kid or two playing, but, the weather being so hot, most everyone stayed inside.

"Here. This must be the new development," Mom said with what sounded like a sigh of relief.

On one side of the street sat a row of apartments, on the other a field of dirt and construction materials. Here and there a leafless tree had been plopped down, it seemed, by someone who didn't want to carry it any further. We slowly drove by while Mom wrote down a couple of phone numbers. With that we were done finding a place to live.

Maybe Dad felt bad because we'd been in the car all day, or because the man on the street had scared the bejesus out of us. Whatever the reason, I was glad he picked the Corona since we didn't eat in fancy places very often. We got to sit in our own little booth with cloth napkins, ketchup in a real Heinz glass bottle, and fancy paper-wrapped straws.

We ate in silence, the noise of the air conditioner not loud enough to drown out the sound of Dad's teeth clicking as he chewed. Red and I shared a soda pop and Little Sister did her best to spill milk whenever she could. I think everyone was wondering what was going to happen to us next.

After Dad found the local drug store he'd be calling on, also closed, there wasn't much to do except drive back to Clear Lake, finish our vacation, and say goodbye to Winnipeg.

▸▸▸◂◂◂

The towns, now fewer and farther between, quickly rolled by the windows of Mom's pride and joy, her '57 Bel Air station wagon; the pad of paper beside me listing the towns we'd already passed—Portage la Prairie, Westbourne, Neepawa, Minnedosa, Russell, after which, according to the folded map in my lap, we made a sharp turn into Saskatchewan. We were headed back to Yorkton, this time to live. There were towns I'd missed, but we'd been in the car for hours and I was too tired and hot to write any more.

I sat in the back between the suitcases. Little Sister was fast asleep across the middle seat and Red up front, talking a mile a minute as usual. The more we drove the more things spread out. Grain elevators and the occasional farmhouse sprouted up now and again before falling back into the horizon, small dots against a flat land.

When we finally arrived, it was in time to hear a loud argument from the apartment across the hall. Dad, having arrived a couple of weeks earlier, mentioned seeing a lady and her son but hadn't introduced himself. According to him, "The best neighbours were the kind that left you alone." And that was exactly what he intended to do.

Our apartment was full of Allied Mover boxes marked *dishes, clothes, bedroom;* their contents emptied, the crumpled Winnipeg newspapers now stuffed back in. Dad's prized possessions, his piano and jazz record collection, sat in the living room waiting for him to decide just exactly where they should be placed. Mom found some boxes meant to be left behind for Goodwill in Winnipeg, toys and books we were told we couldn't take. Dad grumbled something about not watching the movers pack, to which Mom replied since his company paid for the move the movers just loaded up everything in sight.

We tumbled into our new rooms. The girls sharing one, me alone in mine. Within a day we'd gone from our three-bedroom house, with backyard and detached garage, to a three-bedroom apartment. I managed to plug in the radio, but finding only static on the dial, turned it off, rolled over to face the wall, and fell asleep.

▸ ▸ ▸ ◂ ◂ ◂

Sunday morning. If we were going to church Dad would soon be up, and I didn't want to be in the bathroom when he expected to use it. But I couldn't wait any longer. Just as I entered the hallway I heard the bathroom door shut; he was up.

I stood near the door, danced up and down, and tried to think of anything but water. A step or two more and my cowboy pyjamas would be wet. Once he finished I held my nose as I went in, and then flushed the toilet as the last wave of relief rolled over me.

By the time everyone was up and had eaten breakfast, it was clear we weren't going to church today but were instead going to get the apartment in order. At least as much as we could before he left tomorrow morning for the week. Things were going to be different, at least while we lived here. The plan, from listening to Mom and Dad talk when they thought no one was listening, was for Dad to rebuild the territory and then get promoted to Toronto, where the "big money" was.

I'd read about Toronto in the encyclopaedia. If Yorkton was small and Winnipeg was bigger, well, Toronto looked like it could swallow up both quite easily. I hoped things didn't go too well, otherwise we might never get back home to Winnipeg, to my friends and our family.

After getting in their way enough times we were finally told to go out and play, but to be back before it got dark, whenever that was. The three of us sat on the main stairs, halfway between our landing and the front entrance. After asking Red "What do you want to do" a few times, and hearing only "I don't know", it was clear we were bored.

Little Sister, having already gotten her tricycle, started riding it up and down the sidewalk. Across the street, grown-ups came and went from the row of triplexes — but no kids. Not that it mattered since I wasn't the sort to just go up and say, "Hi, do you want to play?"

Finally, a lady dressed in her Sunday best walked up our front walkway, her purse swinging on her arm, pulled the door open with a white-gloved hand, and stepped inside. She ran her finger down the list of names on the mail slots while she asked, "Did you children just move in?"

Was it that easy to see?

I answered, "Yes ma'am. May I ask who you are?"

"I'm Miss Jean Meadows. The Welcome Wagon lady."

I knew we'd moved west, but not so far that a wagon lady welcomed your family. I looked out on the chance I'd missed something, but there wasn't a wagon in sight. Maybe she parked it around the corner.

Placing her gloves inside her purse, she asked which apartment was ours.

"Number 3, the door at the top," Red replied.

I thought I'd test Miss Jean Meadows. "Do you know where we moved from?"

Miss Jean Meadows looked us up and down, a smile breaking the corners of her mouth as her ruby red lips began to form words.

"Why, I'd say Winnipeg. If I had to guess."

Darn it, how did everyone know? Did we look so different that everyone knew we didn't belong here?

She moved toward the steps and we slid over to let her pass. As we did, she smiled and said, "Your Mom put it on her welcome form."

I turned and watched her bright white shoes climbing the red, carpeted stairs. The ruffles of her dress swished, and the smell of perfume washed over us. She smelled fresh and clean, like spring.

Just then the door from across the hall opened and a kid about my age came out. A woman's voice followed, "Don't go too far and don't get dirty!" Turning to come down the stairs, he saw Red and me, froze in his tracks, and stared at us. We stared back.

I heard Mom greet Miss Meadows, asking her inside. She called down to us—me, actually—to stay out of trouble.

Red got up and went outside, leaving me still staring at the boy on the landing. I gave him the once-over: White high-top runners, Lee's rolled up way too high, bright white tee-shirt, and a "Litttle Dab'ill Do Ya" wave about an inch too high. Looked to me like someone figured he was about to grow real tall, real quick.

"You gotta bike?" I asked.

No reply. I asked again, only this time slower.

"You … gotta … bike?"

"Yes," he replied in a voice so low I wondered if I'd really heard him say something.

"Pardon?" I asked.

"Yeah, I have a bike. Why?"

Why? Because I wanted to know. Why else do you ask a question?

"No reason," I replied. "What kind of bike is it?"

"Nothin' special. Just a bike."

Questions like, "Where you from?" "What's your name?" and "What school do you go to?" suddenly spilled out of my mouth. He looked at me like I was crazy, but I was just happy to have someone to talk to. I finally stopped to catch my breath.

"I'm Mark. Not sure which question you want me to answer first, or if I can even remember them all."

"Doesn't matter," I replied, pleased he'd at least spoken. "Where ya from?"

By the look on his face he was figuring on me winding myself up again, but I surprised him and stopped talking. He blinked a couple of times before replying, "Winnipeg. We're from Winnipeg."

What were the chances of anyone else around here being from Winnipeg? Yorkton was the middle of nowhere. I figured everyone here must have grown up here. Why else would they be here?

"Heck," I replied. "You can't be from Winnipeg."

"Why not?"

"*We're* from Winnipeg; how can you also be from Winnipeg?"

Mark's face turned red and he clenched his fists. "Listen you," he stammered. "We *are* from Winnipeg. My dad got transferred. He's a travelling salesman."

Now it was my turn to get mad — he must have heard about my Dad and was trying to make fun of me. A quick punch to the nose would take care of this! But just before I got up to take a swing I thought, why can't it be true? He deserved the chance to tell his story before I gave him a bloody nose.

"Okay. Who does your Dad work for?"

"Scott-Bathgate."

"Scott who?"

"Scott-Bathgate. The Nutty Club candy company."

I remembered the factory in Winnipeg, with the giant walking candy cane painted on one side. "You mean your Dad works for the dancing candy cane man?"

Now *he* kept on talking. "That's what I've been trying to tell you. He got transferred here from head office. Dad said it was a promotion; Mom said it was a demotion. They don't agree on much anymore."

Dad had already made a small office in our apartment storage room and loaded it up with vitamins, shampoos, and product samples. I wondered what kind of samples Nutty Club salesmen had, and hoped the question would just sort of slide out of my mouth.

"My dad's a travelling salesman, too. Got his own little office with samples and stuff. Your Dad have samples?"

"Course he does: candy, popcorn, sunflower seeds. All kinds of stuff."

Today was shaping up to be a really good day. First no church, and now meeting this Nutty Club kid. Maybe things weren't going to be so bad here after all.

"Want to play catch?" Mark asked.

"I don't have a glove. Dad promised to buy me one, but I'm still waiting."

"I got a glove and bat. Let's go to the school. We can hit pop flies to each other."

Seeing as there really wasn't much else to do I waited for Mark to get his glove and bat. When he came back he'd changed into scuffed runners and a pair of patched, worn Lee's.

"Why did ya change?"

"These are my getting-dirty clothes."

Getting-dirty clothes?

I didn't have enough clothes to change twice in one day, let alone for getting dirty. A new shirt and pants for the first day of school, and maybe something for Christmas or my birthday, meant I pretty much wore the same things all day long. With the exception of my Sunday best, they were all for getting dirty.

We walked along the street, the sunlight from the bright blue sky almost giving me a headache.

"Where are we going to play?"

"The field behind the school; Columbia, where I go. Figure you'll go there too." Mark stopped. "Unless you're Catholic. There's a Catholic school round the corner. You're not Catholic are you?"

I wasn't sure what to say. I didn't think I was, but I could tell from the way he said *are you* that it wasn't something he wanted me to be.

"No," I quickly replied. "I'm sure we're going to the same school." At least then I'd know one person in class. Mark carried on as if it wasn't a big deal, but I figured sooner or later I'd have to find out about this Catholic thing.

"Well, anyway, the school's on Bradbrooke near Independent. It's got a big gym and a paved lot out back. There's also a baseball diamond and a soccer field."

I followed along, trying to remember the way in case I had to walk home by myself.

▶▶▶◀◀◀

Monday morning, and Dad had left to start covering his territory before we were up. After breakfast Mom packed us into the car and we drove off to our first day at our new school. For Red and me this was our second "first day" of school this month, since we'd started school in Winnipeg right after Labour Day. We'd also moved twice already when we lived in Winnipeg, so this would be my third new school since grade one. I was getting used to the first-day feeling.

We went in through the main entrance doors and Mom's heels clicked as we walked down the shiny hall floor. I heard a duplicator running and soon enough the fumes of which had crawled up and into my nose as we got to the main office door.

The glass rattled in its frame as we closed the door behind us. Mom told us to sit while she talked to the secretary. An engraved metal "Secretary" sign sat on the front of her desk and I wondered what would happen if someone changed the wording on the sign.

Would she just become someone else?

Picking up the phone the secretary had a hushed conversation before leading Mom through the door marked Principal's Office in gold block letters. The last two words one would see if one were in trouble.

The sunshine outlined Mom and the principal against the frosted glass, the sun's rays interrupted each time they moved. After a few minutes the door opened, the waiting room flooded with light again. Little Sister slid off of her chair and grabbed Mom's hand.

"Don't worry. These two will be just fine," the principal said as he led Mom out by the arm. She in turn pulled Little Sister along, telling Red and I to remain sitting as they stepped out of the office and started down the hall. The principal's aftershave, Brut, I thought, just like Uncle's, lingered as the click of Mom's heels grew softer and softer. Soon enough they trailed off completely. I supposed she was on her way back home with Little Sister.

I looked back at the secretary and wondered how much Aqua Net had been used to keep her beehive hair wound up that high, her head and hair keeping perfect rhythm as she typed. It was like the rumble of a far-off train rolling down the track. I imagined the keys flinging themselves against the page, the carriage moving closer and closer to the return bell. I shut my eyes and listened for the wail of a whistle, like the ones I heard in Winnipeg at night. I wanted to be on that train.

From somewhere in the back of my head I heard, "Ricky, come this way." Judging from the way the principal was staring at me he must have repeated it two or three times before I realized he was back. Red, good as ever, already stood at attention beside him. He had a rather square face that was topped off by short grey hair and a kind of stern look that didn't invite any sort of pleasantries.

In his grey suit, white shirt, and skinny black tie, he could have just as easily been selling insurance.

"No point in going outside to play now, I'll walk you both to your rooms." As he walked he talked, and the faster he walked the faster he talked. "The bell will ring at nine. Everyone will line up and file in quietly *after* a teacher has opened the door. Once inside, line up single file along the wall outside your class and enter your room *only* after your teacher has greeted you. Do you have any questions?"

I couldn't tell if it was the way he spoke, the way he walked, or the way he looked at me, but whatever questions I may have had were lost at the bottom of my throat. I shook my head no.

"Your teacher is Mr. Long," he said to me. "Stand and wait for the bell."

I didn't want to get caught leaning up against the wall and shifted back and forth as Red and the principal walked to the end of the hall, opened the door, and disappeared from sight. The overhead lights hummed and made two reflected lines off the floor straight down the hall. I wanted to follow the lines out the front door, but knew better. Besides, I might get lost.

The silence soon became filled as I realized things were going on all around me: chalk on a board, coughing from one of the nearby rooms, the sound of a fish tank bubbling. The bell sounded to bring everyone in from outside, and as much as I was ready for it to ring it was closer and louder than I expected. I jumped, then quickly looked around to make sure no one had seen me snap to attention. The hall was still empty, but I could hear voices getting closer. Boys and girls talking, a teacher telling them to be quiet.

The hall doors swung open and kids spilled in like a wave threatening to sweep me away. I stood frozen against the wall. Most just brushed by. One or two stared. I wanted to be back in Winnipeg with Grant—my best friend. A girl's voice brought me back from wondering what he was doing at this particular moment.

"Oh, you're the new boy Mr. Long told us about. "What's your name?"

I turned to look at, or rather down, at the girl. She was short, had dark black hair, wore glasses that now fogged up as she spoke, and her nose was runny.

"Ricky," I replied. "Ricky Doornink."

"Doornink? What kind of name is that?"

"It's *my* name." I made sure she really heard the word *my* when I said it.

"That's not what I meant," she replied. "Where do you come from?"

What was she asking? Did I look as strange as I felt? Had I suddenly sprouted horns?

"Winnipeg; I'm from Winnipeg and it's a Dutch name. I'm Dutch."

The other kids had moved from a single line along the wall to a semi-circle around the girl and me. All of a sudden I didn't feel so good, and wished I hadn't eaten so much Puffed Wheat for breakfast. I was confused by her question. I mean, you have a name all your life and don't really think about it until someone corners you and starts asking a lot of questions.

"Well then," she continued. "What's your middle name?"

"William."

I noticed the fog had lifted from her glasses as she wiped her nose along her polka-dotted sleeve. "I know what," she said. "We'll call you

Donkey. That's easy to remember."

Donkey? That's the name of an animal!

I was about to yell "Anything but Donkey!", but it was too late, the other kids now whispered the name. Before I could say anything the classroom door opened and a man stepped out, to which a "good morning Mr. Long" was now heard from the kids around me.

He stood tall, straight and crew-cut topped, tie and shirt just so, his black pants creased sharp enough to cut a piece of lined paper across them. He looked like he just stepped out of an Eaton's catalogue. The only thing out of place were the large Chuck Taylors he was wearing, a size, I thought, just below clown feet.

"You may all come in now."

As kids walked past some said "Hello," some "Hello Donkey," and some walked by without saying anything. I went in last, and as I did, Mr. Long put his hands on my shoulders and directed me to the only empty desk in the room.

"Sit here; behind Debra."

She turned around and I felt my face get hot. She was cute! I wasn't sure how I'd missed seeing her in the hallway just then, and wondered if she'd heard the Donkey comment. When she whispered "Hi, Donkey," I had my answer. Debra turned back around, her long hair hanging over the back side of her chair. I waited for my face to cool off.

The desk rocked back and forth as I sat, the rubber foot from the front leg gone. Running my hand under my seat I found a couple of good-sized chunks of gum and dug into a piece with my wooden ruler. I wiggled the ruler back and forth, and with a final twist popped the gum free. I lifted my head just in time to watch the gum fly down the aisle and land under Mr. Long's desk. At the same time the ruler flipped back and, with a loud smack, hit the leg of the kid beside me.

"Sorry," I mouthed as I picked up the ruler. He just shrugged. Proper introductions could come later.

I glanced up the aisle. Mr. Long shifted in his chair then leaned forward. As he did his foot came down square on the gum. I held my breath and prayed he'd pass it off as a small dragged-in stone. My prayer went unanswered. Mr. Long lifted his foot, with some effort to release the shoe from the gum's grip. His knee pounded the underside of the large wooden desk, causing everything on top to jump. The globe on the corner toppled off, but he quickly caught it as if reaching for a loose basketball.

I was sure I heard him start to say, "What the hell?" but Mr. Long trailed off as he pushed his chair back and lifted his leg. I slouched, hoping Mr. Long didn't see me or my look of guilt. He picked up the gum and put it in the garbage can by the desk. I let out a sigh of relief. I'd already tested my chances of being sent to the principal's office on the first day. No, the first hour!

"Please rise for the singing of 'O Canada'," echoed from the speakers. Once the song, the Lord's Prayer, and the announcements had finished, everyone sat back down. Mr. Long stood up and cleared his throat.

"As you know we have a new student, please stand up and welcome Ricky to our class." Feet shuffled as everyone stood. I didn't know whether I should stand as well, so remained in my seat and stared at the floor while everyone said, "Welcome Ricky" in unison. I was sure I heard a "Donkey" or two spoken under someone's breath. Embarrassed at being singled out I didn't dare look to see who. It didn't matter at this point; I was just going to have to get used to hearing that name.

"Please sit and take out your social studies book. Last week we talked about Confederation. Next year Canada will be one hundred years old and a very special event, Expo '67, will be held in the province of Quebec."

Key beck?

All I knew about Quebec was that it was on the other side of Ontario. And all I knew about Ontario was that Toronto was in the middle of it; Toronto, of course, being the centre of Canada. He passed out the assignment to those at the front, who then handed them back until the last person in each row had one. Mr. Long started the lesson, and before I knew it the bell rang for recess.

I followed Mark out of the class and by the time we reached the schoolyard most of the kids were already in small groups, a few off by themselves. I saw some guys from our class standing by the edge of the pavement and walked over. Mark followed far enough behind that he could stop and go his own way if anyone spoke to him. I kicked the dirt around, hoping one of the boys would speak up and say something, but no one did. I finally said, "I'm Ricky," and with a wave of my hand back toward him added, "This is Mark."

I knew as soon as the words rolled out how dumb they were. Everyone knew Mark already, and I'd been introduced this morning. There were a couple of laughs, then silence. I was about to walk away when one of them stepped forward.

"I'm Chad. This is Kyle, Billy, Randy, and Ricky."

Great, another Ricky in class. For sure I was going to be Donkey.

"So who's your favourite football team, Donkey?" Randy asked, stepping closer. Without thinking I replied, "The Blue Bombers. Why?" Billy and Chad snickered and I knew the Bombers was the wrong answer.

"The Bombers? That's a laugh," Randy said. "You know Ricky's uncle plays for the Ti-Cats, don't you?"

I didn't, and wasn't really sure what difference that made. Other than maybe his uncle was famous.

Since Mark and I were both from Winnipeg I blurted out, "You know, Mark likes the Bombers, too." I turned to Mark, the look of surprise on his face told me he wondered why I had dragged him into this.

Randy took another step closer, until we were almost face-to-face. "Around here, you're either a Roughriders fan or you're not a fan at all. Unless your uncle's on another team, then it's okay. Even then, Ricky puts the Roughriders first and the Ti-Cats second. Besides, everyone knows the Roughriders are going to win the Grey Cup."

I should have kept my mouth shut, but I didn't. "Well, we'll see. There's still some football to go."

I hoped the Bombers would come out ahead, but the Roughriders had already kicked their butt twice and there was only one game left in the regular season. Even if the Bombers won, Randy could still say the Roughriders were the better team. The Bombers, I thought, would just have to beat them in the playoffs.

Before they could ask anything else, the recess bell went off and we started back to the school doors to line up. I glanced over at Mark as we walked, but he didn't say anything, grateful, I guess, it was me and not him they'd cornered.

▸▸▸◂◂◂

Within a couple of weeks it seemed as if we'd always lived here. In the mornings Mark would knock on my door if he was ready first, or I'd walk across to his place and wait for him.

It was hard to tell that fall was approaching as we walked to school since the lack of trees meant there weren't much changing colour, but once in a while the chill of the wind—a wisp of which crawled under my jacket and up the back of my neck, told me winter wasn't too far behind.

After Monday morning announcements, Mr. Long shuffled some papers on his desk then stood up. Looking straight ahead he rocked back and forth on his feet before finally clearing his throat and curling the papers into a tight roll. He headed down our aisle. I looked over to see David's hands inside his desk—this was going to hurt! As quickly as I had the thought David glanced up, saw Mr. Long, closed the desk lid, and clasped his hands as if he'd been paying attention all along.

Mr. Long stopped beside David. I waited for Mr. Long to swat the desk to make a point, but instead he just stared at David. David's feet now swung back and forth under his desk. The longer Mr. Long stood there, the faster David's feet swung. Soon enough whispers could be heard around the room.

Finally, Mr. Long leaned over. "David, is there something interesting in your desk? I mean besides books, papers, and your lunch."

David stopped rocking his feet and with a nervous laugh replied, "No, sir. I mean those things are certainly of interest, but nothing else in my desk is."

I knew by now David was one of those people who always tried to make a joke out of everything, this being no exception. The roll of papers came down hard, hitting the only open spot on the desk and missing David's nose by a fraction of an inch. The smack of the papers was enough to scare away any fly within miles. But as much as the class jumped, David did not. If possible, he sat even more still than before. Mr. Long walked back to the front, turned, and continued to stare at David as he began to address us all.

"Next week, as we move indoors for winter, we'll have gym class inside. We'll walk together to the gym, then split up for either the girls or boys locker room, where each of *you* will change into your gym clothes."

Mr. Long emphasized *you* as if talking to each of us directly. I wondered if anyone else was worried about having to change in public. I thought of saying something, but after looking around could see no one had raised their hand. Both of my hands remained on my desk.

"You will be given your own basket," continued Mr. Long. "Please bring a combination lock so you can keep your gym clothes here during the week. Remember the combination. I do not want to start class late because someone has forgotten it, is that clear?"

I'd learned quickly that, just like when Dad asked a question, Mr. Long didn't always want an answer. Sure enough, without waiting, he continued. "Please bring the following and keep them here so you can participate without excuse."

I tried to keep up with the list of things we needed to bring, but quickly fell behind as I wondered how I was going to undress in a room full of boys. I thought about wearing my gym shorts under my jeans then remembered swimming with my uncle and cousin at the Y in Winnipeg last year.

I'd worn my trunks under my jeans. Aside from a tight fit that made me squirm on the bus ride over, it wasn't a big deal. It was only after we'd finished swimming, as I stood dripping onto the change room tiles, cold water squishing up between my toes, that I realized I had a problem: I couldn't change in front of strangers. My uncle and cousin didn't seem to have a problem. Nor did any of the old men going about their business wearing just a towel or nothing at all, their fat, wrinkled skin on display. Some bent over to put on sandals, others rubbed areas I never knew needed to be rubbed dry. I waited as long as I could then reached into my plastic bag for my towel, patting myself and my bathing suit as dry as possible. I grabbed my underwear from the bag, rolled it up inside the towel, put both back into the bag, pulled the plastic through my hand, and closed the bag tight.

"Geez," I sighed. "Mom forgot to pack my underwear."

"You're kidding," Uncle said in a tone that told me he didn't believe me.

"No," I replied quickly as I pulled my jeans over my damp trunks. "Doesn't matter anyway, trunks are almost dry!"

If the bus ride over wasn't so bad the ride home was really unpleasant, the trunks now creating a telltale wet outline. Annoyed earlier about having to shift once in a while to pull the dry trunks out of my butt was nothing compared to the damp trunks now stuck to my skin, growing colder and colder the longer we sat on the bus.

A chill came over me just thinking about it. I drifted back in time to hear Mr. Long say, "Since we'll be running around and working up a sweat you are expected to bring your clothes home at least once a month to be washed. Is that clear?" After a moment's silence he got on with the lessons for the day, while I wondered what I was going to do.

►►►◄◄◄

The days sailed by, the exact opposite of when time slowed while waiting for a birthday or Christmas, and before I knew it we were lined up: boys on the left, girls on the right.

Mr. Long called out, "Boys, into your room. Get changed then line up in the gym along the wall closest to your door. Girls, go to your locker room where Mrs. Reed, the school nurse, is waiting." Like a human caterpillar, we all marched forward. Of course someone near the front couldn't pull the door open fast enough and we moaned as the weight of our bodies pressed against each other. I waited for Mr. Long to bark out an order to stop, but it was clear he wasn't looking at us since no such order came.

The pushing and shoving ended as we made it through the door. As one, we walked toward our baskets along the back wall, past rows of lockers meant for the older kids, then stood around awkwardly. It didn't look like anyone wanted to change first, but finally Kyle and Chad, off to the side, undid their shirts and pants. After that everyone stopped talking and started to get undressed. The room was quiet, the only noise the buzz of overhead lights.

After a few moments someone giggled, then outright laughter could be heard. I looked up to see that Kyle and Chad had stopped mid-change, their white tee-shirts covering their underwear, but didn't look too long in case someone caught me looking. Chad was pointing at Robert, who now stood behind the large cardboard barrel normally used for garbage. He stared up at the ceiling, his clothes carefully folded in his basket balanced on the edge of the open barrel, and his shorts in his hands.

Chad laughed. "Undressing behind the barrel. What a chicken!"

Kyle soon joined in. "Yeah chicken. What's the matter with you?"

Robert's face turned beet red and I felt bad since I knew he wasn't the only one who wanted privacy. I was just glad he had thought of it first. As Robert continued to change, they started toward the barrel. It looked like they were going to push it out of the way, leaving Robert with nowhere to hide. I was angry and wanted to speak up, but couldn't find my voice. Just then the gym door swung open and Mr. Long poked his head in.

"Come on boys; time's a-wasting. Hurry up."

Robert, now fully changed, slid his basket into his slot and walked out, leaving Kyle and Chad standing there. I quickly finished, threw my clothes into my basket, and ran out into the gym as Mr. Long blew his whistle.

"Everyone spread out. Make sure you can't touch anyone in front, behind, or beside you. We're going to start with jumping jacks. Legs apart, hands up and out at your sides." Of course everyone had to try and touch the person around them as he counted out, "One, two, three, four."

I grew hotter and hotter as we continued through calisthenics and wondered if I was going to smell after class. Though the thought bothered me, I knew there wasn't much I could do about it. Finally, Mr.

Long blew his whistle. "Everyone gather round. Girls in this half of the gym, boys in that half. Chad, Kyle, Debra, and Cindy; please go get three balls each from the storage room. We're going to play dodge ball."

As they came running back Mr. Long told the girls to play on one end of the gym while the boys were to play on the other end, and to make sure there were three balls on each side. He reminded us to aim for the feet, and not the head. With a "Ready, set, go," he blew his whistle. There was a lot of shuffling as everyone tried not to get hit first. Some hid behind others, but that only worked until the slow ones—like Mark—got knocked out. Soon there were only a few of us left; Robert, surprisingly, was one of them. I didn't want to be next out, I wanted to win!

As players left the game Mr. Long took away balls until the boys only had three left. I looked over to see Chad and Kyle each with a ball in hand, which meant only one ball on our side. I reached down as it rolled toward me, a good move for me and bad one for Robert, for as I did Chad and Kyle threw their balls. Kyle's hit Robert in the stomach so hard Robert bent forward. Chad's ball then hit Robert in the face, the force of which sent Robert's glasses one way and his body back against the wall.

Robert slid to the floor and tried to catch his breath as Kyle laughed. A bright red mark appeared across his cheek; another across his nose where his glasses once sat.

Mr. Long blew his whistle again then yelled, "Enough! Time to get into the locker room." He threw in a, "Are you okay, son?" for good measure.

Robert picked himself up and retrieved his glasses, stepping back as a still-laughing Chad and Kyle walked by. Robert started to stammer a reply, but before he could get any words out Mr. Long patted him on the back and pushed him toward the door. "Atta boy, let's get changed." It seemed to me that Mr. Long was more interested in getting everyone out of the gym than whether Robert was hurt or not.

We dressed in silence, most of the boys far off to either side. No one asked Robert how he was, probably afraid that Chad or Kyle would pick on them next. Chickens! I went over and asked Robert, "How's your face? It's pretty red."

"Not too bad," Robert stammered. "I'll be okay."

"Ooooh. How's your face?" Kyle imitated. "It's pretty red."

Some of the boys laughed, but most remained quiet as I turned to give Kyle a look. Out of the corner of my eye I caught Chad down on one knee, his foot sticking out from behind the same barrel Robert had earlier stood behind. Now I started to laugh. Kyle stepped forward, standing inches from my nose.

"What's so funny?" he asked.

I pointed toward Chad. "Look everyone, Chad's so embarrassed he hid behind the barrel to tie his shoes!" The room burst into laughter.

"That's not what happened," he protested. "I just bent down to tie my laces."

I wasn't going to let this go. Not after how they had treated Robert.

"Sure, Chad, sure," I said. "You were only hiding to tie your laces." Everyone laughed harder.

"It's true," he said, getting angry.

"Listen here," Kyle started, but again Mr. Long saved the day, this time for Chad and Kyle. "Come on boys, the girls are done and waiting. Let's move on to math class."

Kyle turned to walk away then called over his shoulder, "You wait. We'll get you."

Most of us were still laughing as we walked back to class.

▸ ▸ ▸ ◂ ◂ ◂

I knew we'd be going to church as Dad had announced yesterday it was "time for us to be attending again." He added that Red and I would be taking Bible Study classes with the minister's wife. It wasn't that I didn't like church, but I hated going downstairs halfway through service for Sunday school with the little kids.

As we drove up I had expected to see a big, old church, with lots of wood and stained-glass windows like our church in Winnipeg. But for the small Knox Presbyterian Church sign out front, this one looked less like a church and more like a hall. With a small tower off to the side, a plain front, and a couple steps up to the doors, it didn't even look like it had a bell to ring.

We walked in just as the service was about to start and took a seat at the back. I was sure in the weeks ahead we'd end up at the front, Dad's favourite place, on display. I closed my eyes and listened. As the minister spoke it was as if we were back home in Winnipeg, only this time there wouldn't be any cake and cookies after the service with aunts and uncles and our Oma and Opa.

Asked to stand during the announcements, everyone turned in their pews to take a good look. Singled out, it was like the first day of school all over again.

When the time came, I went downstairs with the little kids and waited for the service to be over so I would be allowed back up. As we walked past the minister on our way out I made sure to shake his hand and say hello. He held on to it so I was forced to stop.

"We look forward," he said, "to seeing you and your sister attend Bible classes with Mrs. Martin in a few weeks." I thought better of saying what I really felt about having to attend Bible class, mumbled a "me too," then waited for him to let go of my hand. All I wanted to do at this point was get home, and get changed.

▸▸▸◂◂◂

Lately, all Billy had talked about was watching *Mission Impossible, Star Trek*, and *The Monkees* on his new colour TV—for which his dad paid almost nine hundred dollars. His dad even had to go out and buy a special antenna, he bragged. At least in Winnipeg we had had two stations to choose from; here there was only one. The only good thing was having something to talk about with everyone else since we'd all have seen the same program if something good had been on.

Even so, I ran most of the way to Billy's house to see the TV for myself. His was a newer house—it even had a two-car garage attached. I rang the bell and heard it echo behind the wooden doors. A lady opened the door, curlers in her hair and a cigarette in her mouth. Billy's mom, I figured.

"Hi, I'm Ricky. Billy said it was okay for me to come over and watch TV."

"Oh sure," she replied. "Billy, Randy, and Ricky are already downstairs. Take off your coat and runners, and go on down."

Those three hung around so much they were the Three Musketeers. Truth was, I was jealous. The only person I had really made friends with was Mark, and from what I could tell he was happy to spend most of his time alone in his bedroom, door closed, reading. When we did play together it was mostly on weekends; when neither of us wanted to be home.

It was dark, the stairs carpeted, and I made it down without slipping. I quietly said, "Hi" then sat on the carpeted floor in front of the sofa. All eyes were glued to the screen in the middle of a large wooden cabinet. Billy spoke without moving.

"It has instant on, just click the button, wait eight seconds, and presto, your show is on. It's so fast! You can tune the picture, set up the volume, and then sit back and watch. Hardly have to get up at all. Not like the old days." He was excited and it sounded like he was trying to sell us all colour TVs.

"It is a contemporary design in oiled walnut with matching veneers and solids that really lend elegance to the simple design. The doors actually cover the screen when not in use. I give you," he commanded with a wave of his hand, "the Princess TV Console."

The set glowed. The screen was clean, yet the colours just didn't seem quite right. Faces appeared washed out, and sometimes the clothes; once in a while someone's hair colour was completely wrong, but it didn't matter.

The light of the screen fell across his face and I could see he was beaming. For a minute I thought he had this speech memorized, but after my eyes had finally adjusted to the dark I realized he'd just read from a brochure in his lap. I watched until it was time to go home for dinner. It was going to be hard to watch black-and-white TV again.

CHAPTER TWO

October, 1966

I rolled away from the wall and looked over at the clock. Early enough to get up. I wasn't sure why, but Dad had promised to take me to a football game in Regina. This would be the first time we'd ever been away together overnight and I was already packed.

I walked quietly down the hall and looked back toward their bedroom, the door slightly open, the room dark since it faced the back of the building. I heard him, as he put it, "breathing deeply," since he refused to admit he snored.

I liked being up early, all alone. It was as if the apartment building, with everyone fast asleep, was waiting to spring to life like flies on a window sill waking on a warm winter day. Since we'd already eaten our way through the Cap'n Crunch, breakfast was either Puffed Wheat with powdered skim milk or peanut butter and jam sandwiches. The good and bad was Puffed Wheat had the same plain taste and feel in your mouth no matter how long the bag had been opened. As for powdered milk, as long as it had a chance to sit in the fridge for a while, it wasn't too bad. But if we ran out that meant milk was cold tap water and lumpy powder.

We rarely had prize-filled cereal. "Too expensive," Mom said. When we did get a box we would run a knife under the top flap, so it could be re-folded perfectly, then we were sure to cut, not rip, the bag so cereal wouldn't fall between the bag and box. The prize had to tumble out on its own, no digging, otherwise we'd get the sugar coating under our nails or the box would be bent out of shape—all of which would make Dad mad. Red and I would hold off eating it right away so Dad couldn't say we wolfed it down too quickly, even agreeing to leave a little in the box so it looked like we had lost interest in eating any more.

Sometimes the prize would be glued to the inside of the box. Then we'd argue about who was the rightful owner. Even more disappointing was reading the fine print only to find out we had to actually send away for the prize, which meant money for postage. The worst, however, was every once in a while, no matter how hard we dug, there wasn't a prize to be found. Then we'd feel cheated by the person in charge of putting a prize in each box, thinking they maybe kept the prize for themselves.

It was better when we slept over at Grandma's. She let us empty the entire box into her biggest bowl, from which we would then grab the prize from the mound of cereal. After that, she simply left the cereal in the bowl and let us take as much as we wanted, even if it meant feeling sick right after the last spoonful.

I ate quietly, enjoyed the silence, and waited for him to get up so we could go.

▸▸▸◂◂◂

I glanced at Dad's watch; we'd already driven for over half an hour, Yorkton now a dot on the map unfolded on my lap. Other than to ask if I'd packed my toothbrush, toothpaste, and pyjamas he hadn't spoken. I'd never had him all to myself, and, happy to be in the front seat, I sat quietly and wondered what to talk about.

We all had our places in the car: mine directly behind Dad, Red behind Mom, and Little Sister in the middle. Although Dad could see me in the rear-view mirror, he had a hard time turning to hit me when he was mad; Red was another matter. He could reach her legs over the seat, so that meant she got slapped a lot. Since she was red-headed and pale-skinned it didn't take much of a slap for her legs to turn red.

I worked up the nerve to ask how much longer until we got to Regina. I didn't get an answer right away, so turned my head slightly toward him. This was a game we played—when he was in a game-playing mood—looking sideways to see if the other person would look, but not enough to make direct eye contact. Wearing sunglasses to block the glare of the sun, Dad's gaze remained fixed on the road ahead. It was clear he was not in a game-playing mood.

Sometimes, on long car trips, Mom would bark out his name and Dad's head would snap up, a string of Dutch swear words tumbling out. He'd struggle to pull the car from where it had strayed to the side of the road and back onto the highway. The three of us in the back would roll slightly left, then right, then back again, like bowling pins unable to make up their minds whether or not to fall. He'd then spend the next few minutes insisting he hadn't dozed off.

The longer we drove, the more excited I got. As much as I had heard about the Roughriders the Bombers were still my team—though I now made sure to keep my mouth shut about it at school. I had been so excited about going away I'd forgotten to ask who the Roughriders were playing. After a long pause he cleared his throat. "The Stampeders," he said. I sat back and watched as farms now gave way to the city of Regina.

By the time we got to Taylor Field, parked, walked, found our seats, and waited for the game to start, it was clear I wasn't going to be warm enough. I wedged myself between Dad and the large, cigar-smoking man beside me, leaning as far back from the wind as I could to hold off the chill. Soon enough there were whistles, pushing and shoving; footballs were thrown and even caught once in a while. It seemed to me the players on both sides spent a lot of time huddled together before lining up across from each other, and very little time doing anything else. That is except to crash into the person in front or run away from everyone else. I found it hard to follow what was going on and asked what was happening. Dad replied he didn't know the rules since football in Holland was a game played without equipment, and with a round ball kicked up and down a field. That just made things more confusing.

Watching a game in person sure was different than watching on TV, what with the noise of the crowd, the announcer's voice echoing around the stadium, and the cold beginning to set into my bones. I mentioned Ricky's uncle played for Hamilton, but Dad didn't seem interested. Perhaps he couldn't hear me through his ear muffs.

At half-time we left the stands for a pee break and a hot chocolate, returning to our seats in time to hear the announcer stating there were over sixteen thousand people in the stands. That was about three thousand more than the whole of Yorkton!

Once the game was over, we quickly made our way back onto the highway and headed toward the motel. I asked how far we had to drive and after a few minutes, without turning his head, he replied, "About half an hour. Reach over and get my cigarettes."

I opened the glove box with one hand, pushed the lighter into the dash with the other, undid the plastic wrap, and handed over the pack of cigarettes. Without taking his hands from the wheel he pushed the deck up, the flap flipped open, and he pulled the silver foil from the pack. The smell of fresh tobacco drifted up from the neat rows of cigarettes and flooded my nose as I stuffed the plastic wrap in my coat pocket. He pulled out a cigarette, tapped it several times on the dash, slid it into his mouth, and tossed the pack to me just as the lighter popped like a jack-in-the box; a red-hot coil instead of a bobbing clown head. We both reached for it at the same time, which meant neither of us got it and the light coil fell beneath Dad's feet. The car swerved from side-to-side as he felt around the floor with one hand while trying to drive with the other. His "Jesus Christ" told me this hadn't been a good idea.

I spotted it on the mat and reached down just as he moved his foot back. His boot heel pressed my hand against the lighter, the red tip still hot enough to do its job. My brain screamed every swear word I'd ever heard but my mouth only managed a quiet, "Sorry, Dad."

The car, finally back on track, stopped rocking. Other than my palm feeling like it was on fire, everything seemed okay. At least until the pain increased and a "Jesus Christ that hurts" slipped out of my mouth. I froze, but it was too late to take the words back. Dad stared at me while the car again divided its time between the road and the soft shoulder.

"What did you say?"

I watched as he went to swing his arm toward my head. I like to think the smell of burnt skin reaching his nose was the reason he didn't follow through. Instead, he pulled over, reached down, and popped the lighter back in.

"What were you thinking, grabbing the lighter? You should have known I was getting it myself!"

Thinking things couldn't get any worse I replied, "I was just … I wanted to help."

I squeezed my wrist and tried not to let any tears run down my face. I was sure he was looking at me out of the corners of his eyes, but I wasn't going to look back.

"Burn yourself?"

My lips parted, words ready, but I was going to cry and nodded yes instead.

"Let me see."

I opened my hand: little round circles had started to blister my palm.

"Probably looks worse than it hurts," he said.

I was sure it looked worse to him since he couldn't actually feel it.

"Come on, I'll buy you a pop at the next gas station. You can wrap your hand around the cold bottle." We sat in silence while my hand throbbed.

A Shell station soon appeared on the right. I waited for the car to slow, but as we passed the entrance it was clear we weren't stopping. Finally, he spoke. "Don't need gas yet. Besides, I want an Esso. There's one ahead."

I leaned my head against the cold metal of the door and closed my eyes. The next thing I knew the car came to a hard stop and I pulled my head back up, my neck now stiff. The inside of the car glowed red as a neon vacancy sign slowly flashed on and off. It was clear we were at the motel and not an Esso station.

Dad looked over. "You were asleep when I got gas. I figured your hand didn't hurt much and didn't want to waste time waking you up, so after I gassed up I just kept on driving." He was right. By now I was used to the pain and my hand probably wasn't going to hurt any more than it already did.

He stepped out into a rush of crisp fall air, a reminder winter was on its way. I watched as he entered the front office and shook hands with a man behind the counter, the light from the front window spilling out across our hood. The longer they talked, the colder I got. I tried not to fog up the windows any more than they already were in case we had to move the car. I picked at the plastic sheet stuck to my window and had managed to rip a good chunk of the corner off before I realized what I had done. I put my hands under my legs to keep my fingers away from trouble.

I was startled by the sudden, hard rap of knuckles against my window. "Come on, let's get our stuff into the room and get dinner before they close," came Dad's muffled voice. I watched as he disappeared below the front of the car, reaching down, no doubt, to plug in the block heater. I grabbed my bag, opened the door, and made to get out.

"Don't step on the cord," he snapped. "Supposed to get cold tonight. Can't wait to turn this car in and get a new one."

The car—the "son of a bitch" as Dad sometimes called it—had belonged to the guy he'd replaced. According to Dad, the Pontiac Parisienne took forever to start whether it was "damp, cold, or sometimes just plain didn't feel like it."

"Last thing I want is to be stuck in the morning, so we're not taking any chances, are we?" It was one of those questions I knew didn't require an answer.

We stopped in front of room number six. As Dad opened the green painted door, stepped in, and flicked on the light, I felt the cold air outside meet the cold air inside. Along one wall were two beds, and a table with a single lamp between them. Against the opposite wall sat a TV on a metal stand and a desk hardly big enough for a man like Dad to sit and work, and a single clothes bar fixed to the wall. The cinder-block walls were painted the same bright green as the door, the light from the overhead fixture not quite reaching the corners of the room.

I wanted to use the bathroom, but knew I needed to wait and see if he was going first. Instead I asked which bed was mine. He pointed to the one closest to the bathroom. It had a little box with slots for quarters attached to the top, the words *Magic Fingers Relaxation Service* in big letters. *Quarters only, fifteen minutes. Try it, you'll feel great!*

"What's that for?" I asked as I put my bag on the bed.

"That, ah," he replied, "is a bed massager."

"What does it do?"

Dad didn't answer. I knew when a question was going to be answered and when it wasn't, and followed him back out.

I could always go pee in the restaurant.

We walked along the row of doors; some rooms had lights on, one or two with shadowy figures moving about. Still others appeared empty: no lights, no shadows, no noise. I knew it wasn't polite to stare, but I wanted to see who was here and what they were doing.

Dad opened the door to an almost-empty diner, directing me by my shoulders towards an empty booth, Pine-Sol and fried food the first smells to hit my nose. My runners squeaked as I walked across the freshly mopped floor, and I worried about the footprints I was surely leaving behind.

The waitress behind the counter looked up, smiled, and started around and towards us. "How are you, hon? I didn't expect to see you for another few weeks." She continued in a slightly sweeter voice. "This is a pleasant surprise." Dad gave her a quick smile and a wink as we settled into the booth.

"Pleasure, not business this time. Took my son to the game today."

She looked at me, placing her free hand across mine and pressing it firmly down on the table, my burnt palm now fully stretched out.

No tears, no tears.

"Little Ricky! It's nice to finally meet you. Your Dad has told me all about you. I almost feel as if you're one of mine." I wanted her to take her hand off of mine, but she held it down as if to keep me in place. "I hope you had a nice time."

I looked up, thinking she was talking to me, but she wasn't. She was talking to Dad. My face got warm and I knew it was turning red. I wanted to slide under the table and out the door.

"Liver and onions?" she asked. Dad nodded yes and she looked back at me. "And what will you have, hon?"

The few times we did eat out we never got to choose and always ended up sharing a pop; half for me, half for Red. Not this time! Just as my mouth started to water at the possibilities Dad answered for me.

"He'll have a hamburger, fries with gravy, and a glass of milk." A hamburger, fries and gravy, okay—but a glass of milk? And all to myself?

The waitress turned, the soles of her shoes squeaking as she walked behind the counter and tucked the order up onto the carousel. A hairy arm reached through the window, snapping the paper off the clip with a quick flick before disappearing while the carousel continued to wobble.

She returned with a pot of coffee, flipping Dad's mug over to pour a cup. With an "I'll be back," she squeaked away. We sat quietly; nothing said, nothing asked. It was as if we were around our table at home.

After several dings of the bell, she returned from behind the counter carrying our food. Her outfit crinkled as she leaned against the table and put a plate of liver and onions in front of Dad. As she put my plate and the glass of milk in front of me she said, "Make sure to drink your milk. It gives you good bones and will make you big and strong." For good measure she added, "Just like your father."

I noticed she didn't have any rings on her fingers, her nails painted a bright red. I felt my face getting warm again, and kept my head down as I reached for the hamburger. I just wanted to eat and get back to our room.

Dad dug into the liver and onions as if he hadn't eaten in days, each chewed mouthful louder than the last until all I heard was the sound of gnashing, chomping teeth. Finally, a low, rumbled burp of appreciation welled from within. He was finished and ready to leave.

"Come on. Hurry up and clear your plate," he said.

The juice from the last bite of burger ran down my chin, and before I could grab my napkin Dad had his hanky out and was swiping it across my mouth. I hated that hanky. Lord knows how many times he'd blown his nose before carefully folding it up and putting it back in his pocket. I slid the last of the fries down as quickly as I could, now a soggy, cold mess of pulpy potato. Once done, we silently walked back to our room.

Though now under the sheets, I realized I still had to pee and wished I'd gone when we were in the restaurant. I slid out of bed, my feet now colder as I walked across the linoleum floor. Sitting on the toilet, icy air swept across the back of my neck through the open window. No matter how Mom complained, Dad always wanted the place, any place, colder.

I finished up, closing the window as much as I dared. Looking out I could see nothing but a moonlit field. It was as if we'd been plucked from someplace and plopped here, in the middle of nowhere.

Jumping back into bed I looked up to read the instructions on the coin box. I wanted to try it, but was afraid to ask on the chance I'd have to give up my allowance. Finally, I worked up the courage. "So, if you put a quarter in, what happens?"

Without looking away from the TV, Dad replied, "Shakes you to sleep. If you're ready to sleep. Otherwise it might take several quarters."

That was a lot of allowance to spend on falling asleep.

"Grab a quarter from the change on the desk." Not having to be told twice, I jumped out of bed, grabbed a quarter, and crawled back under the covers. Dad was staring at me and I realized the quarter was clutched in the palm of my good hand under the blankets. I slid my hand out.

"Can you please put it in for me?"

He leaned over and dropped the quarter in the slot. Nothing happened.

"Goddammit, that's why you don't bother with these things. I wasted a whole quarter." But as the word "quarter" left his lips the bed roared to life.

"It's working," I shouted. "It's working! I'm getting relaxed!" Each word echoed as the bed shook me around and I tried to concentrate on the ceiling light. The lamp on the table shimmied to the front edge as the bed pounded against the wall.

"Jesus, if anyone's next door I'm going to have to explain *this* in the morning."

Twenty-five cents and fifteen minutes later, the bed fizzled to a stop like a balloon with a slow leak. I tried to remain still, but my dinner started to roll around my now upset stomach.

Oh no; please, God, don't let me barf. If having dropped the lighter wasn't bad enough, barfing certainly would be.

"I think, uh, I think I have to go to the bathroom."

He looked at me with a slight smile. "You won't be asking for any more quarters then?"

No, right now I just need a toilet.

I closed the door with just enough time to open the window and take a swallow of crisp, fresh air before kneeling in front of the bowl. Once the burger, fries, and gravy came up I washed my face, brushed my teeth, and made my way back to bed in the dark. Dad was already breathing heavily.

In the morning a blinding beam of light cut across both beds from the open front drapes. I put my hand up across my forehead to look around. He was up and I should be too.

"Come on," he said. "Let's get some breakfast and then head home."

The cars were dusted with frost. As we stepped outside I felt my face tighten with the chill, the bright fall sunshine having given a false promise of warmth.

Since our waitress wasn't in, Dad decided we could sit at the counter. The man serving greeted Dad with a "Hi Bart," followed quickly with "What'll ya have?" I was surprised when Dad ordered toast and soft-boiled eggs for both of us.

Man oh man, if his wasn't cooked exactly right….

The waiter repeated back our order and Dad replied, "Thanks George." Dad seemed to know everyone, and everyone seemed to know him. I looked at the faded stains on George's white shirt and pants as he reached out to pour the coffee. His sleeves were rolled up, the faint outline of a tattoo and the words HMCS Bonaventure just visible.

This was a funny place for a sailor to end up: in the middle of the flattest land you could find, far away from the sea.

Dad drank his coffee while I spun around and watched as cars and trucks passed by on the highway. George came back almost as soon as the cook hit the bell, and placed our food in front of us. "Here you go, Bart."

The toast was firm but not burned, cut into thin strips Dad could dip into the yolk. Little soldiers, we called them. He carefully tapped around the egg's shell with his knife, pulling the top off without causing any bits to break off. The white of the egg was solid, the yoke slightly liquid. It was now clear he'd trained them to cook a soft-boiled egg and make toast *his* way.

The yolk disappeared with the last sliver of toast. Dad slipped his spoon between the white of the egg and the shell, pulled out the white, and slid it into his mouth. As usual he finished before me, and I needed to shove in my eggs and toast without dripping any runny yolk on my chin as he sat and sighed.

In short order Dad paid our bill and told George he'd see him again in a few weeks. After giving our room a once over he closed the door behind us and sat behind the wheel. I unplugged the block heater, wrapping the stiff cord so it wouldn't dangle beneath the car as we drove off.

"We've got about another hour and a half," he said before losing himself in silence. Listening to the radio recap yesterday's game made me certain Winnipeg would be the Western Conference champs in a few weeks. Then I'd tell Ricky and the others how I really felt about their team.

▸▸▸◂◂◂

In the excitement of the trip I'd forgotten we'd be celebrating Thanksgiving a day early as Dad still intended to hit the road tomorrow as usual, rather than Tuesday. As soon as we had made it home, parked the car, and headed upstairs, he rushed to the bathroom while I poked my head into the kitchen to see Mom straining vegetables from a can and Red mashing potatoes.

I wasn't sure why, but we'd been promised duck for dinner instead of turkey. There in front of me on the counter sat a very small and crispy black bird in the middle of a large platter, bits of foil stuck to its skin. It looked like a chicken, but slightly longer and not so plump, with a smell I didn't recognize. I went into the dining room and took my seat at the table, wondering how that little bird was going to feed five of us tonight *and* make a couple of days' worth of leftovers Mom always planned on having.

Dad came down the hall and took his seat at the head of the table. Red and Mom carried out the vegetables and mashed potatoes, and then Mom brought out the bird. Dad looked down while she stood and stared at him. It reminded me of two gunslingers waiting for the other to draw first.

My stomach tightened and all of a sudden I remembered a doozy of an argument just before Little Sister was born. For some reason, dinner that night had been a large plate of sandwiches: peanut butter, liverwurst, and Kam with lettuce and tomato. Back then Red and I sat across from each other, with Mom and Dad at either end.

I can't remember who said what to start it off, only that time seemed to slow down all of a sudden. One of the sandwiches—liverwurst I think—flew across the table, followed by another sandwich and then another. It was as if Red and I didn't exist. We sat quietly as Mom and Dad removed the carefully stacked sandwiches, layer by layer, hitting each other in the chest or face; in some cases the wall in the too small kitchen.

Red kept her head bowed while tears flowed from her eyes. As quickly as it started, it stopped. They just picked up what had fallen into their laps and put them back on their plate. Mom grabbed Red by the arm and left the room. Dad picked up a sandwich, cut it into bite size pieces with his knife and fork, and then slid them into his mouth. No words. No apologies.

I looked at the thinly sliced duck in front of us now, and for a brief second wished for a fight so we wouldn't have to eat it. Only this time Dad just muttered in Dutch, got up from the table, sat in his chair in the living room, and lit up a cigarette. Smoke soon drifted across the table. I looked at the girls. By now Little Sister had eaten her mashed potatoes and peas.

"Come on," Mom said. "Let's clear the table." I spooned the remaining potatoes and peas down my throat as fast as I could.

"I'll make some peanut butter and jam sandwiches for you guys."

▸▸▸◂◂◂

Mr. Long stopped in front of the gym, his high tops squeaking on the polished floor as he turned to face us.

"I have hockey registration forms here. If you're interested, raise your hand as I walk by."

Everyone raised their hands except Billy, Robert, and the girls. The guys said Billy, skinny and pale, had a twin who died at birth and so was excused from all types of physical activity. Robert simply turned away and stared down the empty hall. Of course the girls weren't allowed to play hockey.

I'd never actually played before. I had in fact only been on skates once, but didn't want any of the guys to know. I raised my hand to get one and after the forms were handed out, we were told to "walk quickly and quietly, get changed, and get into the gym."

▸▸▸◂◂◂

I brought my form home and left it on the dining-room table, knowing if I could convince Mom, I was more than halfway to convincing Dad. When I went to set the table for dinner the form was gone. I started to say something, then wondered if Red had taken it. If she did, I was going to pound her!

After dinner I waited until we were ready for bed then called to Red as she walked by my room. "Did you take my form?"

"What form?"

"You know what form!"

I pretended to leap out of bed as if to get her. She stepped back, looked over her shoulder, and laughed. "Mom has it," she said, pulling my door shut. I pulled the blankets back up before cold air got between me and the sheets. Wanting to stay awake I turned the radio on, but all I could find was *The World Tomorrow* and the voice of Garner Ted

Armstrong booming out of the transistor.

Finally, Mom came to kiss me on the cheek. Her hair fell over me and I breathed in her perfume.

"Will I be able to sign up?" I waited anxiously for her answer.

"I'll see what your father says. Now go to sleep."

That was the last thing I remembered until the nightmare. I'd had the dream before, but now the feelings were stronger, the furniture bigger, me smaller. I was in our old house, alone in the living room. I watched as the furniture began to grow, and as it did I shrank. It was as if everything was pulled and stretched, while I became smaller and smaller. I tried to speak. I tried to scream. Nothing came out. I awoke and lay frozen in bed, unable to move.

▸▸▸◂◂◂

It was getting colder every day, snow expected sooner rather than later. At recess the guys were up against the school wall, out of the wind, trying to stay warm. I wasn't looking forward to carrying a bag of candy through the snow or having to wear my parka over my costume, and hoped the first real snowfall would wait at least until after Hallowe'en.

Since Mom didn't sew and she never seemed to have extra cash, the choice of what to wear for Hallowe'en was always somewhat limited. The easiest thing to do was to stitch some patches on an old pair of pants, rub burnt cork on my face for make-believe dirt, and find a long stick from which I could sling a cloth bag over my shoulder. Oh, and a kerchief to wrap around my neck.

A hobo—again.

The guys stopped talking as Mark and I walked up but after a few minutes of silence and some looks between David and the guys, he asked if we wanted to come out for Devil's Night. I had no idea what they were talking about, but didn't want to seem dumb and said, "Sure we're in" before Mark had a chance to say anything.

I wanted to be part of their group and didn't need to be asked twice.

David kept on talking. "We need to decide where and when on Sunday we're going to meet."

"What about the field behind St. Paul's?" Billy spoke up, surprising us all. I figured he'd be the first to say he wasn't coming.

"Fine," David replied. "We'll meet at six-thirty. Should be dark enough by then. Everyone needs to bring something: toilet paper, matches, soap, eggs, paper bags, gloves, spoons. Make sure you don't get caught taking this stuff, and if someone tries to catch you when we're out run as fast as you can. Whatever you do, make sure the coast is clear before you go home. There'll be lots of cops out trying to catch us."

Cops? Who said anything about cops? They'd done this before and hadn't got caught, why would anyone get caught now? What if they were just trying to see if I'd chicken out?

"No problem," I replied. "I'll be there. I can bring eggs and paper bags." I knew what the eggs were for, but wasn't sure about the paper bags. I kept quiet as I didn't want to let on this was my first time. I knew no one at home would miss some lunch bags, but eggs, easy to count in the carton, required some planning. That meant I'd have to bake on the Saturday before Devil's Night instead of playing with Mark. Since Mom didn't spend much time in the kitchen, I learned to bake from handed-down recipe cards. Even if Red caught on she wasn't going to say anything since she could eat the rewards of my plan.

"Remember," David continued. "No one talks about this 'til we meet Sunday."

We formed a circle, put our hands in the middle, and said in unison, "Swear it out loud." Though I was the new kid, I knew enough that if you swore something out loud you were doomed if you broke the oath.

▸▸▸◂◂◂

Dad and I entered the arena, a big old wooden building they said used to be the old airport hangar, the smell of oil and gasoline replaced by coffee, popcorn, and sweat. I'd heard about the local men's senior hockey team, the Terriers, at school. *Lots of fights. Real tough guys. Some on their way up, some on their way down.*

We were here for the Women's Auxiliary annual used hockey equipment sale. Long rows of tables were filled with used equipment, handmade signs taped to the table fronts, some with sizes, and some with ages written on them.

"What do you need?" Dad asked.

How did I know? I'd never done this before.

I stood and stared at the nearest table. Finally, one of the ladies came over. "First time playing hockey?"

"Yes," Dad replied. His voice always seemed louder just when I didn't want anyone overhearing what he had to say.

"Here's a list," she said. "We have everything except hockey sticks. I'd suggest you purchase a new jock strap, although we have used ones over there." My eyes followed her outstretched finger to a nearby table, a small pile of white cloth-covered mounds with straps attached. I looked at Dad; he looked at me.

"You know," she continued in a motherly voice, "you'll need to protect yourself ... in case you get hit by a puck." Nothing looked as though it would protect me from much, but who was I to argue?

Dad poked at the pile. "What's your waist size?" I shrugged my shoulders and the lady stepped closer.

"Take off your jacket, turn around, and hold still dear." I did as I was told and felt her pull the back of my shirt out, then tug open the back of my jeans.

"Looks like a size twenty-four or so. Maybe a twenty-two, but jocks stretch and will fit a range of sizes." My face was hot.

Dad leaned over, pulled one out of the pile, and handed it to me. I felt something hard and rapped it with my knuckles, then looked up at the lady. She smiled and my face got even hotter. I wanted to run, but seeing as I was holding the jock strap stayed put.

"Come on," Dad said. "Pick out some skates."

I hoped to find a new pair from someone who didn't want to play, or who had two pairs and never used the second. As I picked through the pile I could see I wasn't going to get that lucky; they were all used. I grabbed a pair that wasn't too scuffed, just a little bit of rust that should come off with a good sharpening. Soon I had everything but a hockey stick and bag. I looked at Dad just as he spied a cardboard box over in the corner, the words *Indian River Oranges* printed on its side.

"I need to get my haircut. Grab that box so I can pay and get out of here."

I managed to squeak out, "I still need a stick."

But I knew from his reply—"I'll get you one later"—we were done. That was his give and take; you were with him the whole day if you needed something, or you made sure you were out of the house before he got up if you didn't.

I carried the box to the cash table, where one of the ladies cut the tags off and another wrote up the items in a receipt book. Dad took out his customary roll of bills to pay.

He held open the trunk as I lifted the orange box into the back. I still didn't know how to skate and would only have a few weeks to learn. At least I'd get a new stick.

▸▸▸◂◂◂

Mr. Long called the class to order with roll call. Everyone replied with a "here" as their name was called, until David answered instead with a "yo".

"I beg your pardon?" Mr. Long asked. Snickering was replaced by silence as he stood and started toward David.

David froze, his hands gripping the corners of his desk as a whisper rose from the back of this throat. "Here. Sir." Before the last roll of the "r" had left his lips Mr. Long's wooden ruler fell across the top of David's desk, missing David's fingers by a fraction of an inch.

"That," Mr. Long said as he headed back up to the front, "is what I thought you said."

After singing the national anthem and reciting the Lord's Prayer, we took our seats and listened to announcements from the principal and then Mr. Long.

"Mr. Gazdewich, the school janitor, will put the boards up for the rink this week. Once the temperature drops he'll start to flood the area. Only then can you use it, not before. Also, as Hallowe'en is on Monday, we'll have the party in our classroom at four this Friday. Who'd like to stay after school today and help decorate the room?"

The usual hands went up, including Cindy's and Debra's. Debra was the most popular girl in class. All the guys talked about her, at least when her cousin Dale wasn't in ear shot. This was my chance to spend time with her and I quickly raised my hand.

"Ok then, all set. See you after class today."

At lunch I joined the line at the milk cooler. This was the one place I could get chocolate milk, and I'd learned to line up quickly as there were never enough half-pint cartons for all of us. As I waited Mark walked up, punched me in the arm, and asked, "Why'd you volunteer? I thought we were playing after school."

The best excuse I could come up with was, "We were, but I figured maybe Mr. Long won't be so hard on me at test time if I helped out a little."

Robert, off to the side, spoke up. "Or maybe you just wanted to help Debra." I was going to push him, but didn't want to lose my spot so I kept quiet, got my chocolate milk, and walked away. Mark followed quietly behind.

At the end of the day, after we put our books away and the rest of the class filed out, Mr. Long brought in orange and brown construction paper, along with glue, tape, scissors, and black markers. I spent the next hour trying to figure out how to work with Debra, but every time I came up with a suggestion Cindy butted in and said, "What a great idea" before proceeding to ignore me.

So I sat alone and made paper chains. When they were long enough, I stood on the desks and taped them to the lights. Soon the room was filled with orange and brown loops. Along with Debra's and Cindy's paper pumpkins, and some badly drawn outlines of cats and ghosts taped to the walls, the room was decorated for Hallowe'en.

I never did get a chance to talk to Debra alone, but at least we'd spent some time together.

▸ ▸ ▸ ◂ ◂ ◂

The next morning we filed into class, and the first thing I noticed was that the chains were missing. After announcements Mr. Long thanked us for staying behind last night, and then went on to say that Mr. Gazdewich removed the chains from the lights this morning as he feared it was a fire hazard. It didn't look as much like Hallowe'en this morning as it did the night before.

Once we were back from afternoon recess we put away our books and pushed the desks to one side. Kyle, whose family didn't celebrate anything, was excused from class and sent to sit in the nurse's office. After the candies, cakes, and cookies were eaten, Mark and I headed home and talked all the while about Hallowe'en, our plans for trick-or-treating, hockey, and football.

Once home, I entered the apartment just in time to hear Dad, already home for the weekend, arguing with Mom about signing up for curling. I quietly closed the apartment door behind me and waited in the kitchen.

"Lookit, the deadline to register is coming up and I'm going to register. There's nothing for me to do except take care of the kids." I couldn't hear Dad's reply. I wasn't sure he replied at all.

As hard as it had been on us kids to move maybe it was just as hard on them—or at least Mom.

"Since you won't let me work I need to do something, especially when winter sets in. There's no way I'm staying indoors 'til spring just 'cause you want me to stay at home."

Mom was as quick to anger as Dad, and once she'd made up her mind arguing with her wasn't going to get him anywhere.

"And you know," she continued, "maybe you ought to consider joining in on the weekends. You've got to start making some friends here eventually."

"Fine, I'll write the cheque. You can play." Dad knew when he was beat.

I heard someone walk toward the living room. Dad, I guessed, hearing his chair groan. I popped my head around the corner and said hello then headed down the hall to my room, closed the door behind me, and waited to be called to set the table for dinner.

▸▸▸◂◂◂

On Saturday I baked as planned, and was able to pocket four fresh eggs. After dinner on Sunday I left the apartment, saying Mark and I were going over to Randy's house to play for a while. By six-thirty all but Bradly had shown up. We took a vote and agreed there wasn't any point in waiting for him; he'd clearly chickened out. Besides, it didn't make any sense for him to come. If we had to run he'd be the last to start, and the first to be caught.

David gathered us around. "Let's see what we have. Everyone pull your stuff out." One by one we put in our contributions. Although I was only required to bring the bags and eggs, I wanted to make a good impression and brought a roll of toilet paper too. Soon the pile contained wooden matches, bars of Ivory soap, eggs, paper bags, two large spoons, and about a dozen rolls of toilet paper.

"Load up your pockets. We'll start with the soap and toilet paper," David ordered. "Let's start down the street, find a car, and write all over it with the soap."

"What'll we write?" Randy asked.

"Write anything you want—it's Devil's Night! Draw all over the car. If you run out of things to say, just rub the soap all over the windows. It's hard to wash off. Make sure to throw the rolls of toilet paper over and under the car, over and over, until the roll runs out."

"The eggs," David went on, his smile now a wide grin, "are for passing cars. But don't throw them until the car goes past us. If they want to come after us they'll have to turn around, giving us time to run away."

It wasn't long before we spotted our target: a new two-door Impala parked directly ahead, her sleek lines sharpened by the street light above. It was a beauty!

"Come on," David whispered. "Soap her up, paper her over, and then run like heck."

We peeled the paper off the Ivory bars Mark had supplied, and soon enough the windows were streaked. A couple of rolls of toilet paper were unwrapped and tossed between us. Finished, we ran between the houses and down back lanes, laughing as fenced-in dogs howled and barked.

Several cars later we were out of eggs, having missed all of our moving targets. Soon after that we ran out of toilet paper, so after wrapping and soaping our last car we headed back toward the park. That's when I asked David what the paper bags were for.

"The grand finale! How many do we have again?"

I pulled them out. "I have four; Randy and Mark each have one."

"Okay, who has the spoons and the matches?" Dale reached into his jacket and pulled out two large salad spoons, while Randy fished the matches out of his pants pocket. David took the matches and broke one in half. Counting out five more, he clenched them in his fist and made sure all six match heads were even.

"Now we draw."

I wasn't sure what we were drawing for, but I managed to pull out an unbroken one. After going around the circle it came down to Dale and Mark. We watched as Mark drew his turn. He was it!

"Perfect," David said. "Now, all we need are some piles of dog poo."

Silence.

"What do ya mean some piles of dog poo?" Dale asked.

David turned to face Dale. "We're going to fill the bags with poo and put the bag at someone's front door. Then ...," he paused, an evil look on his face. "We're gonna light the bag, ring the bell, watch 'em stomp out the fire, and squish the poo." You had to hand it to him: he knew how to end the night on a high note.

"Mark pulled the short match. He has to scoop up the first bag." I looked over at Mark. He didn't seem too keen on the idea.

As we walked, we started singing, "All we have to do is get some poo." Repeating the words over and over until someone suggested a yard.

"How about McVicar's? They have a Golden Retriever. Bet it poops a lot."

"Yeah," Dale chimed. "If the dog's in the house, Mark can scoop up some poo and we can be on our way."

"Alright. McVicar's it is," said David.

Gathering round in the lane behind their house we listened closely. The coast was clear; the dog was nowhere to be heard.

"Here's a spoon," Dale whispered to Mark. "It belonged to my grandmother. Don't lose it. And make sure whatever you pick up is hard, not fresh."

We crouched behind the fence and peered through the slats as Mark slowly opened the gate, then followed his zig-zagged shadow around the back yard as he pushed the spoon along the grass. I heard him gag a couple of times, but he never barfed. Finally, he came back through the gate. In one hand a tightly closed bag, in the other the spoon. Mark waved both dangerously around, neither an item with which anyone wanted to be tagged.

"Here, put the spoon in here and hand me the poo bag," David said. "Everyone else cut through the neighbour's yard, get across the street, and hide."

Off we went, ready to break into a run if needed. We watched as David broke through the shadows, climbed the front steps of the McVicar's house, and tried to light the bag. On the third try the bag burned bright. David rang the McVicar's doorbell and ran off.

The porch light flicked on, the door opened, and a man looked down at the burning bag. He turned his head left, then right, then disappeared, only to return with a pot of water. Within seconds the fire was out, the front door closed, and the porch light turned off. So much for that!

David circled back and now joined us in the shadows. "Did he stomp it? Did he get shit all over the place? Was he swearing?" No one answered. "Come on. What did I miss?"

Mark finally spoke up. "Not much."

David took a step toward Mark. "Whattaya mean, not much? That bag was on fire. He *must* have stepped on it!"

"Well, um, no," Mark said. "He didn't. All he did was get some water, throw it on the bag, and close the door. That's it. That's all. The bag's still there."

"Bull crap," David barked out, spitting a little on Mark. "Don't tell me he didn't step on it after all the work we did?"

Mark took a step back and wiped his cheek. "Stop spitting. Actually I scooped up the dog poo, and yes, that's what happened." We all nodded in agreement.

"Well I'll be dammed," David said. "Let's see if we can find someone else."

"No," Mark replied. "I get the idea, but I've had enough. I'm going home." The others sort of shrugged in agreement, but this didn't stop David.

"Come on, guys. Who wants to see someone stomp on a flaming bag of poo?"

I was with Mark; it was getting late and Hallowe'en was tomorrow. "I'll walk home with you," I said.

David stood alone. "Chickens. Next year I'm going to go with guys who know what Devil's Night is all about."

If it's about watching a man put out a fire with a pot of water and leaving it until morning to clean up, I'll be doing something else too.

▸ ▸ ▸ ◂ ◂ ◂

I was ready to start trick-or-treating. I listened for Mark to leave his apartment and opened our door before he finished knocking. I looked at him. We were supposed to be hobos with dirt on our faces and patches on our clothes, and here he was with a carefully drawn beard, makeup under his eyelids, and bits of broom straw sticking out from under a black bowler hat. With a licorice cigar in his mouth he looked like Red Skelton, except for the floral-patterned cloth bag he was holding that looked like the one his Mom used to hold her knitting stuff. Lord knows how long his Mom had saved those clothes since she was now okay with him carefully cutting them with scissors.

"Where's your pillow case?"

"Well, um," he stammered. "I couldn't get one."

"You mean your Mom said 'no', didn't she?" I didn't need an answer. I knew by now she wouldn't let Mark do anything that wasn't proper. Me, I just went ahead and did it. I showed him my pillow case.

"Come on," I said. "We're wasting time and I want to fill this to the top. We can do all the apartments real quick, then head over to the streets where the guys told us give out real candy, no apples or popcorn."

I wanted to get to as many places as possible before Mark got cold or it started to snow, so I pushed him to get in and get out as quickly as possible. We'd made it up and down our street in no time and headed over to the big houses a few streets over. We had to walk more, but I had on extra clothes under my costume so I could stay out as long as possible.

Soon enough it was clear there weren't any little kids running around with their parents, just us older kids out. It was easier to go door-to-door, but because it was getting late it also meant most of the candy was gone or people weren't so free in giving out what little they had left.

Mark, out of breath, finally said, "Come on, we have enough candy. Besides, if I want more I can always take some from Dad's samples." True, but I couldn't. I reached down, pulled out some stuff I knew Mom wouldn't let me keep and started to eat them.

"Alright, let's go home."

I left the apples and unwrapped items alone; we'd already been warned not to eat those. I also knew we'd have to give up some of our candy, so Mom could take them to the hospital for the sick kids who didn't get out for Hallowe'en. I wondered how they felt getting our throwaways.

CHAPTER THREE

November, 1966

"Oh, I had a call yesterday from Mrs. Martin," Mom said as I walked into the kitchen to make breakfast. "You and Red start Bible class after school today."

I'd forgotten, or at least tried to forget. I wasn't sure if I needed more God in my life, or if I was being punished for something I'd done. I didn't know who, if anyone, from school would be there, but figured since it was Bible class it wasn't going to be anyone too popular. I had to figure out something to tell the guys in case anyone asked what I was doing after school.

"Don't forget to wait for your sister so you can walk over together. Mrs. Martin's expecting you at four-thirty. If you get into any trouble your sister will tell me, understand?"

Of course I understood. I was supposed to pretend I enjoyed sitting in someone's house learning about Jesus when my friends were out playing.

"Yes," I replied with a sigh, "I'll make sure we're there on time."

▶▶▶◀◀◀

At the end of the day I stood near the side entrance of the school and waited for Red. I'd made sure I was one of the first ones out of class before anyone asked what I was doing. Red was the slowest person I knew, and also the most stubborn. The more I pushed, the more stubborn she became. Heaven forbid I pushed too hard. She'd turn on me in an instant, a flash of fire in her eyes that meant run, and run fast.

It had started snowing by the time she came out, but that didn't stop anyone from playing road hockey. Goals were being scored; everyone but us having fun. Minister Martin's house was in the opposite direction from school, so that meant walking down streets we hadn't crossed before. This, I thought, would make for a long, dark walk home.

We finally found the house and walked up to the front door. Taped to the window was a handwritten note on flowery paper: *Bible class around the corner through the gate. Come in the side door and take your boots off. We're downstairs in the basement.*

We walked around the side and, Red being closest, opened the gate. As soon as her hand raised the latch I heard the bark of a dog. There was no way to tell if it was loose, chained, or even if it was in this yard or the neighbour's. As scared of dogs as I was, Red was even more so. We always made sure to walk around a dog whenever we saw one—to the point of crossing the street if we could. To make matters worse, when Red spotted one she usually yelled "dog ahead" which meant, "Here we are, chase us as we go screaming down the road."

Red froze, her hand firmly on the latch and the gate still open. On the chance the dog was loose I went to pull the gate shut, then realized why she hadn't pulled it closed: her mitt was caught in the latch and she couldn't pull it free. If I slammed the gate her hand would get squished. If I didn't, the dog's mouth could come through the opening and around her fingers.

I pulled the gate shut and instantly heard, "My fingers are caught! My fingers are caught!" I felt bad, but at least her fingers weren't being chewed up in a dog's mouth. Red looked at me as if I'd know what to do next. I didn't.

The light over the side door flicked on, and the side door swung open. A soft but firm voice called out, "Sugar, back into your house." In the distance I heard a dog pad away toward the back of the yard.

"Come on in before all the heat gets out," Mrs. Martin urged. I pushed the latch down, reaching around to tug Red's glove loose.

"I'm afraid my sister caught her hand," I explained as Red glanced around; trying, no doubt, to see exactly where Sugar had gone. I turned to Mrs. Martin. "You ought to have a sign warning people about your dog."

"But we do," Mrs. Martin replied. "It's on the front window, right below the note I taped for you to come around the back."

"Well, I'm sorry, but there's no note there. I can tell you for certain 'cause had we seen a note we wouldn't have come around to the back on account of my sister being afraid of dogs." I didn't think it necessary to mention this included me, too. We took off our boots, coats, hats, and mitts, and hung them up on the wall pegs.

"Here dear," Mrs. Martin said softly to Red. "Let me have a look." She took Red's hands one by one, turned them over, and examined both sides. Mrs. Martin's hands looked soft, her nails perfectly trimmed and as clean as fine china.

"Looks to me like this one here took a real pinching," she said. "Let me get some ice and a towel so we can wrap your hand before it swells."

Mrs. Martin disappeared around the corner and I looked at Red. Some of the colour had returned to her face, and her tears had started to dry up. After Mrs. Martin came back, wrapped up Red's hand and made sure she was okay, she shooed us toward the basement stairs with a, "Come on children, the others are already here." Her dress swished against her legs and a trail of perfume lingered. It reminded me of the way Mom looked and smelled when she got dressed up. Only then did I realize Mom hadn't got dressed up once since we'd moved here.

Down in the basement I recognized a couple of kids from church, but since they didn't go to our school there wasn't much to say except hello. We sat on a large Hudson's Bay blanket spread over the carpet, a plate of milk and cookies in the centre. Mrs. Martin's nylons swooshed as she drew her legs around and spread her skirt out. She patted the blanket. "Come and sit on either side of me. Today we'll start at the beginning and talk about Adam and Eve, the first two people on earth."

▸ ▸ ▸ ◂ ◂ ◂

"It's Remembrance Day next week so we're going to be learning about the war, as well as making poppies to wear," Mr. Long announced. "We'll also be reading 'In Flanders Fields', and each of you will memorize a stanza from the poem."

My stomach fell. I might have heard just about everyone else's stomach fall too, except Cindy's. Her hand shot up to get Mr. Long's attention, and she wiggled in her chair, unable to contain her excitement. She waved her arm so hard she had to prop it up with her other hand. Mr. Long swept the room for a reaction to his announcement. As hers was the only hand raised, he could clearly see it; I think he wanted to see how long she'd last before he finally looked at her.

"Yes, Cindy. What's the question this time?" His voice trailed off as she talked over his last words.

"Instead of just one stanza, can some of us memorize the whole poem and recite it back to the class?"

Sun streamed in from the windows and lit up bits of dust that swirled around, the hum of the florescent lights the only noise heard as the class held its breath waiting for an answer no one wanted to hear. It was bad enough we had to learn a stanza, no way did I want to stand alone in front of the class and recite the entire poem. If she wanted to memorize the whole poem, she could go ahead. I stared at Cindy as she pushed her glasses back to the top of her nose.

She reminded me of a girl brought round to our first grade class in Winnipeg. Funny thing was I couldn't remember her name, only that she wore black shoes, white socks, blue-checked jumper, frilly white shirt, and thick glasses. She reminded me of Shirley Temple, and from then on she was Little Miss Temple to me.

The teacher had her sit down at an open desk near the front of our class. The teacher handed the girl a book and said the girl was going to show us the joys of reading. The little girl asked where to start, to which the teacher smiled and said, "Wherever you like." Little Miss Temple crossed her legs under the desk and swung them back and forth, keeping time as she spoke sentence after perfect sentence. I wasn't sure how she could read without first sounding out the words.

It must be some kind of trick. Maybe someone taught her the story and she was just repeating it. Maybe she's making parts of it up.

As she spoke, her face inched closer toward the book and her feet stopped rocking. Finally, she uncrossed her legs and then stopped speaking. The teacher asked if everything was okay, but she didn't reply. The teacher stood, the legs of her chair scraping the tile and echoing through the room. She walked toward Little Miss Temple and started to ask the question again, but stopped halfway through. A puddle had formed on the floor below the little girl's desk.

"Oh, honey," the teacher said quietly, "it's okay. That's enough for today." She then helped the girl out of her chair and they walked hand-in-hand to the door, wet shoe prints tracing their path. "Class, we'll be back in a minute. Please remain quiet."

No one spoke. No one laughed. Soon the rumble of wheels and banging metal could be heard. The janitor came in, pushing a bucket with the mop handle, and stood in front of the class as he glanced about. Spotting the empty chair he walked over, stuck the mop in the wringer, and swirled it round the floor, the yellow replaced with grey water that dripped from the mop. A couple of more swirls left only the smell of Pine-Sol. It got right up into my nose, clear through the back of my throat and down into my stomach. It was a smell I loved and hated because it meant something was now clean, but it felt as though you'd just had a drink of it and wanted to throw up. As quickly as the janitor removed all signs of the girl ever having been here, the teacher walked back in. She talked about what we were going to do today, and acted as if nothing had happened while I wondered if reading so well was worth it. We never heard about Little Miss Temple again.

I pushed the thought of Little Miss Temple back to where it had come from just in time to hear Cindy get her wish. Mr. Long said we were all to memorize the whole poem and he'd decide which stanza's we'd recite as we were called up in class.

There's no way to get out of this by just memorizing a few lines.

I vowed to make sure, when Remembrance Day came, not to have anything to drink until after I'd recited the poem. One less thing to worry about.

A few days later I'd written out the entire poem on three by five index cards and had been practicing after dinner in my room, door closed. I wanted to make sure I could get through it without making a fool of myself, but kept getting stuck on one set of lines.

We are the Dead. Short days ago

We lived, felt dawn, saw sunset glow.

I heard a knock at my door and figured it was Mom. "Come on in," I said just as she opened the door.

"May I come in? I heard you reciting a poem and wondered if I could hear you say it."

On the one hand, I didn't want anyone watching me anymore than I had to. On the other hand, maybe it would help me get past the lines I was stuck on.

"Okay, have a seat on the bed."

I put the cards in the back pocket of my jeans, cleared my throat, and started to speak.

"Stand up straight," she interrupted. "Put your hands together in front of you. Say it like you're the only one in class. Everyone will be just as nervous as you."

My back stiffened. I picked a spot on the wall ahead of me, held my hands together, and started over. Before I could get through a couple of lines she interrupted again.

"Louder. Say it louder. Start again please."

I was pretty sure Mr. Long wasn't going to say much about where I looked or what I did with my hands. He just wanted us to memorize and recite, but I started again, louder and clearer. Almost, I was sure, shouting. I never took my eyes off the spot on the wall, waiting for her to interrupt me with what I'd done wrong.

Instead there was silence. A long silence. I looked down and saw she was crying. She never cried and I wasn't sure what to do. So I sat down beside her and waited.

Finally, she stopped and asked, "Do you know what happened to your grandfather?"

The answer to that question is no. How could I when nothing had ever been talked about?

All I knew was that we only had a Grandma but no Grandpa, and for some reason that didn't seem odd. But we did have an Oma and Opa, and that didn't seem odd either. The more I thought about my friends and their grandparents, the more I realized if they had only one grandparent it was usually their Grandma.

Just where had all the Grandpas gone?

"Your grandma always says, 'You never know what tomorrow brings, so enjoy what you can today.' They met in Winnipeg, before the war. My Grammy, your Great Grandma, never wanted them to get married. Said he was no good, but I think she just didn't want to see your grandmother's heart broken so early in life. Grammy believed in spirits. She talked to them, said they already knew how things were going to turn out. But it was no use."

A shiver ran down my back as she continued.

"Your grandfather shipped out for the war. No one knew when he'd be back, though in their minds he would be back. At the last minute, to make it official, they got married. As your grandfather travelled across Canada to the east coast he wrote Grandma along the way, and mailed the postcards whenever the train stopped to pick up more troops. Then he boarded a ship for England. Neither of them knew I was already on *my* way. I was the baby he'd never see; he a father I'd never know. Our only real connection was his name—Robert. That's why your grandmother named me Roberta. It's our name, together.

"He got a telegram when I was born; Grandma got a telegram when he was killed. He's buried over in England. Never made it home."

Mom's voice trailed off, and she wiped a couple of tears from the corners of her eyes. Slowly, she started up again.

"I grew up in a house full of aunts and uncles. Went to Catholic school as soon as I could, which was kind of funny when you think about it."

I wasn't sure why it was funny, so I asked.

"Your grandmother! That's what was so funny," Mom replied. "She raised holy hell to get me into that school. Told them the church had an obligation to take me regardless of how *she* felt about God. I can still hear her telling the priest: 'It's bad enough God took my husband. Goddammit, I expect something in return.' That was the only time I ever heard her raise her voice. The Sisters took me in and the rest, as they say, is history."

I went to give her a hug, but before I could reach her she got up and turned to leave.

"Thanks for reciting the poem. I'm sure you'll do okay in class. It's bedtime now. Go brush your teeth. I'll come back after I tuck the girls in."

I wanted to talk more, but knew better than to ask questions about something that hadn't been brought up before. I also didn't want to see her cry again.

►►►◄◄◄

By the time the conference finals came around, I still thought Winnipeg would be able to beat Saskatchewan—no matter how much the guys at school said otherwise. And I still believed even after Winnipeg lost game one to Saskatchewan, fourteen to seven. At least there were two more games, and Winnipeg could pull it off by winning both. Then I'd be able to give Randy, Ricky, and Billy as much of a hard time about their team as they had been giving me about mine. You don't just change teams because you move.

►►►◄◄◄

We'd been told not to use the outdoor rink until the ice was finished, but here I was, in the dark, skates in one hand and hockey gloves in the other, trying to see any reflection of light across the ice. I sat in the snow, took off my boots, and put on my skates. They were well broken in, but it took a while to get the lace ends through the eyelets seeing how the tips were frayed.

My fingers were cold and stiff by the time I was ready. I tiptoed toward the opening, stepping carefully onto the ice. I started to skate, or rather walk, around the inside of the boards. Slowly at first, then a little faster as I managed to keep my balance. The best I could do was remain standing upright. I'd worry about holding a stick later.

It didn't take long before I had my balance, but, being inside four-foot walls with only a laneway light meant I couldn't see very well. I'd forgotten the rink was only on half of the paved play area, the other half was on gravel. When I reached a spot where Mr. Gazdewich hadn't yet put down enough water, my skates hit the hard, dry gravel and stopped. I didn't.

It was all I could do to keep from hitting the boards, throwing my hands out in front as my knees skidded along the pebbled ground. I ripped a hole in my jeans, both knees scraped. They were brand new, having just got them at the start of school, and I wondered what Mom would say. I hoped not much other than that a patch would have to be sewn on.

I brushed off as much of the gravel as I could and checked for blood. Finding none I made my way back to the opening, sat down, undid my laces, took my skates off, pulled my cold, stiff boots on and made my way home in the dark.

Once in bed I turned the dial away from the station Garner Ted Armstrong would be on and lay there, fingers crossed, waiting to hear the football score. It was do or die time. My heart sank when the announcer said that Saskatchewan had scored twenty-two points, Winnipeg nineteen. It was all over; Saskatchewan had won the best-of-three series. I'd never hear the end of this. I rolled the dial back and waited for *The World Tomorrow* to come on.

►►►◄◄◄

"Come on, Mark, let's go." I'd never seen anyone move as slow as him, except for Red. We should have given *him* a nickname, like Turtle or something. Sometimes I wondered why I brought him along; if we got into trouble, he'd be the one caught. It was like having a little brother, always making sure he was ahead so you could pull him out of the danger he couldn't see coming.

I'd heard about the annual fair and looked forward to going this summer. Since the fairground was closed all we could do now was walk the grounds and wander among the empty buildings. We were warned not to get caught by the old caretaker who lived in an old house on the grounds. The trick was to find a way in far from where we'd expect to find him. Of course, no one seemed to be able to say exactly where that was.

We crossed over Broadway, through an open field, and started toward the grandstand. We circled the race track, then managed to get in through an open space under the rows of seats in front of the track. I imagined them announcing races over the loudspeakers strung post to post.

"Come on. Nothing's going on here, and we're in the open, easy to spot."

I looked around. Not much of anything moved and Mark *was* right, we were in the open. Still, I didn't want him to think he was leading this adventure.

"Well," I said, "from what I've found in the past, the best place to find something interesting is behind a locked door."

Before Mark got cold feet I walked as quickly as I could toward the other buildings, then started to break into a run. He'd either have to continue on with me or walk home alone. Many of the buildings we passed were marked with various signs: Stables, Exhibit Hall, Dining Hall.

"I'm gonna try the doors and windows," I called over my shoulder.

Mark stayed back while I tried to find an unlocked door. I rounded the last building and was almost back to where we had started when I saw *him.*

The caretaker didn't look that big, at least from a distance. He had on work pants, boots, and a large hat that looked too big to be comfortable.

That seemed to be the normal Ukrainian look.

None of that concerned me. What concerned me was what he had in his hand, slung over his shoulder to be precise: a baseball bat. He wasn't here to field pop flies, no sir. He was here to chase us the heck out. And that he did.

"Come on Mark," I yelled. "Start running!"

Besides being slow, Mark's sense of direction wasn't too good either. He turned directly into me and we came together hard. Mark, being skinnier, bounced off and hit the ground head first.

I stood over him. "Mark, Mark. Get up! Can you get up?" He tried to push himself up but slumped back down, a dazed look on his face.

I tried to pull him up. "Come on. No time to catch your breath. The caretaker looks like he's ready to swing that bat!"

We had to get away before he got a real good look. Last thing I wanted was to feel a tap on my shoulder during the fair and have him ask if I remembered who he was.

I dragged Mark until he said, "Let go. You're gonna pull my arm out of its socket!"

We started running full out. Even after we broke through the fence neither of us stopped until I said, "Need … need to catch … breath." For a turtle he sure managed to keep up.

▸▸▸◂◂◂

I walked into the change room for my first hockey game and made my way through the room looking for an open spot, stepping over opened hockey bags scattered around the floor. Mostly Montreal Canadiens and a few Toronto Maple Leafs bags; someone even had a Red Wings bag. I carried what equipment I hadn't put on at home in the *Indian River Oranges* box from the used equipment sale. I knew when Dad said we'd get a hockey bag later on that I'd never actually get one.

Finding an empty spot I slid the box underneath the bench so no one would see. I managed to get myself dressed and, with some help from the coach, laced up my skates, got on the ice, and played my first game without falling over any more than most everyone else.

After the game I pulled the box out just enough to put my stuff inside. Suddenly, a kid I didn't know seemed to think it'd be funny to yell out, "Someone's selling oranges!" then flicked a puck toward me. I could have handled him myself, but the coach quickly stepped in and told the kid to pipe down. I was looking forward to playing against that kid next year and lining him up for a check against the boards.

If that wasn't bad enough, coach announced we'd all be goalie for one game. Since I had just started to play hockey I wasn't too sure how I was going to play net. I figured most of the shots would just hit me and bounce off. At least when I fell I could just lie there and block the net. I needed to learn to skate, and learn fast.

▸ ▸ ▸ ◂ ◂ ◂

When I told Mark that Eaton's was going to have colour TV sets in their store windows tuned to the Santa Claus Parade in Toronto, his only question was why we couldn't just go over to Billy's house and watch? I'd already asked Billy, but he said he'd already invited too many people so we couldn't come over.

We needed to be downtown before ten in the morning if we didn't want to miss the start. By the time we got there others were already lined up. We stood in front of the first open window we came to and pressed up against the cold glass just in time to see the start of the parade.

"Looks like ducks to me. Five of them," I said as a float went by the screen.

"No, they're not," Mark replied. "Swans, or maybe geese."

Whatever they were, they were soon replaced by the rest of the parade that followed. A giant dolphin seemed to swim, side-to–side, down the road, almost touching the kids waving; some kids sat on curbs, others their father's shoulders. The largest polar bear I'd ever seen rolled by on all fours.

The longer we stood, the colder we became. Trying to keep warm we stamped our feet from side-to-side and slapped our hands together. Bands marched by, seen but not heard behind the glass. Clowns, elves, and other Christmas characters walked behind and between floats.

Cold as we were, Mark and I weren't going to leave without seeing Old Saint Nick himself. Finally, there came Santa: bigger than life and waving as his reindeer pranced and danced. The elves waved to the crowds. I watched him mouth the words, "Ho, ho, ho." Then, as quickly as it started, it was over. Everyone peeled away from the storefront, and Mark and I started along Broadway toward home.

I poked at him. "Come on. Let's stick out our thumbs and see if we can get a ride home."

"Naw," Mark replied. "Mom said not to do that."

I'd already learned Mark's mom told him not to do a lot of things.

"Suit yourself," I said. "I'm cold and I really don't want to walk the rest of the way. You keep walking. I'm going to wait here and see what happens."

I waited for Mark to be far enough ahead so everyone knew I was alone and looking for a ride, then walked over to the curb and stuck out my thumb. The first few cars didn't stop, my face wind-whipped as they sped by. After what seemed like ten or fifteen minutes I wondered if Mark's mom was right. Before I could head up the sidewalk and try to catch him, a horn tooted and a big Mercury pulled over.

I peered into the frosted-over side window. A man was driving, cigarette dangling from the corner of his mouth. I grabbed the handle and pushed the button to release the door, which creaked as metal ground metal. Once open, cigarette smoke poured out.

"Sounds like your door needs oil," I said.

"What?"

I raised my voice over the radio. "Sounds like the door needs oil."

The car chugged up to speed and I realized maybe more than just the door needed to be fixed.

"Been meaning to take care of it, but never get around to it. Not my side of the car." A brief silence between us made the music on the radio seem louder.

"Cash?" he asked.

Cash? Was he asking me for money?

I didn't have any cash and I started to panic as the car continued down Broadway. I counted time as we drove ahead to where I might say, "Just let me out here."

"Cash?" he asked again.

I finally replied, "I don't have any cash, mister."

He turned, eyebrows arched as if thinking about what I just said. He took one long drag of his cigarette and a piece of ash curled up, ready to drop. The man chuckled and I waited for the ash to fall loose.

I began to wonder how slow the car would need to be going for me to jump out and not get hurt. At that precise moment we drove right past Mark. I pressed my face against the window hoping he'd look over, but nothing.

There were holes in the floorboards through which exhaust fumes now travelled up my nose, and I was sure I now smelled of cigarettes and gasoline. Even if I didn't tell Mom what I'd been up to, that alone would tell her it was something no good.

"Cash," he said again. "Johnny Cash. Do you like Johnny Cash?"

Oh, that Cash!

I tried to get the words out without sounding embarrassed. "Yeah, he's okay."

"You got that right. He's helped me through some tough times."

Tough times? What tough times?

As usual, my mouth starting going before I could think. "Do you mean, like, women trouble?"

Women trouble, what did I know about women trouble? Why did I even ask?

"Naw," he said as he turned and looked out the side window. "Other troubles."

The window, now frosting up on my side, was getting harder to see out of.

"Could you turn on the heat?" I asked. "I'm a bit cold."

The man started to laugh again. "I can put the heat on, but it won't do ya no good."

I waited for him to say something more, but nothing else came out. By now his well-smoked cigarette was mighty close to his lips. It looked as if he was determined to suck out every last puff.

"Heater don't work. Cold in the winter, hot in the summer. Ass backward, ain't it?"

"Yeah, ass backward," I replied, turning my head and looking for a building or side street I recognized. The car chugged along, the radio keeping the silence between us comfortable.

Finally, after a long sigh, he said, "Prison."

Prison?

"Yes, sir," he continued. "Know just about every Johnny Cash song there is to know." We were close enough to home that I could walk the rest of the way.

"Mister, I appreciate the ride, but this is where I need to get out."

"What?"

"This is where I need to get out."

He stared at me for a minute then said, "Oh, yeah, sure. Sorry, my mind was somewhere else."

I watched the man take the butt from his lip, the skin pulling as he tugged, and use it to light another cigarette, tilting his head up and take a long first drag. The glowing red tip almost touched the roof fabric as he let out a long exhale, the smoke of which curled and danced across the metal dash before making its way around to me.

He started up again. "Nothing like being able to light up a smoke whenever you feel like it. Yes, sir. Smoke when you want, not when you're told. Thanks for the company kid, but I gotta go. Stay out of trouble 'cause trouble ain't always worth the trouble it brings."

He didn't need to tell me twice; I had my hand on the handle and pushed the door open before the car rolled to a stop.

"Thanks again," I said. "Appreciate you picking me up. See you around." Before he could answer I slammed the door shut and watched the car slowly pull away from the curb.

'See you around?' Why would I want to see him around? Why did I say such dumb things?

▸▸▸◂◂◂

David was one of the two class clowns, Kim being the other. The difference between them was that Kim usually got caught and punished, whereas with David it was usually the person watching him goof off that got into trouble.

We were doing a geography test. With five minutes to go before the end of the test, it started. At first, all I heard was someone humming and didn't pay much attention. But then it became annoying. I looked at David, but he was staring off into space and chewing on the end of his pencil. He was probably wishing, like me, that he'd studied more.

Mr. Long slapped the wooden ruler onto the corner of his desk. "Silence, please! This is a test: no noise, no talking, and no looking around the room."

The stencil machine fumes lifted off the page while I stared at the questions and racked my brain for answers, or even half-answers, that I could write down. The humming had started again and I looked over at Kim. Both of his legs jiggled up and down, and he tapped his fingers on the top of the desk. I didn't recognize the tune, which was a good thing since I didn't want to start humming it myself.

Mr. Long called time and asked for the papers to be handed forward. Once turned in, those at the front placed the papers in a neat pile on the corner of his desk. After the last test paper had been placed on the pile Mr. Long took a rock—his special rock—and placed it on top of the pile.

Kim's humming grew louder and louder.

No one spoke. No one coughed. No one cleared their throat. There were times when Mr. Long's bark was worse than his bite, and there were times his silence scared me—just like being at home. It was best to let him explode so you could get straight to the punishment.

Mr. Long pushed his chair out, stood, and stared down the row at Kim. After a few minutes he started down toward Kim and said, "Everyone remain in their seats."

By the time he got to the end of the sentence, he was beside Kim's desk. Mr. Long put one arm around Kim's shoulder and leaned in, mouth almost touching Kim's ear as he whispered something. Kim's body stiffened and his humming stopped, yet he continued tapping his fingers and jiggling his legs.

Mr. Long took his arm off Kim's shoulder and placed his hands on Kim's hands, forcing them down until all of Kim's fingers went red and his legs stopped moving. Like a landed fish whose fight had gone, Kim slumped forward on his desktop. Mr. Long went to pull him up from his seat and Kim then became so stiff it was almost impossible for Mr. Long to pull him out. Normal punishment was to go and sit at the front of the class, but this wasn't where Kim was headed today. He was pulled instead toward the front door, his feet dragging between Mr. Long's legs.

I waited for Kim to spread his hands out as he passed through the door; one last attempt to remain with the class. But he'd given up and they disappeared together down the hall. The only sound was the soles of Kim's Chuck Taylors being dragged along the highly waxed floor.

Normally, a class without a teacher would go from complete silence to a dull murmur to full-blown conversation within seconds. A daring few might even move about, hoping not to get caught; musical chairs with the risk of staying after class as punishment.

Today no one moved, no words were spoken. Even David sat quietly. Another minute or two and we might have started to fidget, but as silently as he left Mr. Long returned without Kim. He asked us to get out our science books and take notes, and carried on as if nothing had happened.

▸▸▸◂◂◂

As soon as the Eaton's Christmas catalogue came out, the countdown began. If I was quick and got it before Red I could hang onto it for a few days and look at all the toys we didn't have a hope in heck of getting.

I grabbed some paper and a pencil from Dad's sample office and went into my room. Closing the door, I sat on the floor and went through the three hundred and seventy-two-page catalogue page-by-page looking for toys I could add to my Christmas list. There was a battery-powered Mustang convertible with removable top. I looked at the price and knew, at $4.98, it was too expensive. A Ford Lotus at $2.98 was more like it. There was a battery-operated metal robot and a battery-operated spaceship at a price I could ask for as well. It seemed like all the toys now needed batteries, and that just added to the cost of the gift.

I flipped the pages, hoping to find something I'd have a chance of seeing under the tree. Then there it was: a Johnny Seven! I read through the list of guns it came with: a machine gun, a grenade launcher, several rocket launchers, a rifle, and a pistol. All the guns you could ever want rolled up into one big gun. I looked at the price. At $8.88 the toy was way too much money; out of the question, no need to even bother asking.

I continued to thumb through the book. More guns and some spy stuff: Secret Sam, 007, *Man from U.N.C.L.E*—all the spies had their own stuff. I reached the girls section, glanced over the dolls, baby sets, and sewing kits, and closed the catalogue.

I knew we weren't going to get as many gifts this year since no one was coming to visit. I'd already heard Mom and Dad argue about whether or not to go back to Winnipeg for Christmas. It was Mom who wanted to go back, while Dad said no. We'd spent enough money this year, he said, so we were going to stay home.

"It was already agreed," Dad insisted. "We accepted the Watsons' invitation for Christmas dinner, then we'll have a few days to ourselves as a family." That wasn't like Dad. Everything had to be cooked the way *he* liked it, *he* had to carve the turkey; everything had to be done *his* way. Even preparing dinner was good for an argument or two, never mind what might come up during the meal.

CHAPTER FOUR

December, 1966

Winnipeg was cold but Yorkton was, well, just colder. Christmas was closer with each passing day, and we'd finally assembled our silver Christmas tree before Dad left for his last trip of the year. Even though I knew he wasn't real, all our letters to Santa had been written and sent.

▸▸▸◂◂◂

Red and I made it to the minister's house for Bible class, by now the dog safely chained before we arrived. That didn't stop me from slowly opening the gate, Red hanging onto me as we opened it into the backyard. It wasn't so bad coming here anymore, at least once you thawed out. But after listening to Mrs. Martin tell Bible stories while drinking hot chocolate and eating freshly baked cookies there was still the long, cold walk home.

The other kids sat in front of Mrs. Martin, colouring Bible pictures and, being younger, got most of her attention. I'd taken up a spot on the floor close enough to her that I could touch the soft edges of her dress with the tips of my fingers, especially if I leaned back. From there I could look at the side of her face without worrying about getting caught staring. She had a clean smell about her and, like breathing VapoRub when we were sick, I did my best to inhale as much of her perfume as I could. Today's story had been about the baby Jesus, Mother Mary, and Joseph. When Mrs. Martin spoke all was peaceful; she could have been speaking Ukrainian for all I cared.

Once she was done she said, "Since this is our last class before Christmas, I have a present for each of you."

She then started to pull little wrapped gifts from a cloth bag, starting with the younger kids before moving onto Red and me.

"Go on," she said. "It's okay for you to open them now."

I took my gift from her hand and could tell by way it wobbled that it was a book. It was a blue, cloth-bound Bible, with a handwritten "Richard, May Jesus always be with you," signed by Mrs. Martin in what was the most beautiful handwriting I'd ever seen.

"Thank you for the Bible, Mrs. Martin. I never had one of my own."

It occurred to me I'd never heard anyone call Mrs. Martin by her first name, and silently went through a list of names. Nothing I could think of seemed to suit her.

"You're welcome sweetie. I thought it'd be nice for you to read when you have time."

Read it when I have time?

I didn't realize I was expected to read it, I just figured it was something to carry to church, like I'd seen everyone else do. I thought about Aunt and Uncle back in Winnipeg. About how after dinner Uncle would pull the Bible out and read a few verses. I once asked how often he read it, to which he replied, "This is our third time."

I had a long way to go.

I remembered being taught to say prayer the first time Mom, Dad, Red, and I sat for dinner as a family. Before that we just started in as soon as food was put on the table.

I listened as Dad said, "Now that we are a family, we are going to learn to pray each time we eat." He went over each sentence until we had the prayer down just right. "Dear Lord, bless this food we are about to eat, through Jesus's sake for ever and ever, Amen."

I thought about how long dinner was going to take if we had to say grace every time we raised our spoon or fork, and asked if we needed to say this before each bite. Mom and Dad looked at each other and then burst out laughing.

"No, no, no. You only need to say grace at the start of a meal, not for each bite," he replied.

From then on we prayed before meals when we ate at home but never out in public, though I wasn't sure why. I figured God was happy with us doing it in private and there wasn't any need to do it around strangers.

Noises echoed as the little kids marched up the stairs with their new colouring books and crayons in hand. Red followed behind, leaving Mrs. Martin and me alone at the bottom of the steps.

"Is there anything else?" Mrs. Martin asked.

"Well, there is one other thing," I replied, hoping she'd ask what it was. Instead, Mrs. Martin stood and waited for me to speak. Her hair glowed from the ceiling light.

"I wondered," I started, then hesitated. "I wondered what your name is?"

She ran her hands down her dress, flattening out the sides. "Well, you know the answer to that question. It's Mrs. Martin."

My face was hot and, I was sure, very red. She smiled and looked directly at me. "Don't be embarrassed. My name is Mary."

"Thank you again for the Bible, Mrs. Martin. I'll bring it to class with me."

Taking me by the shoulders, she turned me around and gently pushed me toward the stairs. "Upstairs young man. I'm sure your sister is ready to go, and your Mom will be waiting with dinner."

While it was true that Red was probably already dressed and ready to go, I knew she wouldn't step outside without me to protect her from the dog. As for Mom having dinner ready, more often than not I was now the one who did the cooking during the week. It seemed lately she was out more and more, and since Dad wasn't home during the week she'd slowly stopped making dinner. Unless you counted eggs and toast, brown beans, or leftovers. Even then, I was the one heating them up for Red and Little Sister.

▸▸▸◂◂◂

Finally, it was the night before Christmas; how long we'd waited! We ate dinner at our usual time, Mom, the girls, and me cleaning up while Dad played the piano. After, we sat in the living room and listened to NORAD updates on Santa's whereabouts. I knew Santa had already been here, dumping everything under Mom and Dad's bed and in their closet. Red was old enough to have her doubts about the man in red, but Little Sister still believed. If Mom or Dad caught me saying anything about him not being real I was sure to get it quick and good, so I kept my mouth shut.

The clock in the living room seemed to slow as the second hand swept past the six, seven, eight, and nine on its way back up to twelve. I couldn't sit still, and asked Dad if he wanted me to plug in the kettle for coffee. He grunted in my direction so I got up and headed to the kitchen. By now, Little Sister had fallen asleep on the floor and Red looked as if she was ready to follow.

Mom got up at the same time, turned off the radio, and said, "Come on girls, time for bed." The normal pleas to stay up just a little longer wouldn't be heard tonight as Mom picked up Little Sister who twitched, mumbled, and put her head over Mom's shoulder, falling back asleep in no time.

I waited for the kettle to whistle, then poured Nescafé instant coffee and steaming water into each cup. The smell of coffee rose while I stirred down the Carnation powdered cream that floated on the surface.

Once mixed I walked to Dad's chair, careful not to spill. He sipped his coffee without a word; a thank you was out of the question, but it didn't matter. By now I knew silence meant one of two things: either everything was okay and there was no need to talk, or he was mad and was using the silence as punishment. At the moment everything was okay.

Our coffees finished, it was now my turn for bed so Mom and Dad could put out the rest of the gifts. I got up, kissed him on the side of his cheek so not to block his view, and brought the cups to the kitchen sink.

I made my way down the hall, put on my pj's, brushed my teeth, crawled into bed, turned on the radio, and waited for Garner Ted Armstrong's voice. Images of presents I hoped to see in the morning started to run through my head. Soon enough, Garner Ted's voice drifted in and out before he too was slowly replaced by sleep.

I heard the girls talking and looked up at the clock on my dresser; it was too early to go into the living room. Besides, we had to wait until Dad got the Super 8 camera up and running before we would get permission to make our entrance. I lifted my head from the pillow and looked around on my bed for my stocking. No matter how hard I tried to stay awake each year, our stockings were somehow always put into our rooms without us waking. Except this time there wasn't one at the end of the bed. I reached around and as far under the bed as I could without falling off. Still nothing.

Did Mom and Dad think I didn't deserve one anymore? Were they trying to scare me for telling them I knew there wasn't a Santa Claus?

I got up and opened the closet door; still nothing. My room wasn't so big that a Christmas stocking would be this hard to find. If I didn't get a stocking, what about toys? Was I just getting clothes instead? How surprised was I going to look as I unwrapped underwear or long johns?

I should have believed in Santa just a little longer.

I walked quietly down to the girls' room, opened their door, and sat down on Little Sister's bed. Both of them were on the floor, each in front of a dumped-out Christmas stocking and eating chocolates.

Maybe wishing you were older wasn't such a good thing after all.

Realizing I was sitting on something under Little Sister's rumpled bedspread, I tossed the covers aside and was surprised to see the stocking I'd decorated years ago. It was stuffed full, my name in green and red sparkles along the white-furred top. I looked at Red, but before I could say anything she said Little Sister had gotten up, snuck into my room, and taken my stocking to see what was in mine.

I pulled out a Mandarin orange, a chocolate letter, and loose gold foil-wrapped chocolate coins (all the same size but with different amounts on them), before struggling to pull out a Life Savers candy book. Since all three of our names began with "R", it was best to eat the letter as quickly as possible since someone would eat yours after they'd finished their own. After finishing my letter I took a couple of the coins, separated the top foil from the bottom, popped them into my mouth, and wiped chocolate spittle from the corner of my lips with my pyjama sleeve.

It was all over as quickly as it began. The only thing left was to wait for Mom and Dad to get up. Since it was always okay for Little Sister to go into their room I whispered to Red, "What do you think? Time to send Little Sister in?"

Red nodded yes and I turned to Little Sister, "Go into Mommy and Daddy's room and see if they're awake." But before we could send her out I heard the flush of the toilet. Somehow, in our chocolate-and-candy-eating frenzy, we hadn't heard one of them get up.

Mom popped her head through the doorway. "Come on kids, time to open your presents."

We started down the hall, turning the corner as Dad, right on cue, flicked on the Super 8 light. The living room flooded with a bright white light and I felt the heat come off my face as we walked past. Lowering my head, I put one hand across my eyes to shield the light while holding out the other to try and feel what lay ahead. It was too late, I'd lost my sense of direction and stopped dead in my tracks. Unfortunately the girls came up short, Red running into the back of me and Little Sister running into the back of Red. Arms flailed about while we tried to keep our balance. Normally, we wouldn't have such a hard time figuring out what was ahead of us, except we always rearranged the living room furniture to make room for the tree. I didn't want to trip, or worse, crash into the tree.

A couple of Dutch swear words was all it took for the three of us to snap to attention and wait for his next command. Soon enough he barked out, "Sit in front of the tree while your mother hands out the gifts." We did as we were told, and sat while waiting for our eyes to adjust to what was in front of us. A glance around the bottom of the tree showed there wasn't as many gifts as last year, even with those that had arrived by Greyhound parcel post from Winnipeg. Still, there was more than enough to go around, including the one large unwrapped gift for each of us that sat off to the side of the tree.

It was clear a Johnny Seven wasn't here, at least not unwrapped. My large gift was a guitar, something I'd both hoped and not hoped for since I knew I'd have to take lessons. Dad focused the Super 8 on me, telling me to strum the guitar like I knew how to play. He then went on to Red and Little Sister as each played with a doll. Red got the bigger of the two, a walking doll that took a few steps before falling.

By the time we were done the floor was filled with opened gifts, empty boxes, and torn wrapping paper. We played while Dad sat and read his new book and Mom worked in the kitchen.

Finally, Mom yelled out, "Come on and set the table kids." I'd been hoping to hear those words since the candy I'd eaten earlier had done little to fill me up. Red and I set the table while Mom stirred a big pot that contained tinned cream of mushroom soup and a couple of cans of whole button mushrooms. Along with a loaf of toasted, cracked wheat bread, this had become our traditional holiday breakfast. By the time we'd eaten our way down to the last few pieces, the toast was soggy and cold, but that didn't stop us from finishing. I pushed my chair away, wishing I hadn't taken the last piece. Since the rule was you had to finish your plate before leaving the table, I didn't have a choice.

After we'd cleared the table, washed the dishes, and put everything away I went to my room, picked up a Tom Swift book, and waited until I could go over to Mark's place.

▸▸▸◂◂◂

After lunch I went over to Mark's to see what he got for Christmas. Mrs. Watson greeted me at the door, a pair of oven mitts in her hands and a Christmas apron over her dress. I stared at her longer than I should have, thinking she had a little bit too much rouge on her cheeks before noticing one cheek was a little puffier than the other. Having realized what I was looking at, she quickly put her hand to her forehead, covering that side of her face, and told me Mark was in the living room before turning down the hall to their bedroom.

I walked straight through to their living room. Mr. Watson was in his chair enjoying a cigarette, the smoke circling his head. I said "hi" to Mark, then looked at the floor in front of the Christmas tree.

"Look," Mark said. "See what my grandparents got me?"

A Johnny Seven lay spread out before him: a grenade launcher, an anti-tank rocket, missiles, a pistol, and more. A one-man army and Mark was the army. "I even got spare bullets!"

It wasn't enough he got the gun, they even gave him spare ammunition!

I tried to pretend it didn't matter, but it did. "Come on," I replied. "Let's bring this stuff into your room. We can set up some targets to shoot at."

After Mark and I finished playing with all his toys, and his once-full stocking of Nutty Club candy now laid flat with empty wrappers all around us, we sat on his floor and wondered what to do next. Neither of us, we had agreed, wanted to put on all the clothes needed to go outside.

The smell of oven-roasted turkey had only partially entered Mark's room, but by the time we opened his bedroom door in the late afternoon and started down the hall my appetite had come back and I was ready for dinner. I caught the sound of Errol Garner on the Hi-Fi as we entered the living room, and was pretty sure it was Dad's LP as Mr. Watson didn't strike me as a jazz sort of guy.

Dad was sitting on the sofa in front of the coffee table while Mr. Watson sat in his usual chair. The coffee table itself was loaded, not so much with food—although there was a cheese tray with Ritz crackers, Bacon Dippers, and kielbasa—but with other stuff like ashtrays, cigarette packages, Red Cap beer cans, a large bottle of rye, and several Cokes. I couldn't remember seeing so many empty bottles before and wondered who had more to drink, Dad or Mr. Watson. After Mr. Watson's breath cut clear across the room, and he slurred out a question about "why weren't we outside playing in the snow?" I figured it was him.

Mark and I both looked out through the living room window. A full-blown blizzard was blowing so hard you couldn't see past our front sidewalk. As quickly as he was looking and talking to us, Mr. Watson just as quickly turned back to Dad and continued on as if we'd both become invisible.

"How *did* you end up getting this territory?" he asked Dad. "I mean, what brought you out here? I can tell you, after being on the road for two years, you'd better have a good reason for thinking this is where you need to be 'cause otherwise, well, otherwise ..." Mr. Watson's words trailed off and he now appeared lost in thought. I wasn't sure what he was trying to say, but whatever it was it wasn't something we were going to hear.

After a moments silence Dad finally replied, "I was in a bar in Winnipeg one night after work and got to talking to a guy beside me. I was selling life insurance for London Life. Doing quite well at it, in fact. In the President's club and all, but I was looking for something more. Well, the guy said his name was Gus and he was from Toronto. He'd been working his way across the west, looking in on his sales reps. He was also trying to replace a guy they had in Saskatchewan and needed someone to work the territory right away. Could lead to a promotion to Toronto for the right kind of person, he said.

"Well, I thought, maybe I'm that person. The idea of getting to Toronto was appealing. So we talked, and a couple more rye and Cokes later I had the job. Or at least the promise of the job. Gus said he'd talk it over with his boss and would let me know in a couple of weeks. I told him we were due to have our family vacation up in Clear Lake, and agreed if I hadn't heard before we left I'd call in and see if I had the job."

Mr. Watson looked at Dad long and hard, as if going over what had been said word-by-word, then asked Dad about the guy he replaced.

Dad started to laugh, then quickly stopped. "Sorry, it's not really a funny story. I asked Gus the same question. Turns out the guy had a car accident, a really bad one. He was barreling down one of those straight Saskatchewan highways on his way to a call when he spotted a combine on the road, off in the distance. So the guy gets closer, realizes the combine is in his lane, and, since they don't really go that fast, decides to pass him. All of a sudden the combine makes a left turn right in front of the guy and then *bam!*"

Dad stopped and took a breath while I was sure we held all of ours, then he carried on.

"The guy plows headfirst into the side of the combine. Just like that. No brakes, no skidding, no nothing. Just plowed into it full out!

"Well, the combine ended up in the ditch, while the car bounced off and crossed into the other ditch," Dad continued. "Dragged up a fair bit of mud and muck, then came to rest several hundred feet into a field of wheat. The guy was in bad shape. Blood everywhere. Hit the steering wheel with his chest and the windshield with his head, then bounced round inside the car. Lucky he just didn't fly right out through the windshield."

Mr. Watson looked at Dad with raised, thick black eyebrows, taking a long drag on his cigarette and letting out a slow exhale. The smoke made its way down onto the tabletop, swirling around the meat and cheese tray before settling on the crackers. Mr. Watson still favoured the duck tail, his hair slicked back on the sides and up and over his ears. With a wisp of hair always laid forward and flat on his head, and a cigarette usually perched atop his ear, he looked less like James Dean and more like a greaser. At least that's what Dad had said to Mom when he thought no one was listening.

Mr. Watson pulled a piece of tobacco from his lower lip, dragged his finger across the edge of the ashtray and asked Dad, "So what happened to the farmer?"

"He just walked up the driveway he was turning into, called the RCMP, and then went back to try and help the guy. Eventually the RCMP and an ambulance made their way to the accident, but the guy lost a lot of blood. Weren't even sure he was going to make it. Pulled him out and drove him off to the nearest hospital. The RCMP was left to try and figure out who was at fault.

"Well, when the officer asks the farmer to explain what happened. The farmer starts to get agitated, asking questions like who's going to pay for the damage, and who's going to pull the car out of the field? The officer calms him down and the farmer begins answering his questions. Tells him he was driving down the road to his barn, then made the turn into the driveway. The officer makes some notes and then asks the farmer, 'So when you made your turn you signalled, right?'"

Mark and I glanced at each other while Dad stopped talking and took a sip of his rye and Coke, pinching his moustache between his fingers before continuing.

"Well the farmer stands there for a minute with a puzzled look on his face and finally says to the officer, 'Signalled? Why would I signal? Everyone knows I live here!'"

"Well I'll be goddamned," Mr. Watson replied.

"No word of a lie; least as far as what Gus told me the RCMP told him."

"Well," Mr. Watson said, "let me tell you about *my* first week on the job. Mr. Bossman comes out from Winnipeg, tells me he has a weeks' worth of calls lined up, and wants to hit the road first thing Monday morning. Wants to make sure I know the drill.

"Now, I've seen asshole managers before, but what the hell I thought, let's get the week over with. So we hit the road Monday and damn near criss-cross the entire province. Crammed too many things into one week if you ask me, but Mr. Bossman wanted to crack the whip so I'd know what he expected of me while he sat behind his desk back in head office. That's why he insisted on making one last call Friday afternoon."

Dad just sat, listening. No one had asked Mr. Watson for a story, but that didn't stop him from starting this one.

"I kept tellin' him there was a storm coming, asking how the hell he was going to make it back to Winnipeg that night, but he just wanted to make his point. Didn't matter to me. Hell, here I was, first week on the job with a brand new car and all expenses paid, you know: gas, maintenance, meals. If he wanted to make one more call and then hightail it back to Winnipeg so he could tell *his* boss he'd trained me by running my ass ragged across Saskatchewan, well, I didn't give a shit."

While he had started off speaking quietly Mr. Watson was almost yelling by the time he spit out the last word. As if that word had come out of *my* mouth, my back stiffened and I looked at Dad; I may have even flinched and waited for a backhand across my head. Instead, Mrs. Watson poked her head from around the kitchen doorway. "Ted, please watch what you're saying."

"Yes, dear," came his reply, and with a wink and a chuckle directed toward Dad he continued. "As I was sayin', I really didn't give a shit he was running my ass ragged through every small town we could hit since he'd be gone soon enough."

This time Mr. Watson whispered the word *shit*, and somehow that seemed to make it okay to say. If one thing was clear, Mr. Watson *did* give a shit about being run ragged across the back roads of Saskatchewan since it sounded to me like it still bugged him. It was also clear Mr. Watson was used to telling a story with a cigarette in one hand and a bottle of beer in the other. He'd take a drag from one, a sip from the other and continue on without being confused as to whether he was talking, puffing, or swallowing.

"Anyway, we made one last call at one of those variety stores the Chinks run from the front of their house. I'll be goddamned if he didn't place the smallest order we had all week. Even had to wait while he went into the back of the house to collect up some cash to pay us.

"As we're waiting the boss says, 'You know, it's a wonder,' then trails off. Well, I'm waiting for what the wonder was, but he didn't say anything more so I cleared my throat and polite as can be asked, 'Um, what is a wonder?' Finally the boss turns and says, 'It's a wonder how we put them to work building the railroad, then all of a sudden they're in every small town across the land owning restaurants, laundromats, and little stores like this piece of shit. They're the ones making money while we're busting our asses on the road selling them stuff. I bet for every dollar they make there's at least another they don't pay a cent of taxes on.'"

As the word "taxes" rolled off Mr. Watson's lips he took a long drag on his cigarette, the living room now a smoky haze of Player's Plain and Export 'A'. I wondered when we'd be asked to go get more cigarettes from Lee's, the only store open today.

This time Mrs. Watson made no effort to come out from the kitchen, simply yelling, "Ted. Watch what you're saying."

A puzzled look came across Mr. Watson's face. I was sure he was going back over the conversation in his head, wondering what he had said that made her speak up again. "Yes, dear," he finally said, again winking and nodding to Dad.

"Anyway," Mr. Watson went on. "After we were done I was itching to get out of there as fast as we could. Mr. Bossman needed to get his car and drive home to Winnipeg, and I just wanted to be back in my own bed. We started back all right, then ran smack dab in the middle of one of the fiercest thunderstorms I'd ever been in. Saw it rolling up in the distance, but it hadn't been clear which direction it was going. Well, in no time it was damn clear the storm was rolling directly toward us." His voice got louder and I knew this part of the story was going to end with a swear word or two.

"Soon we'd gone from broad daylight to dark as midnight. Then the rain came, hard. So too the hail, and not just any hail. At first, it was small little pellets that hit the car. Melted as they hit the heat of the hood. But then the pellets got bigger and bigger again. I swear they ended up the size of golf balls!"

As Dad quickly sat up it occurred to me then this wasn't the first time Mr. Watson had told this story. I wondered if, like a good fishing tale, the size of the hail got bigger with each telling until it reached a size just this side of believable.

"Hang on Ted, are you telling me the hail was the size of golf balls?"

Mr. Watson put his beer down, moved to the edge of his seat and stared directly at Dad. It was as if a bull and matador had entered the ring and were sizing each other up. The room went quiet, even the sound of dishes moving about in the kitchen stopped. I pictured Mrs. Watson holding her breath while she waited for the conversation to continue.

Mr. Watson took another long drag, a good half inch of the cigarette butt burning red-hot as he waited to exhale. He blew the smoke directly toward Dad's face, as if shooting an arrow straight at him.

"Golf balls. Hail the size of golf balls!" Mr. Watson was off and running again. "We drove directly into the path of the storm. The car was pounded, the front hood dented all over. Some stones hit the windshield, bounced up, and landed on the roof. I never heard a noise like it. It was like being in the middle of a hundred marching bands. Figured the best thing to do was to keep on driving. I mean, how long could it last?" He paused as if inviting a question, but none came.

"Well, it lasted just long enough," he said before growing quiet again. Mark had gone back to playing; from his lack of interest, it was clear he knew how this story ended.

Mr. Watson lit another cigarette with the butt of the one he was smoking, then put the old one out in a ceramic ashtray by dragging it over the words *Happy Father's Day*. From the look of the printing of the letters, I figured Mark had made it.

"I drove faster and faster. At some point, this had to just tail off. But it didn't. I looked over at my boss. He was now pale. Pasty white, to be specific. Served him right. I told him a storm was coming and he didn't care. Anyways, maybe God was listening, or something, 'cause just as I was cursing out my new boss in my head one loud and final crack ripped across the sky. Least that's what I thought.

"Fact was, the windshield of my brand new car couldn't take it anymore; the whole goddamn thing shattered. Fell right into the front seat, covering us in little tiny bits of glass. It was on our shirts, our laps, the seats and floor, even our hair! It was a miracle we weren't talkin' when it happened, or for sure we'd have had a mouth full of glass."

I didn't know about Mark, but I'd had just about enough Bacon Dippers to last me a week. Stuffed, I sat with my hands wrapped around my legs, listening to Mr. Watson go on.

"The wind howled and the rain poured in. I pulled the car onto the side of the road and we just sat there getting wet, wondering if what happened really did just happen. After a few minutes I figured if Mr. Bossman still wanted to get back to Winnipeg I sure as hell wasn't gonna be the cause of him not doing so, and pulled the car back onto the road. Drove straight back as fast as I could. Didn't give a shit about any cops on the highway either. What were they going to do, give me a ticket for speeding with a busted windshield in a hail-dented car?

"By the time we finally got back our clothes were pretty much dried out. 'Course we ate a bug or two on the way back, being as there wasn't a windshield, but damn if we weren't home in time for the boss to get his car. Left him standing in front of the Corona. Told him I enjoyed our week together and said not to worry, I'll produce for ya. He mumbled something about maybe staying over, needing a shower and wanting to get some rest. Served him right, trying to run my ass ragged around the countryside! Anyway, the car was a write-off."

Dad cleared his throat. "Well, that beats the combine story." He sounded disappointed, though I think we all had a bit of trouble believing the full truth of Mr. Watson's story.

"Hell," Mr. Watson replied. "You ain't heard the best one. What time is it?"

Before Dad could answer, Mr. Watson carried on. "Time enough. You're gonna love this one, though it didn't happen to me. Happened to a guy on my last job, also a travelling salesman.

"Guy's driving home one night after a long week on the road. Different province, same old crap. He's tired, trying to stay awake with nothing to look at and not much on the radio to keep his interest. Way off in the distance he sees flashing lights and flares, and gets ready to slow down.

"Before he can stop the car spins out. Figures there's been an oil spill, something he didn't see coming. As he's spinning he passes a tractor-trailer on the other side of the road, in the ditch. Just manages to miss the cop cars. Eventually, he comes to a stop; turned around in the opposite direction, but still on the road. He's shaken up, but everything's okay. He gets out, starts walking, and damn if he doesn't slip and fall in an oil slick.

"He manages to get back up, thinking he's covered in oil. Only thing is, as he catches a look at his clothes in the reflection from the head lights, he realizes his clothes aren't covered in oil: they're covered in blood! Then he looks around the ground and sees blood everywhere. Now he's really confused. He starts to walk toward the cops, being careful not to slip again. As his eyes adjust to the surroundings he tries to figure out if he's maybe in a bad dream. Can't make head nor tail of anything. He gets closer to the truck, sees some limbs hanging about, and realizes something's *really* not right."

Dad burst out laughing. "What do you mean, something's really not right? Come on Ted, this story is bull. That's what's not right!"

Mr. Watson leaned forward, narrowed his eyes, and rubbed the top of his teeth across his bottom lip before saying, "That's what I said to the guy when *he* told me the story. He said, 'Let me finish.' So I let 'em."

Without missing a beat, Mr. Watson continued. "The guy stops and looks down. At first he thinks it's a leg then maybe an arm, but as he stares at it, you know, where toes or fingers oughtta be, he realizes just what he's looking at. Then he starts to laugh."

Like listening to a ghost story, I leaned forward and waited to hear the awful truth.

"He's looking at a pig's foot! He glances around again and realizes he'd spun through the wreck of a fully loaded pig truck on its way to slaughter. Turns out the trucker had fallen asleep at the wheel, hit the shoulder, flipped, and spilled a load of pigs. Those that didn't bust out free and clear ended up mangled as the tractor-trailer skidded and the roof peeled back."

Just then Mrs. Watson came around the corner carrying a plate of food for the table. "Heavens Ted, do you really have to bring up the poor pig story just before we eat?" Mr. Watson slumped back, a new beer in his hand and a satisfied smile across his face. Mrs. Watson turned to me and said, "Would you go over and let your Mom and the girls know dinner's almost ready, please?"

Once we were all seated around the table, it was clear the Watsons were not a family for prayer, as they dug in soon as the food had been passed around without so much as folding their hands together or looking down in silence. Mr. Watson was already into his third or fourth bite; more mashed potato, gravy, and turkey on his fork ready to go in as quickly as the rest had disappeared. Without being asked Red started to pray quietly, but the Watsons continued to eat.

Mrs. Watson soon realized what was going on and softly called out to Mr. Watson. "Ted."

Mr. Watson blurted out, "What the hell?" Then he too realized Red was praying and said, "Oh, yeah. Okay."

The room fell silent just as Red finished up with "Amen." Everyone dug in as if one big, happy family.

And then it started. I hadn't heard it at first, but Mr. Watson did. "What the hell is that, Margaret?"

"I don't know; sounds like it's coming from upstairs," Mrs. Watson replied.

Well, being only a three-storey building, it wasn't hard to figure out from whose place the thumping noise was coming from; the noise was directly above us.

"Please calm down," she said. "Let's just eat."

Mr. Watson pushed his chair out. "I'm not gonna sit through dinner and listen to that racket!"

Dad tried to get Mr. Watson to sit back down. "Come on, Ted. We've all had a few drinks. Calm down."

"I'm fine. I don't need to sit down. I don't need to listen to that racket either."

"Ted. Ted," Mrs. Watson pleaded as she tried to reach him over the table. "That's enough. Just sit down. Please."

"Enough my ass, goddammit. I drive and I drive all week, and then come home. I want a quiet Christmas dinner. I don't want to listen to that shit."

Dad stood and started toward Mr. Watson but Mr. Watson brushed him aside and walked out of the living room, tilting to one side as he made his way down the hall. I'd never seen anyone, besides Dad that is, get this angry this quick. Dad looked at Mrs. Watson but she just shrugged her shoulders, put her head down, and went back to pushing the food around her plate. I looked at Mark. He, too, had his head down, eating as if nothing unusual was going on.

By now we could hear Mr. Watson from all the way down the hall. "No way am I going to listen to that goddamn noise while I'm eating my goddamn Christmas dinner!" It sounded as if things were being pulled out of a closet from the muffled noises making their way back to the dinner table. Mr. Watson muttered, "Here it is," quickly followed by a "This will do." As he came back into view I was sure all our jaws dropped. I know mine did.

There he stood, in full army uniform, stiff as a board and pleased as punch, a cigarette in the corner of his mouth, his shirt partly stuffed into his pants. Where I imagined a rifle should be a broom rested over one shoulder, the straw end pointed toward the ceiling. Mr. Watson, reporting for duty. I got the feeling he was waiting for someone to say how handsome or soldierly he looked, but no one spoke.

Then he started to march around the dining room table. The broom swung as he turned, and everyone moved their head from side-to-side to avoid getting clunked. He finally stopped in front of his chair, swayed back and forth, and stared toward the ceiling while we all held our breaths. Taking the broom off his shoulder, Mr. Watson grabbed it by the straw end and poked up at the ceiling with the wooden tip until a fine powder fell toward the dinner table; it was as if we were inside a snow globe.

On cue, both Dad and Mrs. Watson told him to stop. The rest of us ducked again as Mr. Watson twirled around, then suddenly fell into his chair. From the way he continued to hold onto the broom, it was clear he expected trouble at any minute and needed his weapon at the ready.

"Who else needs wine?" Mr. Watson asked.

No one spoke while Mr. Watson filled his glass, spilling as much around his plate as he got into his glass, the red wine bleeding into the white of the mashed potatoes.

"This is the sound you should hear when you're eating," he said. "Nothing is the sound you should hear. Nothing at all."

He looked pleased for having brought about complete silence, both from the apartment above as well as from everyone around the table, except for the knives and forks scraping against our plates.

But then the thumping started up again, only louder this time. A knot formed in the pit of my stomach as I watched him push his chair away from the table and into the wall. I thought of covering my plate, expecting the snow globe effect again, but instead of reaching for the broom Mr. Watson started around the table, both fists clenched. He navigated forward by dragging one shoulder along the wall, slowly disappearing down the hall. The apartment door slammed shut.

Mrs. Watson looked at Dad. "Can you please try and bring him back?"

I couldn't tell whose face was redder: Mrs. Watson's, who changed from her normal pale white to a deep red, or Dad's, who appeared just about ready to burst. He rose from the table and tossed his napkin onto his plate, one edge landing in the gravy. I watched as Old Saint Nick's jolly red-and-white suit turned a pale grey as the gravy soaked in. It reminded me of how streets looked in April; no longer the white of winter or yet the green of spring, but the dull in-between of changing seasons.

Dad called out, "Ted wait. Wait for me." His words bounced off the empty hallway walls and we sank a little more into our chairs, as if all of our energy had been drained.

Soon, the sound of pounding of footsteps heading up the stairs was replaced by the pounding of a fist on a door. Mr. Watson, I thought, had reached Mr. Wilson's apartment and the source of his anger. From what we could overhear whatever Mr. Watson was saying he said over and over, growing louder and louder, no more understood the last time than he was the first. Then came words we *could* understand.

"I don't care that you spend your time on the road. You, sir, are drunk, and if you don't quiet down, I'll call the police." Mr. Wilson was trying to reason with Mr. Watson, but I couldn't make out what Mr. Watson said in reply.

There was a loud crash as something upstairs fell to the floor. I imagined Mr. Watson now had Mr. Wilson by the neck and was sitting on top of him, both hands firmly making his point as they tightened around the chubby man's neck.

I looked across the table at Mark; his head was down, hands in lap. A single tear rolled down his cheek to the edge of his chin, hanging as if trying to decide whether or not to fall. Another tear followed, then soon a steady stream. Mark got up and left the table.

We could now hear something being dragged across the floor above. The sound of footsteps came slowly down the stairs and toward the Watson's door. Turning as one, we saw Mr. Watson being carried back into the apartment; Dad holding his feet, the building superintendent with his hands hooked under Mr. Watson's armpits.

They brought Mr. Watson into the living room and dumped him in his favourite chair, bumping the end table. An ashtray fell onto the parquet floor, and cigarette butts spilled out as ash floated up. Mr. Watson's head fell forward, like a beaten prize fighter gone one round too many.

As he lifted his head from his chest, Mrs. Watson squealed, "Ted, what happened?" There was blood at the corner of his mouth, and it looked like some had also come from his nose.

"Who hit you Ted?" Mrs. Watson asked. "Did Mr. Wilson do this do you?"

Mark entered the living room before disappearing into the kitchen and coming back with a damp cloth. He handed it to his mom, who then wiped Mr. Watson's nose and mouth, a look of sadness now across her face. Mrs. Watson turned to look Dad, waiting for an explanation. I sure hoped he wasn't the one who had slugged Mr. Watson.

"Ted managed to make it upstairs to Mr. Wilson and Mr. McFarlane's apartment. Ted and Mr. Wilson exchanged words from either side of the closed door. Mr. Wilson opened the door after Ted started to pound on it. Once the door was opened Ted ran out of steam and fell forward, flat onto his face into their entryway.

"The super heard the commotion and came up right behind me; we got there just in time to watch him fall. We apologized to Mr. Wilson and Mr. McFarlane, offering to clean up the mess, but Mr. Wilson said not to worry. So we picked up Ted and carried him back."

"He might have broken his nose," Mrs. Watson said. "I'm going to stuff it with Kleenex. I don't know if I should take him to the hospital or not." I watched Mark make his way back down the hall, then heard his bedroom door close.

Mr. Watson bobbed his head around and gurgled, "I'm okay. I'm okay," before asking us to stay and eat. Then his head tilted off to one side and his breathing slowed. Mrs. Watson apologized for Mr. Watson's behaviour, but Mom waved it away as if it was nothing and asked if Mrs. Watson needed any help.

"No. I'll leave him there to sleep it off. It's not the first night he's spent in that chair. Likely won't be the last either. Take your plates with you, please, and make sure you fill them up."

"Come on, kids," Dad said. "Let's go back to our place while your Mom stays and cleans up." Mom shot Dad a look, then started collecting up plates from the table.

The girls had continued to eat through most of the commotion, so they were almost done. I tried to add a bit more turkey, cranberries, and stuffing to my plate, but by now most of the food was cold and stuck fast to the spoon as I went to shake it onto my plate. Dad, the girls, and I went back to our apartment, sat down at the dining-room table with our plates, and waited.

As Mom walked in, closed the front door, and entered the dining room she looked at Dad and said in a low but clear voice, "I told you we should have had dinner at our place."

I waited for him to reply, wondering if what Mr. Watson had started was going to carry on over here. The stare he gave her was enough to stop any further conversation, at least in front of us, and we ate the rest of our meal in silence.

CHAPTER FIVE

January, 1967

The tinsel, lights, decorations, and silver tree were once again packed away, the living room furniture back in place, everything exactly as it was before we'd counted down the days to Christmas. Back in class we carried on with hockey, gym, preparing for Expo '67, and were already talking about Valentine's Day as if Christmas had only been a dream.

▸ ▸ ▸ ◂ ◂ ◂

Like every other day after school I walked into my room, closed the door and sat on the floor. As soon as Mom came into my room, hairbrush in hand, I knew well enough to lay over her knees, keep still, and close my eyes. I wasn't sure if I had done something wrong, or if she was just mad for being stuck with us all week *and* this weekend since Dad had flown to Toronto for his first national sales meeting. Like the times before, my mind and body separated and I watched from above while she raised the hairbrush up and down, again and again, bringing it down on my now numb behind. My head was buried in a pillow getting wetter by the minute, which meant I only heard bits and pieces of what she said. The more still I lay the more she hit me, and I tried every once and awhile to shift ever so slightly so the hairbrush wouldn't land on the same spot too often.

I thought back to the first time they hit us, in the first house Mom, Dad, Red, and I lived in together, Little Sister not yet born. Before then I couldn't ever remember getting hit, let alone spanked. Dad announced we'd be cleaning the house, top to bottom, the way he wanted it done, the way *his* mother, Oma, had always done it. As he spoke I looked toward the living room window and watched as little dust sparkles floated through the sunlight beaming its way in. I figured that was what we needed to get rid of.

"Both you and Red take your sheets and pillow cases off your beds so your Mom can wash them. We're gonna put summer sheets on, and I'll teach you the proper way to make a bed so you can sleep better. Make sure you vacuum your whole room. That means under your beds and the closet floors, too. When you're done, check to make sure your clothes are hanging neatly and then go through your dresser drawers to make sure everything is laid out nicely."

I'd slept just fine up until now, so I wasn't sure how making the bed any different was going to help, but he knew best.

"One last thing: leave your door open and come when you're called." It was clear Red and I weren't going to be out playing until he was satisfied the house was clean.

Once back in my room I pulled the sheets and pillow cases off my bed, then brought them downstairs to the basement. On the way back I passed by their bedroom and went to poke my head in to ask for the vacuum cleaner.

"Goddammit," Dad said. "Hold the mattress properly so I can clean underneath the bed!"

I could see that the dresser and chair were pulled away from the wall and Mom was on the far side of the bed, holding the mattress up in the air. Dad, vacuum in hand, was running it around the floor underneath the bed.

I quietly stepped back, returned to my room, and tidied up while I waited to hear the vacuum turn off. When all was quiet I went back and pulled the Electrolux through the hall, careful not to bang into the walls on my way. Things were fine as I pushed it around the floor then under the bed, until I felt something quickly make its way up the hose and into the machine. The high-pitched motor whine told everyone within earshot that the vacuum had sucked in something it wasn't supposed to. I prayed whatever it was could be pulled out quickly and easily.

I popped the vacuum open and pulled out the bag and then a sock I'd managed to pick up from somewhere deep beneath the back of my bed. Pulling the bag out wasn't hard, it just made a mess on the floor when the dirt fell out with the sock. I started to sneeze, held my breath, waited for the feeling to pass, then snapped the front back on and flicked the switch. The vacuum sounded as good as new, at least as good as it would get considering how old and dented it already looked.

The room seemed clean to me, but I knew Dad would find something wrong. I was about to sit on the floor and play when I heard him yell, "Down to the basement now, both of you kids!"

After Red and I scrambled down the stairs we stood in front of Mom and Dad, waiting for instructions. Dad held a broom and pan, and a garbage pail stood between them, but neither seemed to want our help. Dad started directly at me.

"Who played with matches?"

I looked around; the floor was clean, no matches to be found. I was sure the right answer was "No one," and said so without thinking.

Dad went for Red first, grabbing her arm and pushing her into the space between the furnace and the wall. I waited to hear her bang into something, but somehow she didn't.

Red, in the shaky voice she got just before she started to cry, blurted out, "Sorry, Daddy. Sorry for lying, Daddy. *We* played with matches." Red always confessed too quickly, too afraid of making him any angrier.

In my mind, I'd told the truth. I'd forgotten about the wet wooden matches I had found months ago. I'd waited for them to dry out, then, being out of things to do one day, called Red down to the basement when Mom and Dad were outside. We—well I,—lit the matches and, once burned, threw them behind the furnace.

Who cleans behind a furnace?

Dad pulled Red back out, then went for me. The best he could do was drag me forward, but it was enough. I hit the side of the furnace, then the cinder-block wall, as he pushed me forward and down onto my knees. After being told to sweep the burnt matches, he dragged me up the stairs. Mom followed close behind, Red firmly in her grip.

Once in their bedroom Red and I were pushed down on either side of the bare mattress. I figured on getting yelled at until Dad was red in the face, but instead I got pulled over his knee. I looked over to see that Mom now had Red across her knees, with Red's dress up and her panties down, her skin a pale white.

Then it started; Dad with his bare hands, Mom with her hairbrush. There was a lot of crying and begging to stop, and eventually I couldn't tell whether it was coming from me or Red or both of us. In the end it really didn't matter. I silently counted the time between when he lifted his hand into the air and then back down, so I could brace myself until I couldn't feel him hitting me anymore. I floated up and looked down, watching his hand hitting me until he was done. Finally, he stood up and rolled me off his knees.

By now Red, her face red and wet from crying, was also standing. She held both hands behind her back, rubbing her bum. Mom remained on the bed, hands in her lap and holding the hairbrush, a dazed look on her face.

"Both of you to your rooms," he barked out. "And don't come out until I say so."

That was the first time we were hit. This time, however, it was different. All I could do was to try and stop myself from laughing as Mom hit me, but the more she hit me the more I laughed. Then she suddenly stopped.

"This won't work anymore, will it," she asked.

No, I thought, *it won't*.

While it still hurt I was now big enough that the pain didn't bother me as it once did. As quickly as she'd come in she got up and left the room. Within a few minutes she returned, saying she needed to go out. As soon as she left the apartment I put on my parka, boots, hat, and mitts, and, without stopping, ran across the street, through the windswept open field, over the highway, and onto the golf course.

Somewhere around the eighth hole the snow got too deep and it was becoming harder and harder to get through the knee-deep snow. I stopped and looked straight ahead. I couldn't tell where the land, wide open except for small patches of stick-figure trees, ended and the dull grey sky started. All was quiet and still.

Without thinking much beyond needing a place to stay and keep warm I stuck my mitts, still damp from playing outside before, into the snow to carve out little blocks from the field around me. The top couple of inches of snow was wind-hardened, but under the icy edge it was soft and fluffy, making it easy to lift out the jagged little blocks. Soon enough I had a walled fort big enough for one. If I crouched way down, that is. I tried to carve some blocks on an angle to make a curved roof, but they caved in as quickly as I went to put them in place. I sat down in my little house, colder by the minute. It was clear I needed more of a plan than just running out of the house.

Being an Eskimo sure wasn't easy.

Building a fire was out of the question since I hadn't brought any matches. Besides, there wasn't much around me to burn even if I had. I started to think about the things I'd need: matches and maybe a flashlight. Food—where could I get food? I could take milk out of the milk boxes from different houses each morning. At least it would be cold. If I was lucky, I might even find a house that had chocolate milk delivered. I could get bread, peanut butter, and jam from the corner store, telling them to put it on our tab.

How long could I stay away? How long could I last? How long before Mom would come looking for me, or maybe call the police?

I stood up. Where once everything was light and white, darkness had now settled in.

Was it possible to go home without a fuss being made?

I started back toward the distant lights across the highway, through the deep tracks I'd made earlier in the day. My hands and feet were now numb, my fingertips hard against the ends of my unbending, frozen mittens.

As I reached the front of our building the light from inside spilled out across the darkness. No cop car in front. Maybe they were driving around looking for me. I walked into our apartment and smelled dinner. My fingers and toes tingled as they met the warmth.

"Get undressed," Mom said quietly. "Dinner's almost ready."

I couldn't tell from the tone of her voice whether or not she even knew I'd run away.

▸▸▸◂◂◂

After the holidays, Red and I picked right back up with Bible class. We had gotten good at slipping into the house before the dog realized we were at the gate; we just let ourselves in, shook off the snow, and put everything away as if coming home.

"Who knows the story of Noah's Ark?" Mrs. Martin asked. Some hands went up, but mostly everyone continued to colour or sit and sniffle. I could have raised mine, but that would have meant leaning forward and I was comfortable just sitting back listening to her tell the story.

"Well," she continued. "Today we're going to learn about Noah. Let's begin at the beginning, back when God decided to punish some people for being bad. Now, God came to Noah one night in a dream and said, 'Noah, I want you to build a boat. A really big boat. Then I want you to collect up two animals of every kind, because it's going to rain and I've chosen you to save these animals.'

"God then told Noah how big to make the boat and what materials to use. He told Noah how many floors it should have, the little rooms needed to make sure the animals would be safe from the floods. Can you image if Noah hadn't built the ark so big?" she asked. "Think of all of the animals we wouldn't have if Noah hadn't listened to God."

One of the girls stopped colouring, looked up, and said, "Maybe we wouldn't have any cats or dogs." I didn't mind cats, but the dogs I could have lived without. The more Mrs. Martin talked, the more I thought about the flood. It seemed to me a lot of people must have drowned.

Did God just leave piles of bodies somewhere when he was done flooding the earth? How come no one ever found all those bones?

I wanted to ask, but Mrs. Martin just carried on. "So, Noah started to build the ark. He needed to finish it by the time the rain would come. His friends and his neighbours didn't believe that God had talked to him, and told Noah he was silly for building the boat, for believing a flood was coming. They didn't believe that everything on earth would be covered with water. But Noah did, and he built the ark just as God had told him to."

She put the book down. As with all the stories she told, she was about to make a point.

"Children, it's important for you to listen to God and do what he says. People will try and tell you not to believe in things, but like Noah's friends and neighbours you don't want to find out a flood is coming and not be on the ark."

I thought about Garner Ted Armstrong and wondered why everyone was always worried about God and Jesus. About someone you couldn't see or touch.

We're in the middle of the flattest part of the prairies; not much water to speak of. How long would it take for that much water to come in and sweep us away? Wouldn't we get a warning, an announcement on the TV or radio? Farmers were always looking for rain; what if they prayed too hard and by the time God realized we had enough he'd given us too much—then what?

When Mrs. Martin was done I was left with more questions than answers. I wanted to stay and talk, but it was well past dark. After a long walk home in the cold, and then beans and toast for dinner, I thawed out just in time for bed.

►►►◄◄◄

I overheard Billy and Randy talking during recess about going to Dale's place to snowmobile in the schoolyard near his house on Sunday. I wanted to go, not so much because I wanted to go snowmobiling, which I'd never done, but because Debra and Dale were cousins and I might have a chance of seeing her there.

I asked Randy if he thought Dale would mind. He looked at Billy, who just shrugged his shoulders and then looked back at me.

"I think it'll be okay," Randy replied. "Just one thing."

Randy leaned in and quietly whispered, "Whatever you do, if you see his sister June, don't look at her funny or say anything. You got that? If she starts talking to you just nod your head, but whatever you do don't get her riled up. Else we won't be able to use the Ski-Doo." From the look on his face I could tell he knew I hadn't understood what he was saying.

"Lookit," Randy said a little louder, "June's a retard. All she does is laugh and make noises. When she gets really worked up she waves her arms all over. Don't get her worked up!"

I looked at each of them to see if they were kidding, then blurted out, "What do you mean she's a retard?"

Randy looked around before speaking in an even lower voice than he had used the first time. I could barely make out what he was saying. "She can't speak properly. She can't think properly. Dale's mom and dad keep her at home 'cause she can't go to school." I thought about this, then wondered if I even wanted to go over anymore.

"If she can't go to school and she spends most of her time at home, wouldn't that just make her crazier?" Randy looked at Billy, while Billy just stared at me as if *I* was retarded.

"If you're going to make a big deal out of it, don't bother coming. Dale doesn't speak about June because that's just the way it is. If you want to come, come. But when you walk into the house, pretend everything's normal. Can you do that?"

Like a lot of talk during recess this one ended as soon as the bell rang. We ran up to the line forming along the wall and waited to go back into the school, nothing more said.

▸▸▸◂◂◂

Once Sunday had rolled around, we'd gone to church and then had lunch afterward with the Watsons at the Corona Motor Hotel, half of the day was gone. After meeting up at Billy's house, Randy, Billy, and I started toward Dale's. Halfway there, Billy stopped and said he needed to empty his boots and promptly fell backward into a snow bank, unbuckled each boot, and pulled his feet out. Snow clung to his wool socks; I wasn't sure how, since we'd only just started out. He tried to pull the hardened snow off with his mitts on, but it was no use. He finally pulled his mitts off, and being tied together with strings, they dangled at his sides, his fingers turning a deeper shade of purple by the minute.

He was the only one of us who still has his mitts on a string.

"Hurry up," Randy said, "before they start without us!"

We finally made it to Dale's front door, but for some reason no one seemed willing to reach forward and ring the bell. After a few minutes, Randy finally leaned in and pressed the button. Soon enough, the yapping of a very small dog could be heard. The door opened and I was disappointed to see Dale, his snow suit pulled halfway on, top unzipped and hanging at his sides. Truth was, I had no idea what I would have said if it had been Debra who opened the door. I probably would have stepped back, waited for Randy and Billy to go in, then stood there silently.

"Come on in and close the door behind you, and don't let the dog out."

There weren't many windows in the front of the house and, having got used to the light reflecting off of the snow on the walk over, it took a minute for my eyes to now adjust to the dark. The front hall, bigger than my bedroom, opened to the second floor ceiling. A large staircase led to the basement and an equally large, open staircase headed to the second floor. Dale's was one of the most modern houses I'd ever been in. Debra was nowhere to be seen, though that was to be expected since they were cousins and she didn't actually live here.

We stood and waited, growing hotter by the minute, fully dressed as we were in our snow suits. I could make out a shape in the shadows down the hall, then realized someone had poked their head around the corner and was looking straight at us—June! I froze as she slinked her way forward, pressing against the wall as she moved ever closer to where we stood. I went to take a step back, but was already pressed against the front door. June reached out, grabbed a good chunk of my skin, and pinched my cheek hard. I smelt peanut butter on her breath, and started to get hungry again. She beamed a big smile, let go of my skin, stepped back, and then danced up and down on the mat. The more she danced, the more she gurgled.

Randy and Billy turned to me and started to laugh just as Dale barked out, "June, get along now. Go downstairs and watch TV." She got in one last squeeze before his command sent her on her way. I rubbed my cheek. I didn't want to be near those little pinchers of hers again.

Once Dale was finished dressing we walked over to the school. As we rounded the corner of the last house we watched a yellow Ski-Doo cross the open field. Based on the empty gas cans tossed in the snow, it looked like Dale's brother had been out here for hours.

Seeing us approach his brother stopped the Ski-Doo, and he and his friend, who had been sitting on the back, stood up and took their helmets, toques, and mitts off. As we walked up, I could hear Dale's brother making comments about us being little squirts. I couldn't wait to get older, then everyone else would be a squirt.

Dale's brother turned to us and said, "Hang onto the tow bar at the back," then looked back at his friend, adding, "if you can." He started to laugh.

"Whatever you do, don't grab the seat bar. You'll break it off. And if you do, I'll beat you to within an inch of your life 'cause then I gotta tell Pops and he'll ask who'll pay for it. That means me, since none of you squirts have a job. And make sure you don't get near the track at the back. You can lose some fingers!" I started to wonder if this was a good idea.

With that Dale's brother and his friend put their stuff back on, climbed up onto the Ski-Doo, and revved the engine. It didn't take long to know that the more the engine revved, the more snow was flung from the back of the Ski-Doo and into our faces and mouths as we criss-crossed the back of the schoolyard several times. Try as we might, people kept falling off. Those who did hang on had to wait while those who'd fallen off emptied snow from inside the back of their jackets, mitts, and boots.

Then the Ski-Doo stopped suddenly. As we lay there I looked up to see Dale's brother standing over us. His friend wasn't upright any longer on the back of the Ski-Doo, since the rear seat bar, the one we'd been told not to hang on to, now dangled off the back. Realizing we couldn't make out what he was saying through his helmet, Dale's brother removed it then sent a string of swear words our way.

I knew my hands never left the tow bar and, having gotten used to Dad blaming everyone around him every time something went wrong, somehow made it easier to listen to Dale's brother tell us squirts to get back to our mommies while he figured out what to tell Pops.

Served him right. If he wasn't hell bent on dragging us over the snow banks this wouldn't have happened. For once I didn't feel guilty about something someone else had done, but for which I was still getting blamed.

By that time it was getting dark. My boots were packed with snow, my fingers and ears frozen through. I started back home alone, the street lights bright by the time I reached our building.

▸ ▸ ▸ ◂ ◂ ◂

"Whatever you do, don't sit on the bed, sit on the floor." I told Mark.

"Why?" Mark asked. "What's the problem with the bed?"

"No problem," I replied. "I just don't want it messed up. I don't want to have to make it again." Mark just stared at me.

"Sit on the floor. We can play there just as easily." I waited for him to sit down, spreading out the toys he had brought over. "I read in the newspaper that MacLeod's has over a thousand gold fish on sale. Pick-your-own; twenty-five cents each or two for nineteen. They have turtles on sale too! We should build terrariums and see if we can get some turtles. Whattaya say?"

Mark moved his jeep and army trucks into position before replying, "What do I say about what?"

"Jesus. About the turtles!"

"I don't know if Mom would let me have turtles. I asked for fish once. She said pets cost money and are too much trouble, so I'm not sure about a turtle. And please don't use the word 'Jesus'. Mom says you're not supposed to use the Lord's name in vain. She says you should watch what you say."

Since when was he talking to his mother about what I had to say? Didn't they have anything better to do? It didn't matter; if I wanted to say Jesus, or even Jesus Christ, I was going to.

"Well, before you ask her if you can get one we should figure out how to make some quick money."

Mark moved his army men around for a while, then looked up. "Why don't we shovel driveways?"

"Hey, that's not a bad idea. There's a couple of shovels in the basement storage, beside the washing machines. If the door's unlocked we could use 'em and return 'em before anyone knows."

Mark replied slowly, "What if something happens to them?"

By now I knew him well enough to know he was always worried about something going wrong. "Lookit, we take the shovels, walk across the street, and start knocking on doors 'til we find someone who wants their driveway shovelled. What could go wrong? I'm going to get ready. Either you're in and we get some turtles, or you're out."

Mark sighed. "Okay, okay. I'm in, but *you* gotta get the shovels. I'll meet you out front." What he was really saying was if something happened he could tell his parents it was my idea. But nothing was going to happen, and nobody would be blaming me for anything. I got dressed, picked up the two shovels, and went back upstairs to wait for Mark.

A thin sheet of ice had permanently built up inside the lobby windows, making them hard to see through. I leaned forward to lick the frost but thought better of it, my lips already dry and peeling from the cold. Mark's apartment door opened and then closed; his snow pants swished and his galoshes flopped as he walked down the stairs.

Mark looked at the shovels then asked, "Which one are you getting?" I already knew which one I was getting, since I was the one who got them.

"The spade. You can have the shovel," I replied.

I could tell from the look on his face he already knew which one he was going to get. Not only would he have to push the snow away, but he'd also have to try and lift it up over the snow banks. He was going to have to put some muscle into it, and I wondered how long he'd last before he asked for the spade.

"We're going to take turns, anyway. I'll start by digging up the snow. You push it up and over the banks. After a while we'll trade." He shrugged as if to say, "Okay". I handed him the shovel, grabbed the spade, and opened the door. We were immediately hit with a blast of cold air.

"Let's go make some money," I said and started down the front walk. As we climbed over the snowbank and crossed the hard, snow-packed road Mark turned and asked, "How much?"

"How much what?" I replied.

"How much are we going to charge for doing a driveway?" Mark asked.

In my head I added up the stuff needed to build a terrarium: the turtles, food, and maybe some money left over for a movie next Saturday.

"I figure if we ask two dollars a driveway we should only have to do a few today and be able to get what we need."

Mark nodded. "Okay, let's start with two driveways. If we need to, we can borrow the shovels again and do more driveways tomorrow and even next weekend. Then we'd be able to buy anything we want for the next few months."

I shook my head. He was the one who wouldn't get the shovels in the first place, now he was ready to shovel next weekend too.

We stood in front of the building directly across from our apartment, the words "Rohotensky Manor" painted over the front of the blue triplex. I wasn't sure who Rohotensky was I just knew he was Ukrainian, like almost everyone else around here.

"Might as well ring doorbells until we find someone who wants their driveway done," I said.

It wasn't until we reached the second door that someone answered, and not until the third that someone said yes. When the woman opened the door I jumped; it was dark inside, except for the light from the TV. Her hair was in curlers, and she wore a light blue nightgown and pink puffy slippers; one slipper missing its puff. I smelled food cooking, but couldn't be sure what it was.

In a low, quiet voice she said, "My husband's been meaning to shovel the driveway for some time, but he's been very busy lately. He just might appreciate having it done for him when he comes home tonight." A cat ran out the door and I took a step back.

"Oh, never mind her, she just needs to go out. Been cooped up here all day, just like me. Well, actually," she said, "we've been cooped up in here all week, but that's a different story."

I started to back away, ready to start on her driveway, when I realized we hadn't told her our price.

"Ma'am, we haven't told you how much." I said.

"How much what?" she asked.

"How much are we're going to charge for doing the driveway."

"Well then, why don't you tell me how much you're going to charge me?"

I turned to Mark, who had remained silent the whole time. It seemed to me he'd taken a few steps even further back than I did.

"We charge two dollars each per driveway," I said, up front and direct.

The woman stood silently with a blank look on her face, so I asked if our price was okay. Returning from wherever she had gone she replied, "Oh my, two dollars each is too much. You know I could do the driveway myself for free. Why don't you boys think about it, come back, and let me know."

I put my boot into the door before she had a chance to close it. "Ah, for you," I replied, "we could do it for a dollar each." I heard Mark sniffle but didn't turn around.

"I'll tell you what. Let me get my purse and see what's in there." She closed the door and we waited. We waited for what seemed a long time. I wondered if she was standing behind the door, staring off again like she did before. I took off my mitt and put my hand on the cold knob. Just as I went to turn it, it moved on its own. I stepped away and put my mitt back on.

"I have four quarters," she whispered. "I'm sure that will do for our driveway, wouldn't you say?"

I was ready to turn and walk away when Mark opened his mouth.

"Sure," he said. "We'll do it for a dollar. You're our first customer and we're raring to go!"

"Fine. Soon as you're done ring the doorbell and I'll pay you, but make sure you clean the driveway all the way down to the asphalt."

With that she disappeared back behind the door. I turned to Mark. "Let's get going. The sooner we do this, the sooner we can get on to the next house and make some real money."

Once Mark had scraped off a bit of the fresh snow on the driveway we could see her husband hadn't shovelled all winter since there were two clear tire ruts running down the length of the driveway. I turned to Mark. "Come on, you can use the spade." He started in, but try as he might could only break up small chunks of the hardened, densely packed snow.

"Here, let's do around their door first. Then we can dig out the driveway by the road. When it snows in a day or two it'll all just be covered again. Won't matter then anyway."

Mark shrugged and dug the spade into the area around the doorway. As he did, I removed what he had dug up, flipping it over the snowbank lining the driveway. Soon enough we'd cleared around the door, flinging enough chunks into the snow to make it look like we'd dug up a lot of the driveway. We'd worked up a sweat, but neither of us stopped to take any clothing off.

Once in a while the woman peeked out from behind the curtain. At the rate we were going, and as much as we tried to get down to the asphalt, we'd be lucky if we finished just this driveway today. We had managed to dig out a couple parts of the tire ruts and make the entrance a bit wider, but that was about as much energy as either of us had. I wondered if we should have been more careful about picking our first customer.

"What about putting back the parts we've dug out of the ruts, pack it back down, and tell her we're done. She has to pay us something. We can go home, get lunch, then find some easier driveways to do."

Mark mumbled "sure" and by the time we'd packed the chunks down and smoothed them over, the driveway looked good enough to leave.

We rang the bell and waited, then rang the bell again. I followed that up with a knock. Finally, the door swung back and she stood there, a cigarette and glass in one hand. Her other hand firmly gripped the door knob to steady herself. She blinked several times, as if trying to figure out who we were and what we wanted.

"Ma'am, we're done with your driveway." In a way I was being honest; I was careful not to say we'd *finished* the driveway.

She blinked a few more times. I was getting colder by the minute, and it was clear we weren't getting anywhere fast.

"We're done working on your driveway. We'd like to get paid." That was enough to get her moving.

"Oh, yes," she said. "You want some money." She went to close the door, but didn't shut it completely. After a minute or two she came back holding her purse, the drink left somewhere else, the cigarette firmly planted in the corner of her mouth. Smoke curled up around her rollers.

"I hope you boys did the driveway the way I asked," she said, placing each quarter into our hands one at a time. "I want to surprise my husband when he comes home tonight."

Not waiting to see if she was done talking I said, "Yes, just the way you asked."

I turned away as soon as the last quarter was in my hand. Between not wanting her to see our work and feeling so hungry I could eat a horse, I wanted to get the heck out of there.

"Come on," Mark said. "We can have lunch at my place and then get back out."

By the time we'd eaten the Cheez Whiz and bacon sandwiches Mark's mom made and grabbed the shovels from the storage room again, it was late in the afternoon.

Over lunch we had decided driveways were too much work, and looked for sidewalks to do a few streets over. In the end we picked up several more quarters, careful to make sure the money was put safely in the bottom of our pockets. The last thing I wanted was to find out one or both of us had lost our money and needed to shovel some more.

It was dark when we got home. I straightened my stiff fingers out as

I pulled my mitts off, putting them on the landing to dry. I knew better than to bring anything with snow on it into the apartment; Dad would get mad if there were watermarks on the hall floor.

I looked at Mark's ears. They were beet red from the cold, and figured mine looked the same. I pulled off my toque and waited for everything to warm up.

Mark started toward his apartment with a, "See you later."

I figured he didn't want me around, knowing he would cry as things started to thaw. I just wanted the pain in my toes to pass so I could take my boots off.

By the time all feeling had returned, Red stuck her head out the door and said to get inside so we could eat dinner. I piled my wet clothes into the bathtub and sat at the table. After Red said prayers we ate, and other than someone asking for the bread or butter nothing else was said. After dinner I helped with the dishes, washing while Red dried.

Once done I stood in the living room and stared out the front window. The darkness outside completely enclosed everything, unless you looked directly at the street lamp or managed to catch a light on in a window across the way. Somewhere past the triplexes was the highway, and past that, the golf course with an old abandoned farmhouse everyone swore was haunted.

Slowly, the sound of spinning tires reached my ears. Unless the car had hit a snow bank I couldn't see how anyone could be stuck; our street was plowed and the road was clear. As warm as I was now I thought about putting my winter clothes back on, dry or not, to see if I could help push them out. Maybe earn another quarter, or even fifty cents!

I wiped away some frost from the window, pressed my nose against the glass, and looked up and down the road. There it was! In the driveway of Rohotensky Manor the back end of a car glowed red as the driver stepped on and off the brake, the car rocking back and forth in the same spot. Finally a man got out of the car, grabbed a shovel from the snow bank, and dug around the back wheels. He must have turned everything into one big rut of ice as he spun the tires of the stuck car.

Suddenly, the man appeared to glance up at me. I breathed on the glass to fill in the area I'd just wiped off. Pulling the curtains closed I listened as the whine of spinning tires was replaced by the whack of a shovel against ice. He must have hit the car once or twice too, 'cause the sound of metal on metal rang clear through the night.

Did that lady know where we lived? How long would it be before we came face-to-face? Better to use the back door of the building for a while.

▸▸▸◂◂◂

I sat on the landing and watched him go in and out, his hair matted with sweat. The cold obviously didn't bother him as he was down to just his shirt, jeans, and boots. He looked like a bull, all muscle, and when he walked his knees didn't bend—his legs were stiff and straight. The word Mom had used to describe him was "beefy."

His wife was just as big, but looked puffy and marshmallow soft. She wore a lilac-patterned blouse and a pair of capris; both of which appeared to be under a lot of pressure, and I waited for a seam to split every time she bent down to pick something up.

He moved the heavy appliances by himself down into their basement apartment, while she moved the boxes from the front landing. They'd managed to bring in most of their stuff from the moving truck parked out back, some of it now scattered about where I sat watching. Just as I stood to go and find Mark, she stopped and looked my way.

"What's your name, hon?" she asked, her voice deep and gravelly as she pulled her blouse back and forth, trying to cool down. Without waiting for an answer she said her name was Candy. "We don't have any kids. Haven't had time, what with moving from city to city. Love 'em to death when I get near 'em, but, well … like I said … need time to have 'em."

I wanted to ask her where they'd moved from, but didn't get the question in before she continued.

"Bill's a welder, 'cept he can't get his papers. Least he hasn't *gotten* them yet. Need your papers to make the really big money." The skin under her arms jiggled like Jell-O as she moved about, picking up boxes. "He's taken the test and all. Several times in fact. But he gets rattled. Makes mistakes. Before you know it, tests over and he's failed again. Wish I could take it for him." She laughed as she finished. "I'm sure we'd pass then."

He didn't strike me as someone who'd get nervous about anything, then I remembered how I felt having to do our Remembrance Day speeches and wondered if he got the same feelings inside that I did.

"Has a weak stomach, too. Drinks milk by the gallon," she said. "I like to bake, in case you didn't notice." She waved her hands over her front as if to explain her size. Come in any time the door's open and make yourself at home, 'specially if you smell something good! You're always welcome, just so long as Bill isn't asleep. Lord knows he needs his sleep."

I wasn't sure what to say; Dad had a rule about never dropping in on someone. Besides, I didn't know if I had the courage to just walk into someone's place just 'cause the door was open. At the moment, I needn't worry. I heard a door open upstairs and looked up to see Mark come out of his apartment.

"Thanks. I sure will, but I need to go now."

▸ ▸ ▸ ◂ ◂ ◂

Over the next week Mark and I went to the school library and read everything we could about turtle houses, ponds, and rock gardens. Mark made some pretty pencil drawings based on a story he read. It would have been easier to just buy one of the plastic turtle lagoons with the green palm tree in the middle, but we both had it in mind to build our own turtle homes.

Since Mom and the girls were busy, and Dad was off doing errands after he dropped me back home from hockey, Mark's mom had driven us to the store. She promised to come and pick us back up so the turtles wouldn't freeze on the way home.

We walked up and down the aisles until we found the overhead sign that spelled out 'PETS' and turned up the aisle. After staring at the turtles for a few minutes, trying to choose the one I wanted, I realized Mark wasn't with me. I looked up the aisle to find him staring at something in front of him.

"What are you looking at?"

Without turning away he replied, "Here's where they keep the monkey."

This is a five-and-dime store. Why would they have a monkey? And how would it have ended up here, in the middle of nowhere?

I walked over to where he stood. The cage he was staring at was empty except for being lined with fresh copies of last week's grocery specials. I looked up at the sign above the cage: DO NOT FEED THE MONKEY.

How many driveways would I need to shovel to buy a monkey?

It was too much for me to even think about. Grabbing Mark by the coat I said, "Come on, we need to get going. Your mom's going to be coming back for us soon."

I wasn't so much worried about making his mom wait, I just wanted to get away from the monkey cage. I couldn't stop thinking about having one, but knew that was something I never had a hope of getting. By the time we'd selected our red-eared sliders and purchased tins of Hartz Mountain turtle food, plaster, and potting soil, we were ready to get back home.

Once home I left the turtle in the little box it came in, put the box on the dresser, and watched as the box moved when the turtle hit the sides. As soon as dinner was finished I rushed over to Mark's. His turtle house, a box that last contained oranges, sat in the middle of the kitchen table. He'd already scooped out an area for the pond using a small, round cake pan.

Soon enough Mark had everything finished, and water now filled the cake pan. He'd even built small steps leading into the pan using Lego blocks. The dirt had been spread around, and Mark planted a small cactus his mother had taken from one of her window planters. I watched as he opened the box and picked up his turtle; the turtle pulled in its head and legs, leaving Mark with just a shell in his hand. He placed it gently on the dirt, and we waited for the turtle to make himself at home. After a few minutes the turtle's head slowly poked out, followed by his feet. He made a mad dash for the water, missed the stairs, and fell over the edge, landing in the water with a splash.

The turtled floated as the water settled, and we watched it paddle around for a while. Mark threw in a bit of turtle food, careful not to cover the turtle. We watched as it skimmed the surface, grabbing a couple of pieces of lettuce Mark had thrown in for good measure. I thought about my turtle still sitting in its box, and figured it was time for me to get back home and see what I could do with it before bed.

In short order I'd packed enough dirt around an old cake tin Mom let me have, filled the tin with water, and made a little house out of the box the turtle came in. It didn't look as nice as Mark's, but the turtle didn't seem to mind as it splashed around in its new little pond.

▸ ▸ ▸ ◂ ◂ ◂

Since Candy said I was welcome any time the door was open and the smell of food drifted out, I worked up the courage to come in.

I sat on their sofa and watched as she dusted the furniture and watered the plants, her dressing gown floating around as she moved. I'd never seen so many plants in one place. Already a little darker since their apartment was in the basement, these rooms were even darker than they would have been, what with the window high up on the wall and the sills filled end to end with potted plants.

She talked as she worked, asking different questions. Sometimes she seemed to ask something just for the sake of asking, then continued on without waiting for an answer. Finally I realized she'd asked me the same question twice.

"Oh, yes, I'd like some peanut butter and toast. Thank you."

"Well, then come on into the kitchen."

I hadn't realized how tall she was until I sat looking up at her as she moved the cake that sat in the middle of the table and put a plate of toast with peanut butter, along with a glass of milk, in front of me.

"Here, drink your milk just like Bill," she said, laughing. "Or at least the way he's supposed to. I hope you don't mind," she continued, "but we only have crunchy peanut butter."

Mind? Why would I mind? We hardly ever had crunchy peanut butter. "Too expensive," Mom would say as she reached for the lowest-priced, plain peanut butter on the shelf. It wasn't bad, especially when layered on salted crackers pressed together so that the oily peanut butter formed little "worm bits" squished through the holes. More than once I'd eaten my way through a pack of peanut butter-coated cracker sandwiches while waiting for dinner. It was only when the peanut butter sat too long and the oil had risen to the top that there was a problem. You could stir it up but Dad got mad when any peanut butter got around the edge of jar or was left to harden on the sides. He'd rotate the jar slowly in one direction, carefully running his knife up and down until he'd scraped everything clean and back down into the middle.

When you looked into a jar and saw clean lines running up and down, you knew two things: first, he was the last to use the jar; and second, heaven help you if you pulled any up the side again. Once, he'd ran his knife up and down a jar of Cheez Whiz so hard the bottom fell out and onto his plate. Tiny bits of glass peppered his food, the broken bottom sitting on top of his ready-to-eat Cheez Whiz-on-toast sandwich. A stream of choice Dutch swear words followed. None of which we understood but were clearly not, as Grandma said, "Pearls of wisdom."

I finished the toast and milk, too full at the moment for any cake; not that a piece had been offered. I thought I heard the Watson's apartment door close and, using that as my chance to leave, thanked her and said goodbye.

"I'll save you a piece of cake," she replied with a smile. "Be off with you then."

Their place was always quiet and I felt safe around her.

I'd be back for that piece of cake.

CHAPTER SIX

February, 1967

He walked ahead at a slow and steady pace. With the wind coming up Mountview, his toque on and parka hood pulled tight, he probably couldn't hear anything, or anyone, coming up behind.

We were halfway home from school and had been picking up scoops of snow along the way, rubbing our mitts together and pressing the snow into hard balls of packed ice. As quick as we made 'em we put them in our pockets. I'm not sure why we decided on Big Boy. I'm not even sure who yelled out, "Come on boys. Let's go!" But once we started, it didn't matter.

Dale threw out the first pitch. It landed in the back of Big Boy's head, a good throw as far as throws go. Big Boy spun around and the second snowball, Billy's, hit him square in the face. I was surprised Billy had the distance *and* aim to actually hit anything, seeing as how he didn't play baseball or hockey and was almost always the first one out in dodge ball. I could almost feel the impact as Big Boy's head tilted back, after which we whooped and hollered. Another five or six snowballs found their mark and he went down. I'm sure one or two of those must have hit his face again, adding to the mark left by Billy's bullseye. By this time his nose was bleeding and the snow around his face was starting to turn red. Before he could get back up and chase us, we ran off in all directions.

I'd never actually spoken to Big Boy, but everyone said he was retarded. Whenever he came down the street we'd run up the other side, yelling "Retard! Retard!" He'd start to chase us, swearing and running as fast as he could. Since we walked home in a group, or at the very least in pairs, Big Boy had a hard time trying to figure who to go after as we ran off in different directions. I did hear that he caught someone once, but no one knew who or when.

I managed to make it home safely that day, shaking off the bits of snow clinging to my pants, mitts, and socks as small puddles of water marked my trail from the back door and up the stairs.

An envelope had been slipped under our door, an invitation to Robert's birthday party.

That wasn't the way you were supposed to hand out invitations. You did it at school so everyone would know when your birthday was, and to show who you liked from those you invited. Robert skipped all of that.

I looked at the hand-drawn invitation, the writing flowery and easy to read, like it had been written by his mother. The party was three days away and I wondered if Robert had invited me at the last minute. I didn't know what kind of present to buy; most of us liked models or trading cards, but I never heard him talk about either.

When I'd first arrived Robert talked clear as a bell, spoke up in class, was good at math and science, and always had the answer to any question. As each day passed, however, he spoke less and less, and took longer to say anything. Everyone seemed to want to pat him on the back in order to get the words stuck inside of him out. At first we thought he was just trying to be funny, so we laughed. Then one day Mr. Long told us to be quiet and we knew then Robert wasn't clowning around. His stuttering helped me though, since he used to answer questions so quickly that I could never figure out the answer for myself. Now I had more than enough time when he raised his hand and answered Mr. Long with a "The answer to the question is fi-fi-fifty fi-fi-fi-five."

Even though I could see the back of Robert's yard when I looked between the houses across the street we didn't play together, and I hadn't expected the invitation. I'd watched him burn their garbage in a rusty, blackened metal drum. He'd stand in the cold night air, his breath visible through the light of the flames. I wasn't sure why they burnt their garbage; most of us carried ours out to the bins in back and let the garbage man carry it away. It was, in fact, one of the few chores I did in order to get my allowance.

▸ ▸ ▸ ◂ ◂ ◂

On Saturday I walked over to Roberts' house, making sure to be there at noon as the invitation said. I rang the doorbell and was greeted by Robert's mother. As I stepped in and said hello I was met by smells I didn't recognize; they weren't bad, just different.

Robert poked his head through the kitchen doorway while I took off my coat, scarf, mitts, and boots. I walked past his mom into the kitchen, and handed Robert his present. For a birthday party the house was very quiet.

"Am I the first one here?"

Robert looked at me, then over my shoulder toward his mom before looking back at me.

"You are," he said, quietly and slowly, "the only one coming."

I didn't know where to look. I didn't know what to say. I began to hear the noises a house makes when the people who live in them stop moving about. The furnace whirred in the basement and a pot on the stove burbled, not yet at a boil. We both waited for the other to speak.

After a long silence I finally asked, "What do you mean I'm the only one coming?"

Robert didn't answer and instead said, "Let's go downstairs." As he moved toward the basement door his mom said she'd bring down cookies and drinks in a minute, then closed the door behind us.

The stairway was dark. The only bulb hung at the bottom of the stairs and it took a minute for my eyes to adjust. I held onto the railing, careful not to slip as my socks slid over the smooth steps. At each step a different, musty smell replaced the smell from the cooking food upstairs. The basement wasn't finished; bare bulbs hung from the ceiling, their wires strung from socket to socket. The space was filled with old furniture: a dining-room cabinet, chairs, and a reddish-purple sofa that looked too small and stiff to have ever given anyone a comfortable rest.

In one corner sat a large organ of some sort. It had pull knobs, white keys, and a foot rest at the bottom. I walked over, ran my hands along the well-worn keys, turned to Robert, and asked, "How come they don't make a sound when I hit them. Is there a switch somewhere?"

Robert smiled and walked over. "There isn't a switch. To make it p-p-p-play, you have to use your foot to p-p-p-pump the pedal then pull and push these knobs. It's a pump organ. Here, let me show you."

I sat on one of the boxes while Robert sat on the bench, trying to crack his knuckles like I'd seen Victor Borge do on TV. He began to rock one of the foot pedals up and down, and I watched as he pushed in the knobs then pulled out some of the same ones he'd just pushed in as quickly as he could. His hands moved across the keys, as he closed his eyes and tilted his head back.

At first the notes came out slow and choppy, the way he answered questions in school. I listened as the basement filled with music, song after song pumped throughout the room by Robert's feet and hands. I didn't recognize any of the tunes, but they were certainly songs and Robert was certainly playing them.

What would the other kids at school say if they could see Robert now?

All of a sudden I recognized the music. It was church music! The sound echoed in my ears long after he had stopped, and it took me a few minutes to realize he'd asked me a question.

"Well. Wha-wha-what do you think?"

I thought about what Dad played on the piano, and wondered if Robert knew anything else. "I, um, I was wondering if you could play any other type of music?"

I knew as soon as the last word left my lips that wasn't what he wanted to hear. His eyes travelled down to the peeling grey paint on the cement floor. "I'm not allowed to p-p-p-play any other type of music.

Mom says the only type of music meant to be p-p-p-played on an organ is church music. So that's what I p-p-play."

I tried to come up with something to make him feel better but the best I could think of was, "Well, as far as church music goes that was some of the best church music I ever heard."

Robert stared at me. I wanted to look away but couldn't.

"Does it really sound g-g-g-good?"

"Oh, yeah. You could play the organ at our church any Sunday, if you wanted to." I didn't know what else to say.

What did I know anyway?

The basement door opened and Robert's mom called down to ask if we were ready for cookies and Kool Aid, then placed a tray in front of us as she reached the bottom step. "Lunch will be ready soon, so please don't fill up on these treats," she said as she walked back up the stairs

I looked at the tray in front of us. I didn't recognize any of the cookies and wasn't sure where to start.

"Here," Robert said. "These are date cookies. They have b-b-b-brown sugar, shortening, honey, molasses, and some other stuff in them."

I thought about what he had just said. "They have dates in them?"

There was a long pause before he said, "Well, no, actually. They don't have any d-d-dates in them. Mom never makes them that way."

"If they don't have dates, why are they called date cookies?"

Without answering he went on. "These are apricot dainties. They have apricots, coconut, and condensed and evaporated milk."

"Okay, what is condensed *and* evaporated milk?" I asked.

Robert stared at me like I was crazy. "You know, milk in a ca-ca-can."

I pointed to the last of the cookies on the table. "What are those pinkish red things?"

"Mom's favourite," Robert replied. "Cherry winks with real maraschino ch-ch-cherries. We spend a lot of time baking and cooking when my dad is away."

I didn't want to hurt his feelings any more than I had over my church music comment, and asked to try a cherry wink cookie. I poured myself a glass of Kool Aid, the colour of which said it should be lime-flavoured. I figured the cookie could be washed down if it tasted bad, but as I swallowed the first gulp of Kool Aid my mouth puckered as my taste buds realized his mom had skipped the sugar altogether!

I finished the cookie with the least amount of Kool Aid I could manage, and tried not to get either stuck in my throat. Robert went on to eat most of the cookies, a satisfied smile on his face as he finished the last of the Kool Aid and put the glass back down in front of us. The door upstairs opened once again and Robert's mom called down. "Come on boys. Lunch is ready."

I remembered her warning about getting too full and wondered how Robert was going to be able to eat anything else. He bolted up from his seat and ran past me up the stairs, almost knocking me over; it was clear he still had room for more. I wasn't too far behind, not wanting to be left downstairs if the lights were turned off. After the Kool Aid and cookies I didn't know what to expect for lunch, but as I walked into the kitchen I tried to hold back a smile. On the table were two plates: one piled high with plain hot dogs, the other with Old Dutch potato chips.

Robert's mom told us to take our seats, adding, "Robert thought you might like this for lunch, and since it's his birthday he can have what he wants! At least for today. The cabbage rolls I've been making are for tomorrow, when his dad gets back from the farm."

As she poured us each a glass of milk I wondered if it was condensed *and* evaporated, and tried to smell it before it passed my lips. I opened my mouth wide so I wouldn't have any run down my chin and was happy to find out it was plain old milk, my taste buds happy.

Soon enough it was time for cake and ice cream. We waited while Robert's mom lit the candles on his homemade chocolate cake, the icing thick, across the top "Happy Birthday Robert" written in white letters. It reminded me of Mom's cakes, and the little waves of icing she made by rolling the edge of a knife along the cake's top and sides.

Roberts's mom started to slice the cake, warning us, "Careful boys. There's money in this cake!"

I cut through my piece, hoping for dimes or even a quarter, but my fork slid clean down to the plate. I then placed the fork in the middle of one half, but again sliced through without making a sound save for the fork hitting china. I was going for one last stab before giving up. This time I wiggled my fork around the piece in front of me, hoping to hit any coins I might have missed. Still nothing.

I glanced toward Robert's plate. Around the rim lay a penny, a dime, *and* a quarter. Yes, he was halfway through eating his first piece and I had yet to take a bite, trying as I was to find the coins *before* I put them in my mouth. Still, it was odd he had so many on his plate; most cakes usually had only one or two hidden coins. At least the ones I had the chance to try. Robert's mom stood behind him, serving knife in hand and a big, wide grin on her face. Suddenly everything made sense: she cut his piece knowing where the coins were hidden. The chances of me finding anything in this, or any other slice, were probably slim.

After we were both done with our first slice she asked, "Who has room for another piece?" We chimed in with an "I do!" at the same time, quickly followed by "Jinx! Coke's on you; tell me when to stop: one, two, three...."

"Stop!" I yelled.

"Great," Robert replied. "You owe me three Cokes!"

I dug in as soon as the second piece was put in front of me, no longer expecting any coins. However, on the second bite I felt metal hit my teeth; a stray coin, maybe a nickel or a dime, but too small to be a quarter. I sucked it clean and pulled it out; it was a penny.

Robert and I matched each other chew for chew, eating another piece of cake and finding more coins; a dime for me, a quarter for him. I had to admit being the only guest wasn't so bad. By now there was less than half the cake left, and between the hot dogs, chips, and cookies our efforts slowed. I looked up at Robert and at first thought he was holding his hands over his mouth so he wouldn't throw up. Then I realized the colour had left his face.

His mom stepped forward. "What's the matter Robert? What's wrong?"

Robert tried to speak but nothing came out except some whispered wheezing.

"He's choking!" I said. "He's choking on something!"

Silence fell as Robert's mom slapped his back, hard, and the colour of his face changed from a slight blush to a deep red. Then he coughed and one bright and shiny quarter flew across the table. From the look on his face it was hard to tell if he was happy he'd got another quarter, or if choking on it had taken away the joy of finding it.

"You've had enough for now," his mom said. "Why don't you open your present?" Before he could reply, his mom handed him my present. Robert looked at it then slowly peeled off the envelope I'd taped to the box, pulled out the card, and read it to himself. I watched his lips silently form words.

He must have reached the punch line by now.

Finally he said, "Thank you. The card was very f-f-funny." He slid the envelope back in as carefully as he had pulled it out.

Very f-f-funny? I almost peed myself when I read it in the drugstore. He didn't even crack a smile!

Robert's mom handed him a knife and he slid it through the Scotch tape, removing the wrapping paper while his mom carefully folded it and added it to a pile that rose up in the kitchen drawer she had just pulled out.

"Wow! A real model," Robert squealed with more excitement than I'd heard all day. "Lookit, Mom, Frankenstein!"

"I can see that," she replied as she leaned over, picked up the model, and walked into the living room. "I'll put this away for when you're older. When you can use the glue and such."

Older? To use glue? And such?

I wasn't so sure it was the glue and such as maybe she just didn't like the model. Before I could say anything she came back in, brushed her apron down, and said, "Now, boys, why don't you go back downstairs while I clean up?"

Without hesitating Robert got up and headed toward the basement. I followed while his mom closed the door. He sat upright on the stiff sofa and I took a seat on the organ bench.

"What do you want to do?" I asked.

"I don't know," he replied. "What do you want to do?"

I wasn't sure what I wanted to do, other than want to ask why his mom wouldn't let him have the model until he was older. Everyone our age was making models, and here he needed to wait a few more years. I kept that thought to myself and replied, "I don't know."

"Why don't we take out the g-g-garbage?"

It's February; it's already getting dark and it's freezing outside. Who the heck wants to put the garbage out?

"Come on," he said. "It'll be fun."

I slowly followed him back upstairs and watched as he reached into a cupboard and pulled out a box of wooden matches. "Put on your stuff. The garbage's already at the side of the house."

I stared at the box in his hand. If I was lucky to find any matches at all they were usually soggy paper ones. Here Robert had a whole box of dry wooden matches; you could throw them against concrete and they'd light just like that! Try doing that with paper ones.

Once dressed, the two of us dragged a couple of garbage cans from the side door out to the metal drum at the back of the yard. Robert carefully pulled out some garbage and put it in the drum, adding sheets of newsprint every few layers until the drum was full, then slowly dragged a match across the rusted, burnt-out drum. The red tip flickered and burst into flame. As it ate its way down the matchstick, Robert pushed it through one of the jagged holes punched into the side of the drum. He did this a few more times until small flames were evenly spread around. As the sky darkened the colour of the flames deepened, licking the corners of the newspapers and eating at the garbage in the middle. Soon enough, the crack and sizzle of the fire and flames quickly gobbled up what Robert had so carefully put in.

I stared into the drum as flames danced and flickered, the heat increasing against my face. I held my cold hands as close as I could, steam quickly rising from my still-damp mitts. Darkness and a sprinkling of snow had settled around us, and soon enough the fire was so bright nothing could be seen beyond our little area. It got so hot I had to pull my hands away. We stood together, yet separate in our own thoughts.

Robert startled me. "I've something to show you. Swear out l-l-loud you won't tell anyone."

"Swear it out loud," I replied without taking my eyes off the flames.

I turned to look at Robert as he pulled a match from the box and lit it by flicking the end with his thumbnail, bringing the match to an object he now held in his hand.

"What's that?"

"Watch," Robert replied and pressed the button down.

I heard a *swoosh* as something invisible met the burning match, and a jet flame shot out a good foot or two past us. I jumped back; the can hissed, the flame daring anyone or anything to cross its path. As much as I wanted to get closer, my feet remained firmly planted in place. I stared as Robert held the flame out as long as he could before taking his finger off the button. The flame stopped cold.

"That was a can of hair spray. Want to see it again?"

"Yes!"

He repeated the trick again, but this time the flame burned out before his finger lifted from the button.

"Well, that's all we're gonna get out of this one," he said, then threw the can into the drum. We turned and started back toward the house. That show alone made the whole day worthwhile.

Just then we heard a loud hissing noise behind us. Ash and sparks floated up as something inside the drum rattled, and the sound of metal hitting metal soon met our ears. Three or four times the object bounced around inside the drum before a can, engulfed in flames, shot out and landed about fifteen feet away.

"I-I-I guess that last one wasn't emp-emp-empty," Robert stuttered, a big smile across his face.

Before we stepped back inside I found the courage to ask, "Could I have some matches?"

"Sure, take a few. My dad won't miss 'em."

▸▸▸◂◂◂

First thing Monday morning we were told to go to the gym; not for class but to get a vaccination. All of us filed toward the gym, except, of course Kyle. He was sent instead to the principal's office. No one said why, but I figured it had something to do with him not being able to celebrate all of the things we did—like Hallowe'en or Christmas or even his birthday.

Being one of the tallest kids in class I could see over everyone's head and watched what was happening. Ahead was a nurse and her helper. The helper ran a cotton swab over your arm where the needle would go in, then held your arm while the nurse quickly stuck the needle in. Before you could squeeze out any tears it was over, the needle and the cotton swab dumped into a pail, a fresh cotton ball and a Band-Aid stuck on your arm. After, you were sent back to class.

Everything moved along smoothly until someone let out a loud cry. I wasn't sure what the trouble was; all I knew was the line had stopped moving and we all bumped into the person in front. I looked over to see a very pale Billy being held by the nurse's helper. The nurse herself bent down, and it looked like she was whispering something in his ear. But whatever she said was not enough to make him stand up on his own. His legs turned to jelly and they had just enough time to catch his limp body before it hit the floor. The nurse lightly slapped Billy on the cheeks and he rolled his face back and forth as he came to. She then looked up at Mr. Long. "Help me bring him to my office."

Mr. Long nodded, adding, "Kids, wait here quietly until we return."

It didn't take long for the nurse to return, minus Mr. Long, and we picked right up as if nothing happened, getting through the line and returning to class one at a time. Since Mr. Long was still out the noise in the classroom was pretty loud when I got back, and from what I could tell Chad was defending Billy yet again.

"You know, Billy did have a twin who died when they were born," he blurted out to no one in particular. "Billy was the only one who lived. That's why he's so skinny."

Billy *was* pretty skinny; his eyes always puffy and red. Even his skin wasn't the same colour as everyone else's, turning purplish when he was cold, which was most of the time.

Mr. Long finally returned, but without Billy. The rest of us were no worse for wear, other than having been stung on one arm. Mr. Long started to write on the board, the sound of fast-moving chalk a sign he was serious about what was coming next. Before he could finish there was a knock at the door and a white-faced Billy was slowly led to his seat by the nurse.

He'd been crying, that much was clear. As he slid into his seat I looked at his arm, but I didn't see a Band-Aid on either one. Billy leaned forward, putting both arms on his desk and laying his head down while Mr. Long turned back to the chalk board.

▸▸▸◂◂◂

What began with most of us quietly moving from desk to desk ended up with a lot of running around to hand out, and collect, Valentine cards. Chad, Dale, and the popular girls, including Debra, were soon surrounded by cards from the rest of us. Their hands overflowed with valentines, some in envelopes, but most just cut-outs like the ones I had. Kids like Robert stayed in their seats, not having anything to hand out and, I guess, not expecting to receive any.

I walked over to Robert's desk. "Here, this is for you. Happy Valentine's Day." Robert looked at the card, then up at me.

"He-he-here," he replied as he lifted his desktop. "I have one for you, too"

"Thanks," I said as he handed me an envelope. I put my cards down on his desk, and as I did Robert started to go through the pile before suddenly stopping and looking up. He started to stammer an apology, but I said not to worry before he got through his sentence. I looked at the front of the envelope he'd given me. Robert had drawn a little cupid, along with some arrows and a heart. I started to pull the card out, but felt my face turn red and stopped. Robert must have felt my embarrassment.

"I was just trying to draw some Valentine's things. They don't mean anything."

"Thanks and, um, thanks again for inviting me to your birthday party. I really enjoyed everything. 'Specially setting the garbage on fire."

"Please, don't tell people I do that," he said. "P-p-promise?"

"Um, yeah, no problem. Swore it out loud. Remember?"

Before Robert said anything else I asked if he had a chance to build the model I'd given him, hoping his mom had changed her mind about making him wait.

"Well, Mom said she didn't want me to build a model of Frankenstein or any other monster, for that matter," he stammered. "It's okay; it was enough just to get the gift."

That was a really good Revell kit, and I couldn't even trade him something to get it back.

I scooped up my cards, turning to walk back to my chair. "Don't suppose I'll see you at the dance?"

"No," he replied, "I'm expected home right after school."

Mr. Long told us to return to our desks. "Those who aren't going to the dance can stay behind," he said, as if to single out people like Robert. "You can get your coats and boots on after everyone else has left for the gym."

Once the class was dismissed Mark and I started toward the washroom, wanting to make sure we looked okay before heading to the dance. As we turned a corner I stopped so quickly Mark walked into my back, pushing me forward. There she was, bent over the water fountain. She held her long hair behind her back with one hand while the other turned the knob. A stream of water arched up and through her lips as she took a drink.

As we got closer Debra stood, turned, and looked directly at Mark and me. My heart started to pound. I hoped my face wasn't as red as everyone said it got when I was embarrassed, but the heat now rushing over me said otherwise. With one fell swoop Debra wiped her mouth with the back of her hand, letting her hair fall back down onto her shoulders, then walked right past us.

Mark stepped ahead and was about to get a drink when I pushed him aside, bent over, and took in what remained of her scent. Forgetting I was also drinking water I started to choke and ended up spitting some of it out.

"Serves you right," he said, "for cutting in."

It was worth it just to smell her scent.

"Come on. I didn't want any water anyway," Mark said in a tone that told me he did but was too mad at this point to get some. "Let's go to the gym."

Besides Mr. Long, a few other teachers were there to chaperone. The music started but no one was dancing. The girls stood around in circles, laughing and giggling; the guys leaned against the wall, pretending to listen to the music while making jokes and looking over at the girls.

After "Wooly Bully" and "This Diamond Ring," it looked like we were starting to form one long row; girls on one side, boys on the other. I managed to squeeze in between David and Billy, and looked up and down the line for Debra without seeing her. And then there she was; standing right in front of me. I wanted to look at her, but stared down at my runners instead. The next song started and everyone started moving. Everyone except me. I stood frozen on the spot.

Debra finally leaned forward. "Come on, Donkey, everyone's doing the Pony. Start dancing!"

I watched for a minute, then followed what she was doing. It wasn't so hard, and soon I was bouncing from leg to leg like everyone else, hands out, dancing to the music. Debra and I were so close I could almost touch her. One song ran into another, and by the time "These Boots are Made for Walking" started it seemed as if we'd danced forever.

"Cherish" by The Association came on and everyone on the boys' side took a step closer to the girls. Without asking I carefully wrapped my arms around her, and we slowly swayed to the music. Her scent, smelled only in passing at the water fountain, now clung to me as we shuffled around while I tried to make sure I didn't step on her feet. I wanted this dance to last as long as possible, and for a while it felt as though time had stopped. But before I knew it the music was over and the lights were up. In the crush of people leaving I lost sight of Debra and missed my chance to say, "See you in class on Monday."

Mark and I walked home in silence, snow crunching beneath our boots. It was dark and cold, but I was still warm from dancing and that managed to keep the chill off. I put my hand on the apartment building back door to open it as Mark asked, "Well?"

"Well what?" I replied.

"Well, are you and Debra going to be walking home from school together now?"

Though I'd been thinking about her all the way home, a weekend was a long time to wait and see if someone still liked you enough to want to walk home from school with you on Monday. As we climbed the stairs to our apartments the best I could come up with was, "I dunno."

▸ ▸ ▸ ◂ ◂ ◂

It had been a week since the dance and Debra and I walked home together every day after school. This meant I now had to walk about twice as far as I used to, since I had to turn off in a different direction halfway to my building. It didn't matter, it was worth the extra time and distance. Mark sometimes walked with us the whole way, other times he kept on walking home while I walked Debra to her house.

▸ ▸ ▸ ◂ ◂ ◂

In art class we'd been talking about our next project: a cover poster celebrating Canada's Centennial. We'd all brought our paper, Elmer's glue, and tubes of different coloured sparkles: golds, silvers, blues, greens, and reds, all the colours needed for a project. By now we'd used the Centennial Maple Leaf in every possible way, and I wasn't sure what new ideas I could come up with.

Paying attention to my cut-outs and making sure I didn't get sparkles all over the place, I hadn't noticed Kim's humming. He'd been pretty quiet the last few months, walking and talking a little slower and now being excused from gym. If you looked closely you could see his lips were dry and cracked, a bit of white stuff always in the corners of his mouth. No one dared make fun of him, at least not to his face, as we had all become a little scared of him.

He started quietly at first, then louder as if he led a marching band straight down Broadway:

CA-NA-DA,
One little two little three Canadians
We love thee
Now we are twenty million
CA-NA-DA
Four little five little six little Provinces
Proud and free
Now we are ten and the Territories sea to sea

On and on it went until he got down to the part about Frère Jacques. He seemed to get stuck, like a scratched 45 record skipping back to the same part. By the fourth time around Kim now yelled out the words. White spittle shot from his lips and the Centennial Maple Leaf he'd drawn was covered with little wet spots. We'd already heard that song so many times I was sick of it. Worse, there were times I'd hear it my head even when I wasn't at school. And now Kim was stuck on it, too.

Mr. Long leaped up and, quicker than I'd ever seen him move, strode down the aisle. He locked his hands underneath Kim's armpits, pulling him from his desk and walking backward toward the front of the class. Kim's body was very limp. The room quieted on its own. As they approached the door Mr. Long called for it to be opened, adding "Stay in your seats until I return."

We sat in silence, working on our art, waiting.

CHAPTER SEVEN

March, 1967

I'd dressed, eaten, and waited long enough for stores to open so there'd be warm places to stop into while I walked to the movie theatre. By the time I'd gotten past the top of our street and turned toward downtown, the cold wind had already worked its way into my bones. At least now it was at my back and not my face. The clouds, low and full, showed nothing but snow behind the cold.

I walked until I reached MacLeod's, my last stop before reaching the theatre, and entered the store. I stood in front of the nut display, watching the peanut platters rotate inside the heated case. The mixed nuts and cashews were too expensive, so that left ten cents worth of Spanish peanuts to eat before the movie.

The lady behind the counter lifted the glass from the back of the case, dug into the pile with a silver metal scoop, and then let the nuts fall into a bag. A couple more scoops and she was done. I watched as the red line of the scale moved back and forth before settling on fourteen cents. It was more than I wanted to pay, what with the movie being a quarter, plus popcorn and a drink, and I started to ask her to empty some out of the bag. Before I could finish she smiled and said, "That'll be ten cents please."

She pushed a key down on the cash register and the ten cent sign appeared with a ding, the tray sliding out so fast it pushed into her belly. "Here you go, sweetie," she said, handing me the Spanish peanuts along with a dime and nickel back from my quarter.

"Thanks," I said. At least I think I did since I was still trying to figure out if she'd made a mistake or meant to only charge me a dime. I was getting hot but didn't want to take off my jacket since I'd have to stuff my toque and mitts in various pockets and didn't want anything to fall out, leaving me to walk home with only one glove or no hat. I shook some peanuts into my mouth, put the bag in my top pocket, and sucked on the papery shells while I walked up and down the aisles. I wondered what it'd be like to be able to buy anything you wanted.

When I visited MacLeod's it didn't matter where I started, I always ended up in the pet section. Since Mom was afraid of birds (she didn't like them flying around and ending up trapped in the curtains, or worse, her hair) I ignored the budgies. She would say they liked to poop when they flew, and she didn't want poo all over the place. Aunt and Uncle had a budgie named Ringo, and every time we visited it needed to be caged or else Mom would sit hunched over, shoulders up, eyes glued to the bird.

Uncle would put bits of bread or other food in his mouth, then we'd watch as Ringo would land on the table and hop up his arm, bouncing up and down as he hopped forward. I always expected to see blood from the little claws digging into Uncle's skin, but never did. Ringo would then stretch out his colourful neck until his beak reached the corner of Uncle's mouth. Quick as he could, Ringo would snatch up the food and fly to the top of a window, screeching as if he'd swooped down on some poor creature that dared scamper by, upon which Uncle would let out a deep laugh. This went on until one, or both, lost interest.

Since I had the turtle, and we weren't allowed a cat or a dog, that left fish. I knew the sign said not to tap the glass, but I always tapped anyway after making sure no one was around. I watched as the guppies scattered and regrouped, swimming end to end. Further down the aisle I saw what I'd really come for: the monkey cage. I'd wanted a monkey ever since Mark had shown me the cage. I figured a monkey would be better than a cat or dog since you could talk to them and they'd talk back, play catch, you could even dress them up in monkey-sized clothes. You couldn't do that with a cat or a dog. I could see myself taking the monkey for walks down the street and hearing people say, "Hey, there goes the kid with the monkey."

I'd be known as Monkey Kid, surely the most popular kid at school. I only had to figure out how to get enough money. How many driveways would I have to shovel? Were there even enough driveways to do?

And then there it was, in the middle of the store, bordered by pots and pans, tools and clothes. The monkey, mostly black furred, with a little grey and white around its mouth, sat on a yellow-stained newspaper at the bottom of the cage, surrounded by bits of black poo.

Even if I saved the money, how would I ever convince Mom and Dad to let me get a monkey?

I leaned in; the monkey moved closer and I could almost touch its fur. I could certainly smell it. We stared at each other, and I wasn't sure whom was more mesmerizing to whom.

All of a sudden, a long forgotten but familiar smell of pee and animal fur came racing back. A dog! We had a dog once, though I couldn't remember how we came to get it, it just seemed to show up one day; maybe after months of promising I'd take care of it. I soon realized no matter how much you promise something, making good was sometimes harder than you thought. If I put down two or three sheets of newspaper, the dog would miss by at least one sheet. Adding more sheets just meant he pooed or peed further out. Soon it was clear I'd have to paper the whole basement if I didn't want to always be cleaning the floor. What made it worse, whenever the dog got excited he'd just pee on the spot.

The smell of the dog food didn't help either; I didn't know what it was made from, I was just glad I didn't have to eat it. I always took a deep breath before I cut into the can, careful none of the juice ran down the outside. It didn't matter; the smell would make its way down the back of my throat, and I would gag.

In time the dog did what dogs do, and that was chewing up slippers and shoes. Any chance of making the dog change just wasn't going to happen. Then, one night, something did happen and things *did* change. We'd finished dinner and Red and I had the usual argument about who was going to wash and who was going to dry. Since we were in the kitchen I should have heard the door open to the basement, but didn't. What I did hear was Dad walking down the stairs, asking "Did you clean up after the dog?" I could have lied and said yes, but the truth was I hadn't gotten around to it. If I had, maybe we'd still have the dog.

Before I could answer, Dad yelled, "Jesus Christ" followed by a flood of Dutch swear words that hit me as if I had been slapped in the head. He came pounding back up the stairs, the dog yelping as he held it by the scruff of its neck. Its legs dangled as it scrambled to find ground. In Dad's other hand were his slippers, poo on the bottom of each. I wanted to speak, to say "sorry," but words failed. Dad tossed the dog toward me and it was all I could do to catch it without falling over. In one short burst he said, "You and Red, get your shoes on. We're going out. Don't let the dog go, whatever you do."

While my words failed, tears did not. But I didn't chance wiping them away and having the dog fall out of my arms. Dad opened the back door, threw the slippers outside, and pulled on his shoes as he yelled, "Come with me." We formed a line: Dad, me, and Red walking out into the rain toward the backyard, after which he pulled open the garage door with as much force as I had ever seen. Red and I stepped aside as it swung out and up.

Dad grabbed the dog and nodded at the car. "You and Red, get in."

I opened the car door, careful not to hit the garage wall with it, and slid into my side of the back seat. I watched Red get in on her side, her bottom lip quivering. She almost never cried, keeping it in as if doing so meant she remained a good girl in his eyes. I didn't really care what Dad thought when I was getting punished; it was enough that he thought I needed to be punished.

Dad tossed the dog into the back seat, then slammed Red's door shut. The dog settled into my lap, and raised its head to lick me under the chin, happy to be out for a ride. I smelt its damp, wet fur and held on tightly. Dad walked around inside the garage, cursing as he bumped into things along the way. I was sure I'd hear later about all the stuff I hadn't put away.

All of a sudden someone pounded on the back of the car's trunk just as Dad turned back to see out the rear window. It was clear from the scowl on his face that anger was now driving him forward. Wherever we were going, whatever we were doing, in his mind we were already there and he was already doing it.

Mom must have followed us out, as she was now asking, "Where are you going?" Her face glowed red from the brake lights. Dad ignored her, stepping on the gas enough to move the car and her backward. I wasn't sure if he had checked to see if anyone was in the lane, or to make sure he wasn't going to scrape anything on the way out. I was just glad that when the car straightened out and took off he hadn't knocked her, or anything else, over. I glanced back at Mom as she stood in the rain.

Maybe Red didn't know what was going on and thought it was okay to speak. Or maybe she knew I couldn't. She quietly asked, "Where are we going, Daddy?"

He replied in one, even tone that did not invite a reply. "We're returning the dog to the pound. It should never have been brought home in the first place."

At that moment I found my voice. "Please don't take him back. Don't take him back, please!" I started to beg. "Please, Daddy, just one more chance. Please, Daddy, don't do this."

I can't remember how many times I asked. It was possible he reached behind the seat and tried to whack me across the legs so I'd stop talking. When we got to the pound he hit the brakes hard and before the car had stopped moving he was out, a blast of cold air in and over his shoulders. The dog, caught in a tug of war I wasn't going to win, yelped as it struggled to stay put. As hard as I tried, I couldn't hold on. No sooner had Dad pulled the dog from my arms than he was up the stairs, opening the double door and disappearing down the hall.

Rain pounded the car and the wipers slapped back and forth. A car swooshed by, water splashed up, and our car rocked like a sea-tossed boat. I laid my forehead up against the cold glass of my window; I could still smell the dog on my clothes. As we waited for Dad to return our tears slowly stopped. Soon he was marching back to the car through the wind and the rain, dog-less. Not a word was said on the drive back.

I heard myself blurt out, "I want it back." Then I realized someone was yelling at me.

"Can't you read? *DO NOT FEED THE MONKEY!*"

I didn't understand why the clerk was standing in front of me, yelling. I looked at him and then back at the monkey, now sitting in the back corner of its cage. My jaw dropped. In the monkey's hands was *my* bag of Spanish peanuts, the monkey busily chewing away, brown juice seeping out of its mouth.

"You kids are all the same. The monkey will get sick if you feed it!"

"I'm sorry, sir," I stammered. "I must have leaned in too close, and the monkey grabbed the bag out of my pocket."

"I don't want an explanation. Now I have to open the cage and get the bag. That monkey bites like hell. Whoever buys him better be prepared to bleed a lot!" The clerk moved toward the cage and I stepped back. The monkey glared, making louder and wilder noises, no longer my sweet and innocent pet. I didn't want to be here when the man stuck his hand in the cage, so I started quickly toward the main door.

As I did I heard the banging of the cage door followed by, "Goddammit, the monkey's got my tie." I opened the main door and took a deep breath of fresh air to replace the smell of monkey fur, poo, and pee. I walked over to the movie house, where I could be safe and alone in the dark.

▸▸▸◂◂◂

During the week, when Dad was gone and Mom was out, I made sure the girls were in bed on time, and asleep with their door closed. On nights like this, the apartment quiet, waiting for Mom to return, I'd lay in bed and think about what would happen to us if both Mom and Dad died. Once started on the thought, I'd run through my list of aunts and uncles, Grandma, and Opa and Oma, trying to figure out who would take us, who wouldn't, and who I didn't want to go and live with. Sometimes, I wondered if we could just take care of ourselves. How old would we have to be to be left alone? After going through the list a few times I heard the key sliding into the apartment door, and the door open then close.

I listened as Mom walked down the hard parquet floor then stop and open my bedroom door, the hall light slicing through the darkness. I could smell her perfume, soon replaced by the smell of cigarettes, as she entered and asked if I was still awake. She didn't smoke, but the smell clung to her as she sat on the edge of the bed, her back toward me. She pulled her hair up, uncovering her neck and her earnings caught the light as they dangled, swinging back and forth.

"Can you unzip me, please?"

I reached up and pulled the zipper down, stopping just below her brassiere, after which she let her hair fall back down, stood up, reached behind, and finished unzipping the dress. With one hand held across her top to make sure the dress didn't fall forward, she sat back on the corner of the bed.

"How was the woman's curling banquet?"

"It wasn't bad," she replied. "But I don't understand why they serve chicken at functions like that. I mean, all of the ladies were sitting around, looking prim and proper, knife and fork in hand, trying to cut around the bone, when all they really wanted was to pick it up and eat with their fingers." She started to laugh. "Well, most of us were prim and proper, except for Margie London. She had way too much to drink, swaying as she walked and bobbing her head as she talked."

I pictured a chicken-eating lady walking around, swaying to and fro, and started to laugh.

"That's not the funny part! People tried to get her to sit still, but she kept hopping up. Even as she ate people asked her if having so much chicken was a good idea, but she just kept on eating.

"Then she started heaving. After that everyone around her knew it was only a matter of time. Only they didn't realize how little time before everything that had gone down was on its way back up!" Mom now shook with laughter. Her dress fell forward and I could see where her straps had dug into her shoulders, her freckles little dots against pale white skin. "They dragged over a big garbage can, then everyone gasped, moved back, and covered their mouths as she bent over the can and hung onto the rim. Of course the can, being half empty, meant everyone heard the echo of each heave as she tried to breathe in air and exhale alcohol and chicken. Didn't think she had that much to eat but apparently she did."

Mom stopped, took a breath, and continued. "When they thought it was safe, two women came over and held her up by her arms. I think the ladies were afraid she just might fall in, and no one wanted to deal with that."

She was laughing so hard now I was afraid the girls would wake up and she'd slip away to their room. Weeks, maybe months, had passed since I'd seen her laugh or talk like this and I wanted her to stay here with me.

"Finally, one of the ladies asked her if she was okay. I couldn't see her, but I did hear Margie try to mumble an answer. I figured she was past the point of speaking, what with the alcohol and all. It wasn't until they got a good look at her that they realized she was missing her dentures. She'd thrown them up into the can! Not just uppers or lowers, but the full set. Which, until then, no one even knew she had. Well, at that point everyone around just stared at the can. No one wanted to pick through it for a set of false teeth." Mom took a deep breath and stopped talking.

"Well, what happened to her teeth?" I asked, expecting her to start laughing all over, but she appeared to be laughed-out.

"Well, someone grabbed a plastic bag, used it as a glove, and ran their hand through the muck until they pulled out both sets. We washed them, slipped them into her coat pocket, called a cab, and sent her home. She was the highlight of the night." She paused and added, "Well, that and the fact I won a knife sharpener in the raffle."

▶ ▶ ▶ ◀ ◀ ◀

In Winnipeg they had a giant toboggan run. It was packed with snow and ice, and everyone climbed up the hill for the slide of their lives. In Yorkton there weren't any hills to speak of, except where construction around the new hospital had pushed up some piles of dirt before work stopped for the winter. This is where Mark and me had spent the last few hours, sliding down the little mounds on pieces of cardboard we had grabbed from the laundry room. With enough snow on the ground it was possible to slide down without getting a run of dirt up your back; unless of course you were Mark.

After he got up from his last run I'd started to brush him off when Randy, Ricky, and some tall kid I didn't recognize walked toward us, their own pieces of cardboard in their hands, the three of them talking as if they'd known each other forever. Without a word being said the new guy stretched his hand out and started to shake mine; I don't know why he, or I, did that. No one shakes hands when they first meet, unless they're adults. And while he was one of the tallest kids around, taller than me, he certainly wasn't an adult. He shook Mark's hand, too, to which Mark stammered a, "Pleased to meet you." At least Mark had the sense to say something.

Finally, Randy spoke up. "This is the new guy. He moved in down the street from us. He started school last week, but he's a couple of grades higher."

A couple of grades higher? Why is he hanging around us?

Randy carried on as if I had asked the question out loud. "He came over to see if my sister was home, but she's out so he asked if he could tag along with us and we said sure." Randy was on a roll. "He's the son of a preacher," he continued. "His daddy came here to do some preaching."

I waited for someone to tell us his name, but no one said anything. It was as if he, the new kid, couldn't speak for himself. Since it looked like they were getting ready to start sliding down the hill I turned to Randy and asked, "What's his name?"

Without hesitation the new guy stepped forward and in the slowest, deepest voice I'd ever heard said, "My name is John. David. Smith."

Who called themselves by all three of their names, or paused between each name for that matter?

I started to laugh, then realized no one around me had.

Mark again spoke up. "Just where *are* you from?" I wasn't sure why he had put such an emphasis on the word "are".

"Texas," he replied. "Our family's from Texas. Texas, in the United

States of America!"

"Texas," Mark said. "That's, ah, quite a ways from here isn't it?" He acted as if he knew exactly where it was, which I was pretty sure he didn't.

"Yep, took us four days to drive. But we took our time."

We oughtta call him Texas. I got a new name when I came here. Why not him, too?

Without thinking I blurted out, "We oughtta call you Texas." There was silence.

Then, with the same speed he had spoken his name, John David Smith looked up and said, "Okay. Texas it is. You all can call me Texas."

Thank God, and thank you Texas. No need for me to be embarrassed again.

This time *I* shook his hand and said, "Texas it is." Randy and Ricky joined in, and then off they went to slide. Mark turned to me and I waited for him to tell me I was an idiot or something, but he didn't. Instead he said, "Come on. I need to go home and explain how I got all dirty."

We walked back to the apartment, the snow still snapping and crunching under our feet, winter not yet quite ready to give way to spring.

▸ ▸ ▸ ◂ ◂ ◂

Easter was chocolates and turkey, the first turkey since Christmas, the last until next Thanksgiving. Dad said we were going to avoid what happened at Christmas, which was why the Watsons were having Easter dinner at our place. Mom and Mrs. Watson were busy in the kitchen preparing a Canadian-Hungarian dinner, whatever that was, while Dad was in the living room playing the piano. Once in a while the notes made their way down the hall and through my closed bedroom door, a song or two recognized now and then. Mr. Watson had yet to make an appearance.

Dad and Mr. Watson still talked from time to time, but Dad made sure to stay away from Mr. Watson and his booze. Every once in a while

Mr. Watson would say they should meet up on the road, but somehow Dad's schedule always had him, at least according to Dad, heading in the opposite direction. Besides, based on our trip to the football game, it seemed Dad had a routine; always stayed in the same hotels, probably even ate the same food at the same diner every time.

Mark and I had spent most of the day sitting on the floor of my bedroom, unwrapping and eating our way through chocolates. While I was happy slowly pushing my thumb through soft shells and peeling back pieces of chocolate, Mark just bit off the top of his large Easter bunny, pieces of chocolate falling into the hole left from a now-missing head.

As he rolled the head around in his mouth his eyes opened wide, the piece was too big to just easily slide out. I didn't like the thought of having to stick my fingers in his mouth to fish it out, and watched to see if he was going to be able to keep the piece in or have to spit it out. I reached over for my empty bunny box to have it at the ready. After a minute or two of watching his fat cheeks moving around the piece inside, he broke it down enough that the need for my help passed. We both relaxed at the same time; him from the possibility of choking, me from having to step in and help.

Carefully, so nothing would spill out, I picked up the foil wrappers and empty chocolate boxes, wondering how either of us were going to eat any dinner. "Make sure you wash your hands," I said. "And don't get any fingerprints on the wall."

Mark looked directly at me with a stare that made it seem *I* was the one who always had to change into play clothes and then get washed up by my mom. The truth was it had nothing to do with him: I just wanted to make sure if any walls got marked and Dad started to yell, I'd know it wasn't me who was responsible.

"What do you want to do?" I asked when he returned from the bathroom.

"I dunno," Mark replied. "What do you want to do?"

It was clear neither of us wanted to do anything except let the Easter candies settle in our bellies, so we sat back down on the braided carpet and rested against the edge of the bed.

"Before you know it," I said, "hockey will be over and then it's baseball season."

"Yeah, I heard that, but I'm not trying out."

"Why not?"

"Never signed up for baseball," Mark replied. "Mom said there were more important things to be doing in the summer."

Never signed up? More important things than playing baseball?

It was hockey all over again for him; his mom didn't let him play that either as he might get hurt. Besides, she had said, Mark needed to learn to skate, and that's how he ended up in figure skating. I couldn't see Ferguson, Sevard, or Beliveau taking figure skating lessons, that's for sure. Mark had taken some ribbing over that, at least 'til some of us saw him surrounded by all those girls.

Before I could say anything he added, "I mean I've never played on a team before, you know, where it's all organized." Between his mother telling him all the ways he could get hurt and all the other things he needed to do, and him believing her, it was a wonder he got up in the morning. Not that it mattered; I wasn't going to change his mind. Only his mother could do that.

"Well, I'm trying out. But I need to get a baseball glove and, if I'm lucky, maybe even a bat." First, however, I needed to make sure I got registered to play, then I could bring up the fact that I needed a glove. As far as I knew, there wasn't a used equipment sale for baseball, which meant it was going to be expensive. I had to ask Dad at exactly the right time; when work was going well, when I wasn't in trouble, when he was in a good mood. That was a lot to ask. I lay on the floor, looked up at the ceiling, rubbed my chocolate-filled belly, and waited to be called for dinner.

Sooner than Mark and I had room for it, Mom called the girls to set the table for dinner. Mark and I entered the living room and took a spot at the dinner table. Dad and Mr. Watson each sat reading, white puffs of smoke curling their way up and out over their newspapers. Unlike Christmas, each sat in their own little world, no trading of stories or trying to one-up the other. The coffee table was filled with a couple of half-eaten meat and cheese plates, full ashtrays, and several empty bottles of Coke; the beer and booze, it appeared, were safely locked away.

By the time everyone shuffled into place we were ready to say grace. Instead of a turkey sitting in the middle of the dining-room table there was a big bowl with a ladle sticking out of it. Beside the bowl sat a loaf of Mrs. Watson's homemade bread, all sliced and laid out for everyone to grab a piece, along with margarine for spreading. Once "amen" was said we were off and eating; the sound of the ladle hitting the bowl, and the knives, forks, and spoons scraping against plates, making the most noise as us kids remained silent.

"You know," Dad started, "when I grew up, nobody had much meat or food, but no one wanted their neighbours to know, so we all pretended everything was okay."

I waited for someone to ask a question, but no one did so he continued.

"On Sundays we'd put a big, ornate soupterine on the dining-room table, and leave the front window curtains open so anyone walking by could see the family gathered round. Steam would be rising up and out of the soupterine, and the neighbours would figure we had a big meal to eat. Funny thing was, it was just a big bowl of hot water; we didn't have any goddamn food to put in it!"

I started to laugh, then realized I was the only one. I waited for Mr. Watson to call bullshit or butt in with a story of his own, but he just kept on eating. He'd put too much margarine on his bread, and each time he pulled the bread away from his lips it left a glossy shine.

Like when Mr. Watson marched around the table at Christmas, everyone kept their heads down; only this time not for fear of getting hit by a wandering broomstick. I waited for Dad to explode, but as quickly as he started his story he finished talking, blew his nose in his hankie, carefully folded it back up, and put it on the corner of the table.

That needs to be washed. I hated when he used to pull it out of his pocket to wipe something off my face.

It was clear whatever just happened hadn't affected his appetite. Soon enough, he was shovelling mouthful after mouthful of Mrs. Watson's goulash off his plate and into his mouth. I listened to him chew, his back teeth chomping as they cut through each bite. Everyone carried on and finished as quickly, it seemed, as they could.

Once dinner was over, and without being asked, everyone except Dad pushed their chairs back and set about cleaning up. It didn't take long for the table to be cleared and for Mrs. Watson and Mark to leave; Mr. Watson having quietly slipped out as the last piece of over-buttered bread went down his mouth.

Dad remained alone at the table, while Mom got the girls ready for bed and I made my way to my room.

▶ ▶ ▶ ◀ ◀ ◀

I watched as Kim opened his lunch pail under the table, so no one would see what he was doing, then put something in his mouth that he washed down with his milk. Mark got up, and I told him I'd meet him out on the playground. After he left I walked over to Kim, sat close enough to talk quietly, and asked what he'd put in his mouth. He looked up and away toward the ceiling.

"Just a little pill," he replied in a voice just above a whisper.

Other than getting a needle once in a while I didn't ever remember taking a pill, except a pink children's Aspirin or Gravol for the road. "Are you sick?"

"No, not really," he replied. He then changed his mind and said, "Well, sort of. I'm sick, but not the sort of sick you can see."

"Well, if you can't see it, how do you know you're sick?"

He continued to look up at the ceiling. If it was in his legs, he wouldn't be able to walk. If it was his arms, he wouldn't be able to use them. Since he could walk and use his arms just fine, I figured his stomach was as good a guess as any. "Is it your stomach?"

"Look, Donkey," Kim said, sighing as he spoke. "It's in my head. I'm sick in the head. Least that's what they say."

Except for getting in trouble every once in a while, Kim seemed normal. But now that I thought about it, he really didn't act out that much anymore. Trying not to upset him, I asked quietly, "Who says you're sick in the head, and how do they know this?"

"It doesn't matter. I'm okay as long as I take these every day. Then everyone around me is happy, too. All you need to know is I'm taking pills 'cause I'm sick in the head, and if you tell anyone I'll make sure you pay!" The more he talked, the louder he got. I imagined him getting up and putting his hands around my neck, but as quickly as his words came out he slumped back down, a small smile across his face.

I wondered about all the time I spent alone in my head, and the feeling I often had that my head and my body had separated long ago; two unconnected parts. I tried my best to make sure they never drifted too far apart, although there were times—like when we were getting hit—that being able to look down on what was happening made it easier to take the punishment.

Was I sick in the head, too?

I got up from my seat as quietly as I could, and backed away until I could turn, then headed down the hall and went outside to play.

▸ ▸ ▸ ◂ ◂ ◂

I'd been asking Mom if we could go to Yorkton Bowl for my birthday, and had finally worn her down. She said only six friends could come, which made deciding who to invite pretty easy. Besides Mark, I also wanted Kyle, Dale, Ricky, Randy, and of course I'd need to invite Billy.

In my head I could hear Mom telling me I should also ask Robert since he had invited me to his party. I never told her I was the only one who had been invited. I also didn't want anyone at my party making fun of him, or worse, making fun of me for inviting him. We all knew he was the smartest kid in class; but the fact that he now stuttered so much gave everyone one more reason to tease him. When I gave her the list she looked at it quickly before giving me the okay. I was surprised she didn't mention Robert, and figured if I let my next question slip out quickly and quietly she might also say yes before she had a chance to think about what I wanted.

"Maybe we could go to Fletcher's and pick up some printed birthday invitations, so all I have to do is put their names on them?" I thought by mentioning Fletcher's I'd have a chance, seeing as how he was a customer of Dad's. I knew for sure we wouldn't set foot in Baker's, since they were the competition.

But before the last word rolled off my lips, she replied, "Well, I figured you could make them since we only need six." I turned and started to walk to my bedroom, disappointed I had blown my chance at real invitations.

"Wait," Mom said. "I need to go to Fletcher's anyway. Let's see what they have. Let me go ask Mrs. Watson to listen for the girls while we're out." Before she could change her mind I had on my jacket, mitts, and scarf, and was waiting on the landing.

Mom climbed into the Bel Air while I unplugged the block heater and tied the extension cord around her side mirror. Even though it was keeping the engine warmer it still took several tries for her car to start, and I could already feel my feet begin to freeze from the cold air blasting through the heater.

We drove through the snow-packed, tire-grooved back lane, and pulled out onto the main road. The back end swung around as she pressed the gas pedal. A smile crossed her face as she eased off and the car settled in, as if it knew where to go. After a few streets and a couple of turns, we pulled up in front of Fletcher's. Keeping the car running we both got out, stepping over the snowbank and into the store.

I went straight to the stationery section near the back. Mom, after getting what she needed, stood there while I went through the display. Reaching down to the bottom shelf she asked, "What about this? It's a Cowboys and Indians birthday party kit for eight boys. It includes party hats, place mats, candy baskets, napkins, invitations, *and* a Pin the Tail on the Dogie game."

She continued with a laugh, "Your father will love that! I wonder how we can pin it up without poking holes in the wall."

I couldn't believe what I was hearing and quickly replied, "Yes, please."

At the cash register, I bounced back and forth with so much excitement Mom asked if I needed to go to the bathroom. "No," I replied as she handed over a brand new five-dollar bill to the woman behind the counter, wondered where she got the money, but dare didn't ask. As the change was handed back, I picked the paper bag up from the counter and started to turn toward the front door. Just then a hand was placed on my shoulder, stopping me in my tracks. I knew it; something was wrong.

"Are these invitations for you by chance, young man?" I recognized the voice, turned around, and said, "Hello, sir." He was looking at Mom, and she was looking right back at him.

"Why, yes, they're for *my* birthday party." Mr. Fletcher continued to look at Mom while he talked. "Well, I hope you have a nice party. How old will you be; thirteen, fourteen?" He and Mom laughed.

I tried to laugh too, so they knew I knew they were kidding. "No, sir. Not that old."

"Ah," he said. "You're between the ages. Not quite a teenager, not quite a youngster."

My hand had already turned the cold knob on the door, but Mr. Fletcher continued to talk to Mom as I stepped outside, the package held tightly in my hand. The last thing I wanted was for it to slip under the car. The car had heated up while we were in the store, but it was still cold enough inside to see your breath. I looked out through my side window's plastic frost sheet, toward Fletcher's storefront. Like watching a silent movie, Mom and Mr. Fletcher could be seen talking but not heard. Mom finally came out, and a new wave of chilled air flooded the car as she opened the door. The transmission clunked as she slipped the car into gear.

As soon as we were home Mom started dinner while I pulled everything in the kit apart and laid it out on the dining-room table. I wrote out each person's name as neatly as I could, but when I stepped back it still looked like a kid had printed them. No matter! They were done and I was going to have a Cowboys and Indians bowling party!

Now I needed to figure out how to hand them out without having to explain to anyone why they hadn't been invited, least of all Robert. Mom must have read my mind and asked, "Are you handing these out in class?"

I wondered what else she knew about what was going on in my head. "I'll hand them out to people on the way home from school," was the best I could come up with. "That way we know they got them."

CHAPTER EIGHT

April, 1967

I walked into the kitchen as Mom emptied out a box of Duncan Hines into a mixing bowl. "There's an envelope for you on the dining-room table," she said.

I recognized the handwriting—my birthday card from Grandma—and quickly ripped it open. Out floated a brand new five-dollar bill. My head began to spin as I thought of all the stuff I could buy: model cars, trading cards, and all the Bazooka Joe and Blackjack gum I wanted.

Once finished mixing the cake, Mom asked if I wanted to lick the mixing blades with a smile that told me she already knew the answer. I grabbed both blades and carefully licked them, and the bowl, so clean you could almost put them back in the cupboard.

"Your Dad's in his office making a few calls. I need to go out and get a few things. Make sure you and the girls set the table, and don't forget to take the cake out before it burns. It should be ready at five thirty." With that she was gone.

I went to my room and looked at the turtle house, getting close enough to smell the still, greenish water. I now knew what smelled worse than Pine-Sol up the nose. I built a wall of books on the floor, high enough for the turtle to move around in but not climb out of, and put it inside my little book fort. Mom had warned if it got loose it wouldn't last long, but I knew from the way she stepped back whenever I handed it to her that she just didn't like it. If she found it roaming around that would be her chance to get rid of it.

I carried the pond, cleaned and filled with fresh water, back to my room, making sure not to spill along the way. I picked up the turtle, head and feet pulled in, placed it on the edge of the pond, watched it jump in—happy enough, it seemed.

I wasn't sure how much time had passed, but it was long enough for that smell of cake to drift down the hall. I ran into the kitchen, grabbed some toothpicks from the cupboard, opened the oven door, leaned in, and was promptly met with a whoosh of heat. I wondered if I had any eyebrows left. Pulling out the rack I stuck the toothpick in each pan; it came out clean as a whistle. Just then the front door opened, and I put the pans on the oven top and closed the door.

"Well," Mom said as she put a grocery bag on the kitchen counter. "I see you at least took the cakes out. What about setting the table?"

"Just getting to it." Before she could say anything else I asked what she got for dinner.

"Chinese food. Please unpack the grocery bag and open the tins while I get changed."

Between all of us coming and going, getting utensils and plates, it was a wonder we didn't bang into each other like bumper cars. By the time all the tins had been emptied, the food cooked, and everyone sat down, I was hungry. I wanted to talk about my party tomorrow, but knew better than to do so during dinner. As Dad always said, we were meant to be seen and not heard and I wasn't going to do anything to put him in a bad mood.

Once finished dinner and before we were done cleaning up the table, he was already in his chair reading the paper.

I stayed in the kitchen to see what was happening with the cake. Mom looked over and said, "Oh, by the way, I added one person to the list." Before I could ask who, she continued. "I went by Robert's house yesterday and dropped off an invitation, seeing as how he invited you to his party."

I watched her plop spoonful's of icing onto the cake, spreading the knife across the top and sides. She finished by flicking the knife edge to make little waves around the side of the cake. I wondered why Robert hadn't mentioned anything about the invite at school. Maybe he was mad because everyone else had been invited before him; maybe he wouldn't show up.

"There," she said as she stepped back from the cake, knife held high. "One birthday cake for tomorrow." It didn't look like the ones we used to get from Jeanne's Bakery in Winnipeg, but I could already feel my teeth aching from the sweet icing.

No money in that one!

By the time we were done I was ready for bed. I lay there thinking about my party tomorrow, as much as I could what with Garner Ted Armstrong's strong, smooth voice drifting out of the transistor and into my head. He spoke about four horses, about how the world was going to end, and how we could be saved—at least those who listened to the good word. My eyes started to close on their own. I really wanted to believe there was a better place.

▸▸▸◂◂◂

Mark had been here since the crack of dawn and everyone else had arrived around noon, my bedroom now full of people, parkas, and snow pants. Finally, Mom said it was time to go and we piled into her station wagon. Mark and I got in up front while Dale, Ricky, and Randy slid into the back seat, leaving Billy and Robert standing outside. Since the tailgate latch didn't work they both finally pushed their way in and over the seat into the back, snow from their boots falling over us as they did. The car wasn't going to warm up enough for anyone to worry about sitting on melting snow.

We parked in front of the Yorkton Bowl Arena, and before I could ask why it was called an arena I was pushed toward the door by the others. As we entered the building the sound of balls hitting the wooden alleyways greeted us, little torpedoes tossed toward carefully placed wooden targets. I could hear cheers and groans, as now and then a ball skidding down a gutter.

We stood in front of the counter, behind which, judging from the width and length of his chest, sat a very large man smoking a cigar. Without so much as a drop of spit coming out of his mouth, he rolled the lit cigar from one corner to the other and then barked out, "Line up single file. Call out your shoe size. Wait for them, then stand aside." His forehead glistened with tiny beads of sweat, held between the rolls of skin that moved up and down as he spoke. He picked up a pair of shoes with one hand and sprayed the insides with the other, all the while looking up and down the lanes in front of him.

I was first in line, and the smell from the spray went straight up my nose and down the back of my throat. Before I could speak he leaned forward, put his mouth over the microphone, and flipped a switch with his chubby finger, a finger so fat it swallowed up the ring he wore.

"For those of you on lane four: if you'd like to continue bowling, please make an effort to wait until all of the pins have been set before throwing your ball down the lane." He leaned back when finished.

What a polite man.

Just as I opened my mouth to call out my shoe size, he leaned forward once more and whispered into the microphone, "Or else!"

I turned and looked down the rows until I spotted lane four. The people now looked directly back at the man behind the microphone, with heads bowed and shoulders dropped. His message had been received loud and clear. I knew *our* guys wouldn't be throwing a ball too early.

I looked back as smoke from his cigar curled up and over his shiny, bald head. "Well, what's *your* shoe size?"

I called out my shoe size, and lost no time getting out of the line once he handed them to me. He winked at Mom, then asked Mark the same question and so on down the line until we all had our shoes.

Mom spread the score sheet out and wrote our names down while we sat, ready to go; hats, coats, and snow pants off, bowling shoes on. My feet started to itch but I wasn't going to let that stop me from playing. With Robert along, we split into two teams of four. I knew one of the teams would be Dale, Ricky, Randy, and Billy since I'd already heard Billy complain about not being on their team and knew with Mark and Robert on our team we didn't stand a chance.

It didn't take long for it to be all over, their team scoring higher than ours in all three games. We turned in our shoes to the cigar man, who once again sprayed each pair before placing them under the counter for the next bowlers.

The station wagon slipped and slid along the road, and we all laughed as we bumped into each other on our way back to the apartment.

By the time we wolfed down hot dogs, cake, and ice cream, and played Pin the Tail on the Dogie, there was only one thing left to do and that was open the presents. We crammed around the kitchen table, shoulder to shoulder. Everyone wanted to see their gift opened first except for Robert, who leaned in and whispered, "Open mine last." I wasn't sure if he was embarrassed, but it didn't matter, I was happy to open his last and not hurt anyone else's feelings.

With only Robert's gift left to open I stopped and looked at the hockey and baseball cards, Matchbox cars, and a couple of comic books spread out before me. Not bad, I thought, then reached over and picked up his gift. The box was big enough for a model car, but I didn't want to get my hopes up. I started to tear the paper, then remembered how carefully he'd peeled away the paper on the gift I'd given him. Looking at the box again I realized the wrapping paper was decorated with clowns and balloons, then saw where the top coat of the paper had already been torn off.

Robert wrapped my gift with the paper I had used for his gift.

I stopped, put the box down, and went to open the birthday card, half-expecting to see the same monkey card I'd given him, only this time with our names changed around. It wasn't; it was a couple of squirrels talking about being nuts and wishing a Happy Birthday to a lucky boy.

I looked up to find everyone staring at me. "Oh," I said. "I hadn't read the card first and didn't want to be rude."

Robert started to speak, but before he could get his sentence out the box was back in my hands, paper torn off, and the model now clearly visible. I stopped again and looked at Robert, a smile as big as I'd ever seen on his face.

"I don't know what to say," was the best I could do. Robert had given me back the Frankenstein model I'd given him for his birthday, unopened and ready to go. I was now ashamed for thinking before that I'd wasted my gift on him. Everyone stood around, trying to figure out what was going on.

In a slow, clear voice Robert spoke. "I knew you were disappointed when I said I couldn't keep the gift. I said to Mom it'd be rude to throw it away, so I asked if we could keep it. You know, just in case. But I did buy you one thing you didn't buy me." His stutter returned on the second to last word.

"What's that?"

He pulled a tube of Testors glue from his pocket. "Cement," Robert said, his voice now excited. "Mother got some so you can g-g-go ahead and m-m-make it."

Randy and Ricky whispered behind Robert's back about him being an Indian giver. I started to tell them to knock it off, but just then the front door opened and Dad started to work his way through the pile of boots. It was time for me to get them out the door.

"I hope you guys liked the bowling and the food, but it's time for everyone to go home." I wanted to tell Robert how much I liked the gift, but didn't want to say so in front of everyone else. All I could get out was a simple thank you, and told him to say hi to his mom.

Once everyone had gone, Mark and I headed toward my room. As we passed the living room doorway, Dad called out. I rounded the corner to see him sitting in his chair, newspaper in his hands. His hair, cut on the sides about as close as could be, the top puffed high up in a forward wave, shone in the light. "Mom told me you want to play baseball and need a glove."

I waited for him to tell me where we were going to get a used glove from, but before I could come up with a reason why that was a bad idea he continued. "How about we go to the sports store next weekend and pick one up?"

I wasn't going to miss out on the chance for my own baseball glove. "Yes please," I replied, quick as I could.

▸ ▸ ▸ ◂ ◂ ◂

After a slow start to the season our hockey team played well enough, but not well enough to win anything other than last place. Still, everyone on the team got to go to the banquet. By the time we'd filed into the auditorium it was full, loud voices echoing about. We were told to take our seats at our team's table, and after grace was said got up, one table at a time, and picked up a plate containing a hot dog and a handful of potato chips from the buffet. We each received a pop to wash it all down.

After listening to a speech about good sportsmanship and about learning to win *and* lose (pointed out more than once), the teams got their crests and trophies. For my team, having come out on the losing side, this meant we each got a crest but no trophy. Awards were also handed out for most-improved player—it'd be a while before I won one of those—and then the most valuable player on each team.

Last but not least, the president of the hockey association handed out the championship awards, and then we were done, the hockey season was over.

▸ ▸ ▸ ◂ ◂ ◂

It had been a week since I looked in on the turtle, the water in the pond was gone, the pond itself now lined with green mould. That was the least of my worries: what was left of the turtle smelled worse than the dried-out pond. Dad was going to be home tonight and this was one less thing I wanted him, or me, to deal with this weekend.

I was going to flush it down the toilet, but afraid I'd also have to explain how the toilet got plugged, wrapped the turtle in newspaper, placed it in the kitchen garbage, and brought the garbage down to the outside bin. It wasn't often I took the garbage out without being reminded, and when I returned Red poked her head into my room.

"Where's the turtle?"

"None of your business. And if you make it your business I'll punch you!"

In the past she would have run to Mom or Dad, if he was around, but she had changed since we came here; she didn't run off and tattle anymore. I think she finally figured out that things had a way of taking care of themselves. That God, or Dad, would punish me anyway.

"It's dead, isn't it?" She asked quietly. I expected her to tell me I should have done a better job of taking care of it, but she just stared at me before saying, "I'm sorry it died. I know this was the first pet you had for this long."

I wanted to say something about the dog, but I couldn't find the words. Maybe Dad was right. Maybe I didn't deserve to have anything, or maybe God was punishing me. It didn't matter. The dog was gone, the turtle was dead, and I had been responsible for taking care of them.

It'd be a long time before I asked for another pet.

▸▸▸◂◂◂

It was Saturday morning and Dad drove while I listened to him tell me why I'd never get another baseball glove if I lost the one I didn't yet have. We pulled up to the sporting goods store, and I was out and inside before the car stopped rocking, and straight on through to the baseball section. The days of having to borrow a glove from someone heading up to bat or sitting on the bench were almost over.

I didn't know how much Dad had planned on spending and didn't want to pick something too expensive, or too cheap. It had to be priced just right. I settled on a calf-coloured Spalding; it was nice and thick, my fingers already smelling of leather after sliding my hand in and out a few times. Everyone had advice on how to soften a glove and put a "pocket" in it. One trick, they said, was to get a pound of butter, put it in the middle of the glove, and wrap an elastic band around it. The melting butter was supposed to soften the leather.

I'd been trying to figure out how to convince Mom to buy a pound of butter she knew I was going to waste. As we put the glove on the counter my problem was solved before I made a fool of myself; the man behind the counter started giving Dad all kinds of advice. I knew Dad never really listened to anyone, but he at least looked like he was interested in what the man had to say.

"The simplest way to put a pocket in the glove is to get a hard ball, put it in the centre of the glove, and wrap some thick elastic bands, like this, around the glove. Then spray the glove with some water.

Whatever you do, don't listen to those old wives' tales about using butter or oil. Can't tell you how many times parents come back with their kid's gloves stinking of hot, melted butter once they get their fingers up in all the finger holes, fill 'em with sweat, and leave the thing out in the sun. Oh yeah, you'll get the nickname 'butter fingers' in no time."

Which was worse: being called Butter Fingers or Donkey?

I watched Dad take a roll of bills from his pocket, peeling off the cash to pay for the glove. I looked at the elastic bands, but I'd been lucky to get the glove and didn't risk asking for anything else. I didn't have to.

"What about throwing in those elastics?" Dad asked. The man behind the counter shrugged. "Sure, no problem." I thanked Dad for the glove and the man for the elastics.

As we walked to the car Dad tossed me the elastics. I opened the glove to catch them, watching as the wind carried them off in different directions instead.

Dad laughed. "Looks like you need some practice."

▸ ▸ ▸ ◂ ◂ ◂

It wasn't that Mark and me set out to find trouble, exactly, as much as trouble had a way of finding us, even if we only had the rest of a Saturday to find it.

I wasn't supposed to have a BB gun, wasn't even allowed a cap gun. Dad had made it clear that guns weren't even something to talk about, but that didn't stop me from trading for one. It looked real enough: a detective's gun, not a six-shooter. Since I couldn't keep the gun at home I hid it at the back of a dryer or washer in the laundry room.

I loved to slide back the top, pour in some pellets, and start shooting, just like James Bond or Matt Helm, depending on whether or not you felt like singing. It didn't shoot far, so trying to hit birds or prairie dogs was out of the question. Even trying to get close to a stray dog or cat was pretty hard. Besides, the last thing I wanted was a mad dog that would just as likely end up running after me.

Mostly, those of us with guns would just shoot each other, but this didn't last long 'cause we always ran out of things to use for ammunition. The best were BB pellets, but they cost a lot. There wasn't much else to use except soup peas, but there were limits to those too as Mom would make soup sooner or later. It was easier to go to the grocery store with a pen or pencil, poke a hole into a dried pea bag, and fill our pockets 'til we got scared of getting caught.

The problem with that was dried peas weren't round or smooth like BB pellets, and if you weren't careful they'd jam the gun. If you were really unlucky it might break the spring altogether. Then you'd just be yelling "bam, bam" every time you wanted to shoot someone and that never made anyone stop shooting you if they had peas left.

Mark and I walked past the school without coming across anyone or anything to shoot at. That is until we came across Bobby Royce. I watched as he crossed the field at the back of our school. He was a brown-noser, always staying after school and banging out erasers against the outside wall. It was easy to tell the days we had a lot of notes; he'd end up walking home covered in chalk dust. I hoped he'd come alongside the school and over the lane. As soon as he was too far to run back to wherever he'd come from I yelled at Mark, "Let's get him!"

Mark whooped and hollered as we took off, my plan for a surprise attack now lost. We caught up to Bobby just as he tried to hide in the corner of the steps that led up to the front doors of the church next to our school. I sent peas raining down on him as I climbed up the stairs. While shooting someone from the steps of a church might not have been the best idea, I was only thinking about getting Bobby and not about where we were.

Mark stood below, watching Bobby dance around as the peas hit him. Once I was out of peas, I tossed the gun to Mark for him to have his chance. Mark being Mark, and, well, baseball not being something he played, the gun just sailed through his outstretched hands and landed on the cement. Too stunned to do anything he watched Bobby run over and start to stomp up and down on it. The gun snapped under the weight of his boots. By the time he was done there wasn't much left 'cept broken plastic, a bent spring, and a useless trigger. Bobby looked at Mark, then up at me. I quickly realized *I* was the one now trapped, the doors to the church surely locked on a Saturday.

Just then Mark reached into his pocket and grabbed a handful of peas, and threw them at Bobby. It was enough to distract him, and we took off as fast as we could. I kept looking over my shoulder as we ran. When we were far enough away we stopped, caught our breath, and watched Bobby running off in the other direction.

"What do you want to do?"

"I don't know. What do you want to do?" Mark replied.

▸▸▸◂◂◂

Dad said that the Yorkton airport, nothing more than a little white building beside the landing strip, was originally built for training pilots in World War II. It was also, according to him, nothing like the airport in Winnipeg. We were told that Mom had to go into the hospital, though not the reason why, and since he couldn't take any time off–at least that's what he said–Grandma was coming to take care of us.

We all stood and watched as the plane landed and rolled to a stop, Grandma almost close enough to touch as she walked down the steps to the tarmac, her head scarf wrapped tightly over her hair and under her chin, raincoat flapping in the wind. She looked a little older, and was a little more hunched over than I remembered.

We hadn't seen Grandma since we left Winnipeg and I was more than happy to give up my bedroom and sleep on the floor in the girls room if it meant seeing her for a whole week.

▸▸▸◂◂◂

First thing Monday morning Dad was back on the road as happy, I think, to get away from Grandma as she was from him. After having had listen to the two of them argue about anything and everything on

Sunday, including why we had to go to church and why didn't Grandma want to come with us, I think I was also happy he was back on the road.

Grandma never had a driver's license and, left with the job of getting Mom to the new hospital, that meant we had to take a cab, something none of us kids had done before. The old hospital, Mom said, had been turned into an apartment building, and I wondered about living in a place where people had died.

Red, Little Sister, and I remained in the waiting room while Mom and Grandma were called in to fill the forms needed to check Mom in. It took me a few minutes to realize that the sound of raised voices was coming from behind the doors they had just entered. I couldn't make out what the commotion was about, but someone was growing more upset by the minute. I inched closer to the door, listening in.

"Lookit, I'm sorry. There's nothing I can do about it. I know you're scheduled for surgery. I know what the surgery is for, but we still need your husband's signature to go ahead with a tubal ligation so we know he knows."

"Jesus, this is ridiculous. Of course he knows she's here! Why do you think I'm here? I'm here because he can't be here. I'm her mother and that should be good enough for you, the doctor, or this hospital!" Although I'd heard Grandma swear quietly under her breath once or twice I'd never heard her flat out do so, so loud and so clear.

"Tell you what," the unknown voice said. "I'm going to admit you without your husband's signature, but you've got to get a hold of him. He needs to come back and sign. Otherwise we can't do the operation."

I couldn't figure out who was going to be swearing more when Grandma got Dad on the phone; Dad for having to hightail it back, or Grandma who didn't want to see him any more than she had to. I leaned back in time to miss getting hit as the door burst open and Grandma stormed back into the waiting room. "Come on, kids. We'll come back tomorrow after everything is done. That is if we don't have to sign papers to get back in!"

I watched Mom, having been told that sitting in a wheelchair was policy, whatever that meant, get wheeled down the hall, the doors swinging us her goodbye.

▸▸▸◂◂◂

Dad mustn't have gotten too far since he was home by the time we awoke the next morning. None of us were used to him being home on a school day, and getting ready took a bit of dancing around. With Grandma and Dad bumping into each other it was even more difficult.

Whatever it was he had to sign, he said, he was "gonna sign it quick and then get back on the road."

▸▸▸◂◂◂

The first time we visited Mom after her "sugary" as Little Sister called it, Mom was tired and moved slowly, like she was hurt all over. She sat propped up, pillow behind her head, and a white gown drawn around her neck; as much as she smiled and said she was okay, she didn't look or sound it.

I noticed she didn't have any makeup or lipstick on, and her hair was all flattened down. I was pretty sure she hadn't looked at herself in the mirror lately.

I remembered back to the night she'd come home from the curling banquet and wondered where that laughing, dressed-up person had gone.

Visiting hours were short, and what with Little Sister running around, jumping on and off the bed, Grandma grew irritated to the point of finally declaring, "Come on, kids, taxi's waiting. Time to get you home."

Mom returned home a couple of days later, while we were at school, which meant it was now Grandma, and not Dad, telling us to keep quiet and stay in our rooms.

By the end of the week we'd eaten our way through several Swanson's TV dinners, Jiffy Pop, and a whole box of CAP'N CRUNCH. I was beginning to look forward to Mom's baked brown beans, a day I never thought would arrive.

▸ ▸ ▸ ◂ ◂ ◂

I'm not sure why I started pretending to kiss Debra, making kissy faces and hand motions as if rubbing her hair while I sat behind her, but I did. Everyone giggled, but as often happened I went from carrying on to being carried away. When the class started to laugh Mr. Long slammed his wooden ruler down and the room immediately went quiet.

He got up from his chair then started down the aisle with a, "What, if I may ask, is so funny?" He talked to no one in particular, hoping one of us would crack.

Please, dear God, don't let any of them tell on me.

Although he lingered longer at both Mark's and Billy's desks, neither said a word. "It was funny a few minutes ago, but now you can't remember what you were laughing about? Perhaps staying in for recess will give you all time to think about it." Everyone groaned. He waited for the guilty one to save the rest from being punished, but I wasn't falling into his trap. I kept my eyes down. There was some complaining when we stayed in for recess, but no one said much to me.

As Mark and I walked home after school I looked back to see Dale and Kyle walking behind us, further back than usual. It didn't take long to realize something was up as a snowball landed hard on the back of my head. The ringing in my ears told me someone had spent some time making it, 'cause it didn't break apart when it hit.

I turned back just in time to see Dale getting ready to leap up onto my back. I quickly pushed Mark out of my way and stepped aside, which meant Dale flew past and landed on the sidewalk. He took a few silent gasps before taking a couple of gulps and finally a deep breath. I started to laugh while he picked himself up, but should have ran when I had the chance. He started toward me and tried to trap me in a bear hug, but I didn't move much since he was shorter and weighed less. As we tried to push each other over, he grabbed me by the scarf. I'd had enough, pushed him back, and asked what his problem was.

"You! You're the problem. You made fun of Debra. You pretended to kiss her and rub her hair. She doesn't like that and she doesn't want to walk home with you. She doesn't like you anymore." Dale stepped forward, put his hands on my chest, and shoved me.

In listening to Dale I hadn't realized Kyle was behind me, down on all fours and waiting. I fell over backward and lay there dazed, looking up at the dark grey sky, the cold ground against my body. The most popular girl in class had liked me, and now she didn't. I waited for everyone to walk away, listening to them laugh about how I ended up on my back, when Billy's face suddenly appeared over me.

"What happened, Donkey?"

"Nothin'," I replied. "Just slipped and fell."

There was silence before Billy chuckled then said, "Must have been when Dale pushed you backward."

"Shut up and help me up."

Once up I brushed myself off, looking to see who else was around besides Mark and Billy.

I turned to Mark, "Thanks for nothing."

"Whattaya mean, thanks for nothing? My shoulder hurts from you pushing me out of the way. And I had nothing to do with this."

He had a point.

Mark, Billy, and I walked the rest of the way home in silence. It was clear I didn't have a chance of hanging around with Debra anymore, let alone working on a project or class assignment together.

Forget another dance. Forget making jokes with her. Forget she even knew me.

▸▸▸◂◂◂

It was raining when we drove Grandma back to the airport, so we sat in the car and waited for the signal it was time for her to board. Dad was doing his best to convince her she could just as easily get on the plane any time she wanted.

When the stewardess finally stuck her head out of the doorway and waved to come on in, Grandma leaned over and kissed each of us goodbye while Dad jumped out of the car, opened the trunk, and handed over her bag before she'd even closed her door.

She walked up the stairs, turning to wave before disappearing inside the plane. The scent of her perfume remained in the car as she flew off.

▸▸▸◂◂◂

They finished building the triplexes across the street just before winter set in, and before they had a chance to clean up the field behind them. As winter slowly slid into spring, the field was dotted with banks of pushed up mud and melting snow that held small ponds of ice-cold water.

There were plenty of two-by-fours and plywood lying around for us to build rafts, which we had done the past few weekends. Full four-by-eight foot sheets of plywood made them good for staying afloat, but hard to turn once they were in the water. The one I had built, sturdy enough for two people, floated well. However, being so heavy, it was hard to launch and only stayed flat when you stood in the centre of it—otherwise water would rise up from one end.

When it came to using the rafts it was first come, first serve. But that only worked if the kids who showed up to claim "their" raft weren't bigger than you. The only other choice was to leave your raft into the middle of the pond, the only way anyone could get it was to float out on something else.

I knew I wasn't going to get new boots until back-to-school shopping in the fall, and now tied empty plastic bread bags around my feet, held tight with elastic bands to keep the water from seeping through the holes in my boots and reaching my socks.

The sun was out and I was beginning to get warm under my parka. The parka itself made it tough to paddle, getting in the way of a smooth arm stroke. I was thinking about taking it off when a kid I didn't recognize lined me up. Before I knew it, it was wood on wood.

His raft, all four-by-eight feet of it, now rested halfway up my smaller, unfinished raft. He walked forward, trying to swamp me.

By the time I'd regained my balance my boots had sunk below the waterline, and as tight as the elastics were they were no match for the moment when water flooded over the tops of my boots. I now had two soakers. As I dragged my waterlogged feet across the top of the raft, a nail stuck in my boot. I didn't feel anything and hoped it slid in under my foot, which I checked by shifting my weight around. It was bad enough I had another hole in my boot, good enough that I didn't have to explain a nail in my foot.

As my raft sank, the kid claimed victory before pushing off.

Ramming a raft isn't much of a victory when the person being rammed wasn't paying attention. Then again, I'd have done the same thing.

I found a place to sit, pulling off my boots and plastic bags and emptying them of water. Too wet to continue I walked home, and with every step felt the water squish up between my now-cold toes.

▸ ▸ ▸ ◂ ◂ ◂

Grandma had been gone a couple of weeks, Mom was up and about, and it was back to just Mark and me walking home after school. Today, however, I walked alone, Mark having stayed behind for some reason I wasn't interested in hearing about. I wanted to watch TV, and walked as quickly as I could. As I got to the back door of the building and went to step inside, it was clear I'd let my guard down for there, larger than life, stood Big Boy!

I wanted to turn and run, but before I could he reached out, put one of his arms around my neck, and pressed my face against his parka. I couldn't move, or breathe for that matter, my face deep into his chest. After we got him last February I always made sure he never had the chance at an ambush. There were times I saw him in the distance, and when I did I'd run between houses and through back lanes to get away. Today I was alone with him, and now in a headlock.

How could I be so stupid?

I managed a muffled, "Okay you got me. Now what are you going to do?" I waited for an answer while he held me tight. I waited some more.

Maybe he can't speak. Maybe he is retarded after all. Where is Mark when I need him?

"Nothing," Big Boy finally replied, loosening his grip.

"Nothing? What do you mean nothing?"

"I'm not going to do nothing. I just wanted to ask why you guys always run after me and call me names."

He let me go, but still blocked the stairs. I looked at his freckled face, framed by caterpillar-thick eyebrows with a somewhat flattened nose. I was sure he'd have me by the back of my parka long before I could get out the door. The best I could do was stammer out, "I don't know. I did it because everyone else was doing it."

At that moment I realized that wasn't a good enough reason for doing that, for doing anything like that, to someone else. I heard myself start to say I was sorry, but he stopped me. "All I want is for you guys to stop calling me names. My name is James, and I'm not a retard." Until then I hadn't thought about his feelings. If he was hurt only half as bad as I felt stupid, well he must have been hurt pretty bad.

"I'm sorry. I won't do it again."

"Alright then. I'll see you around." It looked like he was going to say something else, but just then the back door opened. Mark took one step in, looked up at Big Boy, and his eyes lit up. Like a jack rabbit he turned and ran. I started to yell out that he didn't have to run, but it was too late. Big Boy and I were left standing in the stairwell, alone again.

"I'll talk to him when I see him," I said.

Big Boy opened the door and went on his way. I stuck my head out. Wherever Mark had run off to, he was far enough not to be seen. I was getting cold, closed the door behind me and went up to our apartment.

CHAPTER NINE

May, 1967

"Every summer the Agricultural and Industrial Exhibition has a competition for school projects. This year, over twenty schools will be entering the competition. There's lots of categories for you to enter. These includes crafts, needlepoint, creative writing, exercise books, and, of course, artwork. We've been working on our Centennial projects in class, so it'd be a good idea if this was incorporated into your project. And yes, everyone is expected to complete a project. We'll have our own school competition first, then those selected will be sent on to the Agricultural and Industrial Exhibition to be judged. So, good luck everyone."

I wasn't sure why Mr. Long insisted on calling the fair by its proper name; everyone else just called it the fair. I wanted to enter, but I wasn't very good at crafts and certainly couldn't sew beyond stitching a patch on a pair of Hallowe'en hobo pants. English wasn't my best class so writing was out, and I really couldn't draw horses, cows, or pioneers so that was out too.

Lost in my day-dreaming I missed all the fuss that followed the announcement. That is until I heard the sound of a desk being dragged across the floor. I looked up just in time to see a tug of war between Mr.

Long and Kim. Whatever had happened it was serious enough that Mr. Long wasn't even going to try to reason with Kim, and from the look of fear on Kim's face, the corners of his mouth filled with white foam, it wouldn't have accomplished much anyway.

Kim's body was stiff as a board, like a little kid who didn't want to be picked up. He jerked up and down before going limp. With one big, final tug Mr. Long pulled Kim from his desk then called for the class door to be opened.

There wasn't any need for us to be told to sit quietly until they returned, and we remained in our seats.

When Mr. Long returned, the sweat stains under his arms showed the effort of having dragged Kim all the way to the principal's office. He pulled Kim's desk back to its spot, opened the lid, and removed everything stuffed into it. When he was done, all of Kim's belonging lay on one corner of Mr. Long's desk.

As he turned his back to us and started to write on the chalkboard, the rattle of pills in his pocket, was the only reminder Kim had ever been here.

▸▸▸◂◂◂

The lady scared the heck out of me when she yelled, "Leave the laundry alone, and get out of our yard!" I'd waited outside the back fence, and when I didn't see anyone moving through the kitchen window figured no one was home. I quickly yanked the laundry line toward me, removed a pair of pants that looked as though they belonged to the man of the house, and tossed them onto the picnic table. I stuffed the wooden clothespins into my pocket, jumped off the steps, and ran toward the back gate.

As I slammed the gate shut behind me I heard part of it splinter when it whacked the post. I watched it swing back out into the laneway before slamming shut on the woman, who now stood just on the other side, cursing me loudly. "I'm gonna call your mother and tell her you've been taking down my laundry. I don't know what your game is boy, but if *I* catch you I'll use the rug beater on your behind!"

I pedalled off, the bicycle wheels clicking loudly as they revved up to speed. It wasn't her laundry I was after, it was the wooden clothespins. Once in a while I'd get some new ones from the store, but full bags were just too big to take so I'd poke a hole a bag and grab a few. Whenever I rode down this back lane and passed her house, the clothes flapping on the laundry line seemed to call out, "Free pegs for the taking!" The dozen or so I'd just picked up would go a long way to making my bike sound faster and louder. I didn't stop pedalling until I reached the back of the school, empty since it was a still-early Saturday morning.

With Mark away for the weekend I had decided to bike across town, following the boundary road up toward the railway yard. I rode along the tracks until I reached the flat cars at the end. In front of me stood a line of brand new Massey Fergusons. I dropped my bike, jumped onto the rails, and climbed into the first combine. The key had been left in the ignition, but I didn't have the nerve to turn it on. Even with the windows covered in a fine layer of dust it wasn't hard to picture myself driving up and down the fields, bringing in the crop. With nothing but time on my hands I made my way through every cab on the flat cars, pushing, pulling, or turning every knob, dial, and fuse I could see.

At the end of the line I was about to turn around and head back when I heard the sound of a car rolling ever so slowly over the gravel of the next track, the rocks crunching under the weight of the car. Jumping down I looked under the flatbeds. I couldn't see anything, but I heard the sound of a car door closing. Railway cops!

I ran along my side of the tracks until I reached the post where I'd laid my bike, got on, and put as much force into pedalling as I could. The wheels spun wildly, the wooden pegs raising a holy racket; they didn't seem so smart now. I heard someone shuffling, then running, through the gravel. Then came a yell: "Hey … kid … stop! I wanna to talk to you. You're on railway property!"

Talk was the last thing I wanted. I put more weight on the pedals. Just as I thought I was free the man poked his head out from between two rail cars and lunged towards me. At that moment I swerved to miss him, heading down the side of the tracks and along a gully. As I sped off I glanced over my shoulder to see a very fat man bent over, hands on his knees, and trying to catch his breath, not me. I slowed down and wondered what to do next.

I wanted to go to the movies, but spent all of my birthday money and already had my allowance taken away for not putting out the garbage. Without thinking I found myself behind the Edwards's house—one of the kids in my class—and pretended I had a reason for being there. I looked around to see if anyone was home. From what I could tell they weren't; the yard was empty, the laundry line clear. I pressed my face up against the dusty garage door window. No car sat inside.

After working up as much courage as I was ever going to have I made my way to the side of the house and pulled on the milk door. It didn't budge. The thought that it was a sign to get the heck out of there crossed my mind, but like other signs God had given me I ignored this one too. This time I pulled on the handle with both hands, the door swung open, and I almost fell backward.

Inside were several coins and a couple of dollar bills for the milk man. I put my hand in to scoop them up just as the back door of the milk box opened. A woman's thin, delicate hand reached in and flailed about while I tried to grab what I could before running for my bike. The pegs attached to the wooden pegs screamed out my location as I broke through the laneway.

Should have taken those off after the railroad cop chased me!

Without stopping to look both ways I almost hit a car coming out of a side street.

Did Mrs. Edwards get a look at me as I pulled the money out?

I'd gone from making a clean getaway to picturing her sitting down with a police sketch artist. I was afraid my heart, what with the way it was now pounding, wasn't going to hold out. I wanted to return the money, but didn't want to go back on the chance Mrs. Edwards, or even the police, would be waiting.

By now I'd ended up downtown near the movie theatre, and figured that no one would spot me in the dark. I'd have the rest of the day to figure out what to do. I left my bike outside and bought a ticket without bothering to see what was playing. By the time I had my popcorn and drink, and had sat through the opening cartoons, my heart had settled down.

After the western had ended, I picked up my bike and headed home. It was getting dark and dinner would soon be ready. After leaning my bike against the side of the apartment building I took a quick look around the corner. No cop cars; at least none I could see. I ran up the stairs and into the apartment. Dinner was on, and Dad was in his chair reading the paper while Little Sister sat in his lap. Everything was as it should be. We ate, cleaned up, and watched TV as usual.

That night, the glow from the radio dial seemed brighter as Garner Ted Armstrong spoke, and I was sure I heard him tell me I was headed toward eternal damnation as I drifted off.

▸▸▸◂◂◂

It was Thursday and pitching tryouts were to be held by the long ditch near the highway. It was close enough to walk to, yet far enough away from houses that nothing could get broken from a badly thrown ball. Since every player had a chance at each position during tryouts I hoped I'd become one of the pitchers on this year's team.

I had made a pocket in my new glove using an apple taken from one of the kids during lunch. By this time half of the apple had turned to mush, leaving a stain in the centre of the glove that I hoped a little dirt from a baseball would make less noticeable. The important thing was that a hard ball would now sail into the pocket and not pop out.

It still got dark pretty early this time of the year, and by the time we'd almost finished tryouts it had started to rain. Randy and Ricky already had their turn pitching. Both were pretty good, and as their dads were the team's coaches they didn't have to make much of an effort to be picked as one of the pitchers. My pitches, however, had to sail across home plate and into the glove of Ricky's dad if I was to have any chance at all. I thought the first few pitches came close, but the laughter behind me told me the guys didn't agree. I stared at the pocket in my glove, the apple stain now replaced by a circle of dirt.

The light drizzle made every pitch a little harder to throw. By now the ball, as well as my glove and hands, were wet and my final pitches sailed so high over Ricky's dad's head he didn't even try to catch them. Before it got too dark they called it a night, promising they'd call us with our starting positions before the first game. I probably wasn't going to be a pitcher, but I sure hoped I wouldn't be stuck in centre field.

▸▸▸◂◂◂

It had been a week since the try-outs and still no call from the coaches about what position I would be playing. Mark and I had, as usual, walked home from school together. What was unusual was seeing Mom waiting outside the back of our building.

"I need to talk to you," she said. As Mom and I went up to our place I told Mark I would see him later, to which Mom added, "not tonight."

"Come to my bedroom," she said as soon as we entered. I followed her down the hall and stood while she closed the door behind me.

"Sit down."

I didn't want to mess the bed cover, but thinking this wasn't a time to argue did as I was told. After a few seconds of staring at each other she started to cry and asked how I could have stolen money?

"What did we do wrong?" she asked. "Why don't you have the common sense to know that wasn't the right thing to do?" I was sorry she was crying because of me and I knew she wanted answers, but these were questions I hadn't thought of when I had my hand flopping around the insides of the milk box.

Grabbing her purse off the dresser she shook out the contents onto the bed and collected up every coin that spilled out. From what I could tell she was about a dollar short of what I'd taken from Mrs. Edwards.

"This," Mom said, "is all the money I have 'til your father gets home on Friday." I stared at her.

How can this be all the money she has?

Every week I watched Dad empty out his pockets, full of change and rolls of bills, which he then arranged into nice, neat piles. Wiping away the tears she told me to come with her. I thought about Dad and what he was going to say, or rather do, when he got home.

I followed her out to the car. After a couple of pumps on the gas and a few turns of the key the engine started up, and she put the car into reverse and backed out. I stared out of the side window, wondering what I'd gotten myself into. When the car finally stopped I looked up and my heart sank; we were in front of the Edwards's house.

"Get out," she said. My feet felt like cement blocks and it was all I could do to step out of the car and walk up behind her. I felt like Frankenstein, all stiff-legged with outstretched wooden arms, one straight leg stepping out at a time. She rang the bell and, after what seemed like hours, Mrs. Edwards finally opened the front door. Reaching into her pocket Mom pulled out all the change she'd collected up. "Here's all the money we have. I hope this makes up for what was stolen."

Stolen? She makes me sound like a criminal!

Mom asked me to apologize to Mrs. Edwards. I started to speak, but I had gone from cement feet to dry throat and it took a couple of tries to find my voice.

"I'm sorry I took your milk money. I won't do it again." Based on their silence I wasn't sure if they were expecting more, but I didn't have anything else to say.

"Dinner's on the table, and I need to get back in before Mr. Edwards starts asking questions," Mrs. Edwards said.

At least he doesn't know.

We got back in the car, waited for it to turn over, and then drove away. As we pulled back into our laneway Mom said, "Not a word."

Not a word? What does she mean, not a word? Who am I going to tell? I'm embarrassed enough as it is.

Both car doors creaked as they were opened. As we walked up the stairs I found the courage to ask. "What do you mean, not a word?"

She stopped so quickly I almost ran into her backside. Mom whirled around and pointed her finger at me. "Not a word of this to your father, understand?" Well, I understood now. I understood this was to be a secret between us, and I was okay with that. I just wasn't sure why she wasn't going to let Dad punish me for what I'd done.

I opened the door for her, light flooding out as I closed it behind us. Nothing more was said as Mom went about making dinner.

▸ ▸ ▸ ◂ ◂ ◂

I stood outside our building, waiting for Mark to come out, watching the moving van at the apartment building next door. I hoped for someone our age to move in so I wouldn't be known as the new guy anymore. I started to ask the movers if there were any kids in the family, but just then a station wagon rolled up and parked in front of the van.

A lady and then a boy got out, and as they headed toward the building the lady took the boy's hand and pulled him along as he stared at me over his shoulder. She was rail-thin with long black shiny hair, her pale white skin making her appear ghostly. He looked to be about my age, but I couldn't be sure. All I knew was that he looked old enough not to be dragged along by his momma.

The movers spent the next few hours walking up and down the plank at the back of the truck, which bounced under the weight of various items. Finally, in the middle of the afternoon, the kid came out and stood on the sidewalk, hands behind his back and looking down at the ground. I waited for him to come closer, but he remained fixed where he was. I finally yelled over, "Hey! What's your name?"

He looked up. I was sure he knew I was talking to him, but he didn't reply. I yelled again, "Hey, you. What's your name?" Again nothing.

I was about to give up when he yelled back, "Dwayne." It was my turn to stand and not say anything. He yelled again, "Dwayne. My name's Dwayne."

"Is Dee Wayne one word or two?" I asked.

"What do you mean?" He quickly shot back.

It was becoming a tennis match, each of us sending questions back and forth and neither hitting anything. Stepping forward he looked directly at me and proceeded to spell out each letter, pausing in between as if to let them roll around my head. When he was done, he said, "One word. Dwayne. It's one word."

We weren't off to a good start if we were going to be friends. With Mark, I knew from the minute we spoke it had just seemed right. With Dwayne, well, it had already got down to him spelling his name very slowly, like I was a retard.

"I'm not a retard," I said. "Just never heard the name Dwayne before."

I changed the subject and asked where his dad was, but that too was a mistake as he replied, "I don't know."

Before my brain could stop my mouth I carried on. "What do you mean, you don't know?"

"We don't know where he is," Dwayne replied in the same slow tone. "He left a few years ago. Went out for milk one day and never came back. Least that's what Mom says, and I believe her."

How could someone go out for milk and never come back? Where do you go? Did he have luggage? Didn't anyone notice?

I had all these questions, but thought it best not to ask and instead asked, "What kind of name is Dwayne anyway?"

Dwayne ignored the question and kept on talking. "We lived at my Grammy's house on the other side of town. She just went up to heaven to be with Grampy. Momma says the bank got the house 'cause of all of the money Daddy owed. So here we are."

I was beginning to feel bad for him. "Momma can't work on account of her condition," he added.

Condition? She looked okay to me; didn't see her limping or carrying a cane. As far as I could see, she doesn't have a "condition".

"On account of her condition," he repeated. "Momma needs to drink in order to get through the day."

He stood there, wound up, I thought, worse than Mark or Kim. I started walking backward, hoping he wouldn't notice. "Oh," was the only reply I could give. Then I noticed he still had his hands behind his back.

"Whattaya got there?" I asked.

He brought one hand around, holding out the box close enough for me to see but far enough back I that couldn't grab it. "It's my new model boat. It's got an electric motor and can drive around the bath tub. I'm going to build it myself. Momma got it for me for us having to move."

Jesus, the closest I ever got to a model with an electric motor was watching Dad build the car model he'd been trying to finish for over a year now. "Very nice," I said, not wanting Dwayne to know I was jealous.

"Maybe when it's finished you can come over and watch me play."

I wanted to swat the box out of his hand, but just then Dwayne's mother appeared in the building entrance. She stood with her feet firmly planted, hands on hips, and the top of her body slightly rotating, like a slowly spinning top about to fall over.

"Come on, we need to unpack," she called out. "Got to have everything unpacked today. Don't want to be unpacking tomorrow. Need to sleep in then."

One sentence ran into the other. At the end she took one big breath and looked as if she was ready to start all over, but didn't say anything more. Dwayne started toward her and said, "Gotta go. Maybe we can play later." He reached the front door, and she grabbed his arm to steady herself as they disappeared inside.

Mark came out just in time to see Dwayne and his mom walk inside and asked who they were. "New kid and his mom. Come on, let's go see if we can find some more slugs from the electrical boxes in the locker area."

We'd already managed to find a few by reaching into the cobweb-filled corners of empty lockers, testing them in the basement laundry machine coin slots. A few seemed to work, but mostly they got stuck in the slot. When that happened we had to wait for someone to call the super to fix the machine.

We'd talked about asking Dale to get some from the houses his dad was building, but I didn't want anyone to know what we were up to. It was bad enough we were up to no good; I wasn't sure Mark could stop himself from confessing if we got caught. The best thing was to ride over to the construction site ourselves, and get in and back out without being noticed. So we grabbed our bikes and took off before Mark had a chance to change his mind.

Most of the houses were already framed, some with siding, which would allow us to keep from being seen. We hid our bikes near a construction shed then found a partially finished house, walking up a wooden plank that sagged as we got to the middle. I told Mark to be careful since the stairs for the basement weren't in yet. I was sure he heard me, but it was hard to know if he replied since he always spoke so quietly.

It didn't take long to see they hadn't yet started the wiring or plumbing, there wasn't anything but nails laying around the floor. "Come on," I said. Let's go to the next house."

We entered the next building and were in luck: the electrical work had been started and slugs were scattered all over. Just as I started to say "bingo" I heard a scream. It was quickly followed by a dull thud, then complete silence. I turned around; Mark wasn't behind me. I spun in all directions until I got dizzy, leaned against an unfinished wall, and waited for my head to catch up with my eyes.

Where in the heck is he?

Unlike the first house we'd entered this one at the side door, the hole in the floor for the basement stairs being near where we jumped up and in. What had happened next wasn't too hard to figure out. I stared down, trying to adjust my eyesight to the darkness below.

"Are you alright? Are you okay?"

Mark, ever so quietly, said, "No, I'm not okay. I just fell through a hole in the floor."

He talked as if nothing was wrong, but I could hear him sniffle between his words.

Good thing the concrete hasn't been poured and he landed on dirt. Probably had the wind knocked out of him.

Finally, in a steadier voice, he said, "I think I broke my arm."

How were we going to explain this? It'd be hard enough telling his mom we were snooping around a construction site, never mind we were looking for slugs. None of that mattered now. I didn't want to go get Mrs. Watson, heaven knows she'd call the police, maybe even the fire department. No, I needed to get Mark out of there myself.

"Can you see anything?" I asked.

"Like what?"

"Like a ladder?"

"No," Mark replied, this time clearly annoyed. "It's dark. I'm on my back and my arm is killing me. Don't you think if they had a ladder it'd have already been up against the hole in the floor?"

Even if there was a ladder leaning up against the hole, I think you still would've fallen in.

"Let me see if I can find something."

Out of the darkness he replied, "I'm not going anywhere."

I walked over to the construction shed. The door was padlocked, the only window also locked. After checking out a few more houses and not finding anything useful, not even any slugs, I wondered about getting help. But then house number five told me I need wonder no more, for there was the top of a two-by-four ladder sticking up and out from the basement hole. I pulled it up, made sure it and me didn't fall in, and dragged it back to the house where Mark was.

"Mark, are you there?" A stupid question, I thought, as soon the words came out.

"I'm still here," Mark replied. "Did you get a ladder?"

"Yes. I'm sliding it down." I felt several slivers slip under my skin as the ladder passed through my hands.

Better slivers than a broken arm.

When it rested on the floor I told Mark to start climbing, but it took a few minutes for him to grab the ladder and steady himself. The ladder shook as he climbed. I held both sides as tight as I could, the last thing I wanted was Mark *and* the ladder falling back in. A bead of blood slowly rolled down my hand. Better not get any of it on my clothes; that would be one more thing I didn't want to have to explain.

"Thanks," he mumbled as he reached the top and stepped off onto the floor. His hair was a mess, his once-white tee-shirt and face now covered in tears and dirt. I was sure he'd try to convince me the tears were really sweat. It didn't matter; we needed to get our story straight before he went to his mom. I made to grab his arm and have a look, but the wince on his face when he pulled away told me he needed help now.

"Come on, let's get going," I said. "We need to figure out what we're going to say."

"Okay. I'm already in enough trouble for getting my clothes dirty." I felt bad that the first thing he worried about was his clothes. I'd seen his dad fly off the handle, and sometimes *I* got a headache watching him swat the back of Mark's head.

We reached the shed where we'd left the bikes and I held Mark's bike steady as he climbed on, telling him not to fall off. He started off by almost losing his balance until he had enough speed to ride with one hand.

"We can tell everyone we were riding near the rafting ponds, up and down the hills, and you fell over your handle bars. You know, landed on the ground and pinned your arm underneath your bike."

Mark remained quiet. Once in while he came too close to my bike, trying as he was to steer with one hand.

Not very good with two hands, even worse with one.

"I dunno," he replied. "If we're going to tell a story, I want it to be a good one. Like I was doing something dangerous so people would say, 'Wow, are you ever brave.' I don't think they'd say that if I just fell over my handlebars."

He had a point, though I wasn't sure what story we could tell that was believable *and* stick to. Fact was, we were looking for slugs and he fell down a hole 'cause he wasn't paying attention.

"No," I said. "I heard if you're going to tell a story it should be sort of based on something true, so when you tell it you'll believe it yourself."

"Okay," Mark replied. "That makes sense."

I kept talking so he wouldn't come up with any more ideas, but he was faster than me. "Where can we find a deep enough hole I could have fallen into?"

"Geez. I didn't mean you needed to fall into a big hole. We just need a hole. Any hole." I wondered what he'd do without me, but then realized most of the time he got into trouble it was trouble I'd gotten him into.

"What about falling out of something, like a tree? Maybe trying to rescue a cat? I mean, I can also fall *out* of something."

"We could try the cat-in-a-tree story, but first we'd have to find a cat, a tree, and a place no one would have been when it happened. Last thing we need is for someone to say they were where we were, except we were never there and why were we lying about being someplace we weren't?"

"I still think falling off the bike is the best story," I finally said. "Why don't we say you pedalled so fast the bike went up into the air, and before you knew it came crashing down and you kept on flying?"

"I like falling out of a tree to rescue a cat better," he replied. Mark paused, then added, "But maybe we'd better stick to this story."

"Done," I said. "Falling off your bike it is." As soon as I said it Mark shot me a look. "What I meant is riding up in the air over a hill then having your bike fly out from under you is what happened."

Reaching the apartment we leaned our bikes against the back wall. That's when things went from bad to worse. Mark stood and felt his pants pockets; first the left, then the right, then the back ones.

He stood there, arm held to his chest, pants pockets pulled out like two floppy bunny ears. What colour he'd gotten back in his face disappeared again.

"What's the matter?"

"I can't find my keys," he stammered. It was like listening to Robert all over. The word "find" became "ffffined" and "keys" became "kezzzzs", ending with a very slow zee sound. "Mom and Dad are out shopping. I need the keys to get in."

Goddammit Mark, how can you be so stupid?

I started to say, "Let's go and see if your keys fell out when you hit the floor." Had I gotten the words out quickly enough we might have been on our way, but at that precise moment his mom pressed her face up against the screen of their bedroom window and called down at us. "There you are! Apparently your father's not yet ready to get up and face the world. I need you upstairs so we can get ready and go grocery shopping."

Just as my words didn't have time to sink in, the words from his mom's mouth didn't quite finish coming out before she realized something wasn't quite right with Mark.

"Oh my Lord!" she yelled. "What happened to you?"

Mark froze. Getting any story out of him, true or not, was iffy at this point. She yelled out his entire name then added, "Get yourself up here this minute!"

"Stick to our story," I said as quietly as I could. "Make sure you remember everything you tell her so you can tell me later. I'll go get the keys."

Since Mark was already marching ahead I wasn't sure how much I'd said had sunk in. I watched as he climbed the stairs, his good hand on the rail. I waited for their door to close before I dashed up the stairs, went into Dad's little office, grabbed a flashlight, and started back to the construction site.

By the time I returned to the site a couple of empty pickups were now parked on the street. Whoever had been in them was either in one, or more, of the houses, the construction shed, or both. From what I could see the shed was still locked. I rode over to the furthest house and hid my bike behind a pile of lumber; boards that would've made good rafting material. If needed, I could run away without worrying about having to get my bike right away.

I should have paid more attention to what was around me instead of the pile of lumber in front of me. I turned to start off for the unfinished house and now stood in front of the biggest, roughest looking men I'd ever seen. One stepped forward and picked me up by my shoulders. My feet dangled. I looked at his unshaven face, the smell of cigarettes and garlic now hanging over us.

"I oughtta beat you to within an inch of your life, kid. Teach you a thing or two about coming around a construction site. Whattaya think, Vic? Should I beat the crap out of the kid?"

Like Fred Flintstone running tippy-toed down the bowling alley it was all I could do to find solid ground, though I wasn't yet sure what I'd have done if I'd been able to stand on my own two feet.

"Tommy, we gotta 'nough to do today without having to beat up a kid," Vic replied. Yet Tommy seemed determined to teach me a lesson. I had enough lessons during the week in school, and more than enough on the weekend when Dad "taught" me a thing or two. I was damned if I was going to let Tommy also teach me something.

"I'm sorry for riding around here, Mister. My friend thinks he dropped his keys. I came back to find them."

I don't know who was more surprised I was talking back: them or me. Either way, they were too stunned to say anything. The hands gripping my shoulders tightened, making it a little harder to breathe. But I wasn't backing down. Tommy broke into a smile, starting to laugh so hard he couldn't continue to hold on. He asked where my friend was as he relaxed his grip and put me down.

Safely attended to by his mom, while I try and bail us out.

"He's, um, he's at home now," I replied, a quiver in my voice.

"At home, eh? What's he doin' there?"

I cleared my throat. "Truth is, he tripped and fell and hurt his arm. That's when he thinks his key must have fallen out."

What I said *was* true. Of course there were some missing parts, but I didn't think confusing the situation with too much detail was necessary. All I wanted were the keys and my bike.

"Funny that," came Tommy's reply.

Funny what?

"Funny that when you trip and fall your keys end up down a basement hole. Your friend must have fallen pretty far forward?"

Okay, maybe more detail was required.

"Sir, it's possible we were inside the house. We didn't mean any harm, and, yes, he did trip, but that was, um, that was off of a ladder." I hoped calling him "sir" showed respect. Maybe I should have called him "sir" from the beginning.

Vic stepped forward, reached into the front pocket of his overalls, and stretched out his beefy hand.

"Here kid," he said. "Take your key and get outta here. Consider yourself lucky we don't lock you up and wait for the cops ta get here. Understand?"

I understood. As fast as I could I picked up my bike and hightailed it out of there. I swear I heard them laughing all the way home, and checked over my shoulder more than once to see if they were following me.

Once home I threw my bike down and ran up the steps, two at a time. As quick as I could I closed my bedroom door, laid on the floor, and waited for my heart to stop pounding. Mark's keys pinched my leg through my pants pocket. He'd have to wait for that.

I spent the rest of the day waiting for Mrs. Watson to come over and punish me, but by dinner she still hadn't come by. After we ate I looked out our front window; Mr. Watson's car was on the street. From what I could see they were still at home. Maybe Mark had stuck to the story. Maybe they believed him after all. I wasn't sure what was worse: waiting for punishment or the punishment itself.

Sunday rolled around, and we'd already been to church and back. I needed to know if I was going to be punished and worked up the nerve to walk across the hall. Mrs. Watson opened the door and I expected to get an earful. Instead, she said Mark was resting and her tone made it clear she didn't want me hanging around. I said I was sorry and walked back to our place, trying to scoot past Mom unnoticed.

"How is Mark?" she asked.

So she knew! That meant she had talked to Mrs. Watson. It also meant that if I hadn't yet been punished, what with Dad being home, they believed whatever story Mark had told them.

"Mrs. Watson said he was resting." I waited for Mom to ask what happened, but she didn't say anything other than it was funny how hurt one could get falling out of a tree.

Dammit! He told the tree story. Just what did he say? Was he climbing a tree and fell, or did he say he was trying to rescue some cat? What tree was he in? What cat was he trying to rescue? I knew I couldn't trust him to stick to our story.

I wasn't sure if Mom thought I'd crack, but I wasn't going to say anything more than I had to. I put a hand on my bedroom door knob, turning back to say, "Yup. Funny how that happens." Before she could reply I was in my room with the door closed.

▸ ▸ ▸ ◂ ◂ ◂

On Monday, after the morning announcements, Mr. Long let everyone crowd around Mark's cast and take turns signing it. Mark was only too happy to tell everyone how we came by a poor cat stuck in the tree, and how he had fallen out of the tree trying to rescue it. He seemed to enjoy being the centre of attention. I stayed back, listening to all of the details that now seemed to come out of Mark without any effort.

By the time I had my chance to sign his cast it was hard to find an open spot, marked up as it was with pen and crayon. I leaned in and grabbed his cast so he wouldn't be able to pull back without it hurting. "Fell out of a tree, did you?" He shrugged as if to say so what, but I was still mad at him. I didn't write anything fancy, just a reminder I was still his best friend.

▸ ▸ ▸ ◂ ◂ ◂

Saturday and the warm sunlight streaming through the windows signalled spring had arrived, and we were another week closer to school being out for the summer. Even though we still had a month and a half to go, the news was already about how hot and dry this summer was going to be. Already, the radio said, the farmers had begun to pray for just the right amount of rain, sun, and crop prices.

Dad and I had eaten breakfast, me careful not to say or do anything to upset him, after which we drove over to the church to help with the annual spring cleanup. As we pulled into the parking lot it was clear many of the people we only saw on Sundays were here to help. I looked around to see if there were any kids I knew, but didn't see anyone I recognized.

The church itself was a plain white building, with only four grey concrete steps to climb before reaching two plain wooden doors set with tiny glass windows. I squinted up at our small bell tower and couldn't help but think about where we shot Bobby. That church had a set of stairs wide enough for people to hang around on, and large, stained-glass windows with images of Jesus, the Mother Mary, and angels descending from heaven.

Our little, yellow-coloured glass widows barely let in enough light to read the Bible during service, let alone cool air once everyone sat for church. Not that I was upstairs for the whole service, still forced as I was to join the little kids in the basement Sunday school. At least when we went over to Minister Martin's house for Bible class we got milk and cookies.

Minister Martin walked toward us, and as he did I gave him the once-over. Usually I only saw him in his flowing black robe; today he strode up in a plaid shirt and denim overalls, a straw hat pulled down on his head. I wondered if he was Ukrainian.

"How'd you like to help me paint the wooden stairs at the side of the church?"

"Sure," I replied as he handed me some sandpaper.

"The first thing is to sand down all of the hand rails, moving to the deck then the steps. After, we'll put on a fresh new coat of white paint and make everything new again. What do you say?"

Truth was I wasn't so sure. I mean I didn't have a problem painting, I just wasn't sure why he asked *me* to work with him.

I wasn't about to argue with God's servant, as he referred to himself every week. I said okay and started sanding, really paying attention to what I was doing. After a long period of silence, and without looking up, he asked, "So, Ricky, how are things at school?" I wasn't sure what to say except to reply that things were fine.

"How'd your first season of hockey go? Heard you scored a couple of goals. Turned out to be quite the defenceman by the end of the season."

I don't remember ever discussing hockey with him.

It was becoming clear that even though I had been in his house for bible class for weeks on end, he knew more about me than I did about him.

"You know," he continued. "When people play with guns, real or toy, they need to be careful. People can get hurt."

I wondered where this was going, the sinking feeling in my stomach telling me I probably wasn't going to like it.

He stopped sanding, looked up directly at me, and said, "And in addition to being careful, we really ought to think about what it is we're shooting at. Wouldn't you agree?" It was one of those questions that had only one right answer.

"Yes, Minister. We shouldn't use guns to shoot people."

"It's funny," he continued. "Somehow I thought you'd agree."

My head started to ache. I felt drops of sweat roll down the back of my neck and along the sides of my face. Minister Martin knew about my hockey season. He knew about me shooting Bobby Royce. It was safe to say he also knew about the milk money.

I brushed my arm over my forehead, the sweat mixing with the dust on my arms and creating a slight paste, my arm hairs holding everything in place.

"I don't know about you, but I'm thirsty. Why don't I get us a couple of soft drinks from the cooler? What would you like, Ricky?"

My mouth had gone completely dry. I knew it wasn't from the work or the sun, but from wondering what was coming next. I managed to squeak out, "If they have any Wink I'd appreciate one, sir."

"Well, Wink sounds just fine. Two bottles of Wink coming right up."

If Dad wasn't there I might have bolted and run all the way home, but I'd see Minister Martin in church tomorrow anyway and didn't want to be singled out any more than I'd already been. I sanded the wood as hard as I could, running through several pieces of sandpaper by the time he returned and to the point that I sanded through to the skin on a finger or two. I never thought a drink could taste so good, and I finished it as fast as I could. The only thing left was to let out a burp, but I knew this wasn't the time or the place.

Finally, Minister Martin said, "You know, Ricky, when we steal from people, especially from people we know, God is watching." He looked right at me while he took a sip from the bottle. "Do you understand what I'm saying?"

I wasn't sure if Minister Martin knew this 'cause God told him, or if he was just letting me know God was watching all the things we do. Or perhaps, more importantly, God was watching the things I did. It didn't matter; Minister Martin would always find out some way, somehow, of that I was now sure. I wanted to disappear, but knew there was no escape. I looked up, the sun behind his head making it appear he was surrounded by a glow.

"Yes," I replied. "I do."

"Good," he said. "I hope then you'll think twice before stealing anything again."

"Yes, sir, I will." As the words came out I realized Minister Martin had gotten me to agree to things without having directly accused me of anything.

"Looks like the stairs are ready to be painted. I think you can handle this on your own. What do you think?"

I wanted to show him I could, and replied without hesitation, "Yes, sir. I can finish up for you."

"Fine," Minister Martin replied. "I'll come back later to see how you've made out. The ladies are in the church basement making sandwiches for lunch. Make sure you stop working when everyone else does and grab one."

I wasn't going to stop until the stairs were as bright and as white as they could be. I swept the deck, the freshly cut grass now full of white powder and sanded wood chips. I opened the paint container, stirring until the film on top had mixed into a fresh white glow, stuck in the brush, covering every bristle, and started with the hand rails.

The wood, hot from the sun, dried the paint before I could make a second pass. No matter; I was going to paint these hand rails, this deck, and those steps like no one had before. I worked right though lunch, not stopping when the ladies called out that sandwiches and drinks were ready. This was my chance to make good for shooting Bobby and for stealing the milk money that Mom had replaced. It was one thing to be punished by Mom or Dad; it was another to have God mad at me, too.

By the time I was done it was late afternoon. I set the brush into the almost empty paint can, and stood back to admire my work. Yes, siree! Minister Martin would be pleased. Just then, two older kids came around the corner, laughing and poking each other as they walked toward the freshly painted steps.

"Hey, don't get so close. They're not dry yet. I painted them myself!"

They looked at each other, laughed, and replied, "Yeah, looks like you did it by yourself too!" Before I could reply they ran off, which was good since all I had was a wet paint brush and an empty can of paint to throw at them and didn't want Minister Martin's sermon to go unheeded. I picked up the brush and can, walking around the front of the church to tell him I'd finished. He was kneeling down in front of the glass-encased Knox Presbyterian Church sign, replacing a burnt-out light bulb. I told him I was finished painting.

"Thanks, Ricky. I appreciate your help today and was glad we had the chance to talk."

While he fiddled with the lights I wondered how they went on and off. The answer, he said, was a timer. I thought about that, and then asked, "We're coming into the summer months. Shouldn't you adjust the timer so it comes on later and turns off earlier?"

Minister Martin rested his arms across one knee. "Well, Ricky, I think you're right. Bet no one's ever changed the time to match the seasons. I can see you're pretty smart." Before my head got too swelled up he brought me back down to earth. "So I'm sure you can understand how God is all around you, and you should do the right thing."

I didn't have a problem understanding God was all around me I just hoped he'd attend to someone else once in a while, so I could catch a break now and then. I was going to reply but heard Dad calling, and said I'd see Minister Martin in church tomorrow. But before I left I asked for one request.

"Sure, son, what's that?"

"I don't want to go downstairs with the little kids anymore. Could you talk to my Dad and see if I can stay upstairs from now on. Maybe help pass out the collection plate or something?" I thought I saw a twinkle in his eye, but wasn't sure if it was that or the light in the sign flickering on and off as he played with the wires in his hands.

"Sure," he said, pausing. "But I think I'll find something else for you to do besides the collection plate. Maybe you can pick up the Bibles after church." It didn't matter to me what I did, or if I did anything at all. I just wanted to be with the adults. "One more thing: we host the food hall at the fair. It'd be nice if you helped out this summer."

It didn't take me long to answer if it meant hanging out at the fair every day. "Yes, sir. I'll be there!"

I walked over to our car and got in, Dad already behind the wheel.

We drove off and without him taking his eyes off the road he asked if the minister and I had had a chance to talk. I turned my head toward my window, leaned on the glass, and said, "Yes, we did."

"Good," he replied, after which we drove home in silence.

CHAPTER TEN

June, 1967

I rounded the front corner of our building and stopped in front of Dad's dust-covered, bug-splattered car. It was report-card time and I was sure it was written somewhere I could do better if I only applied myself. Again.

It seemed to me life was just fine, and applying myself any more than I already did wasn't going to make things better or worse. Besides, Red always had better marks, and there didn't seem to be much point in trying to be better than her. Leaning my bike against the building I walked around to the back, climbing each step a little slower than the last. I pressed my ear against our door, listening and trying to figure out his mood. One way or another punishment was coming, be it the report card or something else.

I opened the door as quietly as I could, and walked around the corner to see all his papers spread out across the dining-room table. Phone in one hand, pen or cigarette in the other, he alternated between taking orders on the phone and puffing a drag. His happy tone told me he'd made his numbers for the week, making the last five days on the road worthwhile. I wasn't sure if he ever wondered if this was worthwhile for any of us, what with him gone and us alone even though things were better when he was away. At least his good mood would help get us through the weekend.

I listened as he rattled off a list of long distance calls he wanted the operator to make. He was calling customers and getting ready for his Friday night check-in with head office. Each call was always the same. He'd say, "Hello, Barry," or Gil, or Ted, then make a joke and ask about their family. It didn't take me long to know all about the pharmacists in his territory, about their wives, their kids, their problems. Once in a while he'd lower his voice and I'd hear, "Well, I hope the doctor has better news next week," or, "I'm sure everything will work out." Sometimes, the tone wouldn't change and he'd say, "I'm really sorry. If there's anything I can do to help, let me know."

After a few minutes, Dad would bring the conversation around to vitamins, hair care, and other products, and ask for the order no matter how serious the family matter. There were times I wished he cared about me as much as he did about those he only visited once or twice a month.

Seeing me, he lifted his head and nodded toward the empty pack of cigarettes on the table; it was my job to make sure he never ran out. During these calls he'd light one cigarette after another, using the one in his mouth to light the next: one long smoke that lasted an hour or two. Depending on the week and the number of orders he needed to call in, by the time he was done the room would swirl with smoke. Heaven forbid he should run out when Lee's was closed.

He waited for the operator to come back on the line, and when she did said, "Hang on before connecting the next call. My son just walked in." Cradling the phone on his shoulder he said, "Your Mom's at church for a women's meeting. We need bread, milk, and cigarettes." He picked the receiver back up, looked down at his papers, and returned his attention to the operator. "You can put the next call through now."

No, "Hi, how are you?" No, "What's been happening?" No, "Do you have all your fingers and toes?" Nothing at all. "What's that Doris?" he asked, pausing. "Oh, yeah. He had a great week in school."

I could have taken my bike to the store, but since Mom wasn't going to be back for a while I decided to walk. The streets were empty, most people already home for the day. I looked inside their places, watching as they ate dinner or cleaned the dishes.

I climbed the well-worn steps of Lee's Supermarket, which was really just a large room built onto the front of their house. The bell over the door clanged and the smell of the Lee's dinner hit my nose. Surrounded by anything and everything you might run out of, Mr. Lee stood on a platform behind the counter. Behind him a wall of cigarettes—Players, Export 'A', Lucky Strike, and Dunhill—as well as bags of tobacco, matches, lighters, flints, lighter fluid, pipes, and cigars.

I looked at the jaw breakers, Popeye Cigarettes, Ruby Red wax lips, Black Cat, Bazooka Joe gum, chocolate bars, and Old Dutch potato chips on the candy counter, trying to decide what I'd buy if I had money. I wanted to put something on our tab, hoping Dad wouldn't ask what the ten cents was for, but didn't dare.

"Yes, how are you tonight?" Mr. Lee asked. "Yes, what you need today?" It was always the same from both of them, asked in a sing-song voice that made me wonder if they spoke in rhymes in China. I looked up at Mr. Lee as he stared down through black horned-rimmed glasses that matched his slick black hair. He was eating something, and whatever it was a bit of it was stuck in the corner of his mouth, the pencil behind his ear bouncing up and down as he chewed. He blinked several times and I realized he was still waiting for me to answer him.

"I need a couple of packs of Players Plain," I said then walked the aisles, returning with two loaves of bread and a big box of powdered milk while he reach behind him for the cigarettes. I asked to have them put on our tab. Mr. Lee pulled out a little book from his front shirt pocket, flipping the pages until he found ours, then slid the pencil from the top of his ear to write up the order.

"Make sure you tell father come tomorrow, pay tab, okay?"

"I will. He's been away all week."

I'm sure Mr. Lee knew that, but force of habit made us repeat the same things back to each other week after week. I started to walk away, thinking about needing money. The Lees worked by themselves, each taking turns behind the counter. I wondered if it was possible to get a job sweeping the floor or stocking shelves. By the time I got home I'd decided to go back in the morning to ask Mr. Lee for a job. I thought about what I could buy with my new-found money: all the comics I wanted, all the candy I needed.

Mom and the girls had returned from the church meeting, and while dinner was being made I overheard Mom talking to Dad about the meeting. "We have a committee working on the Knox Presbyterian Church Centennial cookbook. We're collecting recipes from all of the Knoxonions, and we're going to publish it to raise money for the church."

"Uh, huh," he replied. "I'm sure it'll be quite a mix, what with the Ukrainian, Dutch, German, and whatever else. I'll be finished making my calls in a minute. The girls can set the table then."

We ate in silence, and after clearing the table Red and I did the dishes; it was my turn to wash and hers to dry. I looked over at Dad sitting in his chair, smoking and listening to Dave Brubeck on the Hi-Fi, Little Sister curled up in his lap. I wasn't sure if he'd read my report card and was making me sweat it out, but I wasn't about to ask. Better to let as much time pass as possible, than to bring it up on my own.

What we did with what was left of Friday night was determined by whether or not there was anything good on TV. I'd already checked for any specials but there wasn't one, and none of us were interested in the Tommy Hunter show. I got up, looked over at Dad, and said I was going to bed. I expected to be called back, but reached my room without as much as a grunt from his direction. By the time I was under the sheets I was only thinking about working at Lee's.

The next morning I put on my Wrangler's, Keds, and a tee-shirt, ate some cereal, grabbed the last nickel I'd hidden my old Mummy model that sat on the back corner of my dresser, and rode over to Lee's. Leaning my bike against the wall I ran up the stairs, went to turn the door knob, and promptly froze; I hadn't prepared anything to say. I walked back down, rounded the corner and leaned up against the wall. I could feel the flakes of curled paint against my back. I could say I'd work cheap and sweep, take out garbage, stock shelves, and whatever else he asked.

God, I hope he hasn't heard about the milk money.

I pushed away from the wall, tucked in my shirt and pulled up my pants, walking back up the steps and pulling the door closed before the bell finished clanging. I turned toward the counter, expecting to see Mr. Lee except Mr. Lee wasn't there. Mrs. Lee was. If it was possible she was even shorter than Mr. Lee, and I sometimes wondered if they used the same horn-rimmed glasses or just bought them two pairs at a time. I didn't think she understood English, or if she was very good at pretending she didn't—unless of course someone said they wanted to pay their tab. Then she was quick to pull out the book.

Still, I didn't want her to say no only to wonder if it was because she didn't understand me. I felt her eyes follow me as I started to walk up and down the rows, worried she was thinking I was trying to steal something. Three short aisles later I was done, and still no sign of Mr. Lee. This wasn't going the way I'd hoped.

The bell clanged and another customer came in. I stood still, trying not to look like I was going to grab something and take off. I walked up and down the aisles again, trying to learn all the products in case Mr. Lee wanted to test me on what they stocked. By the time the customer was gone, Mr. Lee still had not appeared. Pulling out my last nickel, I asked for some jaw breakers and went back outside.

The sound of cards clicking against bike spokes came up the street. I looked up to see Billy riding toward the store. He pedalled up, pushed the bike back onto its stand, and got off.

Who uses a bike stand?

"What are you doing, Donkey?"

"Nothin'. Just standing here sucking on jaw breakers. What are you doing?"

"I'm getting some baseball cards and gum. Then I'm going to the diamond for practice. You coming?"

"Yeah, I'll be there later. What cards you got on now?"

"Baseball. Have a look."

Sure enough, crisp new Yankee cards were stuck in the spokes. They were hardly bent at all. In place of cards I was down to taking Dad's old cigarette packages, cutting and folding them to fit.

"Just put these on this morning. We're also going to trade Jell-O pogs later. Make sure you bring yours!"

"I'll bring 'em. See you later."

I popped the last jaw breaker into my mouth, slumped to the ground, and waited for Billy to buy his stuff and pedal off. Once he was gone I ran up the steps. As I went to pull the door open I caught myself in the glass above the sign displaying the store's hours. Beads of sweat lay across my forehead, and the back of my hair was stuck up.

I stepped back, wetted my fingers, rubbed down the cowlick, and then wiped my shirt across my forehead. It was now or never! I pulled the door open and as the bell stopped ringing Mr. Lee's head popped up from behind the counter. I was in luck!

"Yes, yes, you here to pay tab now?" I forgot the tab needed to be paid. My heart pounded, and I wasn't sure words were going to come out so I simply shook my head no.

"What you need then?"

"I'm here," I said, taking a deep breath. "I'm here to ask you for...."

Mr. Lee waited then said, "Yes, yes, hurry up." My throat was dry, the jaw breaker juice now gone. I cleared my throat just in time to hear the door knob rattle and the bell clang once again. "If you no speak, you wait!"

I moved to one side. After the customer paid his tab Mr. Lee asked again, "What you want. Tell me now." With all the air I could bring up I blurted out my request in one long blast.

"I want to be a box boy. I could sweep, take out garbage, dust shelves, move things, anything you say. You could pay me what you think is fair."

By the time I finished speaking I was hot and thought I was going to faint. I peered into Mr. Lee's thick black glasses, but he just blinked several times. Maybe I'd spoken too fast and he didn't understand.

Should I repeat everything, pausing between each word?

I felt the cowlick slowly rise up, like a skunk getting ready to spray, and hoped Mr. Lee wasn't staring at it.

"What a matter with your mouth?"

What a matter with my mouth?

"Mouth all black. Lips all black"

Dammit, the jaw breakers!

I wiped the back of my hand across my mouth, looking down to see a wet, black streak.

"We no need no help," he said. That was it, nothing else. Not "let me think about it" or "Come back tomorrow and you can start." Just a simple no.

I turned, trying to move each leg a little faster to get out of the store before I heard him laugh or say anything else. I pulled on the door so hard I thought the bell was going to clang off. Picking up my bike I pedalled off as fast as I could.

As I rode all I heard was, "We no need no help, we no need no help," over and over. The wheels spun; the bent and broken cigarette packs flapped, keeping time to the words in my head. Once at the apartment building I threw my bike on our lawn, ran up to my room, and grabbed my baseball glove. I was back out before anyone could ask me anything and rode off to the diamond, wheels clicking as I pedalled.

After baseball practice I leaned my bike against the wall just as Red yelled down from her bedroom window. "You'd better get up here quick. Dad's looking for you."

I ran up the stairs, careful not to pound my feet; by now his constant reminder to be quiet since people lived below drilled into my head. Opening the door I walked into the kitchen. He was eating a late breakfast of boiled eggs and toast, peeled shell neatly laid on the edge of the plate. A second egg sat in the cup, cracked through, though top still intact. At the corner of the table lay my report card. The conversation was, as he liked to say, "short and sweet."

"Anything to say?" I knew it wasn't a question. He just wanted to see if I'd say something so he could jump all over it, or if I'd just take whatever was coming next. I decided to take whatever was coming next.

"No, sir."

"I have errands today. You'll be coming with me. After which you're grounded for a week. No allowance. And don't say anything. If I want to hear from you I'll shake a pail of gravel." Since we never had a pail of gravel around to shake I'd learned a long time ago that meant to just keep your mouth shut.

I walked down the hall, closed my door, lay on the floor, and waited to be called. I wasn't sure if I could still play baseball during the week, but I'd wait until he left on Monday and then ask Mom.

▸▸▸◂◂◂

After a full week of not being allowed out except for baseball I was ready for some fun and Mark was along for the ride. The plan was to meet Dale, Billy, Randy, and anyone else who showed up at the back of the mall after church. Using leftover two-by-fours, rubber hoses, and anything else we could find we'd build some go-karts and then run them around on the paved parking lot. Dale always had as much as he needed in the way of tools, nails, or screws, which was good for us. That is, if he wanted to share. What we really needed was something for the wheels. That's when the trouble began.

I wasn't sure who said the shopping carts out front of the mall had wheels we'd be able to pull off, but that was enough to send me sprinting around to the front. By the time I'd come to a full stop one kid had already stood up, a metal bar in one hand and a shiny new wheel in his grease-stained hand. The other three boys remained huddled over the cart they were trying to take apart.

"What are you doing here?" he growled. "This is none of your business. Get it?"

I didn't recognize them and figured they were St. Mary's boys from the Catholic School a few blocks over. They were just as big as everyone said; looked about as mean too. Punks, from what I could see; not a white tee-shirt among them. I'd heard stories about stolen bikes and fights that ended in black eyes.

Never mind that I'd seen them helping themselves to wheels, working beneath a brand new sign saying to "Take a Buggy." In the few seconds I had to think, I figured my business was also none of their business.

"Lookit, we, I mean I, just want some wheels. There seems to be enough to go around."

"Ha!" The kid standing with the pipe and wheel said. "He just wants some wheels."

The other three boys now stood, two of whom started to come around behind me. My stomach rumbled and I was glad breakfast was a few hours ago, and not likely to come up this late in the day.

"Ha!" The kid handed the wheel and pipe off to one of the other punks standing there. "He wants some wheels off of *our* carts!" That was two "ha's" I thought, and wondered if in his mind he was making big discoveries.

The carts didn't belong to any of us, but since they'd already taken a couple apart I could at least see how he viewed the wheels as theirs. "I'm not looking for trouble. All I want are some wheels and there seems to be enough to go around."

Sometimes it just doesn't pay to reason with someone. It just gives them time for whatever they think of doing next. In this case the punk stepped back, brought his hand up, and firmly planted it on my nose. I fell back into one of the guys who now stood behind me. As I did he grabbed me by my shoulders, then pushed me toward the grease-stained fist of the punk; I looked down to see blood on my white tee-shirt. Things had gone from bad to worse: I was now a wobbling, Bozo the Clown punching bag.

The punk's fist started forward and I waited for the next punch, but instead of being hit I felt a big hand settle in around the back of my neck and was suddenly pushed out of the way, landing against the side of the cart corral. I turned around to see the hand that would have hit me caught up instead by a much larger fist that slowly turned the punk's hand clockwise, until the punk bent over and finally dropped to his knees as he let out a cry of pain.

It was Big Boy, seemingly larger than I ever remembered, now standing over the punk, the punk's hand firmly in his grip. I think I winced as I waited for the hand to turn ever so slightly more and hear the crack of a bone breaking.

"Why don't you guys pick on someone your own size," he growled at them. The punk's three friends had stepped back and remained silent.

Big Boy looked at me. "Go on, get out of here."

I didn't need to be told twice. I picked myself up and left Big Boy and the punk to figure things out for themselves, with my money on Big Boy. At that moment I was truly sorry for every bad word I'd ever called him.

I turned around the back of the mall expecting to see Dale, Randy, Mark, and Billy, but only Mark and Billy remained—the weakest of the bunch, the stronger ones long gone. I wiped my hand across my nose and, looking at the blood smeared against my skin, figured I'd gotten off lightly. Now at least when someone asked I could say, "Yeah, they're punks, and yeah, they'll punch you out if you try and take their stuff."

Mark asked where Big Boy was and I replied that as far as I knew he was still out front, taking care of things. When Mark asked about my nose I could have lied and said I got in the first punch. Instead I asked, "Where did Big Boy come from? I'm surprised you guys didn't just say something to get him mad and then run off so he couldn't catch you."

Mark stared silently while Billy answered. "Truth was he surprised us. All of a sudden he just appeared. Wanted to know where you were. We said you were around front. As soon as he was out of sight Dale grabbed his tools and he and Randy took off."

I felt the inside of my nose tightening, the blood drying. I could wash my nose and hands outside the apartment building, but I still needed to figure out how to explain the shirt.

▸ ▸ ▸ ◂ ◂ ◂

With nothing in a brush cut to hold it back, a bead or two of sweat started to roll down my neck. It was eight a.m., too early to start a lawnmower. I went around the side of the building, turned on the water tap, spread my legs to avoid the water and leaned forward for a sip. The water disappeared into the hard, cracked dirt as quickly as it hit the ground while I slurped from the cold metal tap.

I wasn't sure if Mom heard from Mr. Lee that I'd asked for a job or not, but she said it was about time I learned the value of money and had convinced the building superintendent to let me cut the lawns for our two buildings at a quarter each. I also wasn't sure if the super was interested in helping himself, Mom, or me, but it didn't matter. I'd seen him around, even nodded once or twice and got a nod in return, but didn't know his name. If something needed to be fixed, he was there; when it snowed he shovelled the sidewalks and plowed the parking spots.

That's how I came to be standing here, waiting for the time to pass. The yards could be finished in about an hour if I walked fast. I wanted to go to the movies and needed the money today. Unable to wait any longer, I went back into the building and grabbed the gas can and lawnmower from the basement.

Once outside I unscrewed the gas cap and rocked the mower to see how much gas was in the tank.

Looked to be just enough to hold the dirt down in the bottom.

The smell of gas rose up my nose and down the back of my throat as I pulled the wet nozzle out from the gas can. As quickly as I poured gas into the mower it just as quickly dripped wet spots onto the cement from the leaking nozzle, which drew back into themselves until they evaporated. By the time I was done, I wasn't sure if I had more gas in the tank or on the ground.

It took several pulls on the cord before the mower kicked up a cloud of dirt, little stones and blades of grass that hit my bare legs. Soon enough, my socks and sneakers were covered with the leftovers from the last time the mower had been used.

While I stood and decided whether to go up and down each lawn on its own, or across both in one long pass, I looked toward Dwayne's front window just in time to see the bed sheet pulled back. Dwayne's mom stared at me. It was clear some people didn't like the sound of a lawnmower in the morning, but I wasn't going to let her stop me from earning my money.

The lack of rain meant I cut mostly dry, brown grass and the occasional weed I was supposed to pull. I wasn't keen on having to get down on my hands and knees and figured it'd be hard enough to see where they'd been once I ran over everything.

I started up between the two buildings, and saw something caught in the shadows ahead. The closer I got, the clearer the thing became. Dwayne must have finished his model, the now-empty box having been blown out of the garbage bins in the back.

I pushed the lawnmower faster, bore down on the box, and waited to hear the sound of shredding cardboard. Instead the lawnmower sputtered and slowed. I held the handle steady as it decided whether to spit out what was flying 'round inside or conk out altogether. With a loud growl, a stream of multi-coloured material shot out and the blade spun free; after which the motor revved back up to speed. My heart sank and my stomach tightened. I shut the mower off and waited for the blade to stop spinning so I could turn it on its side. Shredded paper and chewed-up plastic now showered the grass around me.

Dwayne hadn't finished his model, and this wasn't an empty box. He must have been carrying it around again, put it down, and forgot to come back and get it. The only thing not yet chewed up was the small, electric motor, which I quickly picked up and put in my shorts pocket. I looked around; from what I could tell, no one had seen me do this.

Upright again I rested my foot on the mower and pulled one, twice, three times. Nothing! I gave it one hard pull with everything I had, and it sprang to life. I went back and forth across the lawns as quickly as I could, until every last blade and weed in sight was reduced to the smallest possible bit, ready to be taken away by any breeze that whistled down between the buildings. My face and arms were now wet with sweat, my legs covered with dirt and grass.

I had the mower cleaned and put back, and had started out the door just as the superintendent walked toward the front of our building.

"Well," he said, "looks like the lawns are done."

"Yes, sir," I replied.

"Any problems?"

"Nothing to speak of."

I reached into my shorts pocket and wrapped my hand around the motor. He was going to have to drag it out of me.

"It's a little hard to get the mower started, but once you do it really chews up the grass." As soon as I spoke I realized those weren't the best words I could have chosen.

"Yeah," he agreed. "She's temperamental, but once she gets going nothing stands in her way. Did you also pull the weeds and pick up the garbage?"

"Sure did." I stared at him, hoping he couldn't tell I was lying. He looked directly at me, narrowing his eyes. It felt like sweat ran down me like a river. I wanted to wipe my face, but didn't dare on the chance he'd know something was up.

"Well," he said, turning to look across the lawns. "Hard to tell where the weeds were. Looks like they were pulled, and that's all that matters. Make sure you do the lawns again in two weeks," he said, handing me a couple of quarters.

"Thanks," I replied, feeling good about getting the money and not having to pull weeds.

"However," he added. "Next time don't just run over the garbage, pick it up."

"Um, yes," I muttered. He must have been close enough to see something, but far enough away not to make it out. Since nothing was said about the model I thanked him again and went into our building, and put running over Dwayne's prized possession behind me.

▸▸▸◂◂◂

It was time for Mr. Long to read the names of the winners for the fair competitions. Since I wasn't interested in making crafts or worried about making sure my handwriting was neat, I didn't hand in anything for those categories. For my project, I'd simply gone to the library and picked through art books. After looking at pictures by the likes of Kandinsky and Pollock, I settled on a book about abstract expressionism. I figured those artists must have had the same problem I did, trying to get the pictures in my head onto the canvas. I wasn't sure who was actually judging the art at the fair, but it really didn't matter. If mine got picked, great; if it didn't I was still going to enjoy the fair.

We were all the way down to the final category—art—before I heard my name called. Yes! It was going to make it into the show. I couldn't wait to see my work on display. I was going to drag everyone and anyone I could over to the picture, saying, "Hey, doesn't that look interesting?" It was then they'd see my name on the winner's tag. But that would have to wait until after school was out.

▸ ▸ ▸ ◂ ◂ ◂

Before we knew it, it was track and field day; the last day before school ended for summer. We were split into small groups, rotating through long jump, high jump, sprints, running, and relay races. The girls were off doing their own events like skipping rope, activities that Billy and Mark, I thought, would have done well in.

As events finished and winners were determined, shirts were pinned (or not) with first-, second-, or third-place ribbons. It didn't take me long to win first-place gold ribbons for long jump, triple jump, and high jump, but I knew the hundred-yard dash, the last event, was going to be the hardest. I ran as hard as I could and qualified for the final race, which included Emanuel and Kyle, two of the fastest runners in class.

It was hot and dry, and the bright overhead sun didn't do much except give us our first burn of the summer. By the time we were lined up and ready to start, I wondered why I'd spent so much energy in the other sports. The last thing I remembered after the starter's pistol went off was my feet slipping on the gravel as I tried to find some traction. While I was sure I'd gotten off before Kyle had, I knew the dust in front of me meant Emanuel was off before both of us.

I waited to hear "false start," but the longer we ran the more I knew it wasn't coming. If we had another fifty or hundred yards I might have caught Emanuel, but he beat all of us, fair and square. I watched as the first-place ribbon was pinned to his chest, while I fell one ribbon short of getting all golds.

After picking up what belongings we had left, we all wandered out of the school and headed home. Most walked, but those with too much to carry were met by their parents. Mark, his arm still in a cast, was one of those who'd already been picked up. I walked alone, thinking about the summer that lay ahead, and in doing so forgot about the past.

Like forgetting about lighting matches, the dog, and taking money that doesn't belong to you; like forgetting we'd hit someone with snowballs, I'd forgotten all about running over Dwayne's model. That is, until I opened our back door.

Just like Big Boy had waited, months before, on the other side of our back door, Dwayne's mom now stood in front of me. She wore a tattered and torn dressing gown that had seen better days, the flowered pattern all faded. A cigarette in her mouth and her hair in curlers completed the look.

How is it possible that two different people could patiently stand behind a windowless door waiting for me to come home? And why in the world doesn't this door have a window? If it had I wouldn't have walked directly into a trap not once, but twice!

Before I could say hello, she reached out and grabbed me. I felt the yellow snap-buttons of my cowboy shirt start to pop as I tried to breathe. Although it was my last good shirt, that wasn't what really bothered me.

What bothered me was the smell of cigarettes, beer, and garlic that sailed out when she opened her mouth with a "Why did you do what you did?" and "What are you going to do about it?"

I waited for her to blow herself out, but it soon became clear that, as thin and bony as she was, she had enough energy to keep on letting me have it for a little while longer. I looked at the red lines around her eyeballs, and wondered if she leaned over and kissed Dwayne goodnight; I felt sorry for him.

Having to look at that before lights out is worse than any eternal damnation Garner Ted Armstrong could dream up.

I tried to get a word in edgewise, and it took a few tries before she caught her breath, blinked, and realized I was talking.

"Look, it was an accident. I didn't know the model was still in the box; I figured the lawnmower would just chew up the box."

She leaned forward and we were now nose-to-nose, my cowboy shirt clenched tighter in her fist as she sneered, "I knew you did it! I knew you ran over that model!"

Dammit! She didn't know for sure, and I just confessed. For

someone who didn't look like she knew the time of day, she was pretty smart. Here she was, waiting behind the door, keeping me prisoner by holding my shirt, and tricking me into a confession. If Mark could see me, he'd pee his pants laughing.

"I'm sorry. There's nothing I can do now." It was the best I could offer.

The upstairs door opened before she could reply. I hoped it was someone who could get me out of this jam, and not ask why I was in it in the first place. Mrs. Watson yelled down, asking what all the yelling was about.

Dwayne's mom shot back a quick reply. "Why don't you mind your own business and close your door. Nothin' here concerns you!"

I'd never seen Mrs. Watson really get mad at anyone, 'cept at me for whatever I'd last done to get Mark in trouble. Somehow, she could really light into me and yet I still liked her at the end of it all. Mrs. Watson could have just as easily gone back into her apartment and left well enough alone, but like a prize fighter springing up at the sound of the bell she ran to the railing and shook it until it rattled.

"If you don't let him go this instant," she now yelled, "I'll call the police and have you arrested for drunk and disorderly."

Without looking up, Dwayne's mom replied, "If you'd like to come down here and talk, I'm all ears. Or, if you like, I'll see you at the top of the landing!"

This wasn't an offer to sit and have tea. Mrs. Watson quickly turned around and went back into their apartment. For a minute I thought Dwayne's mom scared Mrs. Watson, as much as Dwayne's mom scared me. Before Dwayne's mom could get herself back in gear and finish me off, Mrs. Watson burst back out, carrying the broom Mr. Watson had used to poke the neighbour's ceiling. I'd never seen a family so good at swinging around a broom.

Mrs. Watson started down the stairs but there wasn't enough room for the three of us at the bottom, especially with her swinging around that broom. She stopped halfway, broom at the ready.

Turning to look at Mrs. Watson, Dwayne's mom loosened her grip on my shirt, and I caught my breath. She then leaned forward and whispered in my ear, "This ain't over."

Using what heft she had, she pushed me aside and fumbled with the back door handle. After remembering how to use it, she opened the door and the outside light flooded in. She was gone in a flash, hopefully off to brush her teeth and take out her curlers.

Jesus, am I going to have to check the back door every time I come home? Better to use the front, at least with all the glass I'd see someone standing there.

Mrs. Watson looked at me, clearly trying to figure out what to do. "Dare I ask what kind of trouble you're in this time, mister?"

As quick as I could, I answered in my most polite and respectful tone. "I'd appreciate it if you didn't. Can we leave it at that?"

Mrs. Watson thought about it for a minute then said, "Well, making sure you don't run into her any time soon is probably punishment enough. If she ever gets a hold of you, she'll likely punish you more than I ever would. Get yourself upstairs." She walked back up, closing the door behind her.

▸ ▸ ▸ ◂ ◂ ◂

I'd finished cutting the lawns for another couple of weeks, and since Mark still had to stay inside I went for a bike ride by myself. I rode until I ended up by the new airport, and peddled up to the tarmac to watch a man working on one of the planes for the Yorkton Flying Services. I wondered if he was one of the pilots looking for the missing plane I'd read about in Wednesday's paper.

"What are you doing?" I asked. He jumped, almost banging his head against the top of the cowling as he pulled back from the engine. "Sorry. I didn't mean to scare you."

"Aw, think nothin' of it," he replied. "Just a little jumpy, that's all. Haven't had much sleep since the weekend. Getting ready to go up again."

"Where you going?" I asked as he stuck his head back under the cowling.

"Goin' back up on the search and rescue for those missin' guys.

The ones returning from Little Bear Lake. You know, north of Flin Flon." He pulled his head back out. I didn't know where either were and figured it showed since he added, "Manitoba."

He wiped his hands on an oil rag, looked at me, and continued. "Supposed to be back last Sunday. Looks like they crashed somewhere between here and there."

He shrugged as if I knew what he was talking about, then stuck his head back under the cowling, careful this time to make sure he had plenty of clearance. He started to talk again, but he was hard to hear, what with his head pressed up inside the engine.

"So far we got four RCAF airplanes out, and an Albatross, if you can believe it. Plus me and another local plane."

I was glad he wasn't looking at me as I didn't know what an Albatross was. I didn't want to look stupid again, so replied as quickly as I could. "So if the plane didn't make it back and you don't know where it crashed, how you gonna find them?"

"Well, that's easy," he replied. "I mean, easy in a manner of speaking. You just keep flying back and forth along the route you figure they flew, hoping someone spots them or the plane." At that point his voice got so low it was almost impossible to hear. "Then again, may have veered so far off their flight plan you just won't find them that way. In that case, we'll have to wait 'til someone comes across them. You know, someone who's already in the bush. That assumes they didn't go down in a lake, 'cause if they did, probably ain't never gonna find them." His voice trailed off. "Least not right away."

"So you mean you might not find them right away, and they'll just have to wait there 'til someone finds them?"

He pulled his head back out, slowly stood up, and turned toward me. "Unless something comes upon some wreckage first and, well, you know."

I didn't know, but then I got the point and quietly replied, "I sure hope you guys find the plane, I mean them, soon."

"Yeah," he replied. "So do I; the alternative ain't so good."

We both stood and stared at our own spot on the ground, concentrating real hard on nothing in particular. The heat rose from the tarmac. I thought about the long ride back and turned, putting my leg over the bike and started off.

"Good luck," I yelled as I pedalled toward town.

"Thanks. We're gonna need it."

▸ ▸ ▸ ◂ ◂ ◂

With his cast finally off, Mark was allowed to play with me again. He had a problem holding onto anything for a little while, but soon enough we forgot his arm had been broken in the first place. I still had the slugs we'd taken from the construction site, and we were ready to go.

We made our way down Bradbrooke and over to Independent, and as we walked I asked Mark to pick up the pace, wanting to get to the laundromat and the Coke machine inside before it got busy with people doing their washing. Soon we were walking along streets with names I didn't recognize, and I made sure to check over my shoulder once in a while for St. Mary's punks.

It would have been easier just to tell Mark where we were going, but then he'd start telling me why we shouldn't. Sure enough, as soon as I did tell him, he replied, "That's a bad idea."

"A really bad idea," I said, to be exact.

He started bellyaching about the whole idea, and I wanted to whack his arm just so he'd have something else to talk about. Instead, I let him talk himself out. Which he did, only to start up again as we reached the laundromat. That's when I let him have it.

"I'm gonna go get a free Coke. If you want one too, you'll be right behind me. Otherwise sit on the steps and wait, but keep your mouth shut on the way home. I don't want to hear any complaining about why I got one and you didn't!"

He shut up long enough for us walk in through the front door, everything fresh and damp at the same time. The place was empty. Whoever owned the clothes now being washed had put their loads in and left. We made our way past dispensers filled with tiny soap boxes, and machines that spun, washed, dried, and generally banged into each other as the stuff inside spun around.

"Let me know when someone comes in," I said as we reached the pop machine.

"What do I do? Do you want me to tell them something, or do you want me to warn you?"

I thought again about hitting his arm, but figured if he broke it here I'd really be in trouble. "Just whistle when someone comes in, so I can pretend to be using the machine."

I had the slugs in my hand and started to load them into the coin slots. The first one went in, the second not so much. Mark looked at me; with each passing second he was closer to saying we needed to get out. But I wasn't leaving without my Coke. I started to bang and rock the machine while trying also to hold the door open and jiggle a bottle out. That's when bad luck stepped in, or rather, the old man.

For one brief instant I was mad at Mark for not telling me someone had come in the front door, then realized the old man had in fact come from behind the wall I'd been rocking the machine against.

"Whada ya boys doing?"

Before I could say why I'd been rocking the machine back and forth, Mark was talking and everything Mark said we weren't doing we *were* doing. I did my best to put myself between Mark and the old man, but he wasn't having any of it. He looked around me and told Mark to keep on talking; sooner or later he'd get a confession without laying a finger on either of us. I started to talk over Mark.

"Listen, mister. We were walking by and we were thirsty, and thought we could get a drink of water from a tap in here. Then we saw the Coke machine and, well, that's when we tried to get a bottle out, but it doesn't seem to want to take our money."

"Well, thatso?" he replied, the two words blending into one. "Why don't you wait right here while I get my keys. We can open this up and I'll not only get you your bottle of Coke, I'll give you your money back."

Normally, anyone would be happy with such an offer. But he knew, and Mark and I knew, that when he opened the machine none of us would be looking at any shiny coins, but rather one dull, stuck slug. Trying to mumble my way out of this by saying a glass of water would be just fine wasn't going to cut it either.

Mark, smart enough by now to realize the person doing the talking usually got punished the most, stopped talking and started slowly stepping back toward the front door. He'd become really good at that, leaving me to deal with whomever or whatever trouble we'd gotten ourselves into. While it made me mad, the good thing was that it gave me room to turn and run without fear of knocking him over.

"I'm tired of you kids coming around here, trying to get Cokes out of my machine. Don't move, or I'll call the cops!"

Geez. You leave the machine unattended and give free coffee and sugar for anyone who wants to walk in and take it, but call the cops over a slug?

By the time he'd disappeared around the corner, Mark and I had already started toward the front door. At that moment I could have beaten Emanuel in any hundred-yard dash! Mark and I both tried to get through the doorway at the same time, each squeezing against the other. After a little pushing and shoving we finally made it out and down the street. By the time we glanced back, we were far enough away that the old man wouldn't come after us. A block later we stopped running, and a block after that we'd finally caught our breath.

"I told you it wasn't a good idea," Mark said. By the time we got home, we were both hot and thirsty. We walked between the buildings, turned on the tap, and put our heads under the running water. Taking turns we gulped the water, and as it ran down my chin I felt my tee-shirt getting soaked.

Once done we walked back round the front, and I looked up to see Dwayne's mom peering through the bed sheets that served as living-room curtains. I shivered in the June heat.

CHAPTER ELEVEN

July, 1967

I heard the click of bike spokes and turned to see Barry riding up, dressed in his Sunday best, his hair slicked back. I hadn't seen him since the last day of school. Like Robert he mostly stuck to himself, not playing sports and sitting quietly at the back of class. I had to ask why he was wearing a suit on a Saturday.

"Because," he replied, out of breath. "Because my brother's getting married. I'm going to Lee's to get him some smokes. He's a nervous wreck."

"Oh, I didn't know he was getting married."

"Well, we didn't either 'til a few weeks ago. But Dad said, 'Sometimes you get married sooner than you expect, you know, to do the right thing.'" Then with a, "Gotta go, I'm the ring bearer and I don't want to be late," he pedalled off. I watched him head down the road and turn out of sight. I too started off, then began to feel uneasy about something I'd never really thought about before. Questions started to tumble around my head.

Red and I were at our parents' wedding! How could that be?

Suddenly, things I'd accepted as being, well, normal now didn't seem so normal. I thought back to living with just Red, Mom, and Grandma.

I could safely say my mother was my mother, at least as far as I could remember her always being around. But now that I thought about it, could I say the same about Dad? It seemed to me that maybe he did just sort of appear one day.

Just how was that possible?

I started to pedal off, with no particular place in mind. I just needed to pedal, and pedal hard.

By the time I had stopped, I'd reached the cemetery outside of town. I leaned my bike against the monument in the middle of the lawn, lay down, and felt the grass as it pushed up against my shirt. My mouth was dry from breathing hard. I listened to the grasshoppers and gazed up at a clear blue sky, split by a small white trail from a plane high above. I wondered what it would be like to be a speck in the sky. I wondered if they could see me, just a speck on the ground.

I pedalled back home, sweating more from worry, than from riding. I wanted to ask questions, but didn't know where to start; which question to ask first and whom I should be asking. During dinner I thought I was going to burst, one pin prick and I would have fizzled up and over the dining-room table. And yet as much as I wanted to ask about the past, I wasn't sure it was the right thing to do. If whatever had happened was that important, surely Mom and Dad would have told us by now.

I lay in bed and waited for Garner Ted Armstrong, drifting in and out as the day's thoughts piled up. I remembered me and Red wandering along city streets in Winnipeg back when we were little; Mom at work and Grandma waiting at home. Short little bursts of memories popped in and out like the hot flash of a Kodak Instamatic. Try as I might, I couldn't picture this man I called Dad being around then.

Of course he wasn't. They weren't married yet, and he isn't my real dad!

Like puzzle pieces that didn't look like they fit but suddenly did when flipped around just the right way, early images of Red, Mom, Grandma, and me now fit with images of Dad, Oma, Opa, and our aunts and uncles; people who one day just seemed to enter our lives.

Why did our real father leave? Did we do something to make him leave?

Why didn't he love us enough to come back?
Was he rich? Was he poor?
Was he dead or alive?
Where, then, is my real father and why can't I remember him?

▸▸▸◂◂◂

Mark's knock, loud enough to be heard down the street, made me jump off the bed. "Come on," he called. "We're going to be late."

I wasn't sure how he got the tickets, but we were off to see the Queen and her Maids play the Yorkton Men's All-Star baseball team. Between the two of us we had fifty cents: enough to buy something to drink and eat. By the time we stood for "O Canada" the stands were full, and the crowd remained standing as the announcer introduced the home team. His words echoed as he ended with, "The best of the best here to defend the honour of our city."

Playing for the honour of the city would have made it exciting, but then the manager of the visiting team came out, introduced himself as Royal Beaird no less, and announced three maids, followed by the Queen. No men, no other players. Just a girl on first, a girl in the field, a girl catcher, and the Queen herself as pitcher.

"How are four girls going to beat nine men?" I asked as we settled in for the first pitch. From the sound of the crowd it was clear everyone else was wondering the same thing. I thought their catcher wasn't much to look at, but the Queen … I just stared at her. She didn't look to be but sixteen years old and was just about the prettiest girl I'd ever seen, even prettier than Debra. I wished we hadn't bought the pop and hot dogs we'd just wolfed down, and had instead bought one of the souvenir booklets that featured her on the cover.

Over the first few innings the men showed just enough hustle to make sure the honour of the city wasn't in question. Then Royal came back on the PA system. "To make things more interesting, the Queen will now pitch from second base."

"No way," I said to Mark. "No way can she do this."

Soon enough, batter after batter went up and then back down. Not only could she pitch from second, she struck them out! The cheers and laughter from the men's dugout was soon gone. Most hung over the dugout fence, watching their teammates walk back with sheepish grins. Finally, one managed a hit. It was hard to tell if the crowd was cheering because he made it on base, or booing for only getting to first.

As the next batter came up, Royal jogged out from the bench to second base and put his arm around the Queen. She bowed her head as the two of them started toward home plate before stopping at the pitcher's mound and having a quiet conversation.

I turned to Mark. "There's only two players in the outfit, they can't pull her." Mark just stared at the Queen. It looked like he, too, had eyes for her. Royal left the pitcher's mound and walked toward home. The crowd started to boo. Halfway there, he stopped and faced the stands.

"Ladies and gentlemen. The Queen will now pitch from her knees!" By the time he returned to the dugout she was on her knees, ready to send out a pitch.

"She can't do that," Mark said. But before he'd finished speaking the ball slapped into the catcher's mitt and the umpire yelled, "Strike one." The crowd went wild, Mark and I included. Strikes two and three sailed right past the batter, and the inning was over.

The two maids in the field ran in, passing the Queen as she lifted her hands up and out, scooped her up, and carried her into the dugout while she remained in a sitting position. The crowd roared even louder!

The final batter shuffled toward the men's dugout, greeted by swats from baseball caps and gloves as he made his way to the end of the bench. It was bad enough to be struck out by a girl, worse to have been struck out from one pitching from her knees. After the Queen and her maids had their turn at bat, Royal trotted back out with a microphone and asked the Queen if she'd really been trying or if she was taking it easy on the men.

"Oh," she yelled out. "I'm just warming up." The benches bounced up and down as the crowd stamped their feet in approval.

"Well," Royal replied. "There's a request for you to consider playing with a slight handicap." She glanced around the outfield and laughed. I was sure I saw her eyes twinkle.

"Do you mean more of a handicap than fielding only three players? Girls, I might add?"

"Well," he answered. "I guess so. I've been asked to blindfold you." The crowd roared as if to cheer the Queen on.

Once blind-folded and turned around to face the plate she got ready for the windup and then let go. We leaned forward to see if the ball would cross home plate, sail overhead, or worse, bean the batter. We needn't have worried. As steady as the Queen pitched at the start of the game, as steady as she pitched from second, she pitched just as steady blind-folded. The crowd cheered louder than at any other time as the men came up and went down swinging.

As the last man struck out, the honour of defending the city's pride was long over. The Queen and her maids knew from the start the men never had a chance, but somehow that was okay when everyone had a good laugh. I don't think anyone felt slighted at having been beaten by four girls by a score of 11 – 4.

Royal came out for one last announcement. To everyone's surprise he pulled a wig off of the catcher to reveal that the big-boned girl was not a girl but the Queen's brother, complete with makeup!

▸ ▸ ▸ ◂ ◂ ◂

An urgent appeal was now underway for donations to the Citizens' Search and Assistance Fund to keep the search for the missing plane going. The story, now down to a few lines on Wednesday's editorial page, told of downed flyers who'd been rescued after a considerable period of time, as well as the RCAF's regret in not yet locating the plane.

I remembered the pilot talking about not finding them 'til something had come upon the wreckage.

Just how long was a considerable period of time?

I hoped they were safe somewhere, sitting and waiting to be rescued.

▸ ▸ ▸ ◂ ◂ ◂

As tired as Dad was when he got home on Fridays, no amount of staying quiet Sunday morning stopped us from going to church. He made sure we were up and out of the house in time to sit in what was now known as our front-row pew. We were back to the same routine we had in Winnipeg, except instead of going to Oma and Opa's after church for cake and coffee with all the aunts and uncles, we now went to the Corona Motor Hotel for coffee and pop with one or two other families.

Minister Martin reminded the congregation to make sure everyone who'd volunteered for the fair followed the dining hall schedules for next week. After the church service he pulled me aside and reminded me about working in the dining hall. I quickly nodded yes, I remembered, before bouncing down the steps to meet up with Dad, Mom, and the girls.

As soon as we were home from church I changed and went across the hall, knocking on Mark's door. "Come, on. The fair doors open at two!"

Mark looked at me. "What's your hurry? Nothin's open 'til tomorrow."

"It'll give us a chance to check things out. Maybe we can make friends with the workers so they'll give us a free ride or shooting game. You'll never know unless you walk around and make friends."

"Dad said they're drunkards who can't hold a job, just grumpy carnies that travel from town to town. Mom told me not to talk to them."

I tried to convince Mark by rolling out a list of things we could do. "They got a new ride called the Tempest, and a junior hot rod track, a Tilt-A-Whirl, a roller coaster, bumper cars, and of course The Octopus, which *I* fully intend to ride."

Mark laughed then said, "I want to be there when you get on and watch it spin you around."

"What's that mean?"

"Seeing is believing, that's all."

"Okay, smarty pants," I replied. "We'll see who's chicken. You won't have a problem going into any of the sideshows with me, will you?" Mark closed up quicker than a clam.

"Suit yourself. Drunkards or not, if I can get a free ride or game I'm gonna talk to them."

"Go ahead. I have to help my Mom, anyway. Just remember, if you talk anyone into giving you something don't forget to tell 'em you have a friend."

Right, you don't want to come now, but you want me to make sure you still get a free ride.

▸▸▸◂◂◂

Without Mark to slow me down I had run over to the fairgrounds, and raced up the steps and into the dining hall as people were setting up rows of tables. A few were already working behind the long serving counter, and running in and out of the rooms at the back of the hall. Minister Martin walked in through the back around to the cooking area, where I stood waiting.

"Hello, Minister Martin. What can I do?"

Before he could answer one of the ladies yelled out, "You can dry the dishes as they're washed, then stack 'em at the start of the serving counter 'cause we expect hungry people through the door at any minute." I looked over at the two ladies, wondering just how many dishes needed to be dried.

"Come on," Minister Martin said. "I'll help." We dried as fast as the ladies washed what looked like already clean dishes.

They haven't served a single meal yet. Where did the dirty dishes come from?

Minister Martin must have read my mind, as he turned and said, "The dishes have been stored since last year so we're washing the dust off. Wait 'til you have to wash them after people have eaten off of them!"

I watched as the ends of my runners got wet from the dripping of each passed item. My mind drifted, causing a plate to slip from my hands.

Bounce, please; bounce and don't break!

Just as I finished the thought, the plate broke. Everyone stopped what they were doing and I felt all eyes turn in my direction. I wanted to run, but had nowhere to go. Someone handed me a broom and pan, and I knelt down and swept up the plate.

"Where should I put this, Minister Martin?"

"Over here, Ricky," he said, pointing to a garbage can by the door. "I'll finish the rest. Why don't you ask one of the ladies if they need help somewhere else?"

"Why don't you come behind the counter?" asked one. "You can serve juice; it's easy. When they slide their tray along all you have to ask is, 'Do you want a large glass or small glass?' That's it!"

Before I could say anything she added, "Trays are down here. When you know what size they want, put the glass under the spout and press this button for large or this button for small. The machine's smart and will fill the glass to just the right level. Can you do this?"

I watched as the machine bubbled with orange juice that floated up the sides of the glass, along the top, and back down. I could do this!

Once finished I wandered out of the hall and over to the midway to see if any of the workers would offer me something while I watched them finish unloading and setting up.

►►►◄◄◄

First thing the next morning, Monday, I was up and on my way to the fairgrounds; half running, half walking. By nine everyone was ready, and as if on cue the doors to the dining hall swung open and in streamed the carnival workers. More than one smelled like Mr. Watson, but none acted drunk. It was clear from their half-asleep, unshaven faces that they'd spent most of last night working.

As each face passed I still wondered if I could somehow get a free ride or game, but none appeared any more interested in talking to me today than they were yesterday when they were setting up. I still hadn't made up my mind if these were bad people to avoid, or just regular folks whose job moved from town to town. For all my talk with Mark,

I still didn't have the courage to strike up a conversation. I'd also hoped to see someone from the freak show, but no one looked like any of the deformed creatures painted on the posters that hung from the trailers.

Maybe too scary for the public to see, outside of buying a ticket and looking behind closed doors.

By the time Mark showed up, breakfast was over. Determined to make sure I saw everything I could for free, I grabbed him by the arm, but he turned his head back toward the food on the counter.

"Can you just eat and drink anything you want?"

"Yes," I replied, quick enough to stop any doubt though it wasn't exactly true. "I can have milk and juice, but no pop. I can have food, but only what was left after the paying customers are served." Truth was, other than taking an orange juice I was too scared to ask for anything, but Mark didn't need to know that.

"Let's go see my art."

The open field had now become a midway full of noise, whirling rides, candy floss, and popcorn, and the workers now offered all kinds of reasons why we should step onto this ride or that sideshow.

"Here's the exhibit hall," I said, stepping into the building. We waited for our eyes to adjust to the darkness, split up, and walked up and down each row until Mark yelled, "Over here. It's here."

I wasn't sure why his voice trailed off on the word here, but when I caught up to him and leaned in for a closer look it was clear why. Someone had smeared relish and ketchup between the thick green and red brush strokes I'd laid down.

"I'm sorry," Mark said. "Maybe we can clean it up."

"Well," I replied. "Whoever did this at least followed the brush strokes. It's okay. At least I got selected. Let's get out of here." It wasn't okay, of course, but I didn't want to stand there any longer so I pulled off my name tag and headed for the door.

We walked out into the light of day, the midway grounds now filled with people, noise, the smell of popped corn and fried food. Smoke bellowed from revved-up engines as carny workers pulled back levers that sent people spinning up, down, and around. Air rifles were cocked and shot, balloons popped, and rock and roll blared from the speakers.

By the time we reached the farm equipment display and climbed around the equipment, I'd pushed the mess of ketchup and relish to the back of my mind.

It was late by the time we finished checking everything out and I was dusty, hot, and tired. I told Mark I was heading back to the dining hall to help clean up, and started off. By the time I got there, the hall was empty. I grabbed a sandwich, a piece of homemade berry pie, and the last of the juice. The sandwich, dry around the edges, was definitely leftover from lunch, but the pie tasted as fresh as if it had just come out of the oven. After, I walked home alone.

That night, with the radio on quietly, I lay on my side and faced the wall as Dad had demanded; another of his rules. While Mom said goodnight after she kissed me, Dad would come in and roll me into this uncomfortable position. In those half-asleep moments I'd lie frozen until he closed the door and left the room.

I wondered who this man really was as old memories pushed forward again. I recalled getting dressed up, Red and I sitting in a church. A handful of people talked quietly. It must have been their wedding but there were no church bells, no throwing of rice; just strangers leaving the church together at the end.

I now understood why Little Sister was the only one who got to curl up in his lap. Dad would poke, tickle, and tease her, his comments to Red and me we were too big weighed now against the thought he just didn't want us that close. He didn't even smell like us.

If he isn't my real Dad, do I still have to do things the way he tells us, his way, the right way? Can I make a bed the way I want, instead of sheets wrapped so tight my toes hurt? Does a table really have to be cleaned in a smooth up and down pattern, hand cupped to carefully catch wiped-up crumbs, the sink rinsed and cleaned right away?

I thought back to when Mom and Dad's friends would come over in Winnipeg. I'd listen from the top of the stairs while he bragged about me, saying things to them he hadn't said to me.

Did he mean any of it? What else were they being silent about?

We'd learned not to speak unless spoken to; to be seen and not heard. I wanted to talk to Red, but was afraid, like in a *Twilight Zone* episode, that she was in on it and would tell them I now realized he wasn't our real Dad. I felt stupid for not thinking about this earlier. Then I got scared; scared that if a dad could leave and a new one could take over, maybe I could be sent away for a new son.

As I started to fall asleep, all of the furniture got bigger. I became smaller and the same nightmare started again. I struggled to speak, but all I could do was gurgle. I wanted to scream for help, but nothing would come out. My heart pounded and I couldn't move away from the wall.

▸▸▸◂◂◂

By now everyone knew what to do as the doors to the hall opened and daylight broke in on the workers who'd managed to get up this early. I wondered if this was what work was like.

A man, clipboard in one hand and cigarette in the other, walked in and made a direct path to Minster Martin. It was hard to overhear, but from the look on the minister's face I figured we weren't being congratulated for our pies.

The man walked over to where I stood. "Son," he said through an exhale of cigarette smoke. "I'm sorry, but the rules state counter help must be at least sixteen years old. I'm afraid you can't serve anymore."

My heart sank as Minister Martin and the man stepped away for one more whispered talk, but it was clear that being on God's side wouldn't convince Mr. Clipboard I could stay. Minister Martin turned back and put his arm across my shoulder. "Sorry, Ricky, but we can't break the rules. It'd be great though if you could help peel potatoes and pull peas off their pods."

Potatoes and peas? I went from being a juice server out front to peeling vegetables in the back! Minister Martin guided me toward the room where, he claimed, "the real work is done."

Sunshine sliced through the slatted wood walls as one of the old men tossed a freshly peeled potato into a large bucket that sat in the middle of the floor. Water splashed over the rim. I watched the potatoes float around and thought about bobbing for apples. The shed was musty, and I felt myself start to sneeze then caught myself before I did.

"Hello, gents," said the minister. "I have here one of the best potato peelers in all of Yorkton, ready and willing to pitch in."

I wasn't sure about being ready or willing, but that didn't stop one of them from turning a bucket upside down, and handing me a potato peeler. Without missing a beat the old man said, "Take a seat, kid." Another man asked me my name before repeating it back, and then everyone resumed peeling. I sat on the bucket until my bum was numb. I'd lost count of the potatoes I'd peeled, and had had just about enough of listening to them talk about how much better things used to be.

This was the year of Expo '67, our country's one-hundredth birthday. We had colour TV, and there was talk of soon having thirteen channels. An air-conditioned, Allis-Chalmers farm tractor of the future was on display, complete with citizens band radio, a stereo cassette player, and AM-FM radio. Things *had* changed, but these old men hadn't.

One of the ladies stuck her head into our little room, saying it was time for me to go. I was only too happy to put down the potato peeler, fingers stiff. I worked my way through overall-covered legs with a, "See you all tomorrow morning." I didn't expect anyone to miss me, though I heard a "Thanks, kid" on the way out.

When I entered the dining room I saw Minister Martin talking to Mom, while Red and Little Sister sat at a nearby table. I said my goodbyes and led Red, Mom, and Little Sister out the front hall door. With forty rides and shows to choose from, both time and money limited what we could do. I had to pick things Red would like, since we'd have to do them together. I figured I'd have to work her up to The Octopus, and looked for something she would like to do first. I spied it up ahead: bumper cars. I gently pushed Red in that direction.

"Mom," Red asked, her voice quivering with excitement as we got closer. "Can we go on the bumper cars? Please?"

"Well, yes," Mom replied, then paused. "But the two of you have to share a car."

I turned to Red. "You can drive if I can pick the next ride." Without thinking she blurted out a "yes" and added, "Keep your hands off the wheel so I can go where I want."

Once everyone cleared the floor and we got the okay to board, Red dashed off and sat in a blue car (her favourite colour). At first we were pinned in a corner, then we spent most of the ride getting hit by riders smart enough to choose a car on location rather than appearance. No matter. From what I could see, she was happier spinning the steering wheel around than trying to move us out of danger.

Finished, it was all I could do not to run off as Mom asked if we wanted to try the Scrambler or the Tilt-A-Whirl, a "how about this one" or "how about that one" thrown in for good measure. Each time I answered no. I knew what I wanted.

Then it stood before us; rather, it stood *over* us. The Octopus! Its arms spinning high above, lit up with what seemed like a thousand shining bulbs. Over the loudspeakers Jefferson Airplane's "Somebody to Love" drowned out all other noise. I grabbed Red's hand and dragged her to the ride, three riders back from the entrance chain. She tried pulling her hand out but I squeezed tighter, and whispered in her ear.

"We made a deal. You *have* to come."

The ticket man stood to the side, clenching a cigarette in his mouth as he picked at a scab. A little blood trickled down his arm, running over a tattoo of some sort. I looked at the "You need to be this tall to ride" sign and back at Red; she didn't measure up! I quickly stepped between her and the sign, but it didn't seem to matter. The man appeared more interested in his scab than her height.

The ride hadn't yet stopped spinning before I pulled her toward the closest bucket. Red climbed in first, which was fine with me. I figured once the ride started I'd just squish up against her. As we began to move, "Up, Up and Away" by the 5th Dimension started to play. Perfect, I thought. That was the last thought I had for a while as the giant octopus arms picked up speed.

Climbing up and down, spinning our little bucket around, I soon realized that what you expected a ride to feel like when you were looking at it on the ground isn't always what it's like when you're strapped in, unable to get out. Sounds rolled around as we spun up, around, and down.

After several gasps I found my voice, or rather it found me. “Mister, mister! Stop this ride. My sister’s scared; she needs to get off!” The midway moved about wildly as I tried to find the scab-picking man who operated the ride.

“Mister, mister. Please. You’ve got to stop this ride right *now*. My sister wants off!”

The speed increased and I waited for our door to spring open and fling us somewhere down the midway. I couldn’t remember if the man even checked our door or, if he did, did he put in the locking pin in.

Why had I been in such a hurry to get on? Maybe Mr. Watson was right, maybe the operator is drunk. Maybe he forgot to make sure we were locked in; clearly the reason the door was rattling in my tightly gripped hands.

“Mister, my sister’s going to be sick!”

Tears squeezed out of Red’s closed eyes. I closed my eyes, too.

As the ride finally slowed I heard music again, and people laughing and talking. After one final spin we stopped and I slumped forward, my arms hanging over the door. What food I’d eaten still spun around inside my stomach.

“Hey,” someone yelled. “Don’t unlock the door. Wait ’til I get there.”

It was the scabby ticket man. He reached up, pulling out the lock pin that had, in fact, remained in place throughout the ride. It didn’t matter. I stepped out, waited for Red to climb down, then walked quietly back to Mom and Little Sister.

“How was it?” Mom asked, a small smile across her lips. Neither of us answered. I hoped Red was so scared she hadn’t heard me screaming, or if she had she wouldn’t say anything. I couldn’t turn the clock back, I was just glad to be back on the ground.

▸▸▸◂◂◂

It was Wednesday. I got up at seven, and not too long after was in the back room of the hall, peeling potatoes as they served breakfast. After what seemed like hours, one of the ladies came back and said there was a “Mark” out front. That was my cue to put down the potato peeler, asking if it was okay to leave.

"Sure, kid. We'll save a spot for yah," one of them replied. I bolted from my overturned pail and into the light of the dining hall.

The hot air balloons were supposed to lift off at ten and I started to run toward the launch site. Mark had to hurry to keep up. We arrived just as the balloons struggled to right themselves, anxious to break free and rise up. We sounded out the balloon names as we walked past, names I hadn't heard before. It wasn't until we reached the Dutch balloon, piloted by a woman, that a name sounded familiar.

"Nimbus," Mark said. "Like a cloud."

We sat and waited for a noise that signalled the start of the race. That was the last thing I remembered 'til I heard Mark say, "Wake up!"

I thought I might still be on The Octopus, 'cause everything in front of me was floating. "What time is it?"

"Around noon. You fell asleep. They waited and waited, and then they just took off." I sat up on my elbows, crossing my legs and watching as they drifted toward northeast. Perhaps they could see some airplane wreckage, if there was any to see. I wasn't sure where the finish line was or how the winner would be declared, since the balloons seemed to be scattered throughout the clouds.

As Mark and I walked back, I asked if he was game on coming back tomorrow after the last of the trucks had driven off.

"Why? There won't be anything to see."

"I heard you can find all kinds of stuff on the ground. Coins and things people dropped and were too lazy to pick up."

"I need to see what Mom's doing," Mark replied. I knew that answer: it was a, "I don't want to come, so I'll find something she needs help with."

"I'll knock on your door at seven-thirty. If you're up, great; if not, whatever I find is mine. I'm only gonna knock once, so you'd better be ready." I was thinking I didn't want him coming along after all.

▸▸▸◂◂◂

As expected Mark didn't answer the next morning, but I was determined to see what had been left behind. As I walked over lawns toward the empty, flattened fairground my runners became green and wet across the top of the canvas.

I couldn't tell if the rain last night had swept everything away, but where once three hundred workers and thirty trucks had laid out a town for us to walk through only tire ruts now proved it had existed at all. Concession trailers once full of hanging candy floss and candy apples on display had now been rolled up like an old carpet. The Scrambler, the Tilt-A-Whirl, the roller coaster, and the bumper cars nowhere to be seen. The Octopus, with its eight long arms flying over people as they walked down the midway–gone. Our little bucket now tucked away on some flatbed truck, exciting any kid lucky enough to see it travel down the highway.

Tickets, good as gold the day before, were now trampled and ripped stubs on the ground. I thought about gluing them together for next year, but the best I could find was a soggy few whose ink hadn't run as much as the others. I gave up and started looking instead for anything shiny on the chance someone had dropped a quarter or a dime.

I walked around remembering the painted freak-show banners, the horribly deformed people and animals hidden in trailers behind the admission booths. I thought about Mom and Dad's wedding, wondering what else had been hidden from us. After only finding a few balloons that could still hold air, along with some leftover BB pellets from rifle-shooting booths, I headed home. Mark had been right.

▸▸▸◂◂◂

After baseball practice Chad invited me to his house to race cars with him. He never talked about his dad, saying only that he lived with his mom and grandparents. Their house was in Long Point, where the big houses were. I rode up the centre of the court to a circular driveway that surrounded a large fountain; a big old Lincoln his grandpa drove, and a brand new, shiny Mustang that belonged to his Mom, on either side of the driveway.

I laid my bike gently down on the front lawn. In front of me were two of the largest wooden doors I'd ever seen. In the centre of each sat a gleaming metal ring hanging from the mouth of a lion's head. I reached up, lifted a ring, and let it knock against the door, the sound echoing.

I waited while the sun beat down, wondering if Chad was inside or out back. I reached out to knock again, but before I could the door swung open and the sunlight lit her up.

She wore a pair of leopard-print shorts and a white dress shirt, tied in a knot at her waist. Her hair was parted in two ponytails. I looked down at her feet, each toe painted a bright pink. The gurgling of the fountain drifted off, and all I heard was a single bird singing. I couldn't speak.

"You must be here to play with Chad. Come in. I'm Chad's mom"

Suddenly I'd gone from being hot to being hot *and* dry, and could only mumble a thanks as I walked through the doorway. I was taught to look at the person when you spoke to them and didn't mean to be rude, but the best I could do was look down and ask if I could have a glass of water—please.

"Yes, sure," she replied. "Follow me to the kitchen."

I wasn't interested in Chad or his racetrack anymore. Water was what interested me, more specifically, Chad's mom getting me the water interested me.

"Here," she said. "Sit on a stool and I'll get you a glass."

I soon realized the bird I'd heard was not outside, but a budgie perched in a cage beside the sliding glass doors.

"Oh," I said my voice returning slightly. "That's the budgie Chad talked about in class."

"Yes," she replied. "Sometimes I think it ought to fly away, but I know the kids like it so we'll keep it until … well, until whenever."

I wasn't sure what she meant, but I liked the sound of her voice and wanted to hear more.

"Here's your water. I need to finish weeding before it gets too hot. When you're done, you can just put the glass on the counter."

As she walked, her sandals flapped against the bottom of her feet. I watched as she opened the sliding door, kicked off the sandals, and stepped out into the backyard. She seemed to be swept up into the light, her sweet perfume the only reminder she'd been in the kitchen.

The sound of laughter came up the stairs.

"Hey," Chad said as he and Kyle reached the top.

I thought I was the only one invited?

"I just got here. Your mom gave me a glass of water."

I looked back toward the sliding doors, seeing her kneel forward in the flowerbed, weeding the marigolds. Her feet were slightly green, loose blades of grass stuck to the soles of her feet.

"Come on," Kyle said. "We've got a real cool track set up. You won't believe it!"

I followed them downstairs, and as I walked past the pool table saw the track; it was clear Kyle hadn't lied. In front of us was a fully laid out Strombecker road-racing set, with more track than I'd ever seen in one place and at one time! I could almost feel myself drool as I asked how many feet of track there was.

"Over thirty-six feet," Chad replied.

I'd be happy if I ever got a simple figure-eight.

We sat on the floor and Chad said I could play the winner. I looked around. In addition to the racetrack and pool table, they also had a sitting area with what looked like a brand new colour TV Kyle was staring at, picture on, and sound down. Besides Billy, Chad was the only other person I knew with a colour TV.

I couldn't figure out why Kyle was staring at the TV, not seeing what the big deal was since this was an old *Roy Rogers* episode. Then I remembered hearing he wasn't allowed to watch TV.

"Hey, Kyle. I can tell you how it ends if you want."

"No thanks, Donkey. I just wanted to watch the pictures. I think someday I'm going to get a horse. You know, when I'm grown up and can do what I want."

"Yeah," Chad added. "When we get older we're going to have a ranch together. We even made a deal that when we die we're going to meet up in heaven, too."

I wasn't sure how they were going to meet up there since they seemed to believe in different things. I'd seen Chad at our church every once in a while with his grandparents. All I knew about Kyle was that he could celebrate Easter but not have chocolates, couldn't celebrate Hallowe'en or go to dances or even have a birthday party. I really didn't care if I met them in heaven or not, but it did bug me that I hadn't been invited to join them.

Just as it was my turn to race we heard, "Boys, do you want some chips and pop?" It was her again; my heart leapt.

"Yes, Mom. We'll be right there."

We ran up, elbows flying and legs kicking, though I was sure we had our different reasons for wanting to be up first. Pulling the chairs out from the island we waited while she grabbed cans of pop from the fridge.

"Chad, there's salt-and-vinegar chips in the cupboard. Why don't you put them in a bowl for you guys?"

Salt and vinegar—they were *rich!*

We were lucky to get plain Old Dutch chips now and then; Chad could just pull salt and vinegar from the cupboard any time he wanted. She stood back up, turning around to close the fridge door with her foot. It took me a few seconds to realize she was looking at me while I stared at her. My face got hot and I hoped neither Kyle nor Chad had noticed.

"Cola or root beer?"

"I uh, I uh, root beer please."

She put the bottle down in front of me; a whole bottle! I held on to it tightly, took one long gulp, and watched her move around the kitchen while Kyle and Chad headed back downstairs.

I stayed as long as I thought I could, then thanked her and started back down the stairs. Chad and Kyle were talking about what they were going to do in heaven, and didn't seem to have missed me. As much as I got angry at Mark for being a chicken, being too slow, or not keeping his mouth shut, I liked doing stuff with him, even if we never thought about hanging out together in heaven.

I cleared my throat, told them I remembered I needed to be back at home, and left. Neither tried to convince me to stay, and that was all I needed to know about spending time with them here on Earth or in heaven for that matter, not that they asked me to.

I pedalled home and listened to the sound of my foot pedal hitting against the bike frame, keeping time as I got closer to home. As I turned down our street I saw someone outside our building, hoped it was Mark, and then prayed it wasn't Dwayne's mother. Getting closer I saw it was Dwayne himself.

Before I could say anything Dwayne yelled, "If you're looking for Mark, last I saw he went up through the houses toward the fields by the highway." A reflection from the window in their building caught my eye and I looked up without thinking. His mom stood in their window, watching us.

"Thanks," I replied and put my bike down without taking my eyes off his mom. It wasn't 'til I was safely through the houses that I stopped looking over my shoulder.

I walked through the open field. What a few short months ago had been a frozen pond was now a knee-deep field of long, dry grass that waved around depending on how the breeze flowed across the top. On the highway past the field cars whistled by, disappearing as highway and horizon met. Sometimes I made out the side of a face through a window, and wondered where they were going.

I called out Mark's name until the top of his head popped up. "What?"

He sat cross-legged, windbreaker spread over flattened grass. Only his mother would have made him wear one in the middle of the summer. I noticed a magnifying glass hanging out of his pocket and realized he was surrounded by blackened matchsticks. Stalks of grass, crispy grasshoppers, and some of his Johnny Seven gun parts were scattered around the ground; all of them were burned.

I wasn't worried about him playing with matches, but the Johnny Seven was his pride and joy and wasn't sure why he'd burn something he liked so much. Especially since I'd have taken it if he didn't want it anymore.

As for the grasshoppers, you had to catch and hang onto them under the magnifying glass as they burned and wriggled around, and I didn't have the stomach for that.

"Whatcha doin?" I asked, though it was plain to see he'd now lit the end of a long stalk of grass in his mouth.

"Smokin' a punk," he replied, his eyes watering as he inhaled through the hollow stalk.

"What's it like?"

"Supposed to be like a cigarette," came Mark's coughed-out answer. "I mean it's a lit piece of grass, but it can't be much different can it?"

"Let me try."

The breeze blowing across the field meant I burned several matches before the stalk remained lit. The first puff burned the back of my throat, and not wanting to choke as Mark watched I tried to hold it in. My eyes watered too, and then I started to feel dizzy. The more air I sucked in, the further down my lungs the burning went. I wanted to quit, but didn't want to give him the satisfaction of seeing me stop. I had to cough. Mark laughed, rolled backward, and hung onto his sides.

Just then I smelled smoke, too much for what we'd just burned. I looked back and yelled, "Fire!" We both jumped up. In our effort to light up we hadn't given any thought to putting out the matches, and had just tossed them over our shoulders. I grabbed Mark's windbreaker, trying to beat it out. It seemed like a good idea, but in short order became a really bad one.

The fire spread quickly, partly from fanning the flames and partly because bits of grass flew off in all directions. In a panic, I tossed the windbreaker away from us.

"We gotta get out of here before someone sees us!" I yelled. We were off without an argument, out of the field and up between the triplexes before we stopped running. I looked out onto the street, and not seeing anyone, motioned Mark forward. We walked toward our apartment, as normal as possible.

"What should we do?" I asked, hoping he didn't hear the panic I felt. "Someone has to put the fire out."

We looked back; grey smoke now curled upward behind the roofline.

"Someone'll call the fire department," Mark said. "If *we* call them, they'll figure out who it was and tell our parents; or worse, arrest us!"

"Mark, we gotta make a pledge. No matter what, we don't tell anyone we started this fire."

Before I could get him to make the pledge he grabbed my arm. "Listen, can you hear it?" Sure enough the sound of a siren could be heard off in the distance, yet close enough to figure out it would arrive before things got really out of hand.

"Quick," he said. "We've got to find out what they know."

Just how will it be possible to find out what they know without giving ourselves away?

"Come on. Let's get our bikes."

Before I could reply, Mark had broken into a run, picked up his windbreaker from where I had tossed it, grabbed his bike, and started off. He pedalled fast and furious, and it was all I could do to keep up. By the time we stopped and I realized where he'd led us, it was too late to turn back. We now stood directly in front of the headquarters of the combined Yorkton fire and police departments. I knew I should have stopped him!

Mark bounded up the stairs, toward the police department's main counter, with me in hot pursuit.

"We need to renew our bike licences," Mark said to the officer sitting behind the desk. The officer opened one of his drawers, taking out some forms and bringing them over to the counter. I now realized what Mark was doing. The licenses were free and weren't really required. It was more a way to keep track of your bike if it was stolen, although that never happened. Mark passed a form to me and began filling out another while the officer went back to his desk.

Mark's hanging around me was beginning to pay off.

The officer's two-way radio sprang to life, and I felt as though we were going to be grabbed by a giant "got you," and told how stupid we were: not once, but twice. First because we started the fire, and second because we rode over to the station.

Mark cleared his throat. "I noticed the pumper's not in the station?" We waited for the officer to reply. Finally, he raised his head slightly, and looking directly at us said, "There's a fire. They just pulled out."

This didn't satisfy Mark. He wouldn't stop until he got the answer he wanted. "What's on fire? A house or something?"

The officer pushed his wooden chair away from the desk and walked toward the counter. He knows something, he can smell the smoke on our hands!

Why didn't we change or at least wash our hands? Better yet, why'd I listen to Mark? What kind of idiots offer themselves up to the police?

The officer looked at me, then back at Mark, and in a slow, deep voice replied, "No, it's just a grass fire. Sometimes they start in the dry weather like we've been having. I guess the farmers didn't pray hard enough for rain."

"Oh," Mark replied, nodding his head and narrowing his eyes as if he knew.

The officer scooped up our forms and as he stamped them asked, "These your correct home addresses?"

"Yup," Mark replied. A nod was the best I could do, my throat still sore. As soon as we got our new bike plates, we turned to walk out as quickly as we could without breaking into a run.

"See," Mark said under his breath. "They think it's because of the weather."

"Great thinking," I whispered. "If anyone asks, we can say we were at the station getting our plates when the fire happened."

"That's the whole point. We were at the station getting our plates while the fire burned."

It took a lot of guts to do what he did.

Days passed, and as far as I could tell from reading the paper, the grass fire didn't even rate a mention.

▸▸▸◂◂◂

Mark and I made our way over to the park to see if anyone was playing pickup. Off in the corner we saw everyone gathered near the playground, nodded a "hello" as we quietly walked up, and then sat down on the grass. Texas talked as he slowly swung back and forth on one of the swings, his Keds making little swirls of dust that drifted toward us as he dragged his feet in the dirt. I wasn't sure why, but it seemed wherever he was light followed him around. I wondered if anyone else got the same feeling.

I leaned over and asked Billy what was going on. "Randy's sister. Truth or dare. Randy's house," he whispered and then said, "Shhh." I looked around; Randy wasn't here.

Texas jumped off, spun around, and fell gently onto his back, one leg over the other as he looked toward the sky. I'd heard if you looked up during an eclipse you'd go blind, and although I wanted to see if I could, I knew I wasn't brave enough to try. Just from the way Texas looked into the sun now, he'd probably still be able to see after an eclipse had come and gone.

"Then," Texas said in the slow and deliberate way he had, "she had a choice. Truth or dare."

We waited.

"She choose dare. So we went into the furnace room, where it was a little darker, and I said, 'Dare you to close your eyes.'"

I'd been in that very basement. Until now it had been just a small dark room with a noisy furnace.

"Then what happened?" I asked, hoping no one heard the excitement in my voice.

"I put my arms around her as she closed her eyes." We waited quietly. "Then I leaned in and kissed her full on the lips—for a long time."

Kissed her? What kind of a dare was that?

"What do ya mean you kissed her? Was that it?" I knew as soon as I blurted it out, someone was going to tell me to shut up; and someone did. Texas sat up, looking directly at me. I got the feeling he wanted to make a point, as he waited before saying, "No, the kiss wasn't it. The kiss was the *start* of it."

"The start of it. I knew that."

I just wish my mouth had. I wanted to hear the rest of his story, figuring if I lay back on the grass he'd continue and my face wouldn't feel so hot. One of the other guys spoke up. "Then what did you do?"

Texas put his leg down, raising the other up and over, staring back up at the sky. I tried to find the same spot in the clouds, hoping it would somehow connect me to the thoughts in his head, but after a few seconds realized I was following the trail of a plane. I was going to miss the story if I didn't start paying attention.

"I slid my hand up her blouse, under her brassiere, and onto her boob for a while."

I was sure on the word boob everyone gasped, then thought maybe *I* was the only one who had. I hadn't noticed Vicki much during winter, but by the time spring had come she wasn't Little Vicki anymore, she was Victoria. All grown up, and with the boobs to prove it. I wanted to see his face and sat up on my elbows.

"Then I pinched my fingers round her nipple."

I wondered if we all had the same picture in our heads, or if someone's picture was better than mine.

"That's when she said, 'Stop it. That hurts.'" There was silence again. That was as far as she went with the dare I thought, but then someone again asked what happened next.

Without hesitation Texas replied. "I stopped pinching her. I said I was sorry. Told her I thought she'd like it, but she just said it hurt. She said if I wanted to touch her I could, but not hurt her."

Well, well, well. Well, she didn't slap him. Well, she didn't tell him to stop, and, well, she just told him touch her if that's what he wanted to do.

I wanted to ask how long you could hold your hand over someone's boob without moving it, only I didn't have to as Dale beat me to it. "How long did you leave it there?" he asked.

"Not long," Texas replied. "I got that far and wasn't going to press my luck. Besides, we got the rest of summer and we're going swimming and stuff. I figured I'd have more chances later."

I admired him for thinking he was going to be able to come back for more, and wondered if he knew how lucky he was that girls always seemed to want to hang around him. Maybe it was because he was older, or maybe because they liked the way he talked. I was jealous, but wasn't going to say anything 'cause I liked hanging round him too.

The sun had pushed the clouds away, leaving nothing but blue sky between us and our thoughts, the only sound from grasshoppers jumping about. Finally, Billy broke the silence. "Swear it out loud."

There were times when swear it out loud was called for, and times when it meant you doubted something someone said. I'm sure if it had been anyone else Texas would have met the challenge to swear with a challenge to fight, but hitting Billy was like hitting your sister. But since dreams were going to be based on the truthfulness of this story, we needed to know.

Texas stared at him then slowly said, "Swear it out loud."

Yes! It *was* true. At that moment, if we were cowboys, we would have thrown our hats into the air!

CHAPTER TWELVE

August, 1967

It was Tuesday, Red's birthday, and Dad had left for the road again, saying that her party could wait 'til the weekend. As mad as I was at him for making us wait, I was angrier at Red since she didn't seem to mind.

I'd been making Red's cake when Mom came into the apartment and rounded the corner, lifted up her hair, leaned forward, and asked me to unzip her dress. Before I could ask where she'd been, she asked where Red was. Beyond saying "outside" I didn't know exactly where she was.

Satisfied, Mom went down the hall while I trimmed the top of one cake to make it flat, smoothed strawberry jam on it, and then placed the other cake on top just as the door opened again.

"Red, please get your sister from the Watson's," Mom yelled down the hall; Red did as she was told. If I was quick, I could ice the cake before they returned.

After the cake was frosted and placed in the fridge, we all met at the front door to go for dinner at the Dog n' Suds; Red's special treat. The car creaked as we piled in, then rocketed off as we passed kids playing in the street. Since we were used to eating quietly, nothing more was said other than requests to pass the ketchup or mustard while our little party ate through our hamburgers and fries. Mom stood first. "Come on, let's get going. We can have cake and ice cream at home."

She stopped at Lee's and picked up Red's favourite ice cream flavour, Neapolitan. As quiet as we'd been at dinner, the three of us now pounded up the stairs, after which Mom told the girls to wait in their room while we got things ready. Once the candles were lit I called the girls, and as Red and Little Sister bounced into the kitchen Mom and I started to sing "Happy Birthday." I stopped halfway through my off-key singing when I saw Red's bottom lip start to quiver.

She didn't like to cry in front of anyone, and always worked hard to keep her feelings to herself. A couple of tears rolled down, then hit the table.

"Come on, hon," Mom said quietly as she too stopped singing and put her arm around Red's shoulder. With a slight squeeze that made Red's head bobble back and forth she added, "Let's blow out the candles together."

Red wrapped her arms around herself, her stubborn streak clearly visible. Like a possum you could poke her with a stick and she wouldn't move, but poke her once too often and she'd run after you like a crazed woman. More than once I went too far and had to take off running, even ripping a tee-shirt or two when she caught me. This time she didn't look crazed or angry, she just looked sad.

Little Sister fidgeted on my lap and I held her tighter while I watched the wax roll down the coloured candles, hardening on the icing. "Hey, blow out the candles before we start a fire," I teased. By the look on Red's face I knew she didn't think it was funny.

She whispered something under her breath that Mom asked her to repeat. In a low, quiet voice Red spoke again. "Why does he have to be away so much?"

I waited for Mom to answer. We all waited. Finally, she sighed and replied. "Things need to be this way, for now. It'll get better. Come on, blow the candles out so we can have cake and ice cream."

Better for Red would be Dad here now, better for me would be him on the road seven days a week.

I put Little Sister down and got out the plates, spoons, and ice cream scoop while Mom sliced the cake. The girls mixed their cake and ice cream 'til it was milky smooth, the once-separate vanilla, chocolate, and strawberry ice cream slices now mixed into one rather brownish looking mess of liquid and cake bits, before lifting their bowls to drink it up.

Once the girls had finished their dessert, Mom got up from the table. "Come on, girls. A bath for you two, then off to bed."

As quickly as our party had started it ended. I washed and dried the dishes then went to my room and got ready for bed. As my head hit the pillow, "The Way I Feel" by Gordon Lightfoot came on. The words rolled around my thoughts as Mom came in, leaning down to kiss me goodnight. Her hair settled like a soft, warm blanket wrapped around me and I began to drift off, only to wake in the middle of the night to the sound of a low static hum from the radio. The station had closed down for the night; I reached up and over to slide the radio button off.

▸ ▸ ▸ ◂ ◂ ◂

Another week passed and Saturday morning rolled around. Dad was up early to take his car in for service. As soon as I finished breakfast, I knocked on Mark's door. Mrs. Watson answered. She'd been crying, and one eye looked like she'd walked into a door again. I glanced over her shoulder but didn't see Mr. Watson. It didn't matter. She'd been crying and he didn't seem to be around.

"Mark's in his room," she said. It was enough for me to brush past along the wall and start down the hall. As I did she added, "We're moving."

I stopped, turning to ask if she meant to a new building. Mrs. Watson leaned against the wall. "No, we're not moving into another building."

Well, maybe they bought a house. Maybe Mr. Watson was done moving them around.

"Is the house close by?"

"No. No, dear," she replied. "We're moving away. To Toronto."

Toronto? That's pretty far.

I knocked on Mark's door, and after I heard a quiet "come in" opened it. He lay on his bed, face down, with his head on a pillow clutched between both arms. A couple of Hardy Boys books lay on the floor. I think Mark always wanted a brother and that's what he liked about them. Me, I liked Tom Swift, he had planes, boats, and his Jetmarine to get around in and go wherever he wanted, whenever he wanted.

Mark's eyes were red, his pillowcase damp with wet spots. I sat down crossed-legged on the floor, thumbed through one of the books, and waited for him to speak. I was sure it was only a minute or two, but it could have been longer.

He raised his head ever so slightly, rolled over, and stared up at the celling. He said they were moving again, only this time it was different.

They've moved before, what was so different this time?

I watched his stomach move up and down as he started to breathe heavily and wondered if he was going to start crying again. I didn't want to watch if he was and glanced around his room, which was bigger than mine since they only had a two-bedroom apartment.

"We're not moving this time 'cause Dad got a new job, and we're not moving this time 'cause he lost his job. We're moving this time 'cause Mom wants to leave. We're gonna move in with my grandparents. I don't think my Dad's coming."

Slowly, Mark turned his head toward me and our eyes locked. I wanted to look away, but couldn't. His face turned redder and redder as he spit out his words faster and louder.

"Mom spent a lot of time on the phone this week, talking to Grandma about coming home. If it was possible for us to do that? Near as I can tell it is possible since this morning Mom said, 'We're moving. Only this time it's for the last time.'"

I could never remember seeing Mark this angry before.

"You should wipe your mouth. You've got spittle at the corners."

He flew off the bed, landing on top of me with such force I was sure I'd broke a rib or two, the book having flown off in the other direction. He now grabbed my neck with both hands and was squeezing harder than I ever thought possible, coming from him. I tried to loosen his grip, but he held on. I knew I was bigger and stronger, but there was no way I was going to win this time.

"I don't give a good goddamn about spittle," he said. "I don't give a good goddamn about anything 'cept why do we need to move again."

Having his hands around my neck made it hard to speak, but I managed to rasp out a few words. His grip finally loosened, a rush of air entered my lungs, and I choked as it came in faster than I expected. He finally stood up and stared down at me. "I'm sorry," he said quietly. "Sorry I jumped on you."

I wanted to hear him say sorry for almost strangling me too, but figured an apology for jumping on me was better than no apology at all.

"Lookit," he said. "Mom said it's for the best. She's tired of doing everything herself. Tired of being alone out here. Tired of being so far away from family."

He stopped for a minute then continued. "I dunno what that means for Dad. Mom called him during the week, trying to reach him. I know he called back a few times, but every time they spoke she told me to go to my room."

Before I could say anything else Mrs. Watson came in and said Red had come to get me, that Dad needed me. I told Mark we'd talk later, but wasn't sure if he replied. I knew I needed to get home before I was called again.

I walked into our apartment. Dad was in his chair, cigarette in hand, Brubeck's "Take Five" back on the Hi-Fi. Little Sister sat on the floor, playing with her dolls. I listened to the piano as the drumbeat kept time, then waited for the sax to come in. Without looking up at me, Dad said, "I brought the car in for service this morning."

Well, that's nice.

"And I ran into Mr. Edwards."

Well, that's not so nice!

I tried to figure out if he knew something, or he was just telling me he'd run into one of my friend's dad. I wanted to speak; I wanted to run, but stood and waited instead for whatever would come next.

"Come on down the hall," was what came next. I followed him into my room, watching as he sat on the corner of the bed.

I'm going to have to make that again once he gets up.

"Pull your pants down and bend over." My stomach dropped while

I did what I was told.

Whatever Mr. Edwards had said, it was more than enough. Dad started to hit me without another word. His first few slaps didn't quite get the soft spot he preferred, so he spread his legs out wider, making me lay flatter over them. Even for this he had his own particular way of making sure everything was just so. Once I was centred and unable to fly off, every hand that swung down hit my bum as cleanly as possible. It wasn't long before everything was numb and tears rolled out on their own. I was sure at some point my skin would break. The last thing I wanted was to get blood on my sheets and be punished for that, too.

In between each slap he retold most of the story, providing a rundown about me stealing the milk money, about what a thief I was, and how embarrassed *he* was to have a son like me.

Halfway through one long sentence about how worthless I was, Mom yelled from the doorway for him to stop. But he was too far into making sure I knew how angry he was to listen to her, or anybody else for that matter. By now he'd had enough practice that nothing affected his rhythm once he started.

"Get out," he snarled at Mom, "and close the door behind you. I'll deal with you later for not telling me the kid's a thief!"

Without missing a beat he continued hitting me, but just as Mom closed the door something flew by, hit the wooden dresser hard, and then fell to the floor. I turned my head to see pieces of his watch lying on the parquet floor; he'd been hitting me so hard his watch strap broke and his watch flew off. I braced myself for things to get worse, then felt as if I was flying. In fact I was flying; he had tossed me off his lap. It was all I could do to pull my pants up over my stinging behind while he got down on his hands and knees, and collected up his broken watch. I wanted to run, but knew I wouldn't get far before he'd drag me back.

"This watch," he said, "was a gift given to me by a girlfriend before I left Holland."

That watch always reminded Mom (as she *liked to remind him) of what he'd left behind, of a part of him that had never completely come over.*

"Don't move an inch," he said. "There'll be no supper for you tonight. You're grounded. Period. No leaving this room without my permission, even to go to the bathroom." He slammed the door with his free hand, the other holding bits of his watch. I lay face down on the bed. My pillow was soon wet with tears and snot. I didn't move an inch. I could make the bed again later.

When I awoke the room was dark, the apartment quiet. Whatever the time was, judging from the rumble coming from my stomach it was well past dinner. Eventually, the door opened a crack and Red's quiet voice asked if I was okay. I tried my best to say yes without letting her know I wasn't.

"Did you guys have dinner?"

"A while ago, but no one ate much. Mom mostly spent the time wiping away tears. Then we were sent to our room while they had another fight."

"What about?" I asked.

"Mostly about you, me, and Mom. That Mom was lucky to be married to *him*, and not that railroad bum Richard she was married to before. How he'd adopted us as his own, and how Oma and Opa didn't want him to marry her. It was bad enough Mom had been married before, they had said, but she also had you and me.

"Mom told him that 'You should have known what you were getting yourself into.' But from the sound of it I don't think Dad did."

Red took a breath, then carried on. "He talked about a girl back in Holland, the one who gave him the watch. How he should have married her like he was supposed to. Mom told Dad to stop bringing that up, but he just went on. Reminded her about Oma and Opa not talking to them for a whole year after he married Mom. How they pretended like he didn't exist because of what he did."

She shrugged and went quiet, then slid to the floor like her body couldn't support her weight. "You said our real dad's name is Richard, what else do you know about him?" I asked Red. After taking a deep breath she looked up.

"They kept on arguing. Well, actually, from what I could hear Dad kept on while Mom just stopped talking. Dad said it should have been a sign that Richard was up to no good when he went hunting with his buddies while I was being born. And if Mom needed more proof, Richard quitting the railroad to go work for June's dad should have told her he was a two-timer."

I wondered who June was, and why Red and I hadn't talked like this before. Then I wondered why I hadn't asked her before if she knew anything. The answer was clear: having got used to not speaking unless spoken to, we no longer spoke to each other unless we needed to keep a secret from Mom or Dad.

Before I could get in another question, footsteps came down the hall and we froze as a door closed. If Red was caught here we were done for. Neither of us said anything as we waited. After the toilet flushed and she felt safe enough to talk, Red started back up.

"Dad started to laugh, then said, 'To top it all off, we had to stop getting our cakes from Jeanne's Bakery' when they found out June, Richard's new wife, now worked there."

I blurted out a quick, "You mean she works at the shop where we used to get our birthday cakes?" I thought back to the store and wondered if I had seen her. I wondered if I'd been that close to *him.*

"Well, all I know is she used to. I better go; if Dad catches me … well, you know."

Yeah, I knew. I also knew my bum would still be sore in the morning. Before I could ask any more questions, she'd gotten up and closed the door behind her, my room quiet again.

Is he still alive? How hard can it be to find him? Could I find him?

I knew he had lived in Winnipeg. I knew where June had worked. I wanted to put Garner Ted Armstrong on, but didn't dare make any noise. I rolled against the wall, curled up, and tried to go back to sleep, but there was too much to think about.

►►►◄◄◄

It was morning, and I woke up determined not to let anyone or anything get in the way of me getting to Winnipeg. The smell of bacon came down the hall and the thought of food made my stomach rumble even more with hunger, but no one called me to breakfast. I heard Mom tell Dad she was going to take the girls shopping. Soon enough there was only the sound of his voice talking to, from what I could tell, customers over the phone. I waited until he'd left to do his Saturday errands before I got dressed and slipped into their room.

On top of the dresser lay his usual roll of bills held together by a big silver money clip, a wad thick enough to make him look rich. I took a twenty dollar bill, packed a small bag with a couple of tee-shirts, socks, and underwear, and then slipped out of the empty apartment. I started off through back lanes and avoided open streets, so I wouldn't be spotted by Mom or Dad if they drove by.

I'd passed the bus station many times on the way to the movie theatre, and now sat and looked around for someone I could slip onto the bus with; someone who looked like a father or mother or maybe even a big brother. As the bus for Winnipeg was called, I spotted an older lady about Mom's age. She'd do. I got in line behind her, waited until she was near the front, and spoke up loud enough for the driver checking tickets to hear me say I needed to go to the bathroom. I sat in a stall, and gathered up the courage needed to get on the bus.

After hearing the last call for the Winnipeg bus, I dashed back out, brushed by the driver, and put my foot on the first step.

"Where do you think *you're* going, kid?" the driver asked as he grabbed my arm and spun me around.

In the steadiest voice I could manage I said, "My mom's already on."

The driver looked at me, then said, "You're gonna make us late. Get on the bus." Without needing to be told twice I grabbed the handrail and climbed aboard.

My eyes adjusted to the darkness as I slowly walked down the rows of seats and looked for my "Mom". She didn't look too pleased when I stopped and asked to sit in the open window seat beside her. She lifted her bag from the seat, putting it in the overhead storage so I could sit down. I closed my eyes, leaned against the window, and tried to keep my heart from pounding its way up through my mouth.

The bus pulled out with a whoosh of air and we lurched forward, on our way back to where it had all started. I figured it'd be late in the afternoon before I was missed by anyone.

After hours of listening to the steady hum of the diesel engine we pulled in at a rest stop. I wanted to get off and stretch my legs, but didn't want to risk getting left behind and waited until most were off the bus before heading to the washroom at the back of the bus. When I heard people getting back on, I slipped back into my spot and waited for my "Mom" to take her seat.

As farms gave way and the city rolled into view, my heart started to pound again. I hadn't thought about what I'd do once I got to Winnipeg. The bus pulled into the station with a last gasp of air; the driver opened the door and the passengers shuffled out, myself included. The last I saw of the woman I'd shared a ride with was her being greeted by a young man and woman with a baby.

Not having eaten since yesterday I felt a little dizzy, so walked over to the lunch counter and stared at the menu. For the first time in my life I could order what I wanted. I looked over the drinks, floats, and sundaes, settling on a hamburger that I ate quickly.

I went over to the pay phones, pulled out a phone book, and flipped through the pages until I found the address for Jeanne's Bakery. Beside the bank of phones was a wall map of Winnipeg, and after finding Notre Dame Street on the list of streets I ran my fingers across and down the letter-number grid until I figured where the bakery would be. As best as I could tell the store was just a few blocks over from the bus station.

With a clear destination in mind, but no map in hand to confirm, I started off. I almost walked past it before a display of cakes caught the corner of my eye, looked into the front window, and then walked a little past the building. Unlike trying to ask Mr. Lee for a job I couldn't wait for courage to find me, I needed to do this now, before they closed.

I walked in as a family walked out, boxed cake in hand, and was met with the smell of baked cakes and icing sugar. My teeth started to ache with the thought of eating through one of their cakes, and hitting the hard cookie-crumb crust upon which their cakes were built. I thought back to how birthdays had been in Winnipeg; how we'd come here, pick out our cake, and have our name written on it in colourful letters.

Back then, our house and backyard were filled with aunts and uncles of all kinds: Oma, Opa, Grandma, and next door neighbours. Everyone played while the barbeque smoked away, fires flared, and the smell of food drifted across the yards. My mouth watered at the thought of tasty burgers, Old Dutch potato chips, and Jeanne's chocolate-curl cake. Our little three-bedroom apartment did little to encourage new happy memories; I wanted those days back.

I wasn't sure how many times the lady behind the counter asked what I wanted before I replied. My body remained rigid while my mouth acted on its own, blurting out, "Does June work here?"

I hadn't thought about what do to if she didn't and started to panic. Fear soon replaced panic as the lady replied, "I'm June. And just who are you?"

She stepped from behind the counter, put her hands on her round hips, and looked me up and down, squinting as if trying to try bring something into focus. All of a sudden she brought an icing-stained hand to her mouth. "Oh, my goodness! You're little Ricky, aren't you? You're the spitting image of Richard. Polish through and through."

My mind was off and running. Here was June, saying I was the spitting image of my real dad. A Polish dad. I thought about when people had asked where we were from, and their replies of, "Oh, I can see now you are Dutch, what with your blue eyes and blonde hair," no longer true in my mind. Now I was Polish.

June put the brakes on more unsettling thoughts bubbling up by asking where my mom was, if she was waiting outside in the car.

"I'm by myself. No one knows I'm here. I came to find my dad."

"Don't move an inch young man," June commanded as she lifted the handset, dialled a number, and ducked around the corner. I only heard bits and pieces as her voice went up and down, the phone cord fully stretched out. She ended by saying she'd be home in a few minutes, then hung the phone back up on the wall.

"Come on, honey. Richard's been waiting a long time for this. All he's ever talked about was if he'd ever get the chance to see you again." She grabbed a cake from inside the display case, shut off the lights, and locked the door. I wondered if the cake would taste as good as I remembered.

A short car ride later we pulled up in front of a small square house on a tree-lined street, the street itself protected by the canopy meeting over the middle of the road. I stepped out of the car and spotted a large man with glasses, a white undershirt, and baggy grey pants standing on the front steps. It looked as if his belt might be losing the struggle to keep everything around it in.

As I walked my stomach tightened. Had the sidewalk been any longer, I'm sure I would have stopped breathing altogether before I reached him. The hair on his head was matted down; thin, flat, and missing in places. He was sweating. It looked like tears had started to form in the corners of his eyes.

"My, my, my. How you've grown. Tall and thin as a rail. You're too skinny, kid. Bet they don't serve you good Polish food like your Grandma used to." I started to answer, then stopped.

My Grandma isn't Polish. Not only that, she doesn't cook Polish food. In fact, she really doesn't cook at all. Toast, coffee, cereal, TV dinners, and take-out fried chicken are the only things she makes.

"You're thinking, aren't you? I'm talking about *my* mother, your babcia." He pronounced it as bop-cha. "She used to cook for you all the time. Real food."

June quietly said, "Richard, why don't you take your son into the living room? I'll go put on some coffee and get some cake." She had her hands on my shoulders and pushed me gently forward, steering me into the living room and asking if I was hungry.

"No, thank you," I replied in a shaky voice. "I had a hamburger a little while ago."

"Come on, kid. Sit on the sofa beside me." He slapped the sofa cushion with his big hand. I looked at him. He sure was big. Not the sort of guy you'd want to tangle with. I wondered if I'd end up wearing glasses one day.

I wanted to sit across from him and take everything in, but did as I was told. I rolled into him a little closer than I was comfortable with, and tried to wiggle my bum away without him noticing. He had a strong smell about him; different than what I was used to, sort of sourish, like onions.

"June, can you go get the old photo albums?" he yelled. "I want to show you some pictures. Your babcia was so proud of you and your sister. All she talked about was you two.

"How's your sister? Last time I saw her she was crying about something. Full of tears and freckles, her red hair blowing in the wind every which way. A tangled mess your mom never tamed."

He wrapped his fat fingers around the open stubby beer bottle that sat in front of us, picking it up and taking a long gulp before letting out a low, long rumble that started deep within his belly. He stared at the empty bottle for a minute, then blurted out "should never have let them cut off contact with you!" after which the empty bottle was put back on the table, and a second one picked up.

"What do you mean, cut off contact? You could have just driven over to see us." I knew I'd spoken, but I was shocked that words were coming out. Angry words at that.

"Oh, I tried," Richard replied. "But your new father was a piece of work. We went to court and he made me sign an agreement to stay away. Not that it had anything to do with you. He just stared at me with a look that said, 'Agree or I'll make your life miserable.' To just cut me off, that's how cruel they were."

It seemed to me that not having his life made miserable was more important to him than trying to see us.

"I used to come around though. When you still lived here. I'd watch you from the street. Stood by your school playground once to see if I could catch a glimpse of you or your sister."

In one fell swoop the second empty bottle was on the table. He was, I thought, a match for Mark's dad.

"Your new father called me a railroad bum, just like your grandma's second husband. Sure I came home drunk now and then. Maybe once in a while didn't come home at all, but your Grandma's husband not only came home drunk, he beat her too! At least I never did that. He went after both your grandma and your mom, though your mom said he chased them in different ways. That's why your grandma sent your mom off to Catholic school, to get her away from him."

Catholic school? Grandma remarried? The only husband of Grandma's

I know of was killed in the war.

"What do you mean Grandma had a husband who worked on the railroad? I thought her husband was killed in the war?"

Richard looked at me, and I wondered if he felt he'd said too much. But then he leaned forward, looked toward the hall, and continued on in a whisper.

"Like I said. Your grandma got married again, but he beat her one time too many and she finally left." Another long, low burp rumbled out.

"It wasn't all rosy for me either you know. I had to work my ass off for the railroad. Then I'd come home and hear all these stories about your mom. And the stories weren't pleasant.

"She had a girlfriend. Name was Shirley, not married. Really good looking, just like your mom. The two of them hung out and the places they hung out weren't really proper for a single girl like Shirley, let alone a married woman like your mom. Didn't seem to matter a hoot to either of them, though.

"By the time I'd get home from work and eat dinner alone at the table the two of them, dressed to the nines, would straggle in as if they didn't have a care in the world. When I'd ask your mom where she'd been, they'd look at each other, laugh, and say, 'Oh, you know. Just out and about.'

"Out and about, my ass. I knew damn well where they were, and if it hadn't been for me getting your mom pregnant they would have likely kept on going until all of Winnipeg was talking about them two."

His face was red; redder then anything I could have matched in my most embarrassed moment. I now knew I came by the colour honestly.

"Well, round about then I'd started working for June's dad. June worked in the office and well, you know, one thing led to another and June got pregnant. After that I had to make a decision. And, well, I decided June was the wife for me. In the end I think your mom was just as happy to be rid of me, so it worked out for everyone. Probably didn't help that she had you when she was seventeen. What did we know back then?"

This wasn't turning out the way I had thought it would, but then again I hadn't really thought about much past finding him. In a low, quiet voice I asked, "If Mom was out so much, who took care of me?"

"Who took care of you? Who indeed! Oh, your grandmother tried but she was out all night playing the piano and arranging music for the big bands that came through Winnipeg. Then she slept most of the day. It was a godsend my mom was still alive back then to take care of you, otherwise I'm sure as shooting the authorities would have found you curled up in some corner with a diaper full of crap.

"My mother, God rest her soul. Cooked. Cleaned. Kept the house inside *and* out, did it all. Left my dad alone to be a man; you know, able to enjoy life without having to worry about anything 'cept work, hunting, and fishing. That's the kind of woman your mother should have been. Could never figure out why the nuns just didn't beat some sense into her.

"My mom's heart was broken the day my father, your dziadek, died. I never really understood how that felt until *she* died, too. Just fell over doing laundry one day. Doctor said it was a heart attack, but I think it killed her when they took you and your sister away from us and cut off all contact."

As I listened, the sound of a deep, low voice rumbled in from the front door. I knew the voice, but this wasn't the place it should have been heard. In time I came to realize whose voice it was as Uncle rounded the corner and entered the living room. June trailed behind, photo album tucked under her arm, a tray of sliced cake and coffee in her hands.

"What are you doing here?" I asked.

"June called. Said you were here. Your parents were worried sick when they found you gone this morning. I've come to take you to our place for the night. Your dad's on his way here."

The room was silent but for the rattling of a window pane as a car whooshed by outside.

June quietly spoke up as she put the tray and then the photo album down on the coffee table. "I'm sorry, Richard, but if I was his mom I'd be worried. I thought it best to call Marc so they'd let his parents know Ricky was safe and sound."

Richard blinked rapidly, trying, it looked, to figure out what to say next. "Well, son, they've come to take you away from me again!"

"That'll be enough from you," snapped Uncle Marc. "Come on son, let's get going."

With that Richard leapt up. His full weight shook the floor and he almost fell forward as he tried to steady himself. Uncle Marc raised his hands, ready to push Richard back, but at the last minute Richard found his balance and stopped inches from Uncle Marc's face. They were close, and it seemed both stood and waited for a punch neither wanted to throw. June barked out Richard's name and that was enough for both of them to drop their shoulders.

Richard picked the photo album off the coffee table, popped out a picture, and slid it into my shirt pocket.

"Take this," he said, then looked at Uncle Marc. "Don't want to begrudge the kid a picture of his grandmother, do you Marc?"

Uncle Marc grabbed my shoulders and turned me around, stopping only to thank June for phoning him before marching me toward the door without answering Richard.

"Just remember, kid; you're Polish not Dutch. Don't ever forgot that!"

I never did get a piece of that cake!

As we pulled away from the curb Uncle Marc asked if I was okay. All I could say was, "It's been a long day."

"Auntie Erna's waiting at home. The way your dad drives, he'll be here later tonight. I suppose you guys will be going back to Yorkton in the morning."

I wondered if Dad knew I'd taken the twenty dollars, and, if he did, what his punishment was going to be. Like not being prepared for what might come after meeting Richard, I hadn't thought about what would happen after I got back home.

It didn't take long to drive the empty downtown streets of Winnipeg, before exiting out toward Kildonan. I thought back to the times Grandma hopped on the cross-town bus to pick me up from our old house in St. Vital. How we'd take the bus back downtown, spending the day walking through all the department stores; in Yorkton, you could do all that in fifteen minutes. We'd go to Eaton's, The Bay, and even Woolworth's to eat at the lunch counter. I could have anything I wanted, and took my time working through the candy counters. Sometimes, having too many choices wasn't a good thing. I'd always end up with a new tee-shirt; the best being a Batman tee-shirt. By the time we'd taken the bus back to our house it was all I could do to keep my eyes open as she then boarded the bus for her own trip back across town.

We pulled into the laneway and I got out to open the garage door. A single bulb over the side door provided the only light as we walked up to the house. Once inside, the familiar smell of their house—a combination of Auntie Erna's sweet perfume and cleaning supplies—hit my nose. It was fresh and inviting.

Uncle Marc flicked on the light to the basement as Auntie Erna appeared at the top step. I wanted to rush up and have her wrap her arms around me, to tell me everything was okay like she used to, but I was too embarrassed to step forward. Soon, everyone would know I'd run away.

A feeling of regret washed over me as I thought about how Dad might feel, knowing I'd met Richard.

Auntie bent down and pulled me close to her chest. I started to shake and, before I could will myself not to cry, tears started. Uncle brushed by on his way up and said, "You should get to bed."

Auntie brought me downstairs. My bed was already made, the sheets cold, crisp, and tight as I slipped between them. She sat on the edge of the bed, a ball of Kleenex in her hands, and started to talk in a very quiet voice.

"Do you remember when you moved down the street and ended up living above us, on Inkster?"

Until she said that I really hadn't, but then I remembered everyone carrying bits of furniture, clothes, and dishes down the street, from one house to the other, a line of furniture-carrying ants. Another tucked-away memory that hadn't made sense until brought back to life now.

"Well, things weren't going so well for your mom and dad back then. You moved upstairs so we could take care of you and Red for a little while. Your mother wasn't too good at doing that. She had you young. Very young, and, well she wasn't quite ready to be a mom. I'm sure she tried the best she could, but when we saw what was going on we asked your dad if we could help. Moving upstairs was the answer."

Images became sharper as memories fitted back into the giant puzzle of the past.

"You need to know it wasn't easy for your dad. Oma and Opa had a hard time, shall we say, with the idea that your dad married a divorced woman. Let alone one with two little kids. I think they felt he should have gotten married, then had kids. Kids of his own.

"In the beginning they weren't too kind to your mother either, refusing to speak English around her. That didn't help things much. Your dad said they did that deliberately, but I think they were just embarrassed. Your mom, for all her troubles, was smart and I think they knew that. Your dad even went so far as to tell them not to come over anymore if they weren't going to speak English. As he put it, 'My house is an English house, and if you don't like it you can stay away.' Well, they stayed away for almost a year. Then your little sister came along and things slowly changed after that."

I wanted to hear more, but felt my breathing start to slow and her words begin to trail off. Unlike Garner Ted Armstrong, who put me to sleep while warning me to keep on the straight and narrow or face eternal damnation, Auntie Erna's smooth voice put me to sleep with a calm that I'd forgotten.

She swept her hand across my hair to set it back straight, pulled the sheets up around my neck, kissed my forehead, and left the room. The lights were out, the basement so black things looked the same whether I had my eyes opened or let them slowly close.

▸▸▸◂◂◂

I awoke to the sound of voices upstairs. It was daylight, though I couldn't be sure of the time, the light bouncing off the top of the basement window curtain hung high near the ceiling. From the sound of it, Uncle Marc, Auntie Erna, and Dad were up and in the kitchen. After making the bed and washing up I slowly climbed the stairs, my legs heavier the closer to the top I got. I rounded the corner, waited 'til they knew I was there, then slipped into the only open spot around the breakfast table. It was large enough for the two of them, tight for the four of us.

I ate while they talked; the clicking of Dad's teeth heard more clearly now than at any other time. The little plates of meat and cheese, Dutch Rusk, honey from a tin, and chocolate sprinkles reminded me of how much I missed being here. Then everything was silent. I looked up at Dad. He was staring directly at me.

"You know," he said. "I had a choice. I was doing all right in Holland. Just out of the army. Had a pretty girlfriend. Then Opa and Oma decided to come to Canada, for a better life. Never been sure why, at their age, they thought they needed one.

"Opa made fine furniture by hand. The coffee table they still have in their living room is one of the pieces he made. One of the few things, besides his tools, he brought over. Back home his partner robbed him blind and put them out of business, so in the end I guess they had nothing to lose.

"They almost didn't get to come. Just as they were getting ready, and all of the papers were in order, Opa had a hernia. The Canadian government wouldn't let him come over, so Auntie Erna and Uncle Marc came here first and made sure everything was set up. All of us followed a year later. Well, all that is 'cept Uncle Phillip and Auntie Ellie. Poor Phillip promised his sick mother he'd never leave her, so that's why he and Ellie never came. Ellie hated us for leaving her behind. Still hates us today, I think, but there wasn't much we could do.

"All of this started, you know, from the war."

I remained silent, head down and looking at a drip of honey on the table while he talked to no one and all of us at the same time.

"While Opa fought, Oma and I spent a very long time, day after day, walking up and down the fields, looking for anything to eat. We dug through dirt. We picked through piles of garbage. Anything to find something that wasn't missed or rotted. But all we could ever find was goddamn tulip bulbs!"

Now I looked up. Auntie had tears in her eyes and Uncle stared off toward the cupboards, his fingers flipping the corner of the Bible they kept on the table. Sitting in an undershirt that showed his muscles, I looked at the freckles and spots that dotted his shoulders and remembered how he used to pick us up and toss us high into the air, only to safely catch us before we hit the ground.

"We didn't know if your Opa was dead or alive, or if the Nazis had him. For all we knew he'd been captured again; only this time shot instead of managing to escape. Erna was sent to a farm in the country. Oma prayed every night. Prayed for the fighting to stop. Prayed for her family to come back. For our apartment building to still be standing. For this nightmare to be over.

"I spent most of the first seven years of my life like that. Then the war ended and everyone tried to pick up the pieces."

He heaved, he shook, and then a cry welled up from deep within, the sound of which I'd never heard before. It roared out like a busted dam, raining water down onto everything in its path, all of us now swept up in the flood of feeling he had just released. He put both hands to his face and cried uncontrollably. No one moved as he bawled louder and louder. I'm not sure anything could have been done to get him to stop anyway, and like a flooding Red River no one dared step in lest we too were swept away.

The man who once picked us up by one hand and swing us about, legs oak-tree strong and steady as he carried us up to bed, cried deeper, harder, and longer than I'd ever heard anyone cry before. His shoulders heaved, the table now wet beneath him. Where once I'd look at him, feel my stomach tighten and my throat close up as I waited for whatever would come next, I now only saw a hunched-over man unable to control his feelings, crying like a baby.

There isn't much to be afraid of anymore.

Uncle got up, brought back a box of tissues, placed it on the kitchen table, and then left the room. Auntie wiped some tears from her eyes, picked up the plates, wrapped an apron around her dress, and started to wash the dishes. I wanted to leave but didn't move. After a while, with one long inhale followed by a long exhale, Dad stopped crying. He pulled out his hanky and blew on what looked like its last clean area. He was back to his silent self.

▸▸▸◂◂◂

Dad and I pulled away from Uncle and Auntie's house, the two of us on the road just like when we'd gone to Regina for the football game. Except this time things were different. I wanted to ask questions. I wanted to know why he had adopted us. I wanted to know why he wanted us as his own yet treated Red and me as if we didn't really exist.

I hoped he'd say something that would start the conversation, but like always he remained silent and fixed on the road ahead. With both windows open, the speedometer past the posted limit, it would have been hard to talk anyway. Even the eight-track player was turned off, the only sound the occasional pop of the lighter as he smoked away his thoughts.

Don't grab it when it pops out!

Each field we passed waved a further goodbye to a Winnipeg long been left behind. As we drove down the highway toward the point where the land met sky, I was only too happy to stare out my side window and not have to explain what I did and why. Our wall of silence now as useful to me as it was to him.

By the time we reached Yorkton and he pulled into his usual spot out in front of our building it was late in the day, the sun having followed us as we made our way west. Other than a stop for gas and a bag of Old Dutch potato chips, we hadn't eaten anything in the five hours or so since we'd left Winnipeg. I hoped I could at least get something to eat before being told to go to my room. I went to get out of the car, but he told me to wait as he stared out the front window of the car. "There's something I want to tell you.

"The first time I met you two little kids, I felt something I'd never felt before. I *wanted* to be your father. I *wanted* to be the man that stepped in and took care of everything. I wanted to make a better life for you and your mom.

"I may not have always been the best father, but I've done what I've done for what I think are the right reasons. And I've done the best I could. You need to remember that."

He used the same tone as he had this morning in the kitchen, and I wondered if he was going to break down again. I held my breath but I needn't have worried. Red bounced down the sidewalk toward the car, Little Sister trailing behind.

"What I'm trying to say is that I had a choice. I *wanted* you and Red."

The girls stood outside the car, waiting for us to step out, Little Sister beside herself with excitement at seeing him.

"Go up to your room. We'll sort things out later."

I obeyed without question and headed toward the front of the building, only this time things were different. I could tell by the look on Red's face she wanted to talk, but knew she couldn't bring herself to do so in front of him.

I entered the apartment, and not seeing Mom in the kitchen, poked my head into the living room. She sat on the end of the sofa. Seeing me she smiled faintly and said, "I'm glad you're home. Please don't run away again."

She'd been crying at some point. The tears were now gone, but a sad look lingered. It was the same look she had after they argued, the same look she had after he left for another week, her with us three kids. It was the same look she had in the few pictures scattered around the house before we moved here.

I went to my room, took the picture from my pocket that Richard had given me, and slipped it into a Tom Swift book. I climbed into bed and rolled toward the wall, happy to lie there clutching my pillow, no longer afraid of him.

►►► ◄◄◄

Dad had gone back out on the road without another word having been said about Winnipeg. Mark had been gone for a week and I sat in my room reading a Hardy Boys book Mark had given me, wondering what to do next. There was a knock on my bedroom door, and I leapt up at the thought of Mark before realizing it would never be him again. Red said I was wanted at the door.

"Who wants me?" I asked, straightening out the bed.

"Robert," she replied.

Robert? He never calls to play. I haven't even seen him since the end of school.

I opened the front door, but didn't see anyone. I poked my head out and saw him standing on the landing below.

"Hey, I haven't seen *you* in a while."

"I won … won … wondered if I could talk to you for a min … min … minute?"

I couldn't tell for sure, but it sounded as if his stuttering had gotten worse. It was clear he had something to say. I just wasn't sure if it wasn't coming out because of the stuttering, or if he wanted to speak with no one around.

"Sure," I replied. "Let's go outside."

We were hit with a wave of warm, dry air as we walked over to the road and sat on the curb. I pushed some of the sand and dirt around with the new Hush Puppies I wasn't supposed to wear before school started.

Robert poked at some ants with a small stick before blurting out, "I know what you and Mark did."

My back stiffened, but I tried not to let anything show. "What do you mean, you know what we did? What did we do?" I knew what he meant, but I didn't want to give away anything I didn't have to.

"I know you started the fi … fi … fire. I know you played with matches in the field and smoked pu ... pu … punks. I watched you and Mark run away."

A car sped by, and a swirl of dust and heat settled on us. I kept my head down, not wanting to let him know he was right. As much trouble as I ever got into, none of it involved a fire that brought out both the police and fire departments. At least I could stop worrying about whether someone had seen us. Now I could start worrying about whether he was going to tell someone. Maybe he already had.

"Don't worry, I won't tell. Accidents happen, you know, but you ga … ga … gatta be careful when it comes to matches."

I didn't know what to say. I never figured him to lie, but that didn't stop me from wanting to know why he wasn't going to tell. He started to get up.

"Why aren't you going to tell anyone?"

Robert sat back down and started playing with the ants again. In one flat tone said, "Because of my birthday. I'm not going to tell anyone be … be … because of my birthday. That was the first party I ever had, and you were the only one I invited."

Robert stopped, put both hands over his forehead, and looked up toward the sun before speaking again. "All I ever wanted was a be … be … best friend. When you told Chad and Kyle to leave me alone in the locker room, you were the only person who stood up for me. When you came to my party and we spent that time together, I had a best friend. It was you. That's why I invited you." The last part came out smoothly and without hesitation.

Everything made sense now. No one else had known about the party and all this time I was worried about everyone making comments, so I'd never told anyone I'd gone.

"I'm sorry. I didn't know you wanted a best friend. I thought you liked being alone."

"It's okay," he replied. "That's why I'm not gonna tell anyone about the fire. Best friends don't tell on best friends."

Before I could say anything he stood up and threw the stick across the street. Dusting off his pants, he turned and said, "I've got to go pack up. I just wanted to say thanks for not making fun of me."

"What do you mean, pack up? Are you going camping or something?"

"No. Dad's decided to move us back to the farm. Says the city's too busy, so we're going back for a year. See how it goes. I've already got a hog to take care of, and I'm starting a new school next week. There's lots of stuff to look forward to."

"Well, I hope you like your new school and you make lots of new friends. I had a good time at your birthday party, even if I was the only one invited."

"Me too," he replied then started across the street. I watched him disappear between the houses.

▸▸▸◂◂◂

Tuesday, the first day of school, rolled around quicker than I wanted but it came nonetheless. We'd bought our back-to-school clothes; two new outfits to choose from. Mark had already been gone for just over a week, their apartment cleaned and painted and ready for the next family. I missed him every day.

I started walking, but hearing footsteps behind me, turned around. It was Big Boy. "Hey! Wanna walk to school with me?" I asked.

Big Boy shrugged his shoulders as if to say it didn't matter, but then a big grin came over his face. "Yeah, okay."

"Well then, come on, hurry up. I don't want you walking a couple of feet behind me."

We walked without talking. Rounding the corner of the school we saw Ricky, Randy, and Billy hanging near the wall. When they saw Big Boy they pressed their backs up against the brick and stood quietly. Big Boy rocked back and forth on his feet. Randy nodded as if to say, "What's up with him?"

"His name is James," I said.

"What?" Randy asked.

"I said his name is James, and he's walking to school with me from now on."